Date with the Perfect Dead Man

ANNIE GRIFFIN

BERKLEY PRIME CRIME, NEW YORK

DATE WITH THE PERFECT DEAD MAN

A Berkley Prime Crime Book / published by arrangement with
the author

PRINTING HISTORY
Berkley Prime Crime edition / August 1999

ISBN: 0-425-16985-5

Berkley Prime Crime Books are published
by The Berkley Publishing Group,
a division of Penguin Putnam Inc.,
375 Hudson Street, New York, New York 10014.
The name BERKLEY PRIME CRIME and the BERKLEY PRIME CRIME
design are trademarks belonging to Penguin Putnam Inc.

PRINTED IN THE UNITED STATES OF AMERICA

10 9 8 7 6 5 4 3 2 1

Caralyn

"Something Shocking Has Happened!"

"Kiki, are you alright?"

"I guess I'm okay."

Hannah's shoulders slumped with relief. "What happened? What shocking thing happened?"

"Well," Kiki began. She started sniffling. "I don't know where to start."

"Start anywhere."

"Well, I went back home with Freddie."

"Freddie who?"

"Freddie Casey. We went back to Wanda's guest room, where he was staying." Kiki took a deep, shuddering breath. "And I went into the bathroom, you know, to freshen up. And when I came back out . . ."

There was a moment of dead air, the suspense for Hannah unbearable. "When you came back out, what?"

"When I came back out, Freddie was lying on the bed, and you won't believe this, Hannah. He was completely naked except for a black cape and this little black eye patch."

"Good Lord," Hannah said. "Shocking is not the word."

"No, that's not what's shocking," Kiki said with a trace of annoyance filtering into her distress. "Hannah, he was dead!"

Date with the Perfect Dead Man

To Codi Medeiros, with love.

Special thanks to Marina Sifuentes Davis, Charlotte Blazei, Jim Osbon, and Kevin Sadlier at Green Jeans Garden Supply.

Date with the Perfect Dead Man

One

HILL CREEK IS A SMALL yet polished sort of town, a combination of quaintness and sophistication lying just beyond the spires of the Golden Gate Bridge.

Mount Tamalpais—lush, deep green, and veiled by mist—rises majestically beyond, hovering over the townspeople like a great talisman. The mountain's magic had served Hill Creek well, for its residents had not seen violence, hunger, or poverty except as momentary scenes on their big-screen televisions. They enjoyed lives of abundance, and though they might cry out against the world's injustices, they did so as spectators only, then forgot it a moment later. They weren't insensitive people. In fact, they were generous and well meaning. It was simply that the evil in the world rarely touched them. It lay far off somewhere beyond the hills and the bay. Still, they loved to fret over it, safe with distance, like dogs wailing at the moon.

All of which made a murder smack-dab in the middle of town so incredibly exciting.

Naomi wore a Buddha-like smile of rapture as she raised one chubby leg, balancing herself on the other. Slowly lifting one hand, she clinked her finger cymbals, their cheerful tinkling cutting through the early-morning quiet.

"We dance high above the heavens," she said, eyes half-closed, voice low and throaty. "We seek illumination. We surrender our hearts into the infinite whole."

Not wanting to hurt the other woman's feelings, Hannah Malloy struggled against chuckling as she mimicked Naomi's movements. But Naomi's somber facial expression, along with her floppy pink tunic and her bare left foot pressed against her right knee, made her look like a fat, drugged flamingo.

"Our She-Spirit, craving union with the earth, embraces the clouds and kisses the sea," Naomi continued. "The earth trembles, possessed by the sky."

At this point Naomi paused. A few seconds later Kiki Goldstein, Hannah's younger sister, tapped Naomi's shoulder.

"Don't stop," Kiki said. "If I keep my eyes closed and pretend I'm someplace else, this is almost sexy."

Hannah finally burst out laughing.

"No mirth, ladies," Naomi told them, annoyed. "This is serious. This is sacred. Focus on your mystical healing centers."

Stifling giggles, Kiki and Hannah bent their knees and raised their arms, following Naomi's movements. Blowing a long strand of auburn hair out of her eyes, Hannah tried her best to focus on her mystical healing center, but it was hard, since she had no idea what it was.

No onlooker would have thought this was sixty-one-year-old Hannah's second tai chi lesson. Her long arms and legs moved smoothly, her natural grace broken only by occasional wobbling. Still, at this time in the morning she preferred to be working in her garden, hunting out snails and grubworms. All that bending and stooping was as good as tai chi for exercise, and there was nothing like squishing a few garden pests to illuminate one's mystical center.

"I was in the library the other day and looked at a tai chi book," Hannah said to Naomi as they all bent their knees, lowering into an uncomfortable squat. "And I didn't see any of the positions we're doing. The books had lots of pictures, but I never saw anything even similar to 'Creeping Snail Dreams of Wings' and 'Naomi Goddess Winks at Sun.'"

"Well, if you must know, I've improvised on the traditional exercises," Naomi said, sounding a bit defensive. "One can't limit one's creative spirit."

Hannah gave Kiki a wink as they all straightened their legs once more and lifted their right knees. From Hannah's time at the library she knew that what they were doing was hardly tai chi at all and that Naomi had made up almost every movement they performed. Not that Hannah minded. In fact, this "naomi fu" wasn't nearly as bad as she thought it would be. The only reason she was taking the lessons was because she had lost to Naomi at five-card stud the previous Wednesday and had been forced into three classes. Kiki decided to take the lessons because she couldn't stand to be left out, plus the fact that Naomi told her that tai chi would improve her sensuality, which was one of Kiki's life goals.

As they synchronized their movements, languidly sweeping their arms, the three women's left feet rose in the air, each foot's shape and condition symbolizing the woman herself. Kiki's was a winsome foot, pale and plump, the toes painted a glossy red, its perfection marred only by a little toe disfigured from years of forcing it into what Kiki called "Joan Crawford Hurt-Me Pumps." Hannah's foot was elegantly practical, long and slender, unadorned by either polish or bunion, the happy result of years of comfortable shoes with good arch support. In contrast, Naomi's foot had only sporadically seen shoes at all. It was broad, with bony toes, its frosted purple nail polish (applied months before in celebration of the spring equinox) now peeling. But her toes had the distinction of being audible, since on her middle one she wore a ring with a small bell attached. This combined with her finger cymbals created a constant racket.

"The leg must go higher, higher, dear Kiki. Think of the sky. Rise toward it like a mountain to the stars," Naomi said, her tone increasingly theatrical, her pink sleeves flapping in the breeze.

Kiki grimaced, her short chunky body starting to shake. "If I raise anything one inch higher, I'm going to bust right out of my capri pants." She teetered precariously and Hannah grabbed her arm to brace her.

"Hold on to me," Hannah suggested with a grin. "In fact, let's all line up and lock arms. I always wanted to be a chorus girl."

Kiki circled her arm around her sister's and the two began doing high kicks, but the frantic clinking of Naomi's finger cymbals quickly interrupted them.

"Ladies, get back into your Moon Chuckling pose this instant. Remember, tai chi gives us a balm for the soul, a marriage to the universe. It must be done in meditative silence. Good. Put your feet a little farther apart. Now sweep your arms to the right, my dears. Slowly. *Slooowwwly*. Take deep breaths and think of gently undulating water."

Again lifting her leg, Kiki's entire sixty-year-old body began undulating, but not so gently, until she was forced to lean on Hannah's arm.

"I guess it's hard to be meditative when I'm a bundle of nerves about tonight," Kiki said excitedly. "Just think, all those movie people right here in Hill Creek."

The opening-night party for the third annual Hill Creek Film Festival was that evening. It was on the smallish side as far as film festivals went, but in Hill Creek it was the event of the year, the locals swooning over the prospect of having movie people in their midst.

"It *is* exhilarating, isn't it?" Naomi said, the possibility of film festival chatter making her forget that tai chi was supposed to be so silent and meditative. "My aura has been brighter the last couple of days."

"And your pocketbook fatter," Hannah said, keeping her eyes aimed at a tree. She found she could balance quite nicely if she focused on one object.

Naomi gave an enthusiastic little hop as her arms raised

skyward, her sleeves flopping down to her shoulders. Hannah and Kiki hopped in tandem.

"Yes, my services are booked up for the next few days," Naomi said, flipping her single black braid of hair off her shoulder. "Apparently word of Red Moon's gifts has reached L.A. And I need the money, you know. My water heater will never last through the winter."

Naomi was a well-known psychic in Hill Creek. She channeled for the spirit of Red Moon, a Hopi snake shaman, dead for five hundred years, who spoke through her body. Apparently there was nothing like being deceased a few centuries for honing one's counseling skills, and Red Moon gave Naomi's clients advice on their personal lives at fifty mystical dollars an hour. Hannah had always been dubious about Red Moon's existence, although she had to admit that several of his predictions had recently been eerily accurate.

With a grunt, Kiki reached upward, following Naomi's lead. "We all have Hannah to thank for the fact that there's a festival at all. I'm so proud of you, Hannah."

Hannah's gaze was still focused on the tree when she heard a plop and looked anxiously at Kiki, finding her collapsed on the grass, legs akimbo.

"Oh, spit! I'll never be any good at chai tea," Kiki said, giving the ground a kick.

"It's tai chi, Kiki dear. Chai tea is what they sell at Starbucks. You'll be fine if you just focus your mental energies. Of course falling down is nothing to be ashamed of. You're just getting in touch with the earth," Naomi told her, then looked at Hannah, who held Kiki's arm, trying to hoist her upward. "I have to agree with her, Hannah. If you hadn't written that wonderful, poignant letter to Frederick Casey, there wouldn't have been a guest of honor at the festival." Naomi clasped her hands under her chin. "It's your naturally creative nature, I suppose. The letter sounded almost like one of your poems. Such good karma."

Hannah couldn't help but feel pride that at least in some respect she *had* saved the festival. Several months earlier

the festival committee thought they had secured Richard
Gere as the guest of honor, a position that required him
giving a series of lectures during the week's activities.
Everyone in Hill Creek was so excited about getting him
that half the people in town spent hours pouring oolong tea
over new "Free Tibet" bumper stickers so it would look
like they had been on the back of their cars for years. But
Gere canceled when a new film project came his way. A
well-known young director had been scheduled to take
Gere's place, but he, too, canceled one week before opening
night when offered a directing job in Wyoming. His last-
minute departure left the festival with an embarrassing gap.

It had been Hannah's idea to invite Casey after reading
an article about him in the *San Francisco Chronicle*. In the
sixties Casey had made *The Liar,* a film still considered a
work of genius. His career had seriously dwindled in the
past ten years, further sullied by some ridiculous beer com-
mercials he had done just for money, but the article said
Casey was trying for a comeback. A phone call to him from
Roger Burke, the film-festival president, had resulted in
Casey's flat refusal. Without the committee's knowledge,
Hannah wrote a letter and faxed it to Casey, and it won
him over. Everyone on the committee had been impressed,
especially since Hannah was only a temporary committee
member, taking the place of her friend John Perez while he
spent two months hiking through South America. Hannah
had been proud of the letter and proud of its results, though
at the time she had no idea how remarkable the results
would be.

"In just a few hours, girls, Kiki Goldstein is going to strut
her stuff," Kiki announced, perched in a pink vinyl chair
at Lady Nails, getting a toenail color change.

Hannah waited in a wicker chair near the front door,
leafing through tattered issues of *People* magazine that
dated back five years. "If you strut your stuff any more,
you're going to wear a trough in the ground," she replied.

"Oh, very funny, ha, ha," Kiki said, but all the women
in the salon tittered. Hannah returned her gaze to her mag-

azine to avoid her sister's disapproving stare. Hannah didn't much like *People* magazine, never fascinated by the celebrity marriages, divorces, and other movie-star foibles that some people found so riveting, but the only other magazines available were two copies of *Macrobiotic Quarterly*. The latter publications had been tossed in the reading rack two months earlier when, in an attempt to be more hip, Ellie, the owner, changed the small salon's name to "One Hand Clapping."

A slick salon called Zen had opened down the street, offering herbal wraps, shiatsu massage, and body piercings as well as manicures and pedicures. Zen's New Age marketing ploys resulted in Ellie losing clients. She battled back by hiring Shiloh, a twenty-five-year-old manicurist with so many studs in her nose, ears, and eyebrows she looked like a pincushion. She claimed to be an aromatherapy specialist, but she had trouble making change and her aromatherapy left almost everybody smelling like licorice. Still, Shiloh worked cheap, so Ellie kept her and used her idea of changing the salon's name.

But Ellie's longtime clients fervently resisted any propulsion into the future and they stubbornly continued to call the salon Lady Nails, throwing hissy fits when Ellie tried to replace the Princess Di altar with drawings of Tibetan temples. Lady Nails was, after all, their social club, their refuge from a perplexing and increasingly youthful world. They liked it just the way it was, for it was much like them—narrow in scope, gossipy, and a bit long in the tooth. They felt comfortable with its pink walls, potted ferns, and constant high chatter, and the last thing they needed was a herd of tight-bodied twenty-year-olds traipsing around making them feel like fossils.

Ellie, petite with a head of wiry red hair, glanced up from Kiki's toes. "Anyone want footwork today?" she asked, hope springing eternal. Everyone in the store shifted uncomfortably in their seats and averted their eyes, becoming suddenly fascinated by the closest magazine or the contents of their handbags. To further compete in the dog-eat-dog manicure market, Ellie had branched out into foot reflexology, an ancient art of curing various ailments by applying pressure to the foot. Ellie, a strong woman, specialized in bending back the large toe to relieve tension, resulting in her clients walking out of her shop with a limp that lasted a good ten minutes. The awkward moment was thankfully interrupted by a repeated and muffled beep.

"Oops, that's me!" Kiki gaily announced. After a few seconds of spelunking through her purse, she found her beeper, and then, donning her red-rhinestoned reading glasses, she examined its readout. "Hmm. Looks like someone urgently needs my input."

Adjusting her own reading glasses and keeping her eyes on *People,* Hannah smiled. Kiki had recently picked up the "input" term from a television talk show and, thinking it sounded professional, began dropping it into conversations. This along with the beeper was contrived to create a supposedly businesslike facade. But Hannah considered it unlikely that anyone urgently needed Kiki's input unless they had encountered a life-or-death situation involving push-up bras and spandex.

Always the drama queen, Kiki loudly sighed to communicate the crushing weight of having people need her attention so badly. With a weary shrug followed by an affectionate pat of her bleached-blond hair, she excused herself, and, with tufts of cotton sticking up between her now gold-tipped toes, waddled on her heels to the rear of the shop where Ellie kept the phone.

Wanda, Hill Creek's most industrious society matron-in-training, tried her best to look disdainful yet indifferent, but a month earlier she had undergone her third face-lift and the most expression she could currently muster was to look vaguely startled, as if she had unexpectedly passed wind.

"Imagine our Kiki with a beeper. It must be so annoying for you," Wanda said to Hannah.

Hannah glanced up from a three-year-old article on Clint Eastwood's palimony problems. "She only bought it a few days ago. I've hardly heard any beeping at all," she replied, not mentioning that at home Kiki kept the beeper switched to vibrate, and Lord only knew what she was doing with it.

"I've never seen two sisters more opposite than you and Kiki," Wanda said. "You're so bookish and responsible, and Kiki is so . . ." She let the sentence hang. "Well, it's like comparing day and night."

"Or an apple to a marshmallow," Ellie said.

"Or ying and yang," Shiloh eagerly added.

"Exactly." Wanda smoothed the sleeves of her Donna Karan sweater. "It's a wonder the two of you have lived together so long."

"We get on each other's nerves a little sometimes," Hannah said, feeling unusually patient with Wanda. She wondered if "Naomi fu" was working, and, like Naomi said, she was feeling some sort of spiritual marriage to the universe. "That's only natural. But I think we complement each other overall."

"Still, the way she chases after men. Everyone's been talking about her going to the Elks Club bingo night in those horrible hot pants. It must be so embarrassing for you," Wanda said, tossing out the remark like a poisoned dart.

The comment chafed Hannah, and her marriage to the universe underwent a quickie divorce. The hot-pants situation had been an embarrassment, but although Hannah occasionally criticized her sister, she wouldn't tolerate anyone else doing it, and she gave Wanda a warning glare. Shifting uncomfortably in her seat, Wanda turned to Bertha Malone, who was next to her getting a manicure and licorice paraffin foot wrap from Shiloh. "I don't know why anyone who doesn't have a job needs a beeper."

"I think beepers are a blight on society," Bertha said loudly. "A technological oppression that ultimately only increases our isolation." To emphasize the point, she whacked the manicure table with her hand, sending the cotton balls flying. Nobody responded to this remark, knowing that if they did, Bertha would bore them stiff with a thirty-minute diatribe. Well known as one of the town's more aggressive and civic-minded activists, Bertha was one of several people in Hannah's group of friends, including Hannah herself, who had been an antiwar protester in the sixties. Later Bertha moved to Santa Fe, where she owned an art gallery, but came back to Hill Creek when her husband, plagued by lower-back problems, ran off with his Navajo masseuse. People claimed that being abandoned by her husband had instilled in Bertha her sense of unilateral outrage, and it was true that she leaped at any chance to protest injustice, real or imagined.

Wanda narrowed her eyes while she contemplated the meaning of Bertha's statement but quickly gave up.

"Well, I suppose it's cute that Kiki bought that silly beeper," Wanda said with a special iciness lurking in the word "cute." "Though the beeper is an interesting idea. I'll have to mention it to Roger. It might come in handy for the new job."

Wanda cast her eyes at Hannah, hoping to elicit a comment, but Hannah quickly buried her face back into *People,* feigning rapt interest in Goldie Hawn's exercise regimen, deciding it best to ignore Wanda.

"What job?" Shiloh asked.

"Roger Burke, the Hill Creek Film Festival president, is looking for an assistant," Bertha informed her, her tone important.

"He's practically promised it to me," Wanda said. Bertha nodded with authority.

Hannah knew from Roger himself that he hadn't yet promised the job to anyone. That was the problem. Both Wanda and Kiki were vying for it, and Hannah had done her best to sway Roger toward her sister, but he was being typically cagey. And this was the reason Wanda was being so atypically shrewish.

In the past week the competition between Wanda and Kiki had taken an ugly turn, culminating in an unfortunate incident at the Urban Farm Nursery. The story, rapidly becoming a Hill Creek folk legend, was this: during an altercation in the organic-fertilizer aisle Wanda *accidentally* dropped a clump of bulk-bin chicken manure into Kiki's cleavage, causing her to release a high-pitched shriek that sent Mrs. Wasserstein's French bulldog, Simone, into a neurotic yapping fit. Furious, Mrs. Wasserstein called Hannah that evening and in tears told her that the incident had catapulted Simone back into pet therapy, a distressing setback since Simone had recently made such breakthroughs. It was up to Hannah, she said, to see that Kiki and Wanda controlled themselves in the future.

The problem was that Kiki and Wanda had never controlled themselves in the past and were unlikely ever to do so, but Hannah showed up at Lady Nails that day to referee if necessary. She couldn't understand their fighting over the job in the first place. The assistant's position was unpaid and consisted of a few hours of grunt work each month, mainly making cappuccinos at committee meetings and returning the phone calls Roger considered irritating. But Wanda felt the position carried prestige, and to Wanda prestige was everything. Although not one to shun prestige herself, Kiki lusted for the job because she lusted for Roger Burke, and she thought the job an excellent way to showcase her feminine charms.

Hannah was mystified by what Kiki saw in Roger. He was a dandified doughboy, the type who would get his money's worth at all-you-can-eat buffets if he would ever lower himself to go to one. She felt sure a faster route to Roger's heart would be for Kiki to cover herself with gravy and make noises like a sizzling pot roast. But Kiki was after him at full steam. Roger had made a point of telling everyone he wanted his assistant to be extremely organized and efficient, hence Kiki's new beeper.

Kiki heel-walked back in and plopped down into the glossy pink chair.

"Important call?" Wanda asked, her tone dripping with sugar.

"Oh, yes," Kiki replied. "My days are so packed with important activities I'm forced to be organized. I have to be efficient."

Hannah stifled a groan. Kiki's idea of organization was putting salt and pepper in separate shakers.

"Of course, Kiki," Wanda said. "It's good to try to

improve yourself that way. To develop potential aptitudes.''

Kiki's lips twisted up, and Hannah knew she was trying to figure out if the comment was intended as an insult. It was plain that Wanda suspected the beeping incident was a scam. "Who beeped you?" Wanda asked sharply.

Kiki had apparently decided that Wanda's previous remark had been an insult and, having had only one face-lift, was still quite able to produce a look of imperious contempt. "None of your beeswax," she said haughtily.

Although it was imprudent to leave Wanda and Kiki on the verge of a squabble and within arm's length of nail files, Hannah could take it no longer. Tossing down her magazine, she walked outside, promising herself that she would run back in if she heard anything actually breaking.

Taking a deep yoga breath, she relished the crisp air. She had lived the better part of her life in Hill Creek. She and Kiki had been born and raised there, each leaving the area for a few years during their marriages but returning in widowhood. After Kiki's second husband, Cecil, died, she moved into Hannah's brown-shingled cottage a few blocks from town. Being on a pension, Hannah welcomed the help with the expenses, and even though she and Kiki bickered on occasion, she welcomed her sister's company as well. Now neither of them would consider living anywhere else.

As always, the town center buzzed with activity, the treasured parking spots packed with BMWs and Volvos, the residents swapping gossip in the coffee bars or hurrying down the sidewalks chatting into their cell phones. But today there was a special dreamy hum in the air. The upcoming festival with that night's opening party, the lectures, the films shown each night, the movie people who would be in town (even though they were second-tier movie people, they were *still* movie people) all served as an opiate to the townspeople.

Evidence of the festival could be seen everywhere. A huge banner announcing it hung across the three giant redwoods that rose out of the middle of Center Avenue. The Book Stop displayed movie-star biographies in the window, and a handwritten sign taped to the glass advertised a new coffee drink called Movie Mocha Madness. The boutiques had put their most elegant dresses out front for the opening-night party, and the Hill Creek Grocery was in the process of receiving a special shipment of fresh tuna (caught dolphin free) for the sashimi platters they were preparing for that night's event.

Though Hannah would have denied it if you asked her, she was as thrilled as anyone about the party. Having admired Frederick Casey for years, she was dying to meet him. Twenty years earlier he had made her favorite movie, a romantic comedy called *Midnight in Manhattan*. Casey was known for suspense-filled action films, but *Midnight in Manhattan* was a departure, and Hannah, although she never admitted it to a single soul, had seen it nine times. Perhaps the movie didn't have the genius of his other films, but Hannah identified with its softhearted hero suffering through his rotten love affairs and his habit of cleaning up the messes other people made. And of course, she adored the love story as well.

A smile on her face, she was remembering the last sweetly sad scene when a frantic beeping interrupted her, followed by a squeal and a curse. Peering back into the salon, she saw Wanda with Kiki's beeper, pressing a button with her thumb so it beeped repeatedly. Kiki grabbed for it, but Wanda held it high, keeping it just out of her reach.

"They're like spoiled girls in a gym class," Hannah said out loud. She was about to go inside when she felt a tap on her shoulder.

"Hannah," said a familiar voice behind her. She turned and saw Ed Kachowski wearing his usual trench coat, tweed hat, and battered Nikes, an outfit he wore every day regardless of the weather.

"Hello, Ed. How are you?" Hannah cheerily asked him, and she immediately heard several hellos come at him from inside the salon. An odd-looking man with a beakish nose and large melancholy eyes, Ed was a longtime Hill Creek resident and a favorite around town, especially with Lady Nails patrons. He nodded, his face breaking into a lopsided smile.

"Aunt Hannah!"

Lauren, Hannah's twenty-eight-year-old niece, rushed up, her face flushed, her long brown hair flying. "Did Kiki get beeped a minute ago? I just called her beeper number from my cell phone."

"Did she ask you to beep her while she was getting her pedicure?"

"Oh, yes. She wanted to make sure Wanda knew she had the beeper."

"Well, it worked."

"Good," Lauren said. "But that's not why I came over. I have to talk to you. I'm so excited about the party tonight. I'm all to bits. What should I wear?"

Lauren was an accountant and her clothes fell into two categories—gray suits and blue suits. Hannah had often tried to liven up her wardrobe, but Lauren had always lacked confidence when it came to dress.

"You have that red outfit I like," Hannah said.

Out of breath, Lauren gasped for air as she continued. "I was considering that one. I left work early so I could take my time getting dressed."

"Party?" Ed asked, a few beats behind in the conversation. The way he said the word, it came out sounding more like "powder," but Lauren and Hannah understood. Five years earlier Ed's son had died of a drug overdose in Southern California and soon afterward Ed's wife died also. It wasn't long before Ed had a stroke that slowed his speech to a barely understandable slur. Most of the town's residents knew him and they all looked out for him, but no one as much as Hannah, since she and Ed had been friends as far back as high school.

"Oh, yes, Ed," Lauren said. "The film-festival party. Movie people!"

"Only a couple," Hannah added.

Ed's head bobbed up and down.

"Would you like to go, Ed?" Hannah asked on impulse.

Ed's smile broadened, and Hannah arranged to meet him at the front door at seven.

"That was sweet of you," Lauren said as Ed walked away, his feet shuffling.

"I didn't do it to be sweet. He's good company and has a wicked sense of humor when you make out what he's saying."

Lauren checked her watch. "Gosh, it's late. I've got to run."

"Don't you want to say hello to Kiki?"

"Is Wanda in there, too?" Lauren asked warily. Hannah nodded. "Then no thanks. I'd rather avoid them. I heard about the chicken-poop incident." She wiggled her fingers at her aunt. "See you tonight."

When Hannah walked back into Lady Nails a voice bellowed, but surprisingly it belonged to neither Kiki nor Wanda.

"I'm telling you he's a has-been. His last three movies flopped," Bertha said loudly, turning a shade of purple that didn't look good on her. Hannah winced. Nature had given Bertha a voice like a bassoon in heat, and when she raised it, which was often, it made your fillings hurt.

"Flops? I don't remember any flops," Wanda said, trying to be polite since Bertha was her best friend.

Bertha turned in her seat, her hands still in the possession of Shiloh, who was applying the clear topcoat. But Shiloh spoke before Bertha could reply.

"So, like, who's Fred Casey?" she asked, wearing an expression that looked like she was receiving alien transmissions. "I never heard of him, and I used to live in L.A."

"A screenwriter and director. A very foul one." Bertha turned back to Wanda. "You don't remember his movies because most of them bombed. He deserves to fail. His treatment of women in his films is disgusting."

The conversation was getting interesting. Hannah dropped into the chair across from the manicure tables. "Are you talking about *Chains of Madagascar*? I saw it as being more symbolic. He used the female character as a symbol for how people can be destroyed by politics."

Bertha exhaled with exasperation. "Symbol my foot. The movie was a slap in the face to women everywhere. That character was a weak, brainless female who was physically abused by every man she met, then finally murdered.''

"But he made that movie fifteen years ago," Wanda told her.

"The movie still has impact. A woman was strangled five years ago with her thong underwear and the killer claimed he got the idea from *Chains of Madagascar*. But Casey didn't stop there.'' At this point Bertha gave the manicure table another rap. Ellie looked up from Kiki's toes.

"Stop it, Bertha. You're going to ruin your polish,'' she warned. "Your cuticles are such a wreck from all that digging.''

Bertha lived only five houses down from Hannah and Kiki, and the previous month she had been in her front yard digging a hole for a new Japanese anemone when she found a pottery shard. Certain that it had been left by Native Americans hundreds of years earlier, Bertha had proclaimed to anyone who would listen that her house was built on an Indian burial site. She was now in the process of excavating, but after weeks of shoveling all she had found besides that one shard were some old beer cans, a broken golf club, and a long-dead cat.

"The wretched state of my cuticles is a small price to pay for local history. I'm close to a real find. Naomi did some channeling for me last week and Red Moon was very encouraging,'' Bertha said. "But regardless of the richness of my personal pursuits, I can't turn a blind eye to a heathen like Frederick Casey. He's degraded women in every movie he's made, and I've heard his new movie is going to be the worst of all. The man's a blight on society, and I'm going to that party tonight to tell him so.'' Shiloh had just finished Bertha's nails, and Bertha rose from her chair. "Where's my purse?''

Wanda's mouth hung open. "You wouldn't do that, Bertha? You wouldn't spout off at Frederick Casey? He's the guest of honor. You'll embarrass everybody.''

Having found her handbag, Bertha let Shiloh get the money out of her wallet. Even in her anger she still had the presence of mind not to destroy a fifteen-dollar manicure. Once Shiloh had the money, Bertha headed for the door, turning back to her friends just as she reached it.

"There are some things more important than a silly party." Lifting her chin proudly and giving her permed gray bob a toss, she departed, slamming the door after her and sending the Buddhist prayer chimes into an apprehensive rattle.

"She's on the warpath," Kiki said. "We'll have to keep her away from Frederick Casey tonight."

Wanda nodded. "I've never seen her in such a snit."

Kiki leaned closer to Wanda. "Has Dr. Leland changed her hormones recently?"

Wanda's mouth, enhanced by collagen injections, pouted while she deliberated. "Don't think so. I can usually tell when that happens because she turns pink in the face. We'll just have to take turns keeping her busy tonight. The Hill Creek Grocery's doing the catering, and if they have those marvelous little pesto pastries she'll be glued to the buffet all night."

Hannah looked at the door Bertha had just exited. Bertha was the type of woman who stayed constantly angry. She always stomped about seething over something someone did or an article she read in the paper. It was one of the reasons Hannah avoided her. But Bertha's anger was usually the blustery sort and nothing to be taken too seriously.

Today Bertha was different. The intensity of her rage worried Hannah, and she doubted that a truckload of pesto pastries would mollify the woman. Besides, if the pastries were that good, Roger was bound to get to them first.

TWO

WITH KIKI IT WAS SELDOM a question of whether or not to show her silicone-enhanced cleavage, only a matter of how much of it to display. And that night for the party she had dished up the full monty, her bounteous breasts pushed up so high that there was only limited room between them and her chin. These man-made wonders, a gift from her long-departed second husband, Cecil, were her most prized possessions.

"She could balance a glass of wine on them and not spill a drop," Hannah said to Ed with a laugh as she glimpsed her sister in the far corner of the room talking animatedly to Wanda.

Hannah stood by the buffet table watching the party crowd, with Ed next to her contentedly munching a goat-cheese crostini. He looked dapper, dressed in gray slacks and a blue sport coat. Hannah had also dressed up for the party, wearing an ankle-length shift in deep blue velvet, her shoulder-length hair pulled back as always but ornamented with a small rose from her garden.

She noticed Kiki now standing on the podium in the center of the room anxiously searching the crowd. From her sister's ardent expression, Hannah assumed she was hunting down Roger Burke, but as soon as she caught Kiki's eye, her sister hurried off the podium, disappearing into the crowd.

The festival committee had expected only two hundred guests, but at least four hundred had shown up, everyone jammed elbow to elbow. The invitation said that dress was cocktail attire, but since it was a film-festival party everyone wanted to look artsy, and the room was a sea of black fabric, the guests blending together in one dark funereal blur.

Hannah caught sight of Kiki weaving through the herd. She was easy to pick out. Always the exception, Kiki had gone decisively Zsa Zsa, her frothy pale hair swept up and lacquered into a French twist with a string of fake pearls clipped horizontally above her bangs. The rest of her was swathed in a short and flouncy orange cocktail dress, the ensemble accessorized by gold spike heels, fake diamond earrings, and a matching necklace that dangled teasingly between her breasts.

Getting a closer view of Kiki's face, Hannah knew something bad had happened. Kiki ducked past the fire chief and the school superintendent, emerging at Hannah's side looking loaded for bear—eyes flashing and nostrils flaring with vexation.

"That darned Wanda!" was the first thing out of her mouth.

"Calm down," Hannah said, checking to make sure Ed wasn't listening, but he had wandered over to the buffet, having taken a serious liking to goat cheese. "Take a deep breath—that is, if you can take a deep breath with that girdle of yours."

"I keep telling you it's not a girdle, Hannah," Kiki said with a stamp of her foot. "It's a body shaper."

"A rose by any other name."

"God, I need a drink."

"And I'd cut back on my liquids if I were you. It took us thirty minutes to get you into that gird—I mean body shaper, and it'll probably take the Jaws of Life to get you out."

"You know, I think I may have eaten too many of those little cheesy things and it's getting hard to breathe, but I don't give a poop. Look how it's flattened my stomach." Kiki gave that part of her anatomy an appreciative pat.

Ed walked up carrying a plate piled with goat-cheese crostini as well as pesto pastries. "Kiki, you look lovely," he said, the words a little garbled but understandable.

"Thanks, Eddie. Those pesto things you've got look scrumptious." She reached for one but Hannah slapped her hand.

"Any more food and we'll have to get you a sign that says 'Warning, Contents Under Pressure.' "

Kiki shot Hannah a look then turned to Ed. "Having a good time?"

Ungluing his eyes from her breasts, he smiled and nodded.

"Now tell me, what's the problem with Wanda?" Hannah asked.

Kiki shivered as if the very name gave her the creeps.

"Is Wanda okay?" Ed asked with concern.

"Oh, she's fine and dandy. She's got Frederick Casey staying in her guest room for the whole week! Can you believe that? It's so sneaky."

"Frederick Casey?" Ed said with amazement.

"How did she manage it?" Hannah asked. "She doesn't even know the man."

"Her ex-husband Carl is on the film committee."

"I didn't realize he was her ex. Is he the oral surgeon?"

"No. That was Sam, her second. Carl was her third. He's an entertainment attorney and knows Casey through a friend of a friend. Turns out Casey was going to stay at his house in San Francisco because he doesn't like hotels or something, and Wanda told Carl that she'd give him back some sculpture she got in the divorce settlement if he could get Casey to stay in her stupid guest room. Now she's broadcasting it to everyone, including Roger, and this will probably get her that assistant job. I spent fifty bucks for that dumb pager, and now I can just get beeped till I scream for mercy and it won't do any good.'' Kiki clamped her fists on her hips.

The four-piece band with a saxophone and conga drum began playing energetic jazz at one end of the room. Hannah smiled when she noticed Ed bobbing to the music.

"I'm sure Roger won't let something so silly sway him,'' she said to her sister.

Kiki gave her a disbelieving look. "Oh, spit. You should have seen his face when she told him. I need an adult beverage and I need it now.'' She grabbed a glass of wine off a waitress's tray as it glided by her. "What do you think, Ed? Do you think it's right to use a personal relationship to step on people just to get what you want?"

"It happens,'' he replied.

Kiki took a gulp of wine. "You bet your sweet bippy it does. Well, I won't let old Wanda win that easily. This means war.''

Hannah felt a jolt of apprehension. "Don't be ridiculous. Just forget it and enjoy the party.''

"I won't forget it. There's bound to be something I can do if I put my mind to it,'' Kiki said, twisting the stem of her wineglass in her fingers. She turned to Ed. "You want to dance?''

He nodded eagerly. Kiki grabbed his hand, pulling him onto the dance floor, where they joined four other couples. Hannah chuckled as she watched Kiki do her unique slowed-down version of the Twist, her sister punctuating her swiveling movements by bending over and shimmying her shoulders. She had been doing the same dance for thirty-five years. In contrast to Kiki's loose movements, Ed gyrated stiffly, but he looked like he was having a good time.

In fact, it looked like such fun, Hannah felt like dancing herself, but she didn't see any stray men in her vicinity, so she just swayed to the music and drank in the elegant atmosphere.

Some of the festival-committee members wanted to have the party at the civic center, and it had been Hannah's idea to rent the rustic barnlike structure where the party ended up being held. In the early part of the century it had been Marin County's only winery. The winery's vineyards had long ago been replaced with expensive houses, and the winery itself was no longer a winery at all. So to add authenticity Hannah suggested they dress up the place with empty oak barrels brought in from Napa and stuff wine-soaked rags under loose floorboards so the room smelled like aged Merlot. Roger contributed the inspiration of filling the empty wine racks with wine borrowed from the committee members and other locals, and both Wanda and Bertha had contributed several cases.

Some people on the committee grumbled that Hannah had way too much influence for only a temporary member, but anyone would have to admit that the room was lovely. Hannah had the stone floors covered with rented Oriental rugs and the wood walls spruced up with garlands of ivy twinkling with tiny white lights. In the center of the room sat a huge rented fountain, the base of it at least eight feet wide, with a large fish rising just as high from its center spewing a glistening arc of water.

While Hannah scanned the room for Frederick Casey, wondering if she would have the nerve to introduce herself, she noticed Wanda glide onto the dance floor with Roger. Wanda had the shape of an underfed cat, and for the party a black jersey sheath draped her elegantly thin form. Much too loaded with understated chic to actually dance, she rotated her shoulders to the music while Roger, in a white dinner jacket that made him look like a snowball, bounced happily, snapping his fingers, eyes closed, his teeth over his lower lip. Tossing his head back, he roared with laughter when Wanda whispered something in his ear. Within moments they were dancing right next to Kiki and Ed.

Hannah could see her sister seething. Kiki began dancing faster, her twisting gestures more exaggerated in apparent hopes of attracting Roger's attention, and Ed speeded his movements as well, trying to keep up. Sensing the competition, Wanda swung her hip into Roger's, doing the old dance Hannah remembered as the Bump. This naturally meant Kiki had to bump also and she almost knocked poor

Ed off the dance floor. Fortunately, before paramedics were needed, the music ended, and Kiki, with Ed in tow, came back to Hannah.

"Did you see her throwing herself at Roger?" Kiki asked with desperation. "And her a married woman. But I'm not going to let her win that easy."

The last thing Hannah needed was an escalation in the feud with Wanda, but she was currently focused on Ed, who was still breathing heavily from the dancing. Hannah was looking around the room for a chair for him when a loud "testing, testing" followed by a microphone's screech interrupted her.

Roger twisted a knob on one of the speakers and the microphone quieted. Pinkie outstretched, he tapped a spoon against his wineglass. "If I could have everyone's attention, please. I'd like to take this opportunity to welcome our guest of honor, Frederick Casey!" he announced, and the room erupted into applause.

Hannah's breath caught in her throat. It was a dramatic moment. Since Casey had agreed to participate only a few days earlier, almost no one knew he was the guest of honor, but the crowd accepted him enthusiastically. Hannah, Kiki, and Ed already stood close to the platform and within seconds the party guests swarmed around them, but Hannah held her position so she could get a good look at Casey.

"Such a handsome man. So virile," Kiki shouted over the clapping as Casey stepped up to the podium. Hannah thought he looked much like his photographs—longish gray hair, western shirt, and fringed suede jacket, an affectation for a man born and raised in New York. But she didn't think him handsome. A heavyset, fleshy man, he looked older than his fifty-eight years. His skin was ruddy, and thick unruly gray eyebrows met above his nose, giving his face a demonic appearance. Hannah imagined that she saw sadness behind his flamboyant smile. Regardless of these impressions, she had to admit he cut a striking figure.

Casey bowed deeply to his audience and waited for the applause to die away. "Thank you, thank you, friends. Such a warm welcome is a treasure to me. I'm delighted to be here in your lovely village." He swept his arm with the flourish of a circus ringmaster, the fringe of his jacket fluttering.

Hannah cringed at the term "village." It made Hill Creek sound so unsophisticated, when it was hardly that. The town had two bookstores, a half-dozen upscale boutiques, and three different cafés that served cappuccino.

Casey continued. "I appreciate the affection—and the good taste," he added with a self-satisfied smirk, "that you've shown in inviting me here. Your film festival is an admirable venture. So many of this country's hamlets exist in cultural isolation."

Hannah bristled. Now, that was downright insulting. The nerve of someone from Los Angeles accusing, however obliquely, a town only thirty minutes from San Francisco of being culturally isolated.

As if she had hexed him, Casey stepped forward and stumbled, saved only by Roger catching his arm. Casey let out a belly laugh.

"And I hope, my fair friends," he went on, "that you will support my newest film project, which I'll be discussing in one of my lectures."

Support him how? Hannah thought. She found herself disappointed in him. He appeared half-drunk, but it was more than that. His manner seemed artificial, as if this were all a big joke for him. Looking at the eager faces of the people around her, she assumed they didn't share her feelings. Though oddly, Roger didn't appear dazzled one bit. He stood a good distance from Casey, and Hannah thought the smile on his face looked forced. In fact, he looked at Casey with what she could only describe as distaste. This was very strange, since Roger typically bowed down to anyone with fame or fortune, constantly maneuvering to be around people he considered "quality."

When Casey finished, Roger stepped forward. "And I'd also like to introduce Mr. Casey's longtime friend and partner, Hinkley Bowden, and Mr. Casey's son, Brad Casey."

Peering through the crowd, Hannah glimpsed an older man she assumed was Bowden raise his hand, but she couldn't see Casey's son. Roger turned again to Casey, opening his mouth to say something else, when suddenly Casey stepped off the platform. Roger watched this with chagrin, not ready to relinquish his guest of honor.

"Uh, well," he said, stammering. "A bit later Mr. Casey will give us a talk on his exciting new film project, *Pirate John*." He hurried off the platform and the crowd began to disperse.

A mass of people pushed by Hannah, Ed, and Kiki, shoving them together. One man tripped and fell into Ed, spilling his Coke onto his jacket and almost knocking him over. Hannah saw a troubled look on Ed's face, and she took hold of his hand.

"Are you all right?" she asked.

He nodded. "Too crowded."

"I agree. Let's find some chairs and sit. You want to join us, Kiki?"

But Kiki didn't hear. Her eyes were riveted to Casey, who now sat in a leather armchair preparing to hold court, already enthralling a small group with a loud pronouncement that caused everyone to laugh. Some people pulled up chairs, others sat cross-legged at his feet. Bowden, in contrast, stood off to one side, looking as if he preferred to be elsewhere. Hannah didn't know much about Bowden. He had been Casey's collaborator and producer for years, but he had always stayed in the background.

Hannah turned her attention to Kiki and saw her staring at Frederick Casey the way a cat stares at a shiny moving object. "I'm not going to let Wanda steal that assistant job right out from under my nose. I'm not going to lose like that."

Hannah's radar went on full alert. "Kiki," she said, a warning lurking in her voice.

Kiki flapped her hand in the air. "Oh, take a chill pill. You're always telling me that a woman's got to go after what she wants. Well, I'm going after what I want and I want to be Roger's assistant. If I could only get to Frederick Casey somehow. I could show Roger I know how to rub elbows with movie people just like Wanda."

Kiki's eyes turned dreamy, her head obviously filled with visions of the glittering future that lay ahead of her if only she could vanquish Wanda. She gulped some wine for courage then handed the glass to Hannah. "I'm going in," she said with the steely determination of an Israeli commando.

Feeling an uneasy twinge in her stomach, Hannah watched her sister head for Casey like a heat-seeking missile. It did not bode well, for when Kiki went after a man this zealously, it usually led to a mess that Hannah would have to clean up.

With a fretful sigh, Hannah took Ed's arm and steered him toward the end of the room near the foyer, where the crowd was sparse. She could only find one chair, but Ed insisted he would be fine alone, so she positioned him where he was on the fringes of the crowd but still had a good view of the party. Hannah then went to the bar.

"Is Ed okay?" Lauren asked, coming up behind Hannah just as a bartender handed her a plain soda. "I saw him dancing with Aunt Kiki. I think she wore him out."

Hannah nodded. "I'll get him home early." She took in Lauren's outfit with approval. Lauren wore a black skirt with a loose gold top and dangling gold earrings. Kiki had recently given her a makeup lesson and she was wearing blush, lipstick, and mascara. She looked astoundingly pretty.

"Have you tried the pesto pastries?" Hannah asked.

"Yes, they're good," Lauren said, "but I could tell the dough they used wasn't fresh and they were a little shy on the garlic."

Lauren was the finest and most creative cook Hannah had ever known, and Hannah had been telling her for years that she should be a chef and not an accountant.

"Do you see that guy over there?" Lauren pointed to a young man about thirty standing near Casey's chair. "That's Frederick Casey's son, Brad. Isn't he great looking? He's working with his father on his film project."

Hannah took a better look. Not at all like his father, Brad Casey was slight with dark hair, vivid brown eyes, thick eyebrows, and a chiseled face too pretty to be handsome.

Unlike the other guests he was dressed casually in dark slacks and a dark sweater. The girl he was talking to looked ecstatically up at him.

"He used to be on the television show *Arrest Warrant*. I was so sorry when it got canceled," Lauren said, her eyes still on him. "If only I could meet him."

Hannah noticed a sick-dog expression on her niece that she had never seen before. "What about Larry? Have you forgotten about him?"

"Of course not, but Larry doesn't act that interested in me. Besides, he's nice, but he's no Brad Casey."

Larry was a young Hill Creek police detective who with Hannah's prodding had asked Lauren out a few weeks earlier. They had gone out twice, and Lauren had seemed infatuated with him, at least until now.

"If you want to meet Brad Casey, then go meet him," Hannah said.

Lauren gave her a quizzical look. "What do you mean?"

"I mean just walk up to him and introduce yourself."

Blushing, Lauren shook her head. "I couldn't."

"Of course you could. Go after what you want. Look at your aunt Kiki over there. She's determined to sit on Frederick Casey's lap and nothing will stop her." Hannah paused. "Not that you should emulate her, of course, but she's an example of someone who's willing to go after what she wants." Saddam Hussein could have taken lessons from Kiki.

Hannah watched with amused affection as Lauren stood frozen by indecision, her eyes locked on Brad Casey, her heart propelling her forward, her head warning her to stay put.

"Go," Hannah urged, giving Lauren a gentle push. "Just do it."

Lauren looked at Hannah, then at the object of her desire. Hesitantly, she moved through the crowd in his direction, her steps at first faltering, then growing stronger. When she got within a few feet of him, she stopped. The woman he had been talking to walked away and he was there alone. Lauren looked over at her aunt for encouragement. Hannah waved her forward. Lauren inched closer. A woman tapped Brad on the shoulder. He turned, stepped backward, bumped slightly into Lauren, and, unbeknownst to him, caught the back of his sweater on Lauren's pierced earring.

Hannah winced. Brad chatted with the woman, both of them unaware of Lauren stooped behind them frantically trying to unhook her earring and her head from him. Hannah moved to help Lauren but stopped herself. Although Lauren was twenty-eight years old, she was amazingly naive, and Hannah thought that she herself was partly to blame. She had been overprotective of Lauren since her mother's death years before. Lauren had to learn to handle situations on her own. All Lauren had to do was poke Brad in the ribs and get his attention.

The woman he was talking to walked away and Brad started in the direction of his father. Lauren followed him, her head bent sideways. Hannah covered her eyes with her hand, peeking through two fingers. Feeling something, Brad turned, forcing Lauren to turn with him to keep her earring from being torn right out of her ear. From the puzzled look on Brad's face, he knew something was attached to him but couldn't see what it was, and he twisted around comically like a dog with a can tied to its tail.

Unable to stand it any longer, Hannah was moving toward them when Brad enlisted help from a man nearby, and Lauren's ear was quickly freed. But although her head was free of him, her mind was not. She stood there staring at him, eyes wide, mouth slightly open, incapable of speech. He smiled, his smile growing wider as he got a good look at her. He said something and the two began to talk.

"Well done," Hannah whispered to herself, although deep down she preferred Detective Larry Morgan for her niece. Morgan was a solid, kind man, as well as excellent husband and father material, which couldn't automatically be said for an actor. Still, every woman needed a little zest in her life. The very notion of zest made Hannah think of Kiki, and she looked around the room, finding her sister still with Frederick Casey. Always savvy, Kiki had scooted into a primo position directly in front of his chair so he was forced to notice her. Although it didn't look like he needed much forcing, since they were chatting.

It was then that Hannah caught sight of Naomi in the crowd near Casey. He must have said something that Naomi found spiritually uplifting because she clinked her finger cymbals, holding her hand high so everyone could see where the sound came from. When Naomi noticed Hannah looking her way, she waved and headed for her.

Naomi always wore loose caftan-style clothing that Hannah joked was designed by Oscar De La Tenta, and tonight she sported a bright red caftan, purple turban, and rings on every finger.

"Well, it looks like our famous director has developed quite an interest in Kiki," Naomi said when she reached Hannah. "He seems quite fascinated with her."

Fascinated? With Kiki? Hannah looked closely at Casey and her sister. It was true that the two of them were deep in conversation, their heads close together. Casey said something, touched the pearls in Kiki's hair, and she girlishly giggled.

Hannah just didn't get it. Granted, Kiki was an unusually buoyant woman for her age, but not the type to inspire interest from someone like Casey. Hannah used to say, to herself only, of course, that you could walk through the ocean of Kiki's mind and not get your ankles wet.

"What are she and Casey talking about?"

"Mostly about the new film project he's working on, from what I overheard. Such an interesting man. So intense. So full of *joie de vivre*," Naomi said with a sweep of her arm. "Red Moon would like him very much, I think. Perhaps I should—" She lifted her hand high, and it froze in midair. A peculiar expression wafted across her face, a mixture of curiosity and wonder. Then she began choking. It wasn't a huge choke. More of a quiet gagging, but it was enough to frighten Hannah. Moving swiftly behind Naomi, she put her arms around her to give her the Heimlich maneuver, but Naomi waved her away.

"What's wrong? Do you need water?"

"No, I'm fine," Naomi said, her voice raspy. She paused, lifting her chin and closing her eyes. "How puzzling. Saying Red Moon's name just now made me feel him. Here." Opening her eyes, she pressed one palm just below her chest. "He wants to come out. He has something to say." She paused again. "He thinks there's some sort of trouble in the room."

"Don't be silly. How many glasses of wine have you had?"

"Only one and three quarters, and it was absolute swill. No, Hannah, there's adversity in this room, and it's connected to you and me somehow."

"I don't see what kind of adversity could be here," Hannah said, a nervous flutter in her chest. She glanced about the room to make sure her family and friends were faring well. Ed was talking to Roger, with Roger leaning his head close to make out what Ed was saying. Lauren was chatting with Brad Casey. Kiki's fingers danced on Frederick Casey's thigh. "Everything in this room looks normal to me."

"It's not normal," Naomi said. "Red Moon wants to speak."

Hannah inhaled sharply. "Naomi, please, not here." Bringing out Red Moon required a great deal of loud Indian chanting, after which he took over Naomi's body. When Naomi started speaking with a deep male voice, it could be disturbing if you weren't prepared for it. Hannah was about to take her outside when Naomi spotted something across the room and grimaced. "Uh-oh. Here comes Wanda to harass me about holding another séance for that dead dog."

"I thought you were charging her extra for the sessions with Bon Bon."

"I am, but even *I* don't need money that bad. It's beneath Red Moon's dignity to talk to that yappy little canine spirit. And Wanda insists on bringing along its former vessel."

"You mean the stuffed version?"

"Yes. It stinks to high heaven, its hair comes out everywhere, and it has fleas."

"Fleas on a stuffed dog?"

"The dog may be dead but the fleas live on. Must be karma. She should have had the dog freeze-dried. Everybody knows you freeze-dry now. Stuffing is old technology. Drat, she's definitely heading this way."

With Wanda making a beeline in their direction, Naomi flew off, her fiery caftan flapping like a behemoth butterfly. To Hannah's surprise, even though Wanda saw Naomi leave, she didn't change course.

"Hannah, I must talk to you." Wanda said it like a command. "You know I have Frederick Casey staying at my house."

"I believe I heard something."

Wanda edged closer. "May we speak in confidence?"

"It depends about what." As a rule Hannah avoided listening to secrets, because if they were juicy, it was so painful not being able to tell Kiki.

"About Frederick Casey."

Who could resist? "Go on."

"Well, the strangest thing happened." She lowered her voice, fingering her opera-length pearls. "Frederick dropped off his luggage this afternoon and then left right away. Being in my house even briefly got his creative juices going, I'm sure, and he probably had to rush off to explore them." She stopped, and if her brow hadn't been surgically rendered incapable of furrowing, it surely would have. "But this evening, before I left for the party, I found this note on my doorstep."

When she was certain no one was watching, Wanda slipped a piece of folded paper out of her small black beaded handbag and handed it to Hannah. The outside had Casey's name printed on it. Unfolding it, Hannah read, *Stop your cruelty. There are people who won't stand for it.* The words had the clear crispness of a laser printer's work.

Hannah looked at Wanda. "What does Casey say about this?"

"I haven't shown it to him yet. I didn't want to spoil the party for him." Wanda cast her eyes at Casey, noticing Kiki next to him, her hand now firmly gripping his thigh. "He's having such fun," she said, her voice acidic.

"You must show it to him," Hannah told her. "He may know who it's from. How many people know he's staying at your house?"

"Quite a few, actually. I made some calls, just to friends, you know." Which meant Wanda had called everyone in her address book.

"Talk to Casey about this right away, Wanda. Promise me."

"Do you think someone wants to hurt him?"

"I don't know, but he should probably call the police. This note is threatening."

Wanda nodded, looking frightened, then put the note back in her handbag and took off.

Needing fresh air, Hannah negotiated her way through the throng toward the patio. The party was growing noisier, the music louder and the dance floor more packed, and she had to bob and weave like a prizefighter to squeeze through. At last, with a sigh of relief, she stepped outside, the din of the party muting when she closed the heavy door behind her.

The flagstone patio ran the length of the winery and was surrounded by towering eucalyptus trees that looked black against the sky. Standing near the railing, she relished being alone for a while. She had never been the type for parties, and since her breast cancer eight years earlier she found herself becoming reclusive. It had only been in the past few months that she started forcing herself to accept invitations and get out more. She liked being with her family and friends, but people were always asking her for advice. It was something in her nature, she supposed, and she didn't really mind it. Although she had never felt much good at figuring out her own life, she felt perfectly competent to advise others on theirs. When you were outside a situation things seemed so straightforward.

She lifted her nose and inhaled the clean aroma of the eucalyptus, and the delight she took in this quiet moment instilled the urge to write a poem. She was the semiofficial local poet, her poems published twice a month in the *Marin*

Sun weekly, and she had a poem due to the newspaper in only two days.

"Let's see now," she murmured, her eyes closed. "I wrap the night around me, a silky purple shawl." She halted, not liking it. She was about to restate the line differently when the sound of a man's voice startled her.

"Outside for a cigarette? I could use another one. I'm out," a male voice said. A spark of red and a puff of smoke emerged from the shadows followed by a man's dark outline.

"I don't smoke," Hannah answered. She heard him take a drag of the cigarette, its tip glowing a brighter red.

"I should have known. No one smokes in this burg. The bars here don't even have matches." His voice was nasal, the words sharp.

A beam of light caught his face as he moved closer. His was a narrow face, all sharp angles, with a slender nose and a judgmental mouth, shrewd eyes gleaming behind small round glasses. She recognized him as Hinkley Bowden, Frederick Casey's partner.

"I guess you're going to spout off about how it's bad for me," he continued. He ran one hand through thick dark hair, which, combined with his thinness, made him look boyish, though he had to be close to Casey's age. "That I'm fouling the air and all that crap."

A marine breeze swept across the patio and Hannah wrapped her arms around herself. "You're a grown man and can make your own decisions." She playfully raised one eyebrow. "Besides, I have a dirty secret."

Bowden stepped closer. "Just the kind I like."

"I enjoy the smell of cigarette smoke."

His mouth curled up at the corners. "That *is* a dirty secret. Makes me want to know you better."

"I wouldn't make any hasty decisions. I also like the smell of steer manure."

She expected him to laugh, but he only shrugged. "The odors are probably similar," he said. Shifting his body so the light from the window struck her, he looked at her fixedly, sucking on his cigarette as if it were his primary oxygen source.

She smiled broadly. "In the sixties, in Haight Ashbury, that's how we smoked dope."

He exhaled, the smoke floating in curls out his nose. "This *is* dope, and I like it better than liquor, food, and most women." He started to say more, but stopped himself. He waited before speaking again. "So how come you're not in there with the rest of the local yokels kissing Fred Casey's ass?"

"I wouldn't call our residents local yokels. And most everybody is dazzled by movie people."

"Not you, I expect."

"I'm talking to you, aren't I?"

"Well, do yourself a favor and be dazzled by something else. These no-talent supposed stars and screenwriters that litter the film screens. They're plastic gods." He threw his cigarette on the flagstone and ground it with his shoe. "Plastic gods," he muttered.

This bitterness surprised Hannah. Bowden had produced Casey's screenplays for over fifteen years before the partnership ended. She had read somewhere that the breakup hadn't been friendly, and she wondered what had drawn the two men back together.

"Hink, buddy!" a thick voice boomed behind them. Bowden squeezed his eyes shut as if hit by a shooting pain. Casey hurried onto the patio, tailed by a short, thick, dark-haired girl in her twenties. In spite of Hannah's earlier disappointment in Casey, her pulse quickened.

Casey went straight to Bowden, not even noticing Hannah's presence, and draped an arm around his shoulder. "I need a real fuggin' drink, buddy. That crap in there is goat piss." The girl gave him a dirty look and slid her eyes to Hannah, causing Casey to notice her. He laughed then took Hannah's hand, pressing it to his wet lips. "Sorry, madam, if I offended. It's first-rate goat piss, but I prefer expensive gin."

With a grin, he pulled a leather-covered flask out of his pocket, put it to his mouth, then tipped his head back. With a howl of disapproval he quickly pulled the flask away, spinning toward the girl. "Angie, this fuggin' thing is practically empty. What the hell do I pay you for?"

His words were slightly slurred. Hannah was well known for her olfactory powers, and taking a good sniff of Casey, she knew he had emptied his flask over the course of the evening.

"The way you drink that stuff it would be a twenty-four-hour job," Angie said. "Get your booze yourself, you sotted, fat, puke-hole has-been."

Bowden chuckled. Hannah was shocked, unable to imagine what Casey's reaction would be to such an insult.

"Angie's a sweet little thing, isn't she?" Casey said with a smile of beautifully capped teeth. He took off his fringed suede jacket, shoving his empty flask in the outside pocket before handing it to her. "Here. Make yourself useful. I'm hot." He blew her a kiss. "And not for you, my love."

Cursing, she grabbed the jacket and stormed to the door, jerking it open and closing it with a moderate slam. An awkward silence engulfed the patio. Hannah felt embarrassed by what had happened and was struggling to think of something lighthearted to say when suddenly Casey giggled.

"That's my dear assistant, Angie. She's just sucking up because she wants a raise. I hate suck-ups, don't you?" he said to Hannah.

"I have no experience with them."

Casey laughed. "Unfortunately I've known many."

The patio door opened and a burst of noise and music spilled out along with Roger.

"Frederick, I'd like you to meet a few of the film festival's major contributors, and after that I thought you could give your little talk."

Roger's use of Casey's first name made Hannah think that perhaps Roger was going to schmooze Casey up after all, falling into that army of suck-ups Casey claimed he detested. She suspected that in reality Casey not only enjoyed groveling attention but that his ego required it.

Casey grunted and followed Roger back into the party,

leaving Hannah alone with Bowden. For a while the two of them were silent, with Bowden staring off into the trees. Casey's presence had been so potent it took a moment for the air to clear of him.

"He and his assistant have an interesting working relationship," Hannah finally said.

"Angie's a good girl, really. No one can be around Fred long and maintain much dignity. But Fred's a destructive man, as much to himself as everyone else."

"What do you mean?"

"His health mostly. He's got heart problems, he's overweight, has high blood pressure, and still he insists on drinking a quart of gin a day." He pulled off the tip of a frond from a large fern growing on the other side of the railing, twisting it in his fingers, his expression grim. "Nice talking with you." He tossed the mangled leaf onto the ground and went back inside.

Hannah followed shortly, ready to go home. Scanning the room, she saw Angie, the scowl still on her face, hanging Casey's jacket on the coatrack in the foyer. Movie people are an odd bunch, Hannah decided. They were cynical and self-obsessed and it was probably best to avoid them.

She wandered around the room for a good ten minutes. She saw Ellie and Shiloh talking to Ed, and then after a few more minutes of looking found Kiki standing next to Casey by the fountain. Hannah gave her a subtle wave, but before she could get Kiki's attention, Bertha marched up to Casey, planting herself in front of him.

"You've done more to degrade women than any man in modern culture," Bertha shouted to be heard over the music. Kiki's eyes widened with shock, her unhappiness quickly spreading to the rest of the room. The chatter slowly silenced as all heads turned to see what was happening.

Bertha, loving to remind everyone of her years in chic Santa Fe, wore her usual denim skirt, cowboy boots, and pound of turquoise jewelry. As she angrily faced Casey, him with his own cowboy boots and western shirt, the scene reminded Hannah of some bad western musical. She envisioned Bertha and Casey shooting Colt .45s into the air, letting loose with a whoop then bursting into a duet about campfires and lassos.

But no duets would be sung. As Bertha glanced around her and saw with unnerving clarity that she was the center of attention, she gathered up all her nerve and spoke with increased potency. "You have depicted women as shallow, willing victims of violence, as dumb animals put on earth only for man's pleasure."

"It was their pleasure, too," Casey said with a chuckle, but no one chuckled with him. "Now, honey, let's not get worked up."

The room was so quiet you could have heard the dropping of a bean sprout. Hannah felt the tension as the guests grappled with the moral perplexities before them. If Casey had been anything less than a respected screenwriter, the emotional tide of the room would have surely turned against him, since there were few things people in Hill Creek relished more than moral outrage. But Casey was an artiste, and that automatically threw the needle of the Politically Correct-O-Meter bouncing to the right, and Hannah felt the crowd's energy wafting his way. The man could have dropped his trousers and everyone most likely would have chalked it up to artistic folly.

Giving Casey an icy glare, Bertha stood proudly erect, chin held high, uncaring of the fact that all eyes were upon her, that all mouths gaped open at her insolence. "I will continue to be worked up as long as men like you are out there making degrading films. You can't do this, Mr. Casey."

"And who's going to stop me?" he asked.

"I am," Bertha answered. "I'll stop you for the sake of my sex."

Hannah watched Bertha with both alarm and admiration. She had dared to confront this man whom everyone in the room idolized, and that took courage. Although Hannah had never cared for Bertha, at that moment she liked her.

But Casey did not. "You're not a woman," he told her. "You're a mastodon with a brassiere."

The following moments of stunned quiet were broken by a few giggles that quickly grew into laughter. Without another word, he walked away, leaving Bertha red-faced with humiliation.

Both Ed and Hannah ran to Bertha's aid. Her face crumpled with embarrassment and fury, she locked her eyes on Casey's backside as he walked, joking with companions, to the buffet. Hannah stretched a friendly hand to her, but Bertha pushed it away, then stomped toward the foyer and the ladies' room.

Hannah couldn't believe Casey's cruelty. Yes, Bertha had confronted him, but he was well known and respected and could easily withstand a rebuke from a comical, rather pathetic local matron. He didn't have to humiliate her in such a personal way. Hannah couldn't believe that the man who wrote *Midnight in Manhattan* could treat someone with so little compassion.

"Let's go," Hannah said, moving alongside Kiki. "I've had enough of this party, and I think I should get Ed home."

"I can't go now. I have to go back and find Frederick." Kiki leaned her head close to her sister's. "I think he likes me."

Hannah raised an eyebrow. "After what he just did to Bertha, who cares?"

"Some people might say she deserved it."

"I'm not one of them. And what about Roger? I thought you were after him."

Kiki smirked. "Don't be silly. Roger's Spam. I've had a taste of filet, honey, and I like it. You go on without me. I'll get home by myself."

Kiki started to leave, but Hannah stopped her.

"Come home with me, please, Kiki. You've had a few drinks and you know you don't do well with alcohol."

But Kiki was adamant, so Hannah gathered up Ed, and together they walked outside. Fog had rolled in, turning the night air chilly. She shivered and put her arm in Ed's for warmth. A few other guests were also leaving, the sounds of car engines cutting through the night.

"Did you have a good time, Ed?"

"Poor Bertha," was all he said.

"I know." Hannah patted his arm. "Try not to worry about her. It will all blow over."

But he didn't look convinced, and they walked to Hannah's Eldorado in silence.

As their feet crunched against the gravel, she remembered what Naomi had said about there being trouble in the room and that somehow it was connected to them. The incident with Bertha proved her right. Hannah only hoped the trouble stopped there.

THREE

$\mathscr{A}$T TWO THAT MORNING KIKI still wasn't home. Too worried to sleep, Hannah paced her small living room, her travels across the carpet broken by worried glances out the window. But Walnut Avenue remained quiet and empty, the rest of its residents all safely asleep. Even Hannah's pet pig, Sylvia Plath, and her dog, Teresa S. Eliot, both SPCA foundlings, lay peacefully in their beds, unaware of Hannah's suffering.

"I never should have left her," she said aloud, running both hands through her hair. She dropped into the chair by the window and looked out at the shadows the street lamp threw on the pavement. Kiki had a way of finding trouble.

The phone rang. She leaped to answer it. "Hello, Kiki?"

A cavernous silence loomed on the other end of the line. Hannah felt her insides wrench.

"Oh, Hannie," a quivering voice said at last. The use of the nickname didn't bode well. Kiki only used it when she badly needed her sister's help. "Something shocking has happened."

"Kiki, where are you? Are you all right?"

"I guess. I guess I'm okay."

Hannah's shoulders slumped with relief. "What happened? What shocking thing happened?"

"Well," Kiki began. She started sniffling. "I don't know where to start."

"Start anywhere."

"Well, I went back home with Freddie."

"Freddie who?"

"Freddie Casey. We went back to Wanda's guest room, where he was staying." Kiki took a deep, shuddering breath. "And I went into the bathroom, you know, to freshen up. And when I came back out . . ."

There was a moment of dead air, the suspense for Hannah unbearable. "When you came back out, what?"

"When I came back out, Freddie was lying on the bed, and you won't believe this, Hannah. He was completely naked except for a black cape and this little black eye patch."

"Good Lord," Hannah said. "Shocking is not the word."

"No, that's not what's shocking," Kiki said with a trace of annoyance filtering into her distress. "Hannah, he was dead!"

Four

The 1972 GOLD CADILLAC ELDORADO convertible sputtered with irritation as Hannah shifted it into second gear. Like Hannah, it wasn't used to being up and out at two in the morning, and she had to coax it up the steep hill that led to Wanda's five-thousand-square-foot monstrosity of a house. She inhaled the car's familiar, comforting aroma of aged vinyl, pressed powder, and perfume, but it didn't calm her anxiety.

Hannah had left home in such a hurry she hadn't even changed her clothes but had just thrown a raincoat over her flannel pajamas and pushed her feet into rubber gardening clogs. There had been no time to dillydally, for once Kiki revealed that Casey was dead, once she had shaped the horrific reality into words, she erupted into a Vesuvius of hysterics.

Struggling to keep herself calm, Hannah steered the car around a curve and studied the houses, trying to remember which one was Wanda's. She had only been there a couple of times for Rose Club luncheons, and she remembered its design as pale stucco and overdone French, like some cheesy Riviera hotel. But in the dark they all looked like cheesy Riviera hotels.

She craned her neck over the steering wheel and looked harder as her mind gyrated with the possibilities of how Kiki had ended up with Fred Casey mostly naked and fully deceased. Truth was, given Kiki's luck in such matters, the situation was believable. Was Kiki cursed? Had some voodoo queen put a spell on her at birth that caused disasters? Hannah made a mental note to never let her sister out of the house ever again. She could buy the type of invisible fence they made for dogs and glue some rhinestones on the special collar so Kiki would wear it, then if Kiki tried to leave the front yard she'd get a mild electrical shock.

Just then something large and orange, bobbing wildly over to the left of the street, startled Hannah. At first she thought it was a huge traffic cone bouncing in the wind, but then realized it was Kiki jumping up and down in her orange chiffon dress, furiously waving.

With a screech of tires Hannah pulled the Cadillac to the curb. Kiki galloped to the car, jerked open the door and hurled herself in.

"Oh God, Hannie!" Kiki threw her arms around her sister.

"It's okay, sweetie. It's okay," Hannah said, holding on to Kiki and patting her back. When they at last separated, Hannah took a good look at Kiki and found her in total disarray—her lipstick smudged, her hair wrecked, the string of pearls previously adorning her coiffure now dangling in front of her nose. "Tell me what happened."

"I can't talk! I'm too upset!"

Hannah took her firmly by the shoulders. "You have to. Take a deep breath. That's right." She paused while Kiki ballooned her cheeks with air. "You'll have to exhale now, sweetie. There you go. Now tell me what happened." Hannah swallowed hard, bracing for the worst.

"Well, things started out so nice. Freddie and I got along really great at the party and he asked me if I wanted to come home with him and—" She paused. "You know, have a drink. So we were in his bedroom and he was going to show me his plans for his new movie, *Pirate John*."

"How did you get in his bedroom?" Hannah asked with

suspicion, since Kiki had frequently been known to succumb to the more animal side of her nature.

Another pregnant hesitation. "Well, that's where the movie plans were. So we had a drink, and we were having oodles of fun, laughing and talking," Kiki said, her voice brightening as she relived the more pleasant part of the evening, when all participants were upright and breathing. "Then Freddie said he wanted to play a game, and I said, 'Gee, that sounds fun.' But I had to go to the little girls' room, so I went in and it took a while because I had awful problems with my body shaper."

"It's amazing you came out at all."

"Whatever," Kiki said coldly. "Anyway, it took me some extra time and when I came out—" She stopped, her mouth quivering as she envisioned the horrible scene. "When I came out Fred was lying on the bed. He was on his back, with his arm to the side kind of funny, like this." She sprawled one arm out against the back of the seat, bending it at the elbow. "He looked perfectly okay, really, and I thought maybe he was asleep. I mean he had been drinking a little. So I tiptoed up to him and I said, 'Oh, Freddie, oh, Freddie.' " She tapped her index finger in the air. "Then I realized that he must have had a heart attack. He was dead!" she blubbered. "Oh God, it was so awful. Let's get out of here!" She was shaking so hard now that the pearls in her hair swayed like a pendulum in front of her face. She reached up and ripped them out.

Hannah patted her shoulder again. "You called 911?" Kiki nodded. "Then we should go back to Wanda's. The paramedics and the police may want to talk to you. They'll want to know what happened."

"What does it matter now? He's dead."

"Are you completely sure?"

"Deader than a doornail."

"You took his pulse?"

Kiki threw up her hands in frustration. "I think I know dead when I see it. Trust me, the man kicked the bucket. Now get me home."

"You can't run away. Wanda will tell them you were there."

"No, Wanda didn't know, I'm sure. We were really quiet. I'll call the police later. I swear I will. I'm just too upset right now. Have pity on me."

Hannah studied her sister. Kiki was shaking, tears filling her eyes, and Hannah could feel herself weakening. She knew she should make her go back to Wanda's house and wait, but Kiki looked so pathetic. Besides, Casey was beyond help, and Kiki was too upset to say anything rational. She might make the paramedics' work that much harder.

"You promise to call them first thing in the morning?"

"On my honor, Hannie."

The Cadillac was too large for a U-turn, so Hannah shifted into reverse, backed into a driveway, then turned back down the hill toward the perceived safety of their home.

Early the next morning a churlish mood had settled inside the little brown-shingled house on Walnut Avenue, an accusatory tension that pervaded the cozy kitchen, recently painted cornflower blue, where Hannah and Kiki sat at the breakfast table. It seemed steeped in their coffee and baked into their muffins. They sat across from each other, Hannah eyeing Kiki, who was still in her fluffy pink chenille robe, hair curlers, and bunny slippers. Hannah was dressed in slacks and a light sweater.

Kiki avoided Hannah's laser gaze by concentrating on piling as much strawberry jam as possible on her third muffin. Stress eating, she slathered the sticky red goo with the back of a teaspoon, her face pinched.

"You have to call the police. You promised," Hannah commanded. Kiki refused to look at her. The room was thick with gloom, and Sylvia and Teresa lay by the back door watching the women, their soft eyes worried.

Hannah was baffled by her sister's recalcitrance. Although it would be embarrassing to explain the previous night's events, Kiki was innocent of any wrongdoing.

When she found Casey dead she had called 911 and gotten help.

"I made that promise under duress," Kiki replied, nervously slathering jam to the point where she was getting more on her fingers than her muffin. "The fact is, no one needs to know I was there. It's terrible that poor Freddie met his Maker so unexpectedly, but it's God's will. It doesn't relate to me directly, and telling the police will just get them in a snit."

Hannah's face turned the color of the strawberry jam, her palm hitting the table so hard the silverware jumped. Sylvia squeaked and hastily trotted out of the room, with Teresa right behind.

"It's not right. It's disgraceful," she said angrily.

Kiki finally looked up. "Don't you dare raise your voice to me when I'm about to fall flat on my face from stress."

"Phooey. I never would have let you come home last night if I'd known—"

A frantic rapping on the back door put the brakes on Hannah's tirade and she got up to open it.

Without waiting for an invitation, Naomi flew in, her face flushed and her bracelets rattling.

"Just got a call from Wanda! She was screeching like a banshee with her butt on fire. You're not going to believe what's happened!"

Hannah and Kiki just stared at her, their eyes popping from the strain of suddenly bottling up emotions that only a few seconds earlier had flowed so freely.

"Frederick Casey is dead!" The words spewed out of Naomi's mouth. After a moment's hesitation Kiki let out an obviously faked gasp followed by a more realistic "My God," pushing her hands against the breakfast table as if she required bracing so not to collapse from the shock.

Hannah gave her sister a sidewise glance. Wanting to see the visitor, Sylvia and Teresa trotted back into the kitchen, the two of them sniffing the hem of Naomi's caftan for the intriguing olfactory traces of her cat.

Naomi looked at Kiki a moment, pressed a comforting

hand on her shoulder, said a "poor dear," then swept over
to the stove. "I need tea."

"Help yourself," Hannah told her, though she hardly
needed to, for Naomi had already opened the cabinet and
gotten out the Red Zinger.

"A heart attack, Wanda guesses it was," Naomi said as
she filled the kettle with water. "He had heart surgery a
few years back. I read about it. Somebody actually filmed
the surgery and put it to music. Though he looked fine at
the party, didn't he?"

She directed this question at Kiki, who nodded energet-
ically, her eyes wide as salad plates. Kiki then jumped out
of her chair and opened the refrigerator door, scanning its
contents for stress-reducing foodstuffs. Naomi continued.
"Who knows what brought it on? Maybe he just got too
excited."

Kiki peeked around the fridge door with a barely sup-
pressed smile.

"Or had a nasty shock," Hannah said with a sarcastic
tone.

"I felt it last night at the party," Naomi said, pressing
her fingers to her temples. "Remember, Hannah, when we
were talking about Casey, and I felt Red Moon wanting to
speak? He was sending out a warning."

A cold leg of chicken in hand, Kiki sat back down and
began to gnaw greedily. While Naomi spooned tea into the
teapot with her back to her friends, the sisters communicated a wealth of information, accusations, and denials via
eye and gesture.

"What was really strange was the timing," Naomi said,
the pantomime continuing behind her. Hannah shook an
accusatory finger at her sister, while Kiki, mouth full, huff-
ily waved a poultry part. "Wanda said he received a threatening letter yesterday. It arrived at Wanda's with his name
on it."

Kiki looked aghast and Hannah's hand rose involuntarily
to her mouth as she suddenly remembered the letter. With
all the tumult, the letter hadn't even entered her mind. But
why should it? she reasoned, since Casey had died of nat-

ural causes. An uncomfortable tingle ran up the back of her
neck. If she believed in Red Moon she might just think that
Casey's death had been from a cause that was unnatural.
Just then Hannah noticed Naomi's hand freeze in midair
over the teapot. Suddenly Naomi spun back around.

"You already knew he was dead, didn't you?" she said,
her tone not one of accusation but of wonderment.

"No! We didn't know anything!" Kiki spit out the
words along with a few bits of chicken in a high-pitched
staccato that only confirmed Naomi's suspicions. "We just
heard it from you."

Hannah stood up, her mind still focused on the letter.
How could she have forgotten about it? Kiki had to talk to
the police and there was no time to lose.

Before Hannah could open her mouth, Naomi pointed a
finger at her and cried out, "You!"

Hannah jumped. "What?"

"Don't be afraid. Don't try to hide it," Naomi said,
throwing her arms around Hannah and clutching her so
tightly Hannah could hardly breathe. "You knew that man
was dead. It's *sooo* fabulous. I've always known you had
psychic abilities. In an underdeveloped, infantile state, of
course, but with time, with nurturing . . . !"

Having her windpipe crushed was one thing, but the idea
of Naomi calling her psychic was way too much to put up
with. Hannah disentangled herself. "I know about Casey
because Kiki told me. She was there last night."

Kiki emitted a tense shriek of astonishment and dismay,
this time authentic. Naomi looked puzzled.

"Last night?" Naomi said, her index finger pressed to
her chin. "I don't understand. Wanda didn't find the poor
man until this morning when she brought him his newspaper and granola."

With dramatic flair, the teakettle announced its boiling
via a piercing whistle. It was now Hannah's turn for authentic emissions of astonishment and dismay, and these
she let loose with abundance as the dismal truth about
Kiki's behavior presented itself.

Naomi, made increasingly thirsty by this unfolding

drama, calmly poured the hot water into the teapot. There was little need to push for information. She didn't have to be psychic to know that juicy details were about to spill forth. The Hoover Dam couldn't have stopped them. But although Naomi was tranquil, Kiki and Hannah were pitching hissy fits.

"Kiki, you told me last night that you called 911!"

"I did! I called them. I wouldn't fib about that."

"Then why didn't they find the body until this morning? What did they do, decide 'oh, gee, the guy's dead anyway, let's just leave him until tomorrow?' "

This created a temporary conversational vacuum, with Hannah and Naomi looking expectantly at Kiki.

"It was like this. You see, I called 911," she said at last, her voice rising to a childish pitch. "They asked me first thing if it was an emergency, and I was so flustered." She took an anxious bite of chicken, then kept talking. "My head was just spinning. So I said, well, no, it wasn't." She turned up one of her palms. "I didn't really know if it was an emergency or not. I mean he was dead. If he was sick or hurt, now that's an emergency, right? I was about to tell them that he was dead, but they put me on hold, and I lost my nerve and hung up."

While Naomi calmly looked on, sipping her tea, Hannah stomped around the small kitchen.

"Kiki Goldstein, I am shocked at your behavior. You just wanted to avoid a scandal. The man might have needed medical assistance. What if he wasn't really dead?" Hannah said with a severity only one notch below ranting.

Kiki threw her sister a nasty look. "Why do you keep asking that? I'm not stupid. If you must know, I put my compact mirror under his nose and it didn't fog up. Fred was dead and that's that."

By this time tears were filling Kiki's eyes, a sight that always turned Hannah's heart to churned butter.

"I believe you," she said, patting Kiki's shoulder. "I'm just so upset. That threatening letter that came to Wanda's house yesterday is such a terrible coincidence. I wonder if he was frightened by it and that caused his heart attack.

Though we can't be sure Wanda got the chance to even tell him about it. Did Casey mention the letter to you?''

Kiki shook her head.

Taking a contemplative sip of tea, Naomi eyed Kiki over the rim of her teacup. ''Are you telling me,'' she said after she had swallowed the last gulp of Red Zinger, ''that *you* actually went back to Wanda's with Frederick Casey?''

Naomi's overtones on the pronoun left no uncertainty of her meaning.

The corners of Kiki's mouth dropped southward. ''Why is that hard to believe?''

''No offense to you, dear, but of all the women in the room throwing themselves at him. Young women. Beautiful women. No offense to you,'' Naomi quickly repeated.

But offense was taken. Kiki drew herself up with righteous indignation, her chin lifted proudly, eyes narrowed. She would have looked almost regal if it hadn't been for her hair curlers and bunny slippers. ''I'll have you know that the man couldn't keep his hands off me. It was probably the sight of me in my Wonderbra that did him in.''

Hannah's face registered concern. ''I thought you said that everything was innocent on your part.''

Kiki pressed her fingers against her cheek. ''It was innocent. Completely innocent.''

Hannah wondered if Kiki was familiar with Webster's definition of that particular word. Kiki continued. ''We were just being silly, you see. I told him I had on a leopard-print Wonderbra and he said he didn't believe me, so I showed him. It was just for giggles. If I'd known what effect it was going to have on him, I never would have done it.''

A wry smile crossed Naomi's face. ''Even if you were there, dear, I doubt that the sight of you in your skivvies sent the man into cardiac arrest.''

Kiki exhaled with exasperation and slammed what was left of the chicken leg down on the table.

''I was there, darn it, and I can prove it!''

Hannah opened her mouth to speak, but Kiki stamped out, her house slippers slapping against the linoleum.

"I was just about to say that I picked her up at Wanda's house last night," Hannah said to Naomi, picking up the chicken bone with two fingers and dropping it in the trash. "And can confirm that she was there."

But more manifest verification was forthcoming. Within seconds Kiki returned with her handbag, from which, after a moment of digging, she pulled out a Polaroid snapshot and shoved it in front of Naomi's face.

"Take a gander at this, missy," she said.

Naomi studied it, her brow knitted, her lips parted in the manner of feeding fish. Able to tolerate the suspense no longer, Hannah moved to Naomi's side and took a look. As the substance of the photo became clear, the expression of dismay on Hannah's face congealed into odious apprehension.

The photograph showed a man lying on his back on a bed. Hannah recognized the lamp on the nightstand as being Wanda's. She remembered her buying it at the Sausalito art festival a year before. What proved less familiar was the man himself, for he had obviously thrown himself into the *Pirate John* film project with eye-popping fervor. Casey was wearing half a pirate's outfit—high black boots, a bandanna around his scalp, a black patch across one eye, a large gold hoop in one ear, and a black cape spreading out across the bed beneath him. The rest of him was unclothed.

"Ahoy there, matey," Naomi muttered as she and Hannah stared at the photo with disbelief.

Fortunately Casey's cape was pulled just barely over his private parts. Kiki was also in the picture, but you could only see her grinning face, slightly blurry and distorted, at an odd angle in the lower right corner of the frame.

Kiki came over and looked at the photo with the other two women. "While I was in the bathroom I heard him say something about a ship approaching and him raising his cannon, but at the time I had no idea what he meant."

"How did you get a camera?" Naomi asked.

"Oh, he had the Polaroid camera in the room right there on the dresser. He was using it to scout locations for his movie. He was thinking about filming the ocean scenes off of Point Reyes.''

Hannah moved her eyes to Kiki. ''So you used his camera to take a picture of him dead?'' Her voice broke; she was so incredulous.

''How can you think that? When I came out of the bathroom I thought he was just asleep. Or passed out. He'd done an awful lot of drinking. I didn't think it would hurt if I took one little photo, just as a keepsake.''

''So why is your hair mussed?'' Hannah asked. ''And the pearls in your hair are at an odd angle.''

''Um, well, I had the car window rolled down on the way there.''

Still holding the photo and wearing a quizzical look, Naomi turned it right then left. ''I don't see how you managed to get both of you in the picture.''

''It wasn't hard,'' Kiki told her. ''I just used the viewfinder and figured out how high the camera needed to be, then held it at arm's length. It's not going to win any awards, I know.''

''What it's going to win you is a couple of days in the county jail,'' Hannah said sternly.

''What do you mean?'' Kiki asked.

''I mean that someone's going to find out you were in Casey's room. The backing on the photo, the part you peeled off. Where did you leave it?''

''In the trash.''

''What if somebody looks in the trash and finds it?''

''Who would do that?''

''Wanda, for one. You know what a snoop she is. She could search the trash looking for something of his to keep as a souvenir. I'm not sure, but I think the back part of a Polaroid is like a negative, and she might be able to see something on it.''

Kiki frowned. ''For her to dig through the trash would be so disgusting.''

''That's ironic coming from someone who sneaked a photo of him naked. You have to talk to the police right away and let them know what happened. The police are bound to know about the threatening letter he received. If he died because the letter frightened him, it could be manslaughter. You can't wait another minute.''

"I know you're right," Kiki said meekly. "Darn, I shouldn't have taken that picture. I knew it was wrong when I did it. Hannie, you'll go with me to talk to the police, won't you?''

"Of course," Hannah said, her tone now reassuring.

"We might as well go to Wanda's," Naomi said. She just called me minutes ago and said the police were there. They probably haven't left yet.''

"You'll come, too, Naomi?" Kiki asked, so grateful for company that she forgot she was miffed at her.

"Naturally. Besides, Wanda wants me to cleanse the death spirits out of her house, and it's best to start right away.'' Naomi gave the photograph one more penetrating look. After a moment she held it closer to her face. "Kiki, dear, I must say to your credit . . .''

"What?" Kiki asked.

"From that small tenting in the cape, I'd say Mr. Casey died happy.''

$\mathscr{F}$IVE

$\mathscr{W}$ANDA BACKUS WAS THE HIGH priestess of Hill Creek social life, but to her continual frustration, no one but her realized it. She had done her best to broadcast the fact that Frederick Casey was staying in her home, feeling sure it would solidify her social rank. Only, short of renting a highway billboard (an act of crudeness that Marin never allowed anyway) there was only so much you could do to get that kind of information disseminated.

But Wanda was not to be thwarted. Having Casey die while he was her houseguest was a terrible tragedy, and the initial shock had been just awful. But once her Valium kicked in, it occurred to her with the clarity that arises from sedation that the event could be a bonanza socially. Of course Casey, by Hollywood standards, was strictly a second-tier celebrity. It wasn't anything like having Paul Newman or Clint Eastwood meet his Maker in your guest bed, but still, let Hill Creek's glitterati try to top it.

While the police and paramedics worked in her guest room, Wanda stood in her front yard wearing her best white silk Dior dressing gown, swathed in layers of frothy silk and looking bereaved yet regal. Normally by eight-thirty she would have already been bathed, dressed, and slathered with a pound of Estée Lauder, but she thought that her usual perfect grooming would denote a lack of shock and grief. So instead she just fluffed her hair and wore her makeup a touch paler than usual in order to look wan.

There was a circus air at Wanda's when Hannah, Kiki, and Naomi pulled up in front of her house, with two squad cars, an ambulance, and three television news vans still on the premises. Not much happened in Hill Creek, and Frederick Casey's death was big news.

A small crowd of neighbors milled about the perimeter of the lawn, and heads turned as Hannah parked the Eldorado at the curb. In a land of BMWs and Volvos, the Eldorado convertible was a novelty and had long been a local landmark in town, but that day it attracted special notice because of Naomi's presence in the backseat. Wearing a pink-and-black polka-dot turban, she loudly chanted, her Hopi war stick held high in preparation for the death cleansing ceremony. The war stick, a vital accessory to all of Naomi's spiritual services, was a yard long and two inches in circumference, with white feathers and bells attached to the top. Every few minutes during the trip to Wanda's she had leaned forward in the backseat and shaken it with an ear-piercing Hopi cry, startling Hannah and causing her to slam on the brakes several times.

As soon as the women spotted the TV news vans, Kiki applied an extra coat of Tahiti Pink lipstick and Naomi got out her finger cymbals.

The three women exited the car and searched the crowd for Wanda, finding her near her hydrangeas in the middle of a television interview.

"Frederick and I were dear, dear friends," Wanda said to the reporter, making sure the camera was getting her left side, where she thought her nose job looked the best.

"Oh, hell, you barely knew the man," her husband, Walter, gurgled from the chair he had dragged from the patio so he could watch the events with minimal effort. Already on his second Bloody Mary, he was feeling his oats and risked ignoring the chilly look his wife cast him. Hannah noticed the cameraman turn the lens on him. With a sleepy smile Walter raised his glass high. "Still, old Casey was a damn good screenwriter and I'm proud to have had him die in my house. Hell, it may raise real-estate values around here."

After shoving the camera away from Walter, Wanda marched over to him, grabbed his glass, and dumped its contents on the ground. Then with a beaming smile she returned to the reporter.

"Just look at her," Kiki said, arms crossed, her mouth in a pout. "She's in the limelight when I was the one who was really there. I'm going to talk to that reporter." She lunged forward, but Hannah grabbed the back of her pink, rhinestone-trimmed jogging suit.

"Not until you talk to the police." Hannah's tone was rigid.

"Oh, all right. How do I look?"

Hannah rolled her eyes upward then approached a police officer standing nearby.

"Is Detective Morgan here?" she asked him.

He stretched a thumb toward the house. "Inside. If you want to see him, you'll have to wait here until he comes out," he told her. War stick in hand, Naomi started toward the house. The officer leaped in front of her. "That means you, too."

Naomi nodded and raised her hand, palm outward, in a Buddha-like fashion. "You don't understand. I'm a professional. I'm here to cleanse the house." She gave him a patronizing smile and added, "May we all be blessed by the sun." She then pulled her finger cymbals from her pocket and clinked them in the air.

The officer looked blankly at her. "You'll have to clean up later," he told her, his tone matter-of-fact. "They're not done inside yet. I don't think it needs it, if you want my opinion. You could eat off the floor in that place, it's so spick-and-span."

Her smile of peace and goodwill momentarily dimming, Naomi took a deep, fortifying inhalation. "I'm a psychic." She clinked her cymbals again, this time with a punitive sharpness. "I'm here to cleanse the house of death spirits."

In many parts of the United States this statement would have been met with incredulity, but not in Hill Creek.

The officer nodded. "Navajo?"

"Hopi shaman," Naomi replied.

"Interesting, but you'll still have to wait."

Naomi's mouth dropped open in vexed bewilderment as the officer walked off, and she gave her war stick an irritated joggling. "What ignorance," she said to Hannah. "I need to get in that house right away. Time is of the essence."

"There's Wanda over there by the television van. Maybe she can help," Hannah suggested.

"This just makes me want to spit," Kiki said as Naomi trotted off to Wanda's, the war stick rattling noisily. "Wanda's got that assistant job sewn up now. Look at her over there, talking her head off to that reporter, basking in the glory."

Hannah frowned. "A man has died in the prime of his life. It's a tragedy. There's no glory attached to it."

Just then she saw Detective Larry Morgan walk out the front door, his face stern. She called out his name, and as soon as he saw her he headed her way, an immediate attention that surprised her.

Morgan was in his mid-thirties, thin, with blond hair and an air of sweet sincerity you didn't expect in a cop. He smiled at Hannah and Kiki, extending his hand to both of them. "Hi, Mrs. Malloy, Mrs. Goldstein. Pretty awful, isn't it? A talented man like that."

"Perfectly tragic."

"Yes, it is." He eyes grazed the ground then he brought them up again. "How's Lauren?"

Hannah now realized the reason behind Morgan taking the time to talk to her. He was still very much interested in her niece, and the fact would have given Hannah immense satisfaction if she hadn't had so many pressing issues on her mind.

Kiki edged in closer to him. "Lauren was at the party last night and spent almost the whole time with that good-looking—ouch!"

Hannah had pinched her hard on the rump. There was no need to broadcast to the eligible and perfectly suitable Morgan that Lauren had had her tongue hanging out over an actor who would be gone in a week.

"Lauren is fine," Hannah said to him. "I'll probably see her later today. I'll tell her you asked about her."

A blush crept up Morgan's Gerber-baby face. "Yeah, if you happen to see her."

"Now, Detective Morgan, my sister Kiki has something she needs to tell you." Seeing Kiki make no move, Hannah placed her hand against the small of Kiki's back and pushed her forward. "It's important to your investigation."

This got Morgan's full attention. Once Kiki started telling her story, Hannah backed away to a discreet distance where she could still eavesdrop in case Kiki left out any salient points. But she was soon distracted by the tinkling of ice and found Walter Backus at her side armed with a fresh Bloody Mary.

"Delicious scandal, isn't it?" he said. He was wearing his usual crisp khakis and golf shirt, accessorized by a gold Rolex. "At first I thought Wanda would be upset, but the old girl's relishing it. Probably right. Probably half the people in this town will be trying to lure sick famous people into their houses, hoping they'll die there." He chuckled and slapped Hannah on the shoulder. "Whadda you think?"

She was about to tell him that an artistic genius had just died and that she couldn't believe the crass way everyone was treating it, thinking only of publicity and property values. But before she could get out a word, Kiki came trotting back.

"That was awfully fast, Kiki," Hannah said with suspicion. "Did you tell Detective Morgan everything?"

"I didn't get the chance to tell it all because another policeman took him away," Kiki replied. "Said it was very, very urgent. That they had found something. Oh, hi, Walter."

Walter waved his glass in salutation while Hannah's brain percolated. What could the police possibly have found that would be urgent if Casey had simply died of a heart attack? Her eyes moved to the house.

"Listen, Hannah," Walter said. "You carry some weight with Wanda, and I was wondering if you could talk her into throwing that stuffed dog in the garbage. One of its eyes is falling out and it's starting to rot. She paid through the nose but I think she got an inferior stuff job. Only found out recently that everybody freeze-dries these days. She never listens to me but she's always respected you and—" Walter stopped in mid-sentence, his eye catching something apparently unpleasant over Hannah's shoulder.

"Kiki Goldstein!" Wanda shouted as she marched in their direction, not realizing she was clomping her white satin house shoes right through her ajuga ground cover and turning the satin green. Walter crept away. "What were you doing in my house last night without my knowing! Why, it's trespassing!"

"I was invited by Freddie," Kiki said defensively. "It was all innocent."

It worried Hannah that the word "innocent" was cropping up so often.

"Innocent? Naomi told me everything. Said you have nude photos."

At the use of the term "nude photos" Walter slipped back into their group.

"Can I see?" he asked. Kiki gave him a dirty look. Wanda advanced on Kiki, but just then a breeze blew across the lawn, blowing the top layer of her Dior robe up over her face. Once she had slapped it into submission, she turned to her next major annoyance, which was her husband, and dumped his second drink of the morning, sending him off to sulk.

Once Walter was out of earshot, Wanda smoothed the folds of her robe and leaned her face close to Kiki's. "What was Frederick Casey like?" she asked, her voice low.

"What do you mean?" Kiki asked.

Wanda smiled. "Was he this?" She held up her pinkie. "Or this?" She held up her index finger.

"I would hardly know," Kiki replied. "You have such a filthy mind."

"You most certainly do," Hannah muttered. At that moment her ears pricked up. She could have sworn she heard a shout coming from inside the house, and she turned to investigate. When she didn't hear anything else she pivoted again to Wanda and Kiki to see if they heard the shout as well, and was appalled to see Kiki holding up her index finger with Wanda staring at it, eyebrows lifted, her mouth rounded into an appreciative "oh."

"Kiki!" Hannah said. Kiki retracted her finger, further discourse terminated by a thunderous screech coming from inside the house. To their amazement they saw a policeman drag Naomi out the front door and down the porch steps, holding her arm in one hand and the Hopi war stick in the other.

With a squawk of indignation, Wanda bounded over to Naomi, with Hannah and Kiki following.

"Police brutality! Fascist pig!" Naomi bellowed with all the grandiose self-righteousness of her younger protest days. Hearing the commotion, three other policemen came to assist their embattled comrade. Since the officers had been born after the early sixties, they completely missed the sociopolitical context of Naomi's rantings and took them as personal insults.

"Unhand her! She's my psychic," Wanda shouted to the policemen, waving her arms and causing her robe to fly up again, this time the frothy stuff sticking to her lip gloss.

"She assaulted me with this stick," the policeman answered.

"I did not," Naomi said. "I was only shaking it to cleanse the house of the death spirit, and you got in the way. I was chanting and my eyes were closed."

After spitting out silk, Wanda shook her head and made a "tsk" sound. "Oh, yes, you shouldn't get in the way when she's shaking the war stick," she told the policeman, using the same tone she would have with a naughty three-year-old. "It was your own fault."

"Give me back my stick this instant. I must return to

that house. It's filled with death," Naomi said.

Hearing the last part, Wanda bit her knuckle and emitted a woeful yelp. "I just had new drapes put in."

"You're not getting this stick, lady," the officer said to Naomi. "It's a weapon and you used it against me."

Things were degenerating rapidly and Hannah felt she should at least attempt to ease the situation. She took Wanda aside. "Detective Morgan is in the house," she told her. "He knows Naomi. Maybe he can help."

Wanda bobbed her head and hurried inside. Naomi continued hurling epithets about police brutality until Hannah managed to calm her down enough so that the police let go of her, though the officer retained possession of the Hopi war stick.

It was then that Wanda emerged from her front door, but with a different visage than when she went in. She came out to the edge of the porch and stood there immobile, her face white. Clutched to her breast was her poor stuffed Bon Bon, his hair patchy and one of his false eyes loose, so that he appeared to be looking in two directions at once.

One glance at Wanda and Hannah forgot about Naomi's police troubles. She immediately went to her.

"Wanda, what's wrong?"

Wanda laid a trembling hand on Hannah's arm. "Oh, Hannah, I should have given Frederick Casey that note."

"You never told him about it?"

"I didn't get the chance. He was always surrounded by people at the party and then he slipped off," she said hurriedly, paused, then added, "With your sister," in a gruffer tone.

"But why does the note matter so much now?" Hannah asked.

"I overheard the policemen in the guest room. They said Frederick Casey was murdered."

Six

*I*F THE FILM FESTIVAL HAD brought Hill Creek a taste of excitement, Frederick Casey's death had trucked in a banquet, and by noon that day the residents were all gorging themselves on mouthwatering gossip.

For this kind of rumor mongering Hill Creek's command central was the Book Stop coffeehouse, a tile-roofed, slightly shabby bookstore and café that had sat sedately in the center of town for forty years. Lately two newer, sleeker coffee bars had sprung up on Center Avenue, but the Book Stop maintained its thriving business. It was the very fact that it was aged and dusty, its salmon-colored paint peeling, that gave it its cachet. The Book Stop had authenticity, a quality increasingly elusive in that particular part of the universe. In Marin everything seemed to be an imitation of something else, occasionally including the residents themselves. But the Book Stop was an original, and Hill Creekers loved to sit at the rickety tables, drink coffee from cracked coffee mugs, and wax philosophical about their liposuctions and mutual funds. Late that morning, when the news of Casey's death hit town, people swarmed there to make sure they wouldn't miss any juicy tidbits, true or false, regarding his tragic demise.

Hannah perused the blackboard above the counter. The blue chalk writing listed the day's specials as tempeh burgers and bulgur wheat salad, but she knew what was the real *spécialité de la maison*.

"You hear about that director?" Randy, the seventeen-year-old working behind the coffee counter, pressed a button on the cappuccino machine, and steam blasted into a metal canister of milk. "He, like, you know, died."

"Yes, so terrible," Hannah said, keeping her eyes on her coin purse as she counted out her money. She was afraid that if she looked Randy in the eye, she might blurt out the awful knowledge that rumbled inside her—that not only had Frederick Casey, like, you know, died, he had been, like, you know, murdered.

Hannah fumbled with her change, accidentally dropping it onto the counter, the quarters rolling across the Formica. It had been one hell of a morning. Once the idea of a murder in her guest room firmly rooted itself in Wanda's head, she began wailing and blathering to anyone who would listen how it wasn't her fault, tearing around her yard until her white satin house slippers were completely green.

Hannah knew the real reason for her anguish. Having a famous person die in your house by natural causes had a certain chic. Having him murdered there was downright slummy, not to mention an insult to Wanda's hostess skills. Martha Stewart would never tolerate a murdered houseguest, and even if she did, the victim would be in clean underwear and a tuxedo and not half-naked, looking like Long John Silver.

The women learned that the police thought Casey had been poisoned, and as soon as Hannah had Wanda quieted, Kiki began screaming to have her stomach pumped, worried that she, too, had been poisoned since she had been with him. It took both Hannah and a paramedic to convince her she would live. Then, as soon as Kiki's hysterics slowed to sniveling, Wanda started up again. It was like a carnival game in which as soon as Hannah hammered down one peg another one popped up.

Then there was Naomi. With help from Detective Mor-

gan she finally got back her war stick and immediately
moved to the center of the lawn. There she began an exaggerated jogging-in-place motion combined with an irritating whooping noise, all part of her death cleansing dance,
which the police still refused to let her perform in the
house. It wouldn't have been so bad except that she kept
her eyes closed while she danced and she kept bumping
into everyone, finally knocking over the coroner.

Once Casey's body was removed from the house, Hannah and Kiki followed Detective Morgan to the police station. In separate interviews the two women bared every
detail they knew about Frederick Casey's actions the night
before. After the police questioning, which took an hour,
Hannah had been in dire need of coffee, the stronger the
better. In her drinking days a couple of red wines would
have done the trick, but now coffee was the strongest drug
she allowed herself, so naturally she headed straight to the
Book Stop.

"You want a biscotti with that?" Randy asked, leaning
a scrawny elbow on the counter. Hannah had known him
since he was three. "I heard Casey had a heart attack during, like, an orgy. The cops have pictures."

Hannah raised an eyebrow. "No biscotti, thank you."
She pushed her money across the counter, took the double
espresso and hot tea, and hurried back to the table where
Kiki waited. The café's chatter was at an unusually high
pitch and it was obvious what the buzz was about. Queasiness welled up inside her. For the past couple of hours
she had been so caught up in the spin of events that only
now did the impact of Casey's death hit her.

She set the mugs on the table and sat down. "Rumors
are flying," she whispered to Kiki.

"I know. I've heard people talking," Kiki whispered
back, guiltily glancing around. "But nobody's mentioned
murder, at least not that I could hear."

"Well, they're mentioning everything else, including that
he died during an orgy and that there are photographs."

Kiki let loose an anguished groan. Knowing every atom
of her sister's being, Hannah could guess what was going

through the tangled wiring inside her fluffy pink brain. Though having a potentially hot boyfriend die in mid-date was dreadful, what was more vexing was Kiki's internal battle over how much of her involvement in Casey's death she should reveal to friends and acquaintances. Kiki would want the world to know that Casey had asked her to go home with him that night. A Hollywood director choosing her over all the other adoring women at the party was her life's crowning moment, second only to the glory of being named Miss Artichoke back in 1959. On the other hand, the fact that he had been found in bed naked except for an eye patch and a cape was the kind of information that could hurt a girl's reputation, even a girl of sixty. Kiki desperately wanted another husband, so her reputation, already tarnished from past blunders of *amore,* needed preserving.

Kiki sighed under the weight of this sad irony. "Life's so hard sometimes. I just don't understand how somebody could have murdered poor Freddie."

"Well, somebody did," Hannah said, more gruffly than she intended, but she was too rattled to be in complete control of herself. "Somebody poisoned his flask."

"I still don't understand why the police told you that and not me."

"I already explained twice. The police didn't tell me. When Wanda went back inside she overheard somebody talking about the flask. One of the officers said he noticed a powdery residue around the inside of the flask's top. Wanda told me about it, and when the police questioned me I had to tell them everything I knew."

Kiki leaned forward. "Which was what?"

After checking to make sure no one was eavesdropping, Hannah moved her face close to her sister's. "At the party last night I heard Casey complain that his flask was empty. You know what that means?" The puzzled look on Kiki's face indicated she hadn't a clue. Hannah leaned closer and whispered. "If someone put a lethal substance in Casey's flask, it had to have happened at the party last night, because you were with him from the time he left. And we know you didn't do it."

Kiki inhaled sharply. Her face crumpled and she pressed her hand to the base of her throat. "That's why Detective Larry asked me so many questions about that flask."

"What did you tell him?"

"Just that Freddie was upset that he didn't have any booze in his car. So after we got to Wanda's he sneaked into her liquor cabinet in her kitchen and poured some gin in his flask. Oh, no. Could Wanda have poisoned her own gin? Was she trying to kill Walter?"

"Don't be ridiculous. Walter's too easy to divorce for her to kill him. She has an ironclad prenuptial. Besides, he's a vodka drinker. No, somebody put whatever it was in Casey's flask at the party while it was empty. Then he filled up the flask at Wanda's house. He drank it and then while you were in the bathroom, so long Freddie."

Kiki lifted up her tea, the mug vibrating so she had to set it down again. "Oh, Hannie, could the police think I did it?"

"You'll definitely be a suspect. But then, everyone at the party is a suspect, I'm sure." Hannah sipped her coffee, her brain blazing with speculation. "How long was it between the time you and Casey left the party and when he poured Wanda's gin into his flask?"

"I don't know."

"Think."

"Twenty minutes maybe."

"Then how long before he died?"

"I'm not sure."

"Go over your actions. What did you do?"

Kiki twisted her lips in concentration. "Well, we left the party. We drove to Wanda's. Then we went inside, he got the gin," she said, counting the events on her fingers. "We tiptoed back to his bedroom. We sat on the bed, kissed a little."

Hannah stiffened. "You kissed?"

"Just a little. Let's see now, then I showed him my Wonderbra, went in the bathroom, came out, and he was stretched out on the bed. It was no more than thirty or forty-five minutes total. Why?"

"Because if you're a suspect the timing may be important. A poison, like arsenic or cyanide, could have killed him, but those things might be hard to come by. It could have just as easily been a drug. That would mean it could have been in pill form and would take some time to dissolve. His flask was in his jacket, and his jacket was sitting unattended in the foyer for a half hour or more. Anybody at the party could have slipped something in his flask."

"But a powder or pills wouldn't start dissolving until he poured in the gin. The police could think I put the poison in at Wanda's house."

"But what's your motive for killing the man? You hadn't even met him until last night. The question is, who at the party had a motive?"

At that very moment the answer to this question manifested itself in the doorway in the form of Bertha Malone. She wore a brown suit and brown fedora, the brim pulled down low on her forehead. Odd outfit, Hannah thought. Once inside, Bertha halted, scanned the room, and made straight for their table. Without an invitation she plopped into a vacant chair. Hannah had never seen her so flummoxed, her face damp with perspiration, her eyes wild and darting about the room as if Nazis were chasing her.

Hannah and Kiki exchanged a glance that communicated volumes. Of course, Bertha had a motive to kill Casey. And if you ever had to pick a murderer out of a crowd, Bertha would be a primo choice, always so pushy and self-righteous. The previous month she practically strangled the bag boy at the grocery store when he put a milk carton on top of her bananas. It had been the hot topic at Lady Nails for two days.

Clutching her leather-fringed handbag in her lap, Bertha leveled her gaze at Hannah. "I thought you'd be here, Hannah. You have to help me."

"With what?" Hannah asked, surprised Bertha would ask for anybody's help with anything.

"I'm on my way to the police station. They want to question me. Someone told them about what I said to Casey at the party last night."

"That shouldn't be a surprise. I'm sure they'll be questioning lots of people." Hannah lowered her voice. "Casey was murdered."

"I'm well aware," Bertha replied, then sucked in some air. "I'm a suspect."

That explained her outfit, Hannah thought. Nothing shouted "I'm innocent" like a conservative gabardine.

"How do you know?" Hannah asked.

"The police want to search my house."

Kiki eagerly leaned her elbows on the table. "To look for what?"

Bertha assumed a look of wide-eyed naïveté. "I have no earthly idea."

But Hannah did. The police had to be looking for drugs or poison. The question was why didn't they ask to search Kiki's house? The only answer could be that she wasn't a suspect.

"It's understandable that the police have their eye on you," Hannah said as she took a sip of her espresso.

Bertha glowered. "How can you say such a thing? I'm a pillar of this community. I may not have lived here as long as some, but I sit on four different charity boards. How could anyone think I could kill?"

"Last night in front of a few hundred people you said you were going to stop Frederick Casey," Hannah said, tapping her finger against the table for emphasis. "Killing someone stops them rather decisively."

Bertha bit her lip, her expression losing its previous haughtiness. "I'll admit that little scene last night was unfortunate, but it was nothing." She attempted a dismissive laugh but couldn't pull it off. "All I meant was that I was going to get up a petition against Casey. Write some letters to the paper, organize a little protest. I didn't mean I was going to kill him."

"If the cops slap you around this afternoon, don't fight back. I hear it's best to just sit there and take it," Kiki said maliciously.

Hannah gave her sister a scolding look but understood Kiki's emotion. When Kiki had had some trouble with the police a few months before, Bertha had been less than kind. Now it was Kiki's turn to give a little back.

It worked, for Bertha turned even paler, her mouth starting to tremble. She closed her eyes and her lips began moving soundlessly.

"Bertha, are you all right?" Hannah asked after a few seconds.

"I'm just so stressed," she answered, eyes still closed. "I'm saying my mantra."

"It looked to me like you were saying 'tortellini' over and over," Kiki said.

Bertha's eyes snapped open. "Well, it's hard remembering those strange Sanskrit words."

Hannah patted Bertha's hand. "Try not to worry so much. The Hill Creek police wouldn't hurt anybody, and I'm sure this will all blow over."

The soothing words didn't ease Bertha's fears, for she began to whimper, an incongruous sight on a woman so large and masculine looking. It was like seeing a bear weep. "Hannah, please help me."

The pleading tone in her voice was unsettling. "What can *I* do?" Hannah asked.

"You have to find out who killed Casey. He was a detestable man with dozens of enemies. Lots of people wanted him dead, surely."

"How can you say that?"

"I've been following his career for years, ever since that dreadful *Chains of Madagascar*. He's been arrested for drug use. He's been sued half a dozen times for breach of contract, twice for palimony, and once for a paternity suit. He's the type of man who uses women then discards them." Bertha shot Kiki a meaningful look then went on. "A little investigating by you would turn up some other suspects, I just know it. You were so helpful to the police during that horrible incident last summer."

Hannah's cheeks flushed with pride. "The police don't need my help," she said with more modesty than she felt.

"Ridiculous. If you hadn't practically handed the killer on a platter to them, they'd still be trying to figure it out.

Around here they're used to tracking down litterers, not murderers."

"I just don't see what I could do."

Bertha gripped Hannah's arm. "Please. We've been friends for such a long time."

Hannah blinked. The truth was that she and Bertha had never really been friends because of their frequent arguments over Rose Club issues. At last month's meeting their discussion over the benefits of organic versus chemical fertilizers became especially heated. But Bertha looked so pitiable with those huge mournful eyes, like some cow that needed pulling out of a ditch.

"I'll do what I can," Hannah told her.

Bertha let out a rush of air. "Thank you. Thank you," she said, rising from her chair. "Got to go. I'm due at the police station. *Ciao*." Her face grim, she kissed her fingers and left.

"Why on earth would you help her?" Kiki said as soon as Bertha was gone. "She's been nothing but rude to us for years."

"She's a neighbor and a fellow Rose Club member. Besides, Bertha is all bark and no bite. She wouldn't hurt anyone," Hannah said, taking a sip of her coffee and frowning because it was now lukewarm. "If there's something I can do to help her, then I should do it."

Kiki drummed her fingernails on the table while she eyed her sister. "That's poop. I can see it in your face. What's the real reason?"

"I need fresh coffee," Hannah said, attempting a distracted tone and picking up her coffee cup. "You want an oatmeal cookie while I'm up?"

"I want to know why you're so interested in helping Bertha," Kiki whispered through gritted teeth.

Hannah's earlier queasiness, which had subsided during the chat with Bertha, now returned in full force. Putting down her cup, she reached for Kiki's hand under the table. "The truth is," she said, pausing to get control of her wavering voice. "The truth is, I feel responsible for what happened to Casey. It was my letter that lured him to Hill

Creek, and if he hadn't come here he might still be alive."

"But Hannah, you had no idea when you wrote that letter that he would be murdered."

"I know that, of course, but I'm always sticking my nose into things when I shouldn't, and now look what's happened. I'm only a temporary member of the film-festival committee. John asked me to simply sit in for him and try to see that they didn't do anything crazy. But I got so involved, pushing my opinions about the festival on the other board members."

"But, honey, that's just you."

Hannah grimaced slightly since this wasn't the type of sisterly support she was looking for. "The point is, my letter started a chain of events that led to Casey's death. I feel I owe him something, and the least I can do is try to find his killer."

"But wouldn't looking for his killer be sticking your nose into things again, which you said you weren't going to do anymore?"

Hannah held up a finger. "Well, yes, but it would be sticking my nose into things in order to undo something that happened from sticking my nose in earlier. So, you see, it's completely justified."

Kiki cogitated on this logic, but before she could make sense of it something caught her attention. "Oh, look," she said with exasperation, tipping her head toward the door. "It's Ed." Hannah turned and saw him standing there in his usual old raincoat and Nikes. "Please don't wave him over, Hannah. I don't feel like talking to him. I know it's unsociable, but he's so hard to understand and it's been too trying a day."

"I have to talk to him. Casey's death may have upset him."

"It's upset everybody."

"I know, but Ed's fragile sometimes. I wish I'd never invited him to that party."

"Which is another example of you sticking your nose in places and bad things happening as a result," Kiki said.

"And here you are getting ready to stick your nose into it again."

"Well, isn't that the cabbage calling the lettuce green? We wouldn't be half as involved in this if you hadn't gone to Casey's bedroom with him. And you know that I know that it wasn't as innocent as you say."

Kiki lifted her chin, indignant. "I did nothing wrong."

"I'm not saying you did, but you have to admit there was kissing, there was nudity."

"Only partial."

"There was partial nudity and there were photographs."

"Well, of course it sounds cheap when you put it that way."

"You have to face the fact that the story may get around town."

"How?" Kiki asked as Hannah rose from her chair, leaving Kiki to self-reflection. Ed was now at the counter, ordering his usual black coffee. Hannah said his name. He saw her just as Randy handed him a cup.

"Have you heard about Frederick Casey, about what happened to him?" Hannah asked. Ed looked at her blankly and Hannah knew he hadn't. After all, there hadn't been time for it to reach the newspaper, and Ed didn't talk to that many people.

"Frederick Casey died last night," Hannah said softly.

Ed's hand, which rested on the counter, began to quiver. "That's terrible," he said, the words coming out only slightly slurred. She led him away from the counter, out of Randy's earshot.

"Yes, it *is* terrible. And it gets worse. You're going to find out if you watch the news tonight. Casey was probably murdered."

Ed shook his head, his eyes at the floor. "Dead too young."

Yes, Casey had died much too young, Hannah thought. He had only been in his late fifties. To die at that age of natural causes would be bad enough, but to die at the hand of someone else was unspeakably horrible. And although

Bertha was a likely suspect, it seemed impossible that she would do such a thing. And if Bertha did murder Casey, she would never ask Hannah to investigate, would she? Unless Bertha wanted her to turn up some new suspects to divert police attention. And Hannah had to admit to herself that it was very odd that Bertha knew so much about the man.

Dressed in her Japanese gardening pants, an old sweatshirt, and a frayed straw hat, Hannah sat that afternoon on a gardening stool by her rosebushes and reread the postcard from John Perez. The front of it showed a colorful bird with a huge beak. His message on the back was brief. *Having a wonderful time. Seen lots of everything. Have very sore knees. Can't wait to see you again. John.*

It was the last sentence she liked the best. She couldn't wait to see him either. Only a few months before she would have been perfectly happy if she had never had a man in her life ever again. After her mastectomy she had assumed no man would be interested. She had been wrong about that.

She put down the postcard and continued trimming the errant canes of her rosa cressida. It was an apricot rose that produced a profusion of cabbage-shaped blossoms. It was wonderfully healthy, so healthy it was starting to take over her redwood fence. With heavy-duty shears Hannah clipped carefully chosen canes, but her concentration on her work was limited, her thoughts drifting back to John. It was interesting how important a man could be in your life, regardless of how independent you assumed you were.

It was this idea that started her thinking about Angie and Frederick Casey. She clipped a withered twig, remembering the conversations on the winery patio the night before. Casey and Angie had traded barbs with a vengeance, indicating their relationship was more than professional. Casey had said that he was hot, then had looked directly at Angie and added, "And not for you."

Bertha had accused Casey of using women then discarding them. If Angie had fallen into this category, perhaps she didn't appreciate being discarded. And that would give her a very good motive for murder, at least one as good as Bertha's.

$\mathscr{S}$EVEN

$\mathscr{I}$T WAS ONE OF LIFE'S little ironies that what had
been catastrophic to the health of Frederick Casey turned
into a tonic for the Hill Creek Film Festival. With the an-
nouncement of Casey's death the fledgling festival became
the hot ticket in Marin, the whole week's lectures and films
sold out by five o'clock.

Although a posthumous *muchas gracias* had to go to
Frederick Casey for getting murdered and providing an
abundance of publicity, some thanks went to Brad Casey
and Hinkley Bowden. They agreed to carry on the week's
activities, the two men volunteering to share the lectures to
be held at the Hill Creek Theater. This offer, so generous
in the face of tragedy, surprised everyone, but Bowden and
Brad insisted that all festival activities continue as planned.
They assured the festival committee and the newspapers
that Frederick Casey would have wanted it that way, since
the festival proceeds would fund local independent film-
makers. Besides, Fred Casey wouldn't have wanted anyone
to miss a party.

That night's coffee reception in the theater was to be
followed by a lecture and film. The Hill Creek Theater was
sixty years old and still had an old-style marquee out front,

twinkling stars on the theater ceiling, and best of all, a
balcony. The reception would be in the lobby. A few days
earlier Hannah hadn't planned to go, but now she eagerly
looked forward to it, since many of the key people from
the opening-night party would be there.

So far Angie was the only real murder suspect, besides
Bertha, she could come up with, and there she had little to
go on. She needed more information about Casey himself,
about his strengths and weaknesses. If she could understand
why somebody wanted to kill him, it could lead her to who
had done it. The problem was how to get the information.
The people currently in town who knew him best were
Bowden, Brad, and Angie, and in less than a week Bowden
and Brad would be gone, and Angie could leave even
sooner. Hannah had to move fast, and she decided Bowden
would be the quickest path to information. A man's longtime business partner, especially a partner he had once had
a falling-out with, knew him well, so it made sense to question Bowden first.

But fortune conspired against her. Hannah planned to get
there early to catch Bowden before he was swarmed with
well-wishers, but instead she and Kiki arrived fifteen
minutes late because Kiki had difficulties with her new
false eyelashes. By the time they got there, with Kiki's eyes
dressed in tiny fur coats, the crowd was already thick and
they maneuvered with difficulty to the coffee table. Origi-
nally the festival board planned to sell champagne at seven
dollars a glass, but with Casey's death champagne seemed
in bad taste, and the business the festival picked up from
extra ticket sales more than made up for lost liquor profits.

Hannah and Kiki, their nerves in tatters, stood by the
coffee urn and searched the crowd. Standing on her tiptoes,
Hannah didn't see Bowden anywhere, nor did she see Lauren, who was supposed to be meeting them. Lauren didn't
do well in large groups, having a tendency to hide in the
ladies' room if left alone too long. But although neither
Bowden nor Lauren had arrived, the rest of Marin County
had. Hannah kept up her surveillance while Kiki prattled
on about the horror of Casey's death, her commentary

punctuated by observations on the attractiveness of men who walked by. But all Hannah could contemplate was the frightening notion that there could easily be a murderer in the crowd. She saw lots of people she knew but more people she didn't. She had heard that Casey's death had upped ticket sales from San Francisco.

Hannah saw her usual group of Rose Club friends, including Bertha and Wanda. Wanda was in one corner of the room schmoozing with Roger, and Bertha was in a conversation with someone Hannah didn't recognize. She noticed Ellie over by the front door looking at someone's hands. She thought things looked normal enough, but then again, something just didn't feel right. It was an eerie tension hanging in the air, a macabre excitement over Casey's death that could only come from people knowing his death hadn't been from natural causes. Hannah thought of Bertha's "tortellini" mantra, and underneath the room's buzz she imagined she could hear a different mantra being repeated, one more deathly—the word "murder."

Hannah took a deep yoga breath to calm herself. She wouldn't be able to gather information if she got worked into a snit. She felt a tug on her sleeve.

"Hannah, have you noticed anyone looking at me funny?" Kiki asked. Hannah ran her eyes over her sister to make sure her breasts were inside her blouse and her miniskirt fully covering her ample derriere. Everything seemed contained.

"What are you talking about?" she asked.

"Well, just now Roger looked my way and made the strangest face, and Mitzi from the Rose Club—"

"The woman with those beautiful lace-cap hydrangeas?"

"Yes, her. I just waved to her and she turned her head like she was avoiding me."

"It's your imagination."

"You think?"

"I wouldn't have said so if I didn't."

Crossing her arms, Kiki seemed only halfway satisfied. Hannah was again hunting for Bowden when she noticed a woman she remembered from the previous night's party look at Kiki then place her hand over her mouth to stifle a snicker. Luckily Kiki didn't see it, but it still perplexed Hannah. Kiki's miniskirt and sparkly sweater were a little unusual for a woman her age but not enough to attract that much attention.

"I'm starving and I see chips over by the stairs. You want some?" Kiki asked. Hannah shook her head and Kiki took off.

Yes, that woman definitely snickered at Kiki, Hannah decided. What was the reason? But the approach of Bertha interrupted any further cogitation. She was back to her Santa Fe look, with a denim skirt and blouse, but her expression was even more tormented than earlier that day at the Book Stop. She grabbed Hannah's arm and pulled her into a secluded corner near a fake palm tree.

"How's the investigation? Any news? Any progress?"

"I've hardly gotten started."

Bertha frowned. "There's no time to dillydally. You've got to find Casey's killer and you've got to do it fast."

"These things take time, Bertha. How did the police interview go?"

"They were rather too assertive, I felt. I'm thinking of writing my congressman. They insinuated the most hideous things. Accused me of writing some ridiculous letter. I had no idea what they were talking about. My lawyer advised me not to answer any more questions." Bertha's eyes began to fill.

Hannah hated to see anyone cry. "Bertha, if you didn't commit the crime, there can't be any real evidence against you."

"I realize that."

But Hannah noticed her flinch at the mention of the word "evidence." "Have you told me everything?"

"Of course." Bertha answered too quickly to be believable. "I mean, there's nothing to tell. Hannah, try to smile. I don't want people to think I'm upset."

"But you *are* upset. It's perfectly reasonable."

"I don't care. I don't want people to know it. Smile,

please, Hannah. Put on that blissful expression you get when you're discussing fish emulsion.''

Hannah pasted a smile on her face while Bertha stretched her mouth into an absurd grin that no one who knew her would fall for. Hannah watched her nervously shred a cocktail napkin in her fingers. She was definitely hiding something.

Bertha went on. ''In order to facilitate your investigation I asked the police as many questions as I dared. I got some interesting info. For instance, I learned that someone suggested to the police that your sister would be a viable suspect.''

''That's ridiculous.''

''Your smile, Hannah. Think fish emulsion.''

But the most Hannah could currently manage was a grimace, since she reasoned it was probably Bertha who made the suggestion about Kiki to the police.

''It's a valid assumption,'' Bertha continued. ''She was with him when he died. Some people—not me, of course— would consider that suspicious.''

''Did the police say anything about her?''

''Apparently she's in the clear. They said that whatever killed him was put in his flask at the party, so she's not under any more suspicion than anyone else. She's probably under less from the fact that she went home with him.''

''Did they say why they think the flask was poisoned at the party?''

''I really pressed them on that one, and from what I gathered, the poison needed time to dissolve enough to have the potency to kill somebody.''

Hannah felt a surge in the electrical activity of her gray matter. Casey had been given pills, which meant he died from a drug and not a poison, and that fact caused her to remember something. That night on the patio Casey had said his flask was ''practically empty.'' Perhaps there hadn't been enough gin in his flask for a swallow, but there had been enough liquid at the bottom to begin dissolving pills.

''What else did they say about Kiki?'' Hannah asked.

"Just that they checked with one of Wanda's neighbors and with the 911 dispatchers and that Kiki's story checked out. They said her behavior was irresponsible but not criminal." Bertha sounded disappointed. Hannah felt certain that the police wouldn't have given this information to Bertha unless she had been pushing forth Kiki as a suspect.

"Did they say anything else about the flask?"

"No. After I asked a few questions the officers weren't interested in chitchat. They only told me what they thought would intimidate me. I must say, their efforts were fruitful." Bertha paused. "So you really haven't come up with some leads?"

"Not really."

Hannah could tell that a criticism was about to hurl from Bertha's mouth, but Bertha checked herself. "We need information, Hannah, dear. We need pathways to the truth."

"I'm sure I'll come up with a pathway soon."

With fresh desperation, Bertha took both of Hannah's hands and squeezed them so hard it hurt. "You just have to. I've got to circulate now and make sure everyone sees me looking calm and collected. Stay sharp, Hannah. Stay tuned to the environment." With that, she walked off.

Armed with this latest information Hannah felt new-sprung energy, and she searched the crowd for Bowden and Angie, hoping to add to her growing pool of knowledge. But she didn't find either one of them. What she did find was Kiki standing near the door to the ladies' room looking like a stunned deer and clutching a newspaper in her hands. When Hannah finally caught her eye, Kiki glanced around guiltily then waved Hannah over, gesturing at waist level so no one would see. When Hannah reached her, Kiki immediately pulled her down a hallway and into the ladies' room.

"What's going on?" Hannah asked. The ladies' room was empty, but Kiki dragged her into a stall, locking the door behind them. Hannah opened her mouth in protest, but before she could utter a syllable, Kiki shoved a San Francisco tabloid into her hands. Hannah's mouth being open saved her the trouble of opening it again, for after seeing what was in front of her, her mouth opened so wide you could have gotten a nice view of her tonsils. The tabloid's headline read DIRECTOR POISONED DURING NIGHT OF PASSION and beneath it was the photo Kiki had snapped of Frederick Casey, with him lying on the bed in his partial Pirate John costume.

"My God, how did they get this?" Hannah asked.

"I don't know. I gave it to the police this morning just like you told me to. Somebody there must have sold it to this horrible newspaper."

"At least they edited out your picture."

"Look harder," Kiki said woefully.

"It's so dark in this stall." Hannah took her reading glasses from her purse and put them on. A closer examination showed the top of Kiki's head in the photo's lower right corner, the string of pearls she had clipped in her bangs plainly visible.

"Oh, my," Hannah muttered.

"That's why people are snickering behind my back. Anyone who noticed my hairdo last night is going to know I was there in Freddie's room with him in this shameful condition. Damn him. Why couldn't he die in something respectable?"

"Rude, I'll admit," Hannah said dryly.

"Hannah, will this make people think I had something to do with his murder?"

"Bertha just told me that the police say Casey's flask was poisoned at the party. Bertha's bound to tell Wanda and that means it'll be common knowledge in a couple of hours. People won't think you're a murderer. They'll only think you're a floozy."

"Don't joke," Kiki said, starting to get teary. "There's more."

"Oh, my God—"

"Don't worry, it's not something that everyone will find out. Hopefully."

"What is it?"

"I overheard that girl who worked for Fred, you know the dark-haired one that looks like Morticia Addams."

"Angie, his assistant."

"That's her. Well, I overheard her tell someone that Fred was seducing rich women to get money from them for his pirate movie. She said he was dressing up like a pirate and romping around, then he'd get them to write big checks. She said it when I was right behind her. I think she was trying to insult me. Could my Freddie have been only using me?"

"But, Kiki, you're not even close to rich. We clip coupons for cereal and frozen yogurt."

Kiki grabbed some toilet paper, not bothering to detach it from the roll, and dabbed her eyes. "Well, you see, he might have thought I had a little money."

"Why would he think that?"

"Because I might have said some things to make him think I had some property."

"What kind of property?"

"The ranch kind. I sort of mentioned I had a ranch in Montana. Not a huge one," she said with a shuddering sniffle. "I said I only went there when I wasn't busy in Hill Creek. Or the south of France. I just wanted to impress him so he'd pay attention to me. Is that so terrible?"

A flood of light entered Hannah's brain and she at last knew why Casey had cut Kiki away from the herd of women at the previous night's party. Her fake diamonds that looked real, her claims of wealth. Casey thought he could give her a tumble in the sack and win a huge check for his movie project.

Kiki fished through her large handbag and pulled out a canned margarita, an item always lurking among her lipsticks and eye shadows when she was under pressure.

"Kiki, put that back. I don't want you tipsy. Besides, you don't need it. Where's your confidence, your self-esteem? It doesn't matter what Casey did with other women. He liked you for yourself."

"You think?"

"I could tell by the way he looked at you. So intense, so completely enamored. His eyes said everything."

Naturally Hannah knew this was poppycock, but she told

her lie with loving intention and it wasn't like Casey was around to contradict her. She wanted Kiki to remember her night with a Hollywood director as something romantic, not tawdry.

Kiki dried her eyes. "He did look at me like I was special. You can't fake that."

"Of course you can't." Hannah handed the newspaper back to her. "Now walk out there with your head held high."

"Oh, yes, you're so right, Hannah. I lost my head for a second. Freddie really cared for me, I know it. He and I weren't together long but our relationship was blooming into something real, something to be treasured." Something nude to be captured in a Polaroid, Hannah thought. "And once people know that," Kiki went on, "they won't think so badly of me even if they know it's me in the picture."

Kiki continued spouting her romance-novel babble as they exited the ladies' room. As soon as they reached the reception, Hannah resumed her search for Hinkley Bowden.

Like in a ballroom dance, people had changed places. Wanda chatted with a man Hannah recognized as a film reviewer for the San Francisco newspaper, while Roger huddled with Hinkley Bowden and three festival-committee members. Roger's mouth moved at lightning speed. The board members listened attentively but Bowden looked bored.

Hannah watched Bowden's face, thinking of what excuse she could use to break into the conversation when she noticed him look over Roger's shoulder. Following his line of sight, she found Angie in the opposite corner. She wore a high-necked long black dress and heavy black boots, an outfit not quite as somber as her face. Her gaze connected to Bowden's, and for a moment their eyes locked in ferocious concentration. Angie tipped her head to one side, her eyes darting to the hallway, then she moved in that direction. She wanted to talk to him, and badly.

Intrigued, Hannah kept her eyes on Bowden while Kiki described the Hollywood wedding she and Casey would have enjoyed had he lived only weeks longer. Hannah wasn't really listening but did catch that Kiki would have worn a tiara as well as something about Wanda and Bertha carrying the end of a ten-foot train and scattering rose petals. Hannah saw Bowden slip from the group but in the opposite direction from Angie, and she wondered if he was avoiding the girl. She decided to follow him, but just as she was excusing herself from her sister, Roger, preceded by his aftershave, appeared beside them and grasped their hands.

"It's all such a calamity. Completely tragic," he said in a manner reminding Hannah of John Barrymore. "And it's so good of you both to be here."

"If you'll excuse me, Roger," Hannah said, anxious to follow Bowden, but to her anguish he held fast to her hand.

"I really must—" Hannah started to say.

"Especially *you,* Kiki," Roger said, not paying the least attention to Hannah except to hold her hand like a vise. "Last night must have been devastating." Hannah looked frantically for Bowden but he had disappeared. She felt like kicking Roger's shin, but she had to be nice to him for Kiki's sake.

"It was all completely harmless with me and Freddie. Really it was," Kiki said, starting to sound panicked. "He was just talking to me about his new movie."

"Oh, don't get your panties in a wad, dear," Roger said, this time in his normal tone of voice, accompanied by a glint in his eye. "No one thinks for a minute that you murdered him."

Hearing this last remark, Hannah turned to Roger. "Does everyone know Casey was murdered?"

Roger let loose a high-pitched hoot. "Of course they do. The police are talking to everyone on the festival committee. We're all being questioned."

"The police questioned me already and they know I didn't do a thing wrong," Kiki said.

"Well, of course you didn't. Don't be silly, you little minx. You'd hardly kill the man then take a party picture, would you? I always thought you were kinky, but not that kinky. The question is, who snapped the photo?" He turned to Hannah. "Was it you? If so, you were very naughty."

"I did not take that picture," she replied, offended. Kiki jumped in and explained to Roger, leaving out a few interesting details, how she took the photograph. Soon there was a small group of festival-committee members giving Kiki their rapt attention. Hannah smiled inwardly. Kiki's indiscretion with Casey hadn't hurt her reputation. It had enhanced it.

"Truth is, I'm thinking of writing a retrospective study of Casey's works," Roger said, interrupting Kiki to get the attention on himself. "It seems appropriate, since it was my great interest in his films which brought him here."

Hannah's eyes grazed the room once more for Bowden but again couldn't find him. She would have to catch him after his lecture.

Roger continued. "Frederick and I were getting rather close, you know. I'd made a little investment in *Pirate John*. It's going to be a wonderful swashbuckler."

Hannah turned to Roger. "When did that happen? Your investment, I mean."

"Yesterday morning. Fred and I got together to discuss the week's activities and we started talking about his new project. Frederick thought I had a unique appreciation of his work." He gave Kiki's shoulder a squeeze. "I thought you might want to give me some tidbits about Casey's last few hours so I could put them in my book's final chapter. What he said, what he did."

"Oh, yes, I remember every second. Frederick and I talked for hours about his art, his plans for the future," Kiki told him, gushing with every word. Hannah held back a groan. It was more likely that Kiki and Casey discussed who got to wear the eye patch. Kiki continued with Roger, liberally using words like "treasured moments" and "passions afire."

Needing an escape, Hannah started for the coffee area and on her way spotted Lauren standing near the front door next to Brad Casey. Lauren gazed at him adoringly as he spoke to a small group clustered around him. She was wearing makeup and had her hair pulled back in a French twist.

She looked quite close to beautiful. Hannah reached her just as a group of admirers pulled Brad away. Lauren looked disappointed that he left, but her smile returned when she saw her aunt.

"I was worried you weren't going to make it. Was the traffic bad?" Hannah asked.

"I've been here awhile. I've been talking to Brad," Lauren said with an embarrassed but beaming smile. "He's so upset about everything."

"I'm sure he is. It was very good of him to take his father's place."

"I know. But he said his father would have wanted it."

"They must have been close."

"Oh, yes, especially in the past few years, Brad said. He didn't really know his father for a long time."

"Why not?"

"Well, Mr. Casey wasn't married to Brad's mother and there were problems."

"You know a lot about Brad for having known him such a short time."

"We talked a lot last night. We sat in my car until two."

"Sat in the car with who?" Kiki said as she bounced up, her previous anxiety now vanished.

"Brad Casey," Hannah explained.

A lurid grin spread across Kiki's face. "How exciting. I bet you did more than talk."

Lauren turned pink. "No, we didn't."

"You're a grown woman," Hannah said, although Lauren's blush looked more like a schoolgirl's. "What you do in your car isn't any of our business."

"Of course it's our business," Kiki said, stepping closer to her niece. "If any one of us has sex or anything even close, it's such a rarity that it's our duty to talk about it."

Lauren looked increasingly uncomfortable, her face turning redder, but Kiki pressed on.

"Was there kissing? You can tell me," she said, nudging Lauren with her elbow. "Anything more than kissing?"

"Please, Aunt Kiki," Lauren said. "Keep your voice

down. And don't talk that way. It's tacky, especially
when . . ." She let the sentence hang.

"When what?" Kiki asked. "What?"

"When I think Brad could be the one," Lauren said,
spitting it out with anguish. She bolted through the crowd
toward the door.

"Look what you did," Hannah said to her sister.

"She's being awfully touchy."

"I know. We have to see what's wrong."

Hannah and Kiki pushed through the crowd and found
Lauren out on the sidewalk.

"Are you all right?" Hannah asked her.

Lauren nodded. "I'm sorry for running off. It's just that
it's hard for me to joke about this."

"You said that Brad could be the one," Hannah said,
using a gentle tone.

"I shouldn't have said that," Lauren said, her hands
twisting together. "Forget it."

"But I can't forget. Do you really think you want to
marry this man after knowing him twenty-four hours?"

Lauren looked shocked. "Don't be ridiculous. I hardly
know him."

"That's a relief," Hannah said with a chuckle. "Then
what did you mean?"

For a moment no words passed between the women.
Then, as if simultaneously struck by the same bolt of lightning, Hannah and Kiki knew what Lauren meant.

Kiki's fingers slapped against her lips. "She's a virgin!"
she said much too loudly. Hannah hushed her as Lauren
covered her face with her hands.

"Good God," Hannah muttered with the disbelief natural to a woman who reached maturity during the age of
free love. Lauren's confession was one of the few things
she could have said that would shock her aunts. If Lauren
had told them she was a communist or a transvestite, her
aunts would have taken it in stride. Hill Creek was an equal
opportunity kind of town with all creeds, colors, and ec-
centricities eagerly accepted. But an adult virgin? Hannah
always knew that Lauren was a little backward, but to be

a virgin at twenty-eight was unheard of in California. The term "virgin" was generally preceded by the word "extra" and only when referring to olive oil, not to grown women. But then, looking at Lauren blushing down to her toes in her rather prim blue pantsuit, maybe the term "extra virgin" applied to her too. Perhaps Lauren's mother shouldn't have sent her to that all-girl Catholic high school.

It took Hannah a moment to recover her composure. "Well, Lauren, dear. It's wonderful that you've saved yourself this way," she said, stammering. "Which makes it doubly important that you not rush into anything with Brad."

Just then from inside the lobby came a loud, deeply pitched bellow, a noise Hannah immediately recognized as coming from Bertha.

Hannah, Kiki, and Lauren rushed into the lobby. The crowd had quieted and moved toward the edges of the room, leaving Bertha and Angie facing each other near the center, the scene looking like a rumble behind the back of a high-school gym's bleachers. Bertha's face had turned white.

"I had nothing to do with it!" she said, her voice wavering.

A foot shorter than Bertha, Angie stepped closer to her, her chin jutting out, her fists clenched at her sides. "Just because your tiny mind couldn't understand his genius, you killed him!"

Bertha tried to reply, but words failed her. The previous night she had been regally confident in confronting Casey before a crowd, but now that she was the one being confronted, her nerve failed her. Her salvation came in the form of Roger, who stepped between her and Angie and took her arm.

"It's time for the lecture to start, everybody!" he said with a cheerfulness that didn't match the expression on his face as he dragged Bertha away.

"Let's go and get seats in the balcony," Hannah said hurriedly, and no one argued. She, Lauren, and Kiki made their way toward the balcony entrance.

"Can you believe what just happened?" Kiki said with more pleasure in her voice than Hannah found tasteful. Hannah paused when she saw Bowden walking with Angie toward the hallway leading to the rest rooms. After telling Lauren and Kiki to go ahead, she started after them. She couldn't see anyone at first because they had turned a corner, but then she heard a muffled voice. Peeking around the corner, she saw Angie and Bowden standing in a closet-sized area reserved for the pay phones. Stepping out of view, she pretended to be looking in her purse while she eavesdropped on the conversation.

"You made an ass out of yourself just now," Bowden said.

Angie said something back but it was in so low a voice that Hannah couldn't understand it. Then she heard Bowden once more.

"He was a jerk but not a crook," he said. This was followed by a response from Angie that again couldn't be heard. Then Bowden said, "I won't accept it until I see it in black-and-white."

Bowden walked toward the theater, moving so fast that he didn't see Hannah standing there. Hannah stepped hurriedly out of the hallway hoping to get away before she could be seen, but she wasn't fast enough. Angie barreled down the hall, and upon seeing Hannah, she halted, frowned, and continued walking.

"You shouldn't listen in on other people's conversations," Angie said angrily as she brushed past.

Probably so, Hannah thought. But her nosiness had given her the first good lead in her investigation. There was something intense and interesting going on between Bowden and Angie, and Hannah had every reason to believe it had something to do with Casey's murder.

EIGHT

HANNAH HURRIED TO THE MAIN theater and up the balcony stairs, grabbed a program from a stack on a small table, then squeezed past people's knees to reach her seat between Lauren and Kiki. Her mind blazed with speculation but she didn't dare tell either of them what she had heard. Lauren would just tell her to stay out of Casey's murder investigation, and Kiki would insist on being included in whatever investigating she did.

The thoughts bouncing around her cranium made it impossible to listen to Roger's introduction. "He was a jerk but not a crook," Bowden had said. Was he referring to Casey? It seemed likely, but she warned herself not to jump to conclusions.

Flushed from her jog up the stairs, she fanned herself with her program, trying her best to look calm. But Kiki knew her too well. She gave Hannah a suspicious look.

"What happened?"

"Nothing," Hannah answered, her tone as innocent as a kitten's. Kiki opened her mouth to protest but the theater lights dimmed, enforcing the hush that accompanies the sudden darkening of a room. A pure blue light bathed the stage. Brad Casey walked out and the audience erupted into applause.

With a single white spotlight shining down upon him, Brad looked handsome, solemn, and proud. He spoke of his father's work, about his father's philosophy regarding screenwriting and the importance of writing from the heart. Frederick Casey had never kowtowed to the studios, Brad said. He had been independent. He had fought for his art.

As Hannah watched Brad on the stage alone in the circle of light, he seemed larger than he had the day before. It was as if overnight he had grown in confidence and self-possession, the life force that had left his father flowing into him.

"My father had his frailties," Brad read from his notes to a riveted audience. "But he lived with passion, with intensity, with the desire to leave something of himself in the world. But I've always felt my father's distinguishing characteristic was in how much he loved. How much he loved life."

"I'll say," Kiki whispered.

Brad continued. "And how much he loved the film industry to which he devoted his life."

When Brad stepped back from the podium the audience rose to their feet, the whole room exploding into applause.

Hannah felt an elbow in her side.

"Isn't he wonderful? Just think," Kiki said, cupping her hand over Hannah's ear, "our little Lauren's going to have sex with him. I'm so proud."

Hannah had always suspected that Kiki's fall off a swing set as a child had done permanent damage, and this last statement confirmed it. But before she could tell Kiki just what an inane comment it was, she felt a nudge on her other side.

"He was great, wasn't he?" Lauren said over the clapping, beating her own hands together so hard her whole body bobbed up and down.

"He certainly was," Hannah said with a smile, but inwardly she thought, Poor Detective Morgan. Larry was such a nice man. If only he had shown his feelings more.

Of course, even if he had showered Lauren with flowers and chocolates, it wouldn't have done any good. How could a policeman compete with a television actor?

Hannah watched Lauren's profile and saw the glow of a woman hopelessly infatuated. Hannah knew the signs. She had been there herself more than once, and it was a wonderful feeling. The problem was that it was a high that couldn't be sustained, and Hannah had an awful premonition that the fall to earth for Lauren would be an extra-hard one, especially if she lost her virginity to this man. Lauren was too inexperienced and sensitive to take such a thing lightly. It wasn't that Hannah thought Brad was a bad person. There just seemed to be an air of vanity about him, which was, she assumed, natural for an actor. But she reminded herself that she didn't know him well enough to judge.

As Brad exited the stage Hinkley Bowden entered it, the two men pausing to shake hands. Standing at the podium illuminated by the same single shaft of light, Bowden's slightly hunched, gaunt form seemed aged and breakable compared with Brad's youthful vigor, but his speech was insightful and entertaining. He spoke of his years of collaboration with Casey, the monologue peppered with funny anecdotes about their work. Although his talk didn't have the emotional power of Brad's, it seemed so heartfelt that Hannah thought Bowden must be truly devastated by the loss of his partner.

Bowden finished to strong applause and Hannah's eyes followed him as he walked off the stage. To her surprise he didn't return to his seat, but instead walked down the aisle toward the exit.

The spotlight faded, leaving the theater in complete darkness. Hannah leaned forward, straining to see where Bowden had gone, praying he wasn't leaving. She still badly wanted to talk to him. Music blasted from the speakers as the film washed the room with gray light. She didn't see Bowden anywhere. Then she saw Angie scurrying down the aisle toward the same exit as Bowden.

Angie was going to talk to him again, Hannah felt sure.

Too curious to sit still, she bolted from her seat, disregard-
ing the expressed annoyance of the people she stepped over
to reach the aisle. Dashing down the stairs, she glanced
around the lobby, but it was empty except for two people
cleaning up coffee cups.

She exited the front door, walking out onto the sidewalk.
Halfway down the block across the street she saw Bowden
and Angie beside a blue Ford Taurus, a typical rental
model. They spoke heatedly a few moments, then they must
have come to some agreement because they both got in the
car. Hannah stepped back into the doorway so they
wouldn't see her as they drove off.

Her back against the glass door, she considered what to
do next. Bowden and Angie were going to discuss something clearly upsetting them both, which meant it most
likely related to Casey's murder. One course of action
would be to visit Detective Morgan first thing in the morning and tell him what she had seen and heard. But what
had she actually learned? Nothing substantial, not by his
measurement. Yet this was precisely the type of situation
where she could be the most useful. She could follow her
nose in an investigation while the police were largely limited to rules and facts. She had no such constraints. She
could be in places where the police could not, could see
interactions between people they couldn't. Plus the fact that
if she saw Detective Morgan, it would only remind him of
Lauren and cause him pain, since Lauren was in love with
someone else. The right choice was obvious from every
angle. It was her civic and moral duty to discover what was
going on between Bowden and Angie. But first she had to
figure out where they had gone.

It occurred to her that if the two wanted to have a private
conversation, they wouldn't go to a restaurant or coffee
shop or even a bar. Bowden's picture had been on the front
page of the local paper and someone might recognize him.
It seemed more likely that he would go back to his hotel.

Her blood pumping, Hannah dashed up the steps to the
balcony and once again irritated the row of film enthusiasts
by jostling their knees.

"Lauren, do you know what hotel the movie people are staying at?" Hannah whispered as she reached her seat.

"Yes. The Marin Inn. At least that's where Brad is." Lauren gave her a curious look. "Why do you want to know?"

A man in the row behind shushed them, and Hannah gave him the expected "so sorry" nod. She was very interested in how Lauren had attained such information. Was it possible she had already gone to the hotel with Brad? But although Lauren's sex life was intriguing, it would have to wait. She leaned close to Lauren.

"I want to send some flowers to Brad Casey and Mr. Bowden on behalf of the festival committee," Hannah said in a barely audible whisper. She took a deep breath to fortify herself for the next fib. She detested lying, but sometimes it was necessary. "Would you mind giving Kiki a ride home tonight? I'm not feeling well. My stomach." She placed her hand on that part of her anatomy.

Lauren looked worried since her aunt wasn't prone to minor ailments. Hannah assured her she would be fine, then left, leaving Lauren to explain to Kiki.

Hannah hurried back down the balcony steps, and as she exited the lobby saw Naomi coming in.

"Have I missed much? I didn't want to be late but I was channeling for Bill Lorenzo and Red Moon was being difficult. Sometimes he's a spoiled child. You'd think he'd have more respect. Where are you going?"

"I'm not well," Hannah said hurriedly, anxious to leave.

Naomi's face scrunched with concern. "I'm so sorry. Can I help? I could do the dance of the blue coyote for you. There's plenty of room out on the sidewalk. It always helps my headaches."

"No, but thank you. Kiki and Lauren are in the balcony on the left. You can take my seat."

Hannah knew Naomi loved a balcony seat, and true to form, Naomi headed for the stairs without further conversation. Hannah exited the theater and walked down the block toward the Eldorado. When she turned the ignition key, the car came to life with more vigor than usual. It seemed that it, too, was enthusiastic at the prospect of a little excitement.

"And we're off," Hannah said cheerfully as she pulled from the curb, giving the steering wheel an affectionate pat.

The Marin Inn was only a few miles away. The term "inn" was too exalted for the establishment, since it was really a two-story motel with a face-lift, but it was the only hotel within the Hill Creek city limits and it enjoyed a good business. Hannah drove through the parking lot and easily found Bowden's blue Ford. The parking lot was only a quarter full, so she reasoned that Bowden had parked near his room. The rooms all faced the parking lot and there were only a few doors close to his car.

Hannah looked around the area to be certain no one was watching before she went to the door closest to his car and pressed her ear to it. She heard nothing, so she moved to the next door and did the same. Still nothing.

She jumped at the sound of a door opening. At the end of that wing of the building a woman exited her room, slamming the door behind her before coming down the walkway in Hannah's direction. A pang of guilt shot through Hannah, and she had to remind herself quickly that she wasn't doing anything illegal, at least that she was aware of. Was pressing your ear against a door breaking the law?

Opening her purse, she pretended she was searching for her room key until the woman got in her car and drove off.

Hannah didn't have to press her ear to the third door, for Bowden's angry voice came through clearly. She didn't hear Angie, but assumed she was in there with him.

Last chance to go back, she warned herself. She could still turn around, return to the theater, and catch the last half of the movie. It was supposed to be a good film. On the other hand, why watch life being acted out on a screen when you could live it?

Hannah rapped on the door before she could change her mind. The room became silent. There were footsteps. The door jerked open so hard that she stepped back, startled.

Bowden looked ruffled emotionally and physically, his

hair askew. Looking stunned by Hannah's presence on his doorstep, he stared at her dumbly.

"What are you doing here?" he asked.

Good question, Hannah thought. What *was* she doing there? But this was no time for self-analysis. There were certain advantages to being a sixty-one-year-old woman, including discounts at the movies, social security payments just around the corner, and the fact that you could occasionally get away with absurd behavior since some people assumed your brain was muddled.

"Please excuse me for not calling first, but I wanted to express my condolences over poor Mr. Casey."

Hannah swept past Bowden and into his room, pretending not to notice his dismay. He stayed by the door while she made her way far enough in so that it would be difficult to get her out again politely.

Looking around her, she saw a basic motel room, an uninspiring box decorated in beige and pale pink, the sofa and chairs upholstered in nondescript, indestructible fabric. It had to be a suite, since there was no bed in the room, only living-room furniture. On the walls hung framed photographs of a tropical paradise Hannah probably would never go to, and on the far wall just to the right of a small wet bar a door stood slightly ajar. Hannah assumed it led to the bedroom. She felt a flush of embarrassment, realizing that Angie could very well be behind that door and in Bowden's bed. Was that why Bowden looked so ruffled? Her previous boldness began seeping out her pores.

She was calculating how many seconds she would stay before making an excuse to leave when she stumbled over Angie, who was sitting on the floor by a coffee table, obscured by a potted plant. It took only one look at Angie's face to realize that sex was the last thing on the girl's mind. She looked even more frazzled than Bowden.

A fresh wave of uneasiness fell over Hannah. Even if she hadn't heard the shouting through the door, she would have known it had just taken place. The room felt suffocating, harsh words hanging in the air with the foul intensity of a spritz of pesticide. Something miserable was going on between these two people.

Somehow Hannah had gotten her foot caught in the handle of a red leather backpack that sat by Angie's side. After extricating herself and saying the appropriate excuse me's, she noticed a folder open on the table directly in front of Angie. Angie had her hand on top of the first page, her finger nervously tapping against the paper. She and Bowden had to have been looking at it. The top paper was a spreadsheet filled with numbers and dollar signs. There was only one thing that could heat up two people more than sex, Hannah realized, and that was money. "I'll have to see it in black-and-white," Bowden had said back at the theater.

"I won't bother you for long," Hannah said with renewed determination, thinking it best to keep up a steady stream of chatter since she had no real idea what she was doing except that she wanted to know more about the spreadsheet. "I feel so terrible. You see, I'm the one who wrote the letter to Mr. Casey asking him to come. He had refused Roger Burke's request over the phone, so I wrote him this letter and it must have had some effect." Hannah let out a sigh that she knew didn't sound convincing. It wasn't like you could rehearse these things.

She sat down on the couch in hopes of getting a better look at the papers on the coffee table. "I write poetry for the *Marin Sun.*" Nothing like telling people you were a small-time poet to convince them you were a harmless goof. "Maybe that had something to do with my letter being compelling. My poems are just small free verse."

Her eyes settled on the papers. They were definitely accounting. The top of the page read *Pirate John* and below that *Expense Summary*. Hannah had seen hundreds of expense sheets in her career as an executive secretary. Somebody didn't much like this one. It had been worked over, with many line items marked in red or highlighted in yellow.

"You want a drink?" Bowden asked, still standing. Angie's eyes shot angrily to him. A drink meant Hannah would be staying awhile. It occurred to Hannah that Bowden now looked relieved that she had interrupted them.

"Just water would be nice," she answered, though if she had ever been in need of a stiff cocktail, the time was then.

He moved to the wet bar that held a bottle of Scotch, two bottles of wine, and an assortment of plastic bottles of water and tonic. He pulled ice cubes from a motel-issue ice bucket, dropped them in a tumbler, and poured in some Evian. Hannah smiled. No one in California drank tap water. He fixed a Scotch on the rocks for himself.

He handed Hannah the glass. "You didn't go to the film tonight?"

"Oh, she was there," Angie said with hostility, but Bowden seemed to miss it.

"Yes, I was at the reception," Hannah said. "I have so much work to do tonight I couldn't stay."

"More poetry?" Bowden said with a patronizing smile.

"What rhymes with 'corpse'?" Angie spat. Bowden's head snapped to her, his expression caustic.

"No, not poetry," Hannah said, avoiding Angie's glare. Angie wasn't buying her Hill Creek matron act even though Bowden appeared to be swallowing it whole. Why were women so much more perceptive than men? Hannah decided she had better hurry and get what information she could before Angie got serious about getting rid of her.

"Do the police have any clues about who murdered Casey?" Hannah asked.

Angie went rigid, her pale cheeks starting to blotch. She was the type whose emotions all showed, Hannah decided, the type who made a lousy poker player. "How do you know he was murdered?" she said, then twisted to Bowden. "How does everyone know this?"

"I heard it from the police," Hannah told her. "I was at Wanda Backus's house this morning."

"You get around, don't you, lady?" Angie stood up and went to the mini-bar, her boots heavy against the carpet. She grabbed a bottle of red wine with a sedate label that looked expensive.

Hannah's earlier uneasiness was growing into a stiff pain in the back of her neck and shoulders. She wasn't one of those people who had to be liked by everybody. Over the years she had grown accustomed to the fact that she occasionally ticked people off. Still, she was used to a brand of polite animosity, a loud clearing of the throat followed by a flashing of the eyes, the type of anger people displayed at the Rose Club when they wanted floribundas planted instead of hybrid teas. Hannah worried that Angie was going to stab her with the wine opener.

"Don't be a bitch," Bowden said to Angie, the negative term having no visible effect on the girl. "Hannah's here just being polite." He sat down next to Hannah, his leg touching hers, giving her a conspiratorial smile she couldn't interpret. Hannah shifted a few inches away from him, re-crossing her legs and wondering why she was getting mixed up with such complicated people.

"It's so hard to imagine who would want to hurt Frederick Casey," she said, trying to regain control of the conversation.

Angie, struggling to get the cork out of the bottle, looked up, her expression pained.

Bowden let out a mirthless laugh. "I can think of plenty of people. Like half of L.A."

"Shut up, you shit-eating bastard," Angie told him. She pulled the cork out of the bottle with a mild pop, then grabbing the bottle by the neck, took a swallow.

Bowden winced. "Use a glass for chrissakes. That's an eighty-six Cabernet."

Angie pretended not to hear him, but carrying the bottle and a glass with her, sat back on the floor by the coffee table, curling her legs beneath her.

"But it wasn't someone in L.A.," Hannah said. "It was someone in Hill Creek. Probably someone at the party. When we were on the patio, Casey said his flask was empty. If someone put poison in it, it had to be done between then and when it was filled again, which was at Wanda's house."

Angie took another swig from the bottle and looked at Hannah with venom. "Nobody knows for sure that something was put in his flask. It's too soon for the police to know.''

"Don't be stupid," Bowden said.

"Don't call me stupid!" Angie shouted, her fingers curling into a fist.

Bowden tensed. "I'll call it as I see it!"

"I can figure things out better than you!"

"You couldn't figure out your phone number if you didn't have me to help you!"

"Asshole!"

"Stupid b—"

"People, please calm down," Hannah said with a nervous smile, wishing she had a garden hose to turn on them.

"She's right," Bowden said, sitting back in his seat, but he and Angie still glowered at each other like two pit bulls. "All I meant was that the cops can get a toxicology report in a few hours if they want to. Fred was poisoned. This is a small town, after all," he said, still breathing hard from the bitter exchange. "The word's out. Half the people at the theater tonight were talking about it. The only remaining question is what he was poisoned with. And from the fact that the police asked me if I had a heart condition, I'm guessing somebody killed him with a dose of heart medication. Maybe even his own." He took a gulp of his drink. "Maybe Fred killed himself."

"Don't say that. It's ridiculous," Angie said, but without her previous heat. "He was out of pills, I'm pretty sure. He forgot to refill his prescription before he left L.A. He could never remember a goddamn fucking thing."

Hannah wondered if Angie's mother knew she had a mouth like a latrine.

Bowden eyed the girl. "Did you tell the police that?"

"Of course." She picked up the bottle and poured wine into her glass.

"You didn't just happen to get a fresh prescription for him yesterday, did you?" he asked.

"Oh, I get it," she said, slamming the bottle down on the table. A few drops sloshed onto the pale carpet and Hannah fought the urge to clean it up before it stained.

"I'm the likely suspect, right? Fred asked me to fill the prescription, but I didn't. I never touched his stupid flask, either. I don't run his stinking errands anymore!" She shouted the last part, tears swelling in her eyes. She grabbed her glass, gulped wine, and began to sob.

Hannah held her breath. There was a moment of dead silence, as if a black hole had opened up in the room and was about to suck them into it.

"No, old Fred won't be needing any more errands run for him," Bowden said softly. "You'll have to excuse us, Hannah. The police gave us quite a grilling today, and naturally we're upset over Fred, so we're not ourselves."

Hannah took a tissue out of her purse and held it out to Angie. "Want this?" Angie reached over the coffee table and took it. Bowden recoiled when she made a honking sound as she blew her nose. Hannah sank a little lower in her seat, her conscience struggling with her tactlessness in imposing on these people.

"Can I get you some water?" Hannah asked her. Angie said she was fine, giving Hannah a mildly grateful look. Hannah decided to leave as soon as she could, but she at least had to try to find out what the spreadsheet was all about. "I apologize for bothering you. And with everything that's going on, the two of you are still hard at work." She picked up the top page of the spreadsheet. "All these numbers. I used to deal with expense sheets at the end of every quarter when I was still working."

The truce was over. Angie grabbed the paper out of Hannah's hand, stuck it in the folder, and closed it.

"I'm out of here," the girl said. She started to pick up the folder but Bowden slid his hand on top of it. It was a subtle gesture, and if Hannah's interest in the scene had been the ordinary type, she wouldn't have noticed. But her interest was keen and she watched Bowden and Angie as their eyes caught. Finally Angie gave the folder a sharp tug and it slipped from under Bowden's fingers. She stuffed it in her backpack. She didn't say good-bye when she left.

The door slammed shut, leaving Hannah and Bowden still on the couch.

"I hope Angie didn't leave because of me," she said, trying to fill the silence, not liking being alone with Bowden.

Bowden leaned back against the sofa with obvious relief at Angie's absence. "Of course she did, as you're well aware. I know why you're here," he continued. Hannah felt a nervous twitter. "In other circumstances I would be more than interested. But right now I'm too drained for a romp in the sack with anyone."

Hannah bolted up from the couch. "That is *not* why I'm here."

"Honey, we're both a little mature for you to pull an act, and you don't have to be embarrassed. I felt it, too. On the patio last night we connected."

"Listen, Mr. Bowden—"

"Hinkley."

"Hinkley, I'm flattered, at least I think I am, that you believe we connected or whatever. But you have my promise that I didn't come here for anything like that."

He was quiet a moment as he computed this new data, then he smiled and shrugged. "Well, it was an honest mistake. I've had about a dozen Hill Creek females of varying ages throw themselves at me in the past twenty-four hours. They all love the movie biz. I'm not flattering myself. I'm sure any one of them would run off screaming once she got to know me better."

"You're too hard on yourself."

"Or not hard enough. So why are you here?"

"I want to know what happened to Casey. What I said before is true. I feel some responsibility for what happened to him."

Bowden kept his eyes on her as he took a cigarette from a pack sitting on an end table, lighting it with an elegant silver pocket lighter that made an expensive-sounding click when he closed it. "I already knew that you were the local poet. I asked someone about you last night." He waited for her to respond. When she didn't he said, "That's a compliment. Of course, you're a little older than my usual taste, but you're one of the few women I've met in the past year that I actually wanted to talk to. Why is that?''

"I'm probably one of the few women you've met who's your own age."

He laughed. "Maybe you're right. You can sit down again if you like. Honestly, I'm too beat to accost you." Hannah sat down in a chair across from him. "So let me put your mind at ease about one thing. You shouldn't worry about being responsible for bringing Fred to Hill Creek. Freddie boy had enemies lined up and taking numbers. Whoever decided to kill him would have done it whether he was in Hill Creek or Timbuktu."

"Why would he have enemies?"

"His career had been on the skids for years. He made some bad movies and lost a lot of investors' money."

"Did his career go sour because your partnership broke up?"

"I like to think so." He laughed softly. "I've done at least some good work in the past ten years. Casey hasn't. When his money began drying up he started borrowing, and when that stopped working he began scamming people to invest in projects that never got off the ground."

Bowden finally seemed relaxed as he put his feet, which were clad in expensive suede loafers, on the coffee table. It might have been the Scotch, but whatever the reason, he seemed in the mood to chat, so Hannah kept the questions coming.

"So why were you working with him again?" she asked.

"My career didn't exactly skyrocket after Fred and I parted ways. I've managed to hang in, but not much else. I'm in my sixties. In the movie business that means you're as good as dead."

"I thought age mattered for actors, not writers and producers."

"These days they like thirty-year-old everything. The target audience is teenagers. They don't trust a sixty-year-old to write and produce a movie targeted at a sixteen-year-old. But *Pirate John* is different. It's the best script I've seen in a long time and it has cross-market appeal."

"I don't see many adventure movies," Hannah said. "What's this one about?"

"It's set in the 1500's. It's about this young farmer boy who falls into being the most feared pirate on the seas. It's got action, humor, a great love story. Fred got the option on the original script and wanted me to help him rewrite it. When it turned out as well as it did, we decided to go ahead and produce. Get the glory as well as control the money." He paused. "You look concerned."

"The police could think you have a decent motive for wanting Casey dead. *Pirate John* is your project now." The police weren't the only ones thinking it.

Bowden stamped out the cigarette in a coffee mug. "Yeah, maybe. But Angie's got a better motive than I do."

"Why's that?"

He raised his eyes to her and smiled. "You're fascinated with all this, aren't you? And I thought you wanted me for my manly charms." He lifted his shoulders. "I don't mind discussing it. I'm an open book. Bottom line, Casey screwed Angie, sexually and otherwise. She's got a film degree from UCLA, and she made a couple of small films that were good. She's a bright girl, a helluva lot brighter than Fred in some ways. Yet she's been his lackey for five years, running his errands, making sure his flask was full, his phone calls answered, and sleeping with him when he so desired. He promised her a year ago that on his next project she'd get to be coproducer. Then, when *Pirate John* came up, he reneged. No surprise to those of us who know him. It's his usual mode of operation. Get some kid to do his dirty work by making promises then dumping them. She's just angrier about it than the others. Very angry, I'd say." He smiled. "She's the type that boils deep within, the type who could slip someone a little poison. Me, I'm a cowardly soul. I'd just pay someone to shoot the bastard."

He got up from the sofa and walked over to her, lifted her from her chair, and kissed her. She shoved him away as soon as she got her senses back.

He stepped back from her, looking smug, like a little boy

who had just done a back flip off the diving board. "Now, what else do you want to know?"

Astounded, she put her hand to her mouth. She didn't know if she should be angry or flattered. Both emotions welled inside her, so she had her pick.

"I heard you and Angie talking at the theater. I heard you say, 'He was a jerk but not a crook.' Were you talking about Casey? Did it have anything to do with that spreadsheet?" Hannah said to him in an uncontrolled rush of words. If he hadn't kissed her so abruptly and without saying "Mother, may I?" she might have put the questions more elegantly, but as it was, it all came flying rudely out of her mouth.

The smugness dropped from his face. "What is this? You were eavesdropping on us back at the theater. You had to be."

Hannah didn't say anything. Suddenly Bowden looked irate. It occurred to her that she hadn't just struck a nerve. She had twanged it and made it play music.

"I don't know what your game is, lady, but you can get the hell out of here."

Then he opened the door and shoved her through it.

NINE

HANNAH ROLLED DOWN THE WINDOW of the Eldorado and breathed in the night air. It had been ten
minutes since she left Bowden's and her heart still knocked
inside her chest. The scene at the hotel had been nerve-
racking. But if she had lost some dignity, so what? It had
been worth it.

She had made progress sooner than she expected. Casey
wasn't even in his grave yet and she already had three
decent suspects for his murder. There was Bertha, of
course, but that was old news. More intriguing was the
discovery that both Bowden and Angie had compelling motives for wanting Casey dead.

Stopped at a red light only a couple of miles from Walnut
Avenue, she conjured up the image of Angie and Bowden
in that beige motel room. There was more going on between them than grief. Hannah knew what grief was like.
It was a brown wad of pain that sat in the pit of your
stomach and numbed you to everything else. Angie and
Bowden had a rawness to their emotions that came from a
more damning sort of trouble, and whatever it was involved
Casey and that spreadsheet.

Both Bowden and Angie knew Casey well enough to

know he carried his flask everywhere with him, so either could easily have planned his murder. But carrying out such a plan had one difficulty. If the poison that killed Casey was really an overdose of heart medication, as Bowden suggested, how did you get such stuff if you didn't have a heart condition yourself? Steal it, she supposed.

The light changed to green and Hannah pressed her foot against the accelerator, the Eldorado surging forward with its usual slow but steady power. If all this new data wasn't enough to get Hannah's pistons pumping, there was the fascinating complication of Bowden's kiss. She turned pink just thinking about it. He did throw her out of his room only a moment later, so any budding interest on his part was quickly squelched. Still, he had kissed her like he had meant it. A woman could tell these things. Would he kiss her again if he knew about her cancer or saw its results? Hannah had chosen not to have reconstructive surgery. Instead she had a garden of roses, lilies, and ivy tattooed across the smooth landscape of her chest. Would Bowden find it lovely or hideous? With John Perez it was different. His wife had died from breast cancer. For him it was familiar territory. But Bowden, a man who spent a lifetime dealing with Technicolor fiction, didn't seem the type who coped so well with reality.

"Don't blow it out of proportion," she warned herself. She turned onto Walnut Avenue, thinking with anticipation about curling up in bed with a cup of cocoa, when she saw Wanda's silver Mercedes parked in front of her house. Strangely, all the house lights were off. Looking closer, Hannah thought she saw shadows moving behind the blinds.

An alarm going off inside her, Hannah pulled the Eldorado into the driveway and sprinted to the back door. She had her keys out, but didn't need them. The door was unlocked. She opened it a few inches then halted. If there was an intruder in the house, the smart thing would be to go to a neighbor's and call the police. She was about to turn around when she heard a shout from inside. Without considering consequences, she rushed into the mudroom that doubled as a laundry area and frantically looked for something that could be used as a weapon. Seeing nothing but a new container of liquid Tide, she picked it up, for the first time fully appreciating its easy-grip handle, and continued on, her pulse racing.

She tiptoed into the kitchen, being as quiet as possible, for if she were going to pummel an intruder with a container of liquid laundry detergent, she would need the advantage of surprise. She froze. Strange flute music drifted from the direction of the living room along with a jumble of voices, followed by a bizarre whooping noise. Sniffing the air, she felt sure she smelled incense.

"What on earth?" she muttered. Visions of ritualistic murder filling her head, she ran into the living room, the container of detergent held high, ready to smash the intruder's skull.

The lights were out, the room lit only by candles, a narrow trail of incense smoke fingering its way through the candles' yellow light. The flute music was coming from the stereo. The coffee table and reading chairs had been pushed against the walls, making room for Wanda, Naomi, and Kiki, who stood together in the center of the room, the three of them naked to the waist, their hands joined and held high. Dancing in a circle, they twisted their hips right and left, kicking out their feet. When Naomi shouted "Rejoice!" all three women performed a coordinated leap, initiating a bouncing of breasts and other fatty tissue that made Hannah hastily check to make sure the blinds were closed. Sylvia and Teresa eagerly watched from a position of safety next to the couch.

Seeing her sister, Kiki froze with her foot in mid-kick. "Hannah, you're home! We were worried sick about you." The sincerity of this statement was mitigated when at that moment Kiki, along with Wanda and Naomi, wiggled forward and made a whooping yell. "You going to do some washing?"

Hannah lowered the detergent, placing it and her purse on an end table.

"We rushed home after the movie to make certain you

were all right,'' Naomi said, out of breath. ''Are you better?''

''I'm fine. I'm more concerned about the three of you. What are you doing?'' Hannah asked, silently adding, And why are you doing it half-naked? She said this from the entry to the dining room, maintaining a safe distance in case Naomi, Kiki, and Wanda were victims of some airborne hallucinogen.

The flute music stopped and the women ended their dancing, all three of them giggling and struggling to catch their breath.

''It's so wonderful!'' Kiki said to Hannah, panting from the exertion. ''This horrible thing with Freddie has left Wanda and me with lots of negative chi.''

''Yes, our life energy is flowing badly,'' Wanda said, emphasizing the statement with a waving of her arms and a small leap. ''We're doing the Druid dance of spring.''

''But it's September,'' Hannah said.

Retrieving her finger cymbals from her pocket, Naomi clinked them. ''Irrelevant. We're getting in harmony with the female life force, dancing in honor of the earth goddess. We're celebrating her glory and in return she will bring us purification and fertility.''

Hannah arched an eyebrow. ''Fertility? That should make the cover of the *National Enquirer*.''

''We're not planning on making babies, silly. We're getting fertile in spirit,'' Kiki said as she twirled on her tiptoes. ''I feel so refreshed. Hannah, you must try this. I feel ten years younger. Take your blouse off and dance with me. We can all see your beautiful tattoo.''

''If you don't mind, I think I'll keep my shirt on,'' Hannah replied.

Although both Naomi and Wanda had put on their tops, Kiki remained unclad, doing small jumps around the living room until she stepped on Teresa's tail and made her squeal.

The doorbell rang. ''Get dressed, Kiki!'' Hannah told her. Grabbing her blouse, Kiki danced back to the bedroom.

After turning on the lights, Hannah opened the door and found Lauren and Brad.

"Aunt Hannah, are you all right?" Lauren asked, stepping in the doorway. "I called you as soon as the movie was over. When you weren't home I was worried."

"I'm fine," Hannah assured her. "I felt better as soon as I got in the fresh air, so I decided to visit a friend."

"Who is it?" Kiki asked, returning to the living room still buttoning up her blouse. When she saw Brad she dashed back in the bedroom.

Hannah was amazed to see Brad on her doorstep since his father had died so recently. She could understand him taking his father's place at the festival but not out making social calls.

"Come in, come in. So glad you two could make it," Naomi said, waving them forward. "We're going to speak to Red Moon in a few minutes."

It surprised Hannah that Brad was there for a séance. He seemed too rational to think he would be able to speak to his father.

When Brad tarried too long on the doorstep, Naomi grabbed his hand and pulled him inside. "It's a shame you couldn't have been here a little earlier for our sacred dance ritual," she told him.

Yes, too bad, Hannah thought. It would have eliminated her worries about Lauren's virginity, since seeing these senior citizens bouncing around bare-breasted would have very likely hurled him into irreversible homosexuality.

"Brad wanted to come over when Kiki and Naomi told us at the theater that you were doing a séance tonight," Lauren said. Hannah wished someone had told *her*. "He's very interested in Red Moon. I'm sorry. You haven't met him, have you, Aunt Hannah? Hannah, Brad. Brad, my aunt Hannah."

Brad nodded. Hannah glanced at Lauren, hoping the lovesick flame might have run out of propane. No such luck. In fact, it seemed stronger.

Hannah studied the man who had so completely captivated her niece's heart. Up close Brad lost the impressiveness he'd had in the theater only hours earlier. Without the lighting and the grandeur of a stage he looked joyless, his face drained of color except for the darkness under his eyes. In him Hannah saw the numbing grief she hadn't noticed in Angie and Bowden. It was natural since it had been his father he had lost.

Despite Hannah's previous misgivings, seeing him in such despair made her heart ache. She wanted to hug him and give him a motherly "there, there," but she didn't know him nearly well enough for that. He didn't give off signals that he wanted sympathy anyway.

Lauren led Brad into the center of the room and introduced Wanda, who gushed appropriately. Now fully dressed and properly augmented by lipstick and heels, Kiki vamped into the living room and headed straight at him. Wanda immediately positioned herself on his other side, each woman trying to outdo the other in slathering him with flattery and condolences. He took it all good-naturedly. In fact, their extravagant attentions seemed to perk him up. This was a man who loved to be the center of attention, Hannah mused. Of course, that quality was a prerequisite for being an actor. Before Hannah could take this analysis further, Naomi interrupted everyone with a clap of her hands.

"Wanda, Kiki, we must prepare the dining room for the séance," she announced, then cast Hannah a crusty eye. "Hannah, you stay where you are." Naomi then moved her gaze to Brad, resuming her best guru smile. "Hannah's a nonbeliever and we can't have that negativity while we're preparing the room. It reduces receptiveness."

Being temporarily ostracized was fine with Hannah, since she was anxious to get to know Brad better. Wanda and Kiki grudgingly left Brad's side and went with Naomi into the dining room, the dog and pig following. Brad glanced at the animals and smiled. Naomi closed the old sliding wood doors for privacy.

"How do they prepare the room?" Brad asked. He sat down on the sofa, seeming more at ease than he had earlier. Lauren, on the other hand, was fidgety.

"They burn herbs, chant, and rearrange the furniture a little," Lauren told him, perching on the seat's edge next to him. It occurred to Hannah that she looked at him the same way a puppy looked at you when you were holding its ball.

Hannah sat down in a chair across from them. "I'm terribly sorry about your father. When is his funeral?"

"Dad didn't want a funeral," Brad answered. "It's in his will. He wanted to be cremated and have his ashes thrown off the Santa Monica pier."

Settling back in her chair, Hannah considered this. "That's a lovely idea. I think I'd like to have my ashes planted with a new rose. With a Double Delight, I think."

"Don't talk dying," Lauren said with a nervous chuckle. "You're going to live forever."

"No one lives forever," Hannah replied, turning her attention to Brad. "We're so glad you decided to stay the week. The festival would have flopped, I'm afraid, without you and Mr. Bowden."

He smiled. "Some people think it's weird of me to not be locked in my room grieving, but Dad would have laughed at that."

"But surely at a time like this you'd prefer to be with family," Hannah said.

"My mother died a long time ago. All I had was Dad. This is where he would have wanted me to be, so I'm here." He paused. "I could use a drink." He said it matter-of-factly, as if upon his command he expected someone to leap up and get him one. Someone did.

"What would you like?" Lauren asked, jumping from her seat.

"Wine, if you've got something decent."

"I'm afraid Kiki is the only wine drinker in the house and her taste runs toward jug rosé," Hannah told him. "How about a vodka tonic?" He agreed. Knowing Hannah and Kiki's house as well as her own, Lauren scurried off to the kitchen to make the drink.

Naomi stuck her head out of the dining room. "Where are your earthquake supplies? We need more candles."

"In the chest next to the wall," Hannah said. The doors slid closed. She was now alone with Brad. By tomorrow either Angie or Bowden would probably tell him how she had made an unrequested and ultimately annoying visit to them. Best to pump him for information now before he had reason to be defensive. But he wasn't in a talkative mood. He sat quietly, staring at the floor.

"Has Lauren been showing you around town?" Hannah asked in an effort to get a conversation going.

He looked up. "We haven't had time, but she's entertained me with stories."

"About what?"

"She's told me about your neighbor who's been digging up her yard thinking it's an Indian burial ground."

"You mean Bertha. You'll need to lower your voice. Wanda's her best friend."

He nodded. "Wanda, yeah, I heard about her, too. She's the one who carries around the stuffed dog. Lauren also told me about Naomi the channeler and about Kiki always hunting for a husband."

He said it good-naturedly but Hannah found herself bristling. Of course, everything he said was true and she didn't think he meant to be rude.

"Can *Pirate John* still be made?" Hannah asked

"It has to be," Lauren said, coming back with Brad's drink. "This movie is going to make Brad famous." She sat down next to him and handed him the glass.

"Your expectations for this movie are very high," Hannah said.

At the mention of the film project, Brad's detached demeanor became more energetic. "The script's genius. Dad made a lot of improvements to it. One of the reasons he liked it so much was because it has such a great part for me. It's only a supporting role, but it should get me a lot of attention. I've been trapped in subpar television up until now."

"You were wonderful on TV," Lauren said adoringly. "You carried that whole show."

Brad smiled at her.

"So the movie will go ahead as planned?" Hannah asked.

Brad lifted his shoulders. "We were having some money problems, but those are over now." He paused a beat. "When does the séance start?"

He wanted to drop the subject, but Hannah wouldn't let him. "Any minute, I'm sure. Tell me more about your movie. It's so fascinating," she said as casually as she could manage. "How come all your money problems are over?"

"The production had insurance on Brad's father," Lauren said, proud to show off her knowledge. Brad shot her a look indicating he wished she hadn't said it, but his expression quickly softened.

"It's not the way I wanted to get money for the movie," he said.

"Of course not," Hannah replied. Lauren looked at him with a worried expression. He did look a bit paler and for a moment Hannah thought he might cry. Just then the dining-room doors slid open and Naomi stuck out her head.

"Lauren, could you come in now?" she asked. "I want you to communicate with Red Moon and it will be better if you sit at the table a few minutes and get in harmony." Her eyes moved to Brad. "Lauren's very sensitive to the spirit world," she told him, her tone full of importance.

Lauren cast an anxious glance in Brad's direction. "I'll take good care of him," Hannah assured her. Lauren smiled, then excused herself and went into the dining room.

"Will Hinkley Bowden also be continuing with *Pirate John*?" Hannah asked Brad as soon as they were alone.

"I guess. Ethically he shouldn't."

"Why do you say that?"

"He and my father have been at each other's throats for months. He's said so many terrible things about Dad behind his back. If he had any scruples he'd back out of the movie altogether."

"So why did your father want to partner with him again?"

"He thought he needed Bowden's help with the production, which he didn't. I guess he thought it would be good publicity. You know, the great team of Casey and Bowden back together. But it wasn't working. Dad was considering breaking their contract. He'd even called a lawyer.''

"Did Bowden know what your father was trying to do?''

Brad shrugged. "If he did, it makes a good motive for murdering him, doesn't it?''

Wanda walked in, her hands clasped solemnly in front of her. "We're ready,'' she said in a grand whisper, then went back into the dining room.

Hannah and Brad rose from the couch. "Have you been to a channeling session before?'' she asked him.

"No.''

"A séance?''

He shook his head.

"Will it upset you if Red Moon says something relating to your father?''

He smiled. "Don't worry, they may believe in this junk, but I don't.''

"Then why did you come tonight?''

"To get my mind off things, I guess. What happened to Dad, it makes me feel sick inside. I'd like to take the next flight out of here but I can't because of the festival. Right now I don't want to be alone, and here is better than my hotel room.'' He looked at Hannah apologetically, knowing he'd made a gaffe. "That didn't come out right. It's nice of you to have me here, and I like Lauren a lot. Her being with me tonight has really helped. She's a sweet girl.''

Hannah knew that Brad was trying to say that he cared about Lauren, that he wasn't just using her as temporary company during a rough time, but his words and the way he said them communicated the opposite. Men didn't use the term "sweet'' for women in whom they were truly interested. Sweet girls were discardable. But how could she blame him? Was he supposed to fall madly in love with Lauren when he had known her only twenty-four hours? Hannah's head said "of course not'' but her heart said "yes.''

Acknowledging her own prejudices, she took his arm,

told him she understood, then led him into the dining room.

Prepared for the séance, the dining room didn't look eerie at all. It was lovely. The lights were out and the
earthquake-preparedness candles sat in the center of the old
oak dining table, all burning and casting flickering shadows
on the walls. Long sticks of incense burned on the side
table, the sweet smoky smell of jasmine filling the air.

Kiki sat on one side of the table. On the other side Lauren and Wanda sat next to each other, with Lauren looking
anxious. She didn't like Naomi's séances any more than
Hannah, not because she didn't believe in them, but rather
because she did. In contrast, Wanda and Kiki both looked
as eager as terriers.

When Hannah saw Naomi she had to stifle a laugh. Obviously for Brad's benefit, she had decided make the séance
more theatrical, and she had put on lots of jewelry and a
long purple scarf that wrapped around her neck. But what
Hannah found most amusing was her hat. It was tall and
white, flat at the top with a tassel on it that made her look
like some sort of bizarre Shriner.

"You two sit here," Naomi said, pointing to two chairs.

Hannah closed Sylvia and Teresa in the kitchen, since if
you thought there might be the spirit of a dead person in
the room, a cold nose suddenly against your leg could be
disconcerting. Brad and Hannah sat in their appointed
places while Naomi touched a lighted match to the small
bundle of sage and pine she called a smudge stick. Tied at
the base with string, the smudge stick was used to spiritually cleanse a room, and Naomi waved it about, filling the
air with smoke and the odor of burning weeds. Hannah
hoped it wouldn't set off the smoke alarm.

Once the dining room was cleansed of negative spirits,
Naomi retrieved her Hopi war stick from the corner.

Settling herself in a chair with the stick leaning against
her leg, she closed her eyes and deeply inhaled and exhaled.
"Now, everyone hold hands."

Hannah sat with Naomi on her left side and Brad on her
right. Naomi took Hannah's hand, and Hannah reached for
Brad's, his hand wrapping loosely around her fingers.

"Focus on the candle flames," Naomi instructed in a soothing, modulated voice. "Concentrate on their light. Capture the image of the flame. Now close your eyes. You still see the flame burning in the darkness. Keep focusing on the flame and clear your mind of all thoughts."

For a moment the room was silent. Hannah tried to play by the rules and did her best to clear her mind, but it was a difficult process. Her head was crowded with ideas about Casey's death and the resulting insurance money the *Pirate John* production would receive. With Casey out of the way Bowden no longer had to worry about Casey cutting him out of the contract, and he could produce the movie with the insurance money to back him.

"Someone in the room isn't concentrating. Someone's thoughts are blocking my pathway," Naomi said with a singsong kindness in her voice, but giving Hannah a little kick under the table.

"If your pathway is blocked, don't blame me," Hannah muttered under her breath.

"Any more negativity and I resmudge," Naomi warned, a threat Hannah took seriously since the smoke stayed in her drapes for days.

Hannah tried harder to clear her mind. She pushed out thoughts of murder, of insurance money and movies, of Lauren's soon-to-vanish virginity. Then Naomi began to chant. The chanting began in her natural voice, the Indian words spoken calmly and rhythmically, sounding like music. Then, as the chanting grew stronger, her voice changed, becoming a deeper throbbing sound, like the steady beat of a drum.

It happened gradually, so gradually that at first you weren't aware of it. You listened to the chanting and after a moment it became hypnotizing, lulling you into dreaminess. Then it dawned on you that it was now a different voice coming from Naomi. It was the voice of a man, a voice so cavernous and masculine you felt certain her vocal cords couldn't possibly have produced it. This was the voice of Red Moon.

Although Hannah had been to Naomi's channeling sessions before, she still found this voice chilling, the sound of it making the hair rise on her arms. She felt Brad's hand tighten around hers and knew it affected him also.

Red Moon's chanting grew louder, filling the room, the sound resonating against the walls. Then the chanting suddenly grew quieter, becoming a barely audible whisper from Naomi's lips. Naomi's hand slipped from Hannah's.

There wasn't a noise in the room except for the now subdued utterances of Red Moon. Opening one eye, Hannah looked around the table. She found it amazing how even Naomi's face changed when she took on the Red Moon persona. If it was an act, and Hannah had to believe it was, it was a good one. Having attended many of Naomi's channeling sessions, Wanda and Kiki looked calm, accepting Red Moon's presence like he was an old high-school chum. Lauren's face was scrunched with anxiety. Brad's eyes were closed, his mouth tight.

"Lauren, it's time for you to talk to him," Wanda said. For some reason Naomi always preferred that Lauren ask Red Moon the necessary questions. It wasn't a task Lauren enjoyed, but she sat straighter in her chair and steeled herself.

"Mr. Red Moon, are you ready to speak?" Lauren asked, her voice high-pitched with nervousness. Red Moon responded with louder chanting that apparently in ancient shaman talk meant he was ready. Lauren audibly gulped. "Naomi, your, uh, your . . ."

"Physical channel," Wanda whispered.

"Your physical channel," Lauren continued, her voice cracking. "She feels you have something to say to us. Please speak to us now."

There was a silence. Hannah had closed her eyes again and she felt Brad's hand loosen.

"Bad mountain!" Red Moon shouted with a thunderous wail, the words bouncing off the walls. Everyone jumped. Lauren shrieked and Hannah heard the pig let out a squeal in the kitchen.

"Bad mountain!" Red Moon repeated. Again Hannah opened one eye. Naomi's head began bobbing forward and she emitted a long, low moan that sent chills up the back of Hannah's neck. "Sun grows dark. Coyote cries," Red Moon said, the words now slow and deep. "Grass dies in shadow."

"What's he getting at?" Wanda whispered, sounding frightened.

Kiki shushed her. "Only Lauren's supposed to speak."

"Well, I don't understand that. Why can't I talk to him?" Wanda asked, starting to sniffle. "I want to speak to Bon Bon. Are you there, baby? Are you there? Want a cookie? Say yip, yip for Mommy, Bon Bon."

"For chrissakes, hush up!" Kiki told her.

Red Moon appeared oblivious to Wanda's need to communicate to her deceased poodle. "Tree and earth," he continued, his voice growing so hoarse and deep it sounded like it came from the bowels of the earth. "Father and son. Roots grow far below."

Brad's hand gripped Hannah's. She peeked at him. His eyes were squeezed shut, his lips tightly pressed together. He's not so casual about this now, Hannah thought. In fact, he looked afraid.

"Bird screams. All hide. All cry to Shawa," Red Moon bellowed. "Vengeance! Vengeance swallows the earth! All cry to Shawa!"

Brad's hand gripped Hannah's so hard it hurt. She tried to wiggle her fingers loose, but he wouldn't let go. She could feel his whole arm trembling. Suddenly he dropped her hand, pushing the chair back noisily and standing. Everyone's eyes popped open.

"What is this?" he said, his voice as well as his eyes angry. His face was pale with perspiration beading over his upper lip.

"Brad, I'm sorry," Lauren said, on the verge of panic herself. "Nobody meant anything—"

He turned, stomping out of the room before she could finish. Lauren ran out after him. A few moments later Hannah heard the front door slam.

Everyone except Naomi stared openmouthed first at the dining-room door then at each other, all wondering what had happened and what would happen next. But despite the commotion, Naomi sat motionless, chanting in Red Moon's voice. She slumped forward, quiet.

"Are you all right, Naomi?" Hannah asked, giving her shoulder a gentle shake. Naomi sat still a moment, then her eyes opened.

"Oh, my, I feel strange," she said. "That was so intense. Did Red Moon say anything?"

"Are you kidding? Brad just ran out of the house because Red Moon said the strangest things," Wanda said excitedly. "Something about a father and son, and then Red Moon got really angry and said the word vengeance a couple of times. I think it upset Brad."

"Upset him?" Hannah said. "He looked wild."

"How very interesting," Naomi said, a strong curiosity in her words. The table then erupted into chatter, everyone spouting out their impressions of why Brad had exited so dramatically. Hannah didn't join in. She moved her eyes down to the tabletop, trying to digest what had just happened. Red Moon hadn't said much and what he did say had been very oblique, yet it had such a powerful impact on Brad.

"I better go check on Lauren," she said.

"I'll go," Kiki offered, then hurried toward the living room. Hannah followed. Both Lauren and Brad were gone.

"I wonder what got Brad so worked up?" Kiki asked.

"I don't know," Hannah said, but she had a sickening feeling that when she found out the answer she wasn't going to like it.

TEN

THAT NIGHT HANNAH DREAMED OF Red Moon, immense and vaporous, a see-through Charlton Heston carrying the Hopi war stick in one huge hand. He held it over her head. She screamed as he brought it crashing down, but as it struck it turned into spreadsheets that suddenly burst apart, floating down around her in bits, fluttering like butterflies.

She lay awake for an hour, her head against her feather pillow, her thoughts jumbled as she watched moonlight create hieroglyphs on her blanket. She finally gave up on sleep and, opening the window, let the cool breeze sweep over her. Her mind alert, she sat up in the tangle of white sheets, hugging her pajama top around her knees, and went over Naomi's séance in her mind.

Brad had initially acted so casually about their tête-à-tête with Red Moon. And though he tensed when Red Moon first began speaking, it wasn't until later that he became distraught. He was upset over his father's death and this might explain his emotional reaction. Yet it wasn't what Brad said or even his running out of the room that intrigued Hannah as much as this—the simple feel of his hand. It had only been when he heard the word ''vengeance'' that his hand gripped hers so tightly she thought her bones would crack.

Later in the morning Hannah mentioned the incident to Kiki, fully expecting her to be as inquisitive as she was. It was sunny and they were having their breakfast in the garden amidst the roses when Hannah asked her sister for her opinion on the matter.

"Actors are emotional. They have mood swings," Kiki said offhandedly. "And I thought it was rude of Red Moon to talk about that stuff when Brad's father had just died." Kiki buried her nose back into her *People* magazine, looking up after a moment and pursing her lips in a cunning smile. "If Lauren marries Brad, do you think their wedding will be in *People*?" She picked up a bran muffin, broke off a chunk, and slathered it with marmalade.

Pouring more coffee into her mug, Hannah understood that murder wasn't first in Kiki's mind. "What on earth made you think of that?"

"Oh, I was just reading this article about Julia Roberts. The article hints that she may be engaged soon and it just got me thinking."

Kiki gazed off in the distance, probably planning her wedding outfit, so wrapped up in her daydream that she didn't notice the dollop of orange marmalade that fell from her muffin onto her favorite silk-simulating polyester robe. She had bought the robe as a gift for herself the previous Valentine's Day.

"I thought you were saving that robe for a special occasion," Hannah said, reaching over and wiping off the marmalade with a napkin.

"I was, but this morning I woke up feeling so upset about Freddie's murder that I put it on just to make myself feel better. I mean, a man that famous getting murdered right here in Hill Creek. So horrible. Still," she continued, her chin resting in her hand. "It's brought us up a few notches in the world. Last night we actually had a film star in our home."

Hannah shook her *New York Times* to straighten the wrinkles. "He's hardly a film star. He's a second-rate actor who made it where he is through nepotism. And I don't think Lauren should be picking out any dinette sets yet.''

Straightening in her chair, Kiki frowned. ''You're so unromantic.''

''I'm quite romantic,'' Hannah answered, her eyes not leaving the newspaper. ''But I don't think Brad is the marrying kind in general, and he certainly doesn't seem madly in love with Lauren.''

''But she's madly in love with him.''

''Correction. She's madly infatuated with him. That's what bothers me. She's going to lose her virginity to him and I don't think he's worth it.''

''Not worth it? He's been on television!''

Hannah gave Kiki a hard look. ''Sometimes your value system chills my blood.''

''Don't preach. Besides, this is all projecture.''

''Conjecture.''

''Whatever. The point is,'' Kiki said, lowering her voice, ''I called Lauren as soon as I woke up this morning to find out if they did, you know, the wild thing last night.''

Hannah cringed at the term but she sat up at attention, dying to know more. ''And?''

''Nothing, zip, nada. He didn't lay a hand on her.'' Kiki leaned forward, her forehead scrunched. ''You think he's gay?''

''No,'' Hannah replied. ''His father was just murdered and I think he's too upset to think about sex.''

''I didn't know men ever got too upset to think about sex. Not at that age anyway.'' Kiki punctuated the comments with a bite of muffin, concentrating as she chewed. ''Lauren told me that Freddie only acknowledged Brad as his son about five years ago. Before that his father never even spoke to him.''

Hannah put down her newspaper. ''When did she tell you that?''

''This morning. We chatted for half an hour while you were spraying the roses. Are you still having an aphid problem?''

''No, just mildew. Did Lauren say why Casey waited so

long to acknowledge his son?'' Kiki shook her head. Hannah picked up the newspaper again, but was no longer interested in it. She laid it on the table. ''Kiki, I know you've been asked this before, but the night Casey died did he act disturbed by anything? Now that some time has passed I thought you might remember something.''

''No, just like I told the police, he acted fine.''

''What did the two of you talk about?''

''His movie and what a great investment it was. Then we talked about my Wonderbra.''

''What else? You were together quite awhile.''

''You know my memory's terrible. I've been taking those ginkgo pills but the only thing I've remembered is the lyrics to 'The Duke of Earl.' You think I got a bad bottle?''

Hannah sighed. ''What about when you were in the car driving to Wanda's? What did you talk about then?''

Kiki pushed out her lips, moving them in and out as she thought. ''Hmm, let's see. He was talking about the movie business and about how cutthroat it is.''

''And what else?''

''He said the movie business ruined people. That's right, Hannah,'' she said eagerly. ''I remember that now. I asked him who it had ruined, you know, trying to get a little Hollywood gossip.''

''What did he say?''

''He said it had ruined lots of people. Then he got kind of quiet and said that it had ruined him. That's very meaningful, isn't it? I'm going to call Roger and tell him so he can use it for the last chapter of his book.''

Kiki rose from her chair just as the phone rang and rushed to get it.

''It's for you,'' she called to Hannah from the kitchen window. Hannah took the call on the kitchen wall phone and was astonished to find Bowden on the other end of the line. When Hannah said, ''Hello, Hinkley'' she saw Kiki's head snap in her direction.

''I want to apologize for last night,'' he said. ''I shouldn't have thrown you out like that.''

"It's all right. I was being too inquisitive."

"Maybe, but I'm the curious type, too, so I understand. I acted like a jerk. The stress, I guess." He paused. "Could I make it up to you by buying you a drink this evening? I've got to do a festival lecture at seven-thirty but we could meet before that. Like around six."

Hannah's heart soared. "All right. Where?"

"There's that little Italian restaurant on the main street in town."

"Café Lucca?"

"That's the one. It has a bar. I'll meet you there."

Hannah hung up, her hand remaining on the phone. What did he want from her?

"It's not fair," Kiki wailed from the garden when Hannah told her what had happened. "You already have one boyfriend and now you're getting another one while I still don't have anybody."

Hannah sat back down at the table. "I'm not interested in Hinkley Bowden for anything other than getting information about the murder," she said confidently, then focused on the newspaper so Kiki couldn't see her face. The truth was that she found something very attractive about Bowden, and it was this idea that currently absorbed her and not the article on Asia's financial crisis that she was struggling to read. Perhaps she wasn't as immune to the Hollywood glamour as she supposed she was. Whatever the reason, she looked forward to meeting him and the fact bothered her.

Hannah felt so uneasy that she went to the mudroom, put on her rubber clogs, her gardening gloves and hat, then headed out to the rose bed for some pruning. For her, working in the garden was the best therapy and the only sure way of clearing her head. With the confidence born of years of practice, she snipped off dead blossoms and errant canes. Kiki always said that it looked like Hannah was hacking away at the plants because she did it so quickly, but in reality the placement and angle of every snip was controlled to encourage new growth.

Out of the corner of her eye Hannah saw Kiki glance at

her with suspicion, since it wasn't Hannah's habit to put down the newspaper before she had finished reading it front to back.

Ignoring her sister's stare, Hannah went to work on her favorite prizewinning "Mr. Lincoln," a bush of deep red blossoms. Roses had a marvelous simplicity compared with humans, Hannah thought as she picked off some yellowed leaves. Why were people so complicated, herself included?

Hannah soon found Kiki standing near her, Kiki's high-heeled slippers digging holes in the lawn.

"Hannah, I know you're really thinking hard about something and it's got to be Freddie's murder. Do you know who killed him?"

"How could I already know? I've only started looking into it," Hannah said, punctuating the statement with a snip of her clippers.

"You're bound to have some ideas."

"I suppose right now," Hannah said, using her clippers to remove some yellowing leaves on her Double Delight rosebush. "There are three reasonable suspects. Bowden." *Snip*. "Angie." *Snip*. "And Bertha." Two more snips took care of the wilting foliage. "All of them had a motive as well as an opportunity to put a drug in Casey's flask."

Clippers resting on her knee, she paused to think a moment, noticing a batch of aphids under a fresh green leaf. Ruthless when it came to garden pests, she squashed them with her thumb. "Then of course you can add Brad to the list as well."

"Not Brad!" Kiki said with the same incredulity she would have shown if Hannah had said she suspected the pope. "He couldn't have had anything to do with the death of his own father."

"Then why did he behave so strangely last night? You said yourself that Brad didn't even know Casey until a few years ago. Maybe there wasn't that strong a bond between the two men."

"Well, I think it's terrible of you to even consider him, Hannah. He's Lauren's boyfriend."

Hannah knew that any hope of a logical conversation on

the subject was as dead as the aphids, but the discussion had reminded her how much work lay ahead. If she were going to make progress she had to break things down into manageable tasks. The task to accomplish that day was to do thorough interrogations of both Bowden and Bertha. Bowden would most likely be easiest, as all men usually were after they had a cocktail in them. But Bertha. There was the challenge.

Hannah heard the phone ring, and Kiki went into the kitchen to answer it. Only seconds later she came back out to the garden, her face distraught.

"Detective Larry wants to see us at the police station," she said. "He wants us there in an hour. He sounded so serious. Good God, Hannah, what could he want?"

The Hill Creek police station was pleasant as far as police stations went. Surrounded by tall trees, the small contemporary building had potted plants in the lobby, framed photos of whales on the walls, and a bowl of potpourri on the information counter. Hill Creek was your basic low-crime area and the station reflected it, which was exactly what worried Hannah. Hill Creek's police force was used to catching kids who broke windows and not cold-blooded murderers.

The youngish male officer at the front desk led her and Kiki into Detective Morgan's cluttered, closet-sized office, gesturing to two chairs as politely as if the women were in a tearoom about to sit down for an herbal brew and biscuits.

After accepting an offer of coffee, the two women parked themselves with trepidation in the bare wooden chairs. Kiki pressed a linen handkerchief against her nose as soon as they were alone.

"What if they arrest me?" she asked, tears forming in her heavily mascara'd eyes.

"Don't be ridiculous," Hannah said. "There's not a single shred of evidence that you could have had anything to do with Casey's murder. You don't have to worry about that."

"It's not the murder I'm worried about." Kiki looked at

the doorway to be certain no one could overhear. "It's pornography." She whispered the last word slowly, enunciating each vexing syllable. "That photo of Freddie. He was practically naked. It could be considered by unenlightened people as, well, dirty." Her chest heaved with a shuddering sigh. "Though we were consenting adults."

"He was dead at the time, so you could hardly say he consented to the photo."

Kiki gurgled with despair just as Detective Morgan walked in. It seemed to be a bad day all around, for he looked as droopy as a wilted petunia. When he said hello he didn't smile or even look at them directly. Hannah braced herself. What ever the news was, it wasn't going to be pleasant.

"Coffee?" he asked. "Oh, you've already got it." He looked disappointed that there wouldn't be an excuse for even a brief delay.

"Why did you call us here?" Hannah asked, wanting to get the bad news over with as quickly as possible.

He sat down behind his desk, leaned back, and pressed his fingers together, looking at her directly. Hannah wondered if they taught that gesture in detective school as a way to rattle witnesses. If so, it was very effective, for she found the suspense excruciating.

"There's been a complaint about you, Mrs. Malloy."

"What?" Hannah opened her mouth to protest but Kiki beat her to it.

"A complaint about Hannah?" she said, bewildered but sounding relieved he hadn't mentioned her. "From who?"

Morgan looked down at his notes. "Angie Brown." He lifted his eyes to Hannah. "She says you've been bothering her and Hinkley Bowden."

"Bothering him? I hardly think so," Kiki said. "Mr. Bowden asked Hannah for a date!"

"Looks like the whole family has gone Hollywood," he said sarcastically, then cleared his throat. "The crux of the matter is that you've been snooping around, Mrs. Malloy. Barging into people's hotel rooms uninvited. Asking too many questions, and even eavesdropping, according to Miss Brown. She got pretty emotional about it.''

Sitting up very straight, Hannah chewed on this information, trying desperately to find a more favorable spin. ''It seems to me that what you should be concerned about is not so much the complaint, but why she made it. Why is she so upset about my asking questions?'' she said. It was then that her eyes grazed a file on Morgan's desk. It had *Frederick Casey* typed on the white label affixed to its front.

Kiki turned to her sister, her eyes wide. ''Because she's the one who murdered my Freddie and she's afraid you'll find out. She's probably heard how you helped the police before and she's scared out of her wits.'' She pressed the handkerchief again to her nose. ''My poor Freddie. We were practically engaged, you know.''

At this last statement, Morgan looked at Hannah with surprise and she mouthed a silent no.

''It's possible, I suppose, that Angie could be worried about my finding out something,'' Hannah said distractedly, looking at the file, eager to know its contents. ''Maybe I should talk to her.''

''Hold on a minute,'' Morgan said loudly.

Hearing his ''I'm in authority'' voice, Hannah returned her attention to him, although she was not intimidated. It was hard to be intimidated by a man with the face of a Gerber baby.

''This is exactly what I don't want happening,'' Morgan said. ''Mrs. Malloy, you can't go around questioning people about Casey's murder. Angie Brown called the chief, but I talked him into letting me handle this. I asked both you and your sister to be here because I know how close you are, and it's important for both of you to understand the seriousness of this matter.''

Being unable to think of a good reason for her behavior with Bowden and Angie, Hannah decided to try an offensive maneuver. ''I have every respect for you and your chief,'' she said. ''But I've done nothing wrong. It seems to me that if someone should be questioning their behavior, it should be this police department for allowing that horrible photograph to be published in a tabloid.''

Both Kiki and Morgan cringed.

"Yes, well, that was certainly our fault," Morgan said, obviously regretful. "I still don't know how it happened. The photograph was missing for about twelve hours, then was sneaked back into the evidence room. Someone sold it to that newspaper. I'm sure it wasn't an officer. No officer here would do such a thing. You have our apologies, Mrs. Goldstein. It should never have happened. But that's not why I asked you here. You're here because that girl complained about you, Mrs. Malloy.''

Hannah pressed her hand to her chest. "I don't see why I should curtail my actions because someone from *out of town* is annoyed with me.''

"I'll tell you why," Morgan said. "The chief was in the Hill Creek Grocery yesterday afternoon and Wanda Backus told him that you were investigating the murder and would be turning over the killer to him shortly.''

"That Wanda," Kiki said, miffed. "She always goes to the grocery to spread gossip. I bet she was in the vegetable section, wasn't she? Right by the yuppie chow?''

Morgan gave her a puzzled look.

"The mixed greens with violet and nasturtium petals," Hannah explained.

"I think the chief did mention lettuce," he said.

Kiki folded her arms, her expression smug. "Wanda likes to stand there because she thinks the vegetable misters are good for her complexion.''

For a moment Morgan wore a look of vague confusion but quickly regained his wits. "Anyway, the chief is really ticked off.''

"I don't understand why," Hannah said. "I was very helpful to you on that other case.''

Morgan leaned forward, clasping his hands in front of him. "Between you and me, I don't think the chief liked that very much. Some of his friends at the Rotary Club made jokes." He stiffened like a choirboy about to do his Sunday solo. "So although we appreciate your concern, we don't require your assistance. You are interfering with a murder investigation. That's against the law and it could get you into big trouble.''

He started to say more, but the phone interrupted. After answering it, he excused himself, assuring them he would be right back.

''Did you hear that? Big trouble!'' Kiki said as soon as Morgan was out of earshot. ''You've got to stop investigating.''

''Ridiculous. I don't respond to threats, even from people I like. Besides, it's my civic duty to help.''

''If you want to do your civic duty, then go pick up some litter or paint over some graffiti or something, but don't get us into trouble.''

Hannah got out of her chair. ''Go to the door, Kiki, and keep a lookout.''

''Why?''

''Just do it,'' Hannah commanded.

''Granny sucking eggs,'' Kiki mumbled with disgust as she got up from her chair and sidled to the doorway. ''You're doing it. You're going to get us into big trouble and the next thing you know we'll both be in the slammer.''

Quickly Hannah reached over Morgan's desk and opened the file. ''I'm the one they'll put in the slammer, not you.''

''Ha. You're the one that Angie Brown complained about, but I got called on the carpet the same as you. That's the way it's always been,'' Kiki said as she peeked out the doorway. ''You do something wrong and we both get punished.''

Thumbing through the papers in the Casey folder, Hannah found a collection of forms filled out in print too small to read without her glasses as well as some notes written in a scrawl that was illegible. What she could read was a yellow note stuck to the inside of the folder that read, *Flask—Digoxin*. Hannah committed the last word to memory.

''Oh Hannah, he's coming,'' Kiki whispered, bouncing with agitation. ''Speed it up!''

''Be calm,'' Hannah said as she quickly sat back down

in her chair, but she, too, was flustered. Kiki plopped back into her chair with one eye still on the door, and hit her rump against the edge of the seat, causing the chair to overturn. When Morgan returned he found two plump legs projected upward, quivering like the antennae of some colossal insect in a grade-B horror movie. His face aghast, he rushed into the room and found the rest of Kiki on the floor in an unflattering position, her arms flapping, her skirt pushed awkwardly up her thighs, exposing her undergarments. It occurred to Hannah that Morgan had never before seen a leopard-print knee-length girdle since he stood there staring like he had stumbled upon a two-headed cow.

Hannah cleared her throat. "If you could help me."

"Of course," he replied hastily, remembering himself. Gallantly he stooped down to assist in hoisting Kiki to a more ladylike position, a difficult maneuver since she was too busy spitting out "granny sucking eggs" to provide much help. Once upright, she assured him with all the dignity she could muster that she was perfectly fine, but the event was humiliating for everyone.

"My poor sister," Hannah said to Morgan, trying her best to think of some excuse for her sister's position on the floor. "She had a dizzy spell. All of this has been a strain on her."

"Yes, a strain," Kiki echoed, though by looking at the odd bunching of Kiki's skirt, Hannah felt certain that the main strain she felt at the moment was a result of her girdle having been jolted out of position.

"Please remember what I said to you. You think you're helping but you're really hindering things," Morgan said, his face still the color of a stewed beet. "The chief has left it up to me to keep you out of this. I've got a possible promotion coming up and it won't be good for me if you get caught questioning anyone else."

Hannah looked at him with concern. "You mean you could lose a promotion over my investigating?" She liked Morgan very much, not only as a person but as a professional. She knew being a policeman, even in Hill Creek, was tough, and he carried out his job with efficiency and compassion. The community needed more policemen like him. The last thing she wanted was to hurt his chances for promotion.

"It's possible," he answered.

He picked up a pencil, nervously twisting it in his fingers. Hannah had a feeling he wanted to say more but was too flustered, having seen so much more of Kiki than he had ever intended. It was amazing the man could utter a syllable.

"I've taken to heart every word you've said," Hannah told him. He thanked them both, then left for another meeting.

"I know you, Hannah Malloy," Kiki said as they walked down the station steps and into the sunshine. "You said 'I'm taking to heart every word you've said,' " she mimicked. "But you never actually said that you would stop snooping into Freddie's murder. That's as good as lying."

"You have me wrong. I *am* going to stop looking into it. I have no desire to hurt their investigation or Detective Morgan's chances for promotion. He's such a nice man."

Kiki came to a halt as she tried mentally to dissect this information, quickly catching up again, her high heels clicking against the sidewalk.

"It's not like you to give in so easily," she said, sounding disturbed at this alteration of her universe.

"I was only going to look into the murder because I was trying to help. I don't want to hurt Morgan's career. Lauren will probably want to date him again once she's over this infatuation with Brad."

"I think you're wrong there. Detective Larry's in her rearview mirror. She's Hollywood bound," Kiki said with renewed cheerfulness.

Hannah kept her eyes on the sidewalk in order to hide her disappointment. Doing her research into Casey's murder had been so invigorating. She hated to give it up, not only because she enjoyed it but also because she honestly thought she could help solve the crime. But she couldn't hurt Detective Morgan.

When they reached the Eldorado, Kiki waited by the passenger door for Hannah to unlock it. "What a disaster," she said, wincing. "Falling down the way I did. I could just die. What if he tells people what happened in there?"

"I imagine it's a memory he doesn't wish to relive through repetition," Hannah said as she got in the car and started the engine, preparing herself mentally for the awful task in front of her. How would she tell Bertha that she could no longer help her?

ELEVEN

HANNAH WALKED AT A DISGRUNTLED clip down
the cracked sidewalk to Bertha's house. Only a few houses
from her own, its front yard was distinguished by three
mounds of earth rising ominously out of the lawn where
Bertha had excavated while searching for Indian artifacts.

Hannah carefully picked her way between the dirt piles
and up to the front door, a massive dark oak slab bearing
a small porcelain sign that read BEWARE THE CRAZY CAT in
French. To broadcast to the world her Santa Fe experience,
Bertha had stuccoed the house's exterior and had fake log
rafters bolted to the outside so it looked like it was made
of rough timber and adobe. The result was hideous, the
house looking to Hannah like a large turd that had been
dropped in the neighborhood. Approaching it always made
her shiver.

She knocked but there was no answer. She checked her
watch. Eleven-thirty. Strange. Bertha had usually com-
pleted her bioenergy bodywork by eleven at the latest.

Hannah walked around the side of the house and opened
the wooden gate that led to the backyard. There she found
Bertha. Dressed in a floppy yellow hat and baggy denim
overalls with the legs stuffed into ankle-high yellow rubber

boots, Bertha looked like a gargantuan Winnie the Pooh.
Her hair hung in damp strings against her forehead as she
vehemently plunged her shovel into the dirt. To Hannah's
consternation she saw freshly dug-up plants heaped high
upon black plastic sheeting. She estimated that half the yard
had been destroyed.

"Why on earth are you digging up your calla lilies?
They're close to the fence and out of the way," Hannah
said.

Bertha stopped shoveling and turned to her visitor.
"Hannah, glad to see you. Coffee?" she asked with the
peculiar lateral widening of the mouth that constituted her
smile.

Funny how a murder suspicion hanging over a person
makes them so sociable, Hannah mused. Bertha had always
viewed Hannah with high-minded disdain, and now all of
sudden here she was acting like they were best friends.

Hannah didn't especially want any coffee, but it seemed
the neighborly thing to do, and Bertha said it was already
made, so she accepted. It was such a lovely day, Hannah
preferred to stay outside, so Bertha removed her shoes and
gloves before entering her back door and came out again
with two Italian pottery mugs of coffee. Bertha always
bragged about the expensive pottery she had shipped from
Italy, and she guarded them like they were the crown jew-
els. For her to allow Hannah to sip liquid from one of the
precious mugs could only mean she was desperate for Hannah's favor. The thought twisted Hannah's stomach into a
knot. She had to tell Bertha that she couldn't help clear her
of Casey's murder, and Bertha was not the type of woman
to take rejection well. Hannah thought that as long as she
hung on to the Italian mug, at least Bertha wouldn't hit her.

Coffee in hand, they settled on a stone bench in front of
a Mexican sage that had yet to hear the executioner's call,
the air smelling of fresh earth and dying roses. Bertha's
hand trembled, driblets of coffee splashing on her overalls.

"I'm ripping out the whole east section of the flower
bed," she said. "Perfect spot for an Indian burial site by

my estimation. The noon sun hits it directly, which could have some sort of religious significance. Someone from the archaeology department at Berkeley is coming out to take a look.''

''But those calla lilies look so healthy.''

''Take them if you want. When I replant I don't want any more namby-pamby flowers. Bushes, that's what I need. Something substantial.''

Hannah looked around the yard with the anguish only a gardener could feel. Once it had been lovely. Now it had the ambience of a gravel pit. With a pang she noticed an eight-foot trench where Bertha's beautiful roses had once bloomed. ''But all this digging. Have you come up with anything new?''

Bertha shook her head. ''Only that one shard. I'm not giving up, though. I've good instincts for this sort of thing. I helped on an archaeological dig in New Mexico, so I'm knowledgeable. Besides, the work is good for me. Keeps my mind off things.'' She said the last part in a gentler tone that made Hannah feel even worse.

''Bertha, if you're innocent . . .'' she said, hoping to soften the blow she planned to deliver momentarily. Bertha grimaced on the ''if'' and Hannah hastily added, ''Which of course you are. The point is, you don't really have that much to worry about. All you did was mildly threaten Casey. There's no hard evidence to connect you to his murder.''

A silence settled on the two women, a silence as gaping as the holes in the yard. Bertha placed her mug safely behind her feet. ''Unfortunately the police are getting, well, information on me.''

''What kind?''

Bertha hesitated. ''I suppose I can tell you. You see, I have a police record from years back.''

Hannah's eyes grew large. Now, this *was* getting interesting. ''Really?''

''If you tell anyone I'll kill you,'' Bertha said quickly, then remembered herself. ''Excuse the terminology. The police record is no big thing really. It happened so long ago, but it was a federal offense and they keep those records around forever.''

"Good God, Bertha, what did you do?"

"Trumped-up charges, that's all they were. It was over twenty years ago when I was doing some postgraduate work. I was quite the radical feminist in those days. Still am.'' She looked at Hannah, her eyes earnest. "But after a while you just have to slap on a little makeup and damn the consequences. A person can't go through life with my sallow skin and never wear blusher, regardless of the political statement.''

"Of course," Hannah replied, not interested in discussing makeup. "Please go on, Bertha."

Bertha inhaled deeply, her overalls heaving. "I was president of a feminist group. Women with Rage we called ourselves. Those were the days," she said wistfully. "Best years of my life. We had a purpose then. We marched. We rallied in Washington. We burned our bras.''

"The police record, Bertha."

"Oh, yes, well, that's the thing really. It was my bra," Bertha said. Hannah raised an eyebrow. "I burned it in Washington.''

"Hardly a crime. In the sixties I set my panties on fire and raised them up a flagpole in front of the San Francisco city hall.''

Bertha's face perked up. "You were in a local Women with Rage chapter?"

"No, Fems for Freedom."

"Ah," Bertha said, nodding. "My problem was that I threw the burning bra into an FBI office. It landed in a wastepaper basket. I wasn't aiming it there, although they accused me of it. Caused quite a blaze. One of the secretaries—no more than a bonded slave, really—had tossed some fingernail polish remover in the trash earlier in the day, and that, of course, proved highly flammable. The fire destroyed half the office, including a silly softball trophy the FBI had won in some testosterone-drenched tournament against the Treasury Department. They were quite livid about it.''

"And the Hill Creek police found this out?"

"Yes. The record makes me sound like a violent radical. Radical, yes. Violent, no. I'm opposed to violence in all forms. I'm vegetarian,". Bertha said. It occurred to Hannah that Bertha had displayed a certain savagery toward the calla lilies. "The point is," she continued, "the police questioned me about it as if they think one silly burning bra makes me a crazed reactionary."

"The idea is ridiculous," Hannah said to comfort her. "We all burned a bra or two back then. I remember the stench of burning fiberfill like it was yesterday. The fact that yours landed in the FBI's trash can is unfortunate. Still, it doesn't make you a killer."

Bertha put her sweaty hand on Hannah's. "You understand. I knew you would. The problem is that I'm the only suspect for Casey's murder."

"That's where you're wrong," Hannah told her with new energy. "There are several other people with excellent motives for wanting Casey dead."

"Like who?" Bertha asked, a glimmer of hope in her eyes.

Hannah explained what she had learned about Bowden, Angie, and Brad, and the fact that all three had decent murder motives.

Bertha clapped her hands. "Oh Hannah, you're too marvelous. You're going to save my reputation, I just know it. I couldn't live in this town if people thought I could do something horrible."

Hannah smiled modestly. Dressed in overalls with garden soil on her chin, Bertha certainly didn't look like a dangerous person. She could be pushy, yes. Obnoxious, yes. Cruel toward landscaping, without question. But a killer?

At this juncture Bertha grabbed Hannah's hand and squeezed it. "I want to thank you, Hannah, for being my friend through all this and for helping me. It means so much, you see. You're respected in this town. People ask me how things are going and I just tell them, 'Hannah's behind me. She's going to find the killer'. It's made all the difference." She took a long, bolstering breath. "And you were right about the organic fertilizer. Since we had that chat at the Rose Club meeting I've been feeding my roses bonemeal.''

Hannah found herself deeply moved, knowing how much this last admission must have cost the other woman.

At this juncture, to Hannah's amazement, big tears of gratitude rained forth from Bertha's eyes, an emotional display Hannah found overwhelming. Looking down at her skirt, she smoothed out its folds and gathered up the nerve to tell Bertha that she couldn't continue with her investigation, that Bertha would no longer be able to say "Hannah's going to find the killer.'' But when she looked again into Bertha's grateful eyes, still spattering water like a garden sprinkler, she opened her mouth and the words stuck in her throat.

Instead she assured Bertha that, as previously promised, she would continue to help her, and with the feeling of a lead brick in her stomach, she arrived home carrying two large calla lilies as well as what seemed to be total responsibility for Bertha's welfare.

Now she was in a pickle. She had told Bertha that she would keep investigating the murder and told Detective Morgan she wouldn't. Bertha claimed that Hannah's investigation was saving her reputation. But only by stopping the investigation could she save Morgan's career.

The conflict weighed heavily as Hannah dropped the calla lilies near the waterspout in her backyard. It was too important an issue for any snap judgment, she decided, and there was always the possibility, remote as it might seem, that she could make both Bertha and Morgan happy. It certainly wouldn't hurt anything if she got a bit of information on digoxin, the drug named in Casey's case file. Morgan didn't tell her that she couldn't look something up in a book.

The bases of the lilies were still encrusted in hard-packed dirt, so Hannah watered them well then hurried into the house to consult her prescription drug manual. Kiki being a hypochondriac, she and Hannah kept a small library of medical manuals. Hannah consulted the index, turned to the specified page, and found what she was looking for. Digoxin was an older heart medication, one of the most commonly prescribed. The manual also said that digoxin could be lethal if a person overdosed with even a small amount.

Hannah closed the heavy book, returning it to the shelf. If the drug was common, then lots of people could have access to it even if they didn't have a heart condition themselves. If you knew someone who used the drug, you could steal enough pills for an overdose.

After donning her rubber clogs and gardening pants, Hannah set to work on finding the orphaned lilies a decent home. Gloved hands on hips, she surveyed her garden. It was stuffed with plants already, but she located a semishady corner next to the house that would suit the lilies if she moved two other plants.

Retrieving her shovel from the garage, Hannah began busily digging, her mind still focused on digoxin and who could have administered it to poor Frederick Casey. Hundreds of people had attended the film-festival party and there was no list of all of them since many people bought their tickets at the door and paid cash. The police had no chance of investigating every guest to determine if he or she had access to the drug. Now more than ever the police needed leads in order to narrow down the possible suspects. Inside information would be critical, Hannah thought as she plunged her shovel into the dirt. And who was better to obtain that than herself? If a policeman questions you, you get defensive. But a sixty-one-year-old woman? Hardly. It would be such a boost to Detective Morgan's career if he solved an important murder case like this one, and he was going to have such trouble getting all the facts himself. Still, he had asked her to stop investigating. But were those the actual words he had used? Hannah paused in her shoveling as she struggled to remember precisely what Morgan had said to her. She was still absorbed in this when she heard a rapping on the fence.

"Any news?" Naomi asked hungrily.

Placing one hand against the small of her back, Hannah straightened, bracing herself against her shovel. The cedar fence between their houses was high enough so that only Naomi's head was visible, and she had to stand on an over-turned bucket to reach that height. She had wrapped a purple scarf around her head and tied it at the top.

"About what?" Hannah asked.

"Don't play dumb. The whole town knows you're look-ing into Frederick Casey's murder. Wanda told everyone."

With a grunt, Hannah again started digging. "So I've heard. The truth is, the case can be handled very well by Detective Morgan."

Naomi scrunched her forehead. "Oh, Detective Mor-gan," she said sadly, the way one talked about an accident victim. "Does he know about Lauren and Brad?"

Hannah gave the soil an especially hard jab with her shovel. "Who doesn't know? But after Red Moon sent Brad running last night, he may not be so interested in Lauren anymore."

"Don't think so. I saw them together this morning at the Book Stop."

Hearing this news, Hannah accidentally decapitated an azalea. "I'm sorry to hear that."

"Don't you like him?"

"It's not a matter of liking him. I simply think he's going to break Lauren's heart."

Naomi made a twiffle sound. "It has to happen some-time. Every woman must feel the pain of an *affaire de coeur.*"

"But Lauren's done very little dating and now all of a sudden here she is with a television actor. A man of the world." She hesitated. "And there's something else."

Naomi lifted her eyebrows. "What?"

"Lauren doesn't know that I know this, but a couple of years ago I found a pile of those silly romance novels stashed under her bed."

"What were you doing scrounging around under her bed in the first place?"

"Looking for mice droppings. She had a rodent problem for a while. The books disturbed me. They showed that her head is filled with ridiculous romantic notions."

"So you're going to protect her from reading material, from mice, and now from men. Hannah, you can't shelter her forever. She went to an all-girl high school and then an all-girl college. It's a handicap. I know that since her mother passed on you feel protective, but as Red Moon says, the hawk must seek the sky and—"

"I know," Hannah said, purposely interrupting.

"But now that you mention it, I think Red Moon has concerns about Brad."

Hannah again stopped digging and looked at Naomi. "How do you know?"

"I felt it last night when I touched his hand. An uncomfortable heat swept through me."

"That was a hot flash." Kneeling, Hannah carefully picked up one freshly dug plant out of the flower bed, cradling its base in her hands, and moved it to the freshly dug hole.

"I'm past that, as you well know," Naomi said testily. "I couldn't tell if Brad was in trouble or linked to trouble or if it was just that vegetarian lasagna I had for dinner. Time will tell." She smiled. "You haven't asked me if *I* have any news."

"That's because if you do, it will come pouring forth with no assistance from me."

"Your chi is terribly blocked sometimes, Hannah Malloy."

"Nothing is blocked in me, dear. I eat so much roughage my problem is rope burn."

"Well, here's my news. Angie Brown is coming to see me this afternoon for a session."

Laying down her shovel, Hannah walked to the fence.

"You're interested, aren't you?" Naomi said with a cagey smile.

"Tell me more. How did she find out about you?"

Naomi put her hands on the fence top, resting her chin on top of them. "Don't know, but she seemed awfully upset when I told her I was booked this afternoon. She seemed so desperate that I moved some appointments so I could fit her in."

"What time is she coming?"

"In a couple of hours."

Hannah cogitated a moment, then said, "Naomi, I need a favor."

A breeze swept through the garden, causing the tied ends of Naomi's scarf to flutter. Hannah never asked for favors and she could tell it made the other woman suspicious.

"What is it?" Naomi asked.

"I want you to have Red Moon say something special to Angie."

"Impossible. I have no control over what Red Moon says."

"You make him say things all the time. You've admitted it to me."

Naomi's lips pressed together. "I regret ever revealing that little secret. At the time I was under duress. I only add a few trifling things occasionally and only if I think it will help somebody. But I can't start throwing things in willy-nilly. It would be unprofessional. And I'm sure Red Moon would disapprove."

"It might help me identify Casey's killer." Hannah noticed a relaxing of Naomi's mouth. She decided to take a more definitive shot at the target.

"What if in exchange I guaranteed you a minimum of three Rose Club members for your tai chi class? We have a meeting next week. I'm sure if I explained all the fantastic benefits of your tai chi they would sign up." Hannah turned her attention once again to her digging, giving Naomi the opportunity to mull over the proposition, but for insurance added, "I think twenty-five dollars an hour would be a good price."

Naomi chewed her thumbnail while she juggled the pros and cons, visions of a real tai chi class and the potential of a new water heater dancing through her head. On the one hand, Hannah had always said she didn't believe in Red Moon, so for her to ask this particular favor took an awful lot of chutzpah. On the other hand, when Hannah really wanted something from you she was like a bulldozer, and it would save time and effort to just give in now. And it *was* for a worthy cause. Naomi stood on her tiptoes, pushing her chin a little farther over the fence.

"What exactly is it you want Red Moon to say?"

TWELVE

"HANNAH, WILL YOU PUT DOWN that silly magazine and pay attention to me!"

So immersed in her own thoughts that she was aware only of a vague whiny noise in the background, Hannah sat in a faded stuffed chair by the front window thumbing through a gardening catalog. But it wasn't the glossy pictures of phlox and lilies that kept her attention off Kiki.

Kiki eyed her sister with the especially potent kind of aggravation that comes from knowing someone a lifetime. "I need your opinion on this outfit."

At last Hannah slid her reading glasses down her nose, looked up at her sister, and immediately wished she hadn't. Kiki was wearing black patent-leather high-heeled boots and bright red leggings that made her thighs look like sausages on the brink of exploding. But the most offensive garment was her sweater, an orange fashion fatality spotted with the dyed-to-match fur of a poor rabbit who had deserved a kinder fate.

"What do you think?" Kiki asked with a kittenish purr, turning from side to side. "I have a date with Bernie Watkins tonight and I want to look special." She raised her eyebrows and lowered her voice to a lusty whisper. "He's started taking Viagra."

Hearing a car, Hannah glanced eagerly out the window, saw the car continue down the street, then, disappointed, returned her eyes to her sister. "I'm afraid he may take one look at you and think he's having a hallucinatory side effect. And did you bathe in perfume? I thought Bernie just had surgery."

"He had it two months ago. He's feeling fine now."

"He won't be when he sees that outfit."

"You've been grumpy for the past hour. And why do you keep looking out that window?" Stomping over to her sister, Kiki peered out the glass.

"I'm looking for a car," Hannah replied.

"Whose car?"

"One of Naomi's clients."

"Why?"

"Why do you need to know?"

"I just do. You better tell me."

Hannah was ready to toss out a childish riposte but stopped herself. It amazed her how she and her sister still resorted to the same juvenile communication patterns they had used when they were ten.

Determined to be adult, Hannah put the catalog in her lap and removed her glasses. "There's no reason you shouldn't know. Casey's assistant—"

"You mean *my* Frederick Casey?"

"I hardly think one brief evening with a man in a pirate suit qualifies the use of a possessive pronoun, but if you insist, then yes, your Frederick Casey. Angie Brown's seeing Naomi for a channeling session, and I want to know when she arrives."

"You told Detective Larry you were going to stay out of the murder investigation."

Hannah raised her index finger. "As I recall, Morgan asked me in general not to interfere with the police investigation and specifically to stop questioning people. He didn't tell me to stop observing, stop listening, or to close off my senses to the world around me. I'm sure he's allowing me the use of my eyes and ears.''

Shaking her head, Kiki made a "tsk-tsk" sound. "You know what he meant."

"I just want to see what Angie looks like when she walks in. To see whether she's calm or agitated."

Kiki's head tilted, aggravation succumbing to curiosity. "Why? You really think she killed Freddie?"

Before Hannah could say she thought it very possible, she jumped at the sound of another car. Both women snapped their attention to the window as a small black BMW pulled into Naomi's driveway. It was a newer model but its paint was already dull and dented, as if it had traveled more than its share of hard miles, and when Angie got out, she looked the same. She wore an ankle-length printed skirt and a dark sweatshirt with a white shirt underneath that straggled out the back. Her hair looked unwashed, hanging limply against her face. Her eyes were cast downward until she reached Naomi's porch, then she looked up. Her face had the vacant look of someone who hadn't slept in days.

"That girl could use some lipstick," Kiki muttered as both she and Hannah watched Angie knock on Naomi's bright red front door. "And her hair."

"I don't think a beauty makeover is what she needs," Hannah replied. The door opened and Naomi's hand and wrist, covered with bracelets, extended out to Angie as she entered.

Hannah shook her head. "When people have trouble, why do they turn to psychics?"

"Angie probably just wants Red Moon to tell her future, like is she or is she not going to jail for murder?"

That wasn't all Red Moon was going to tell Angie. Hannah had coached Naomi on exactly what to say, going over it several times so there would be no mistakes. Not that it was difficult. Just a few simple sentences, but Hannah wanted them said just right. Naomi planned to wait until after she had come out of the Red Moon trance, but she would pretend to still be in the trance and say what Hannah wanted.

Kiki sat down on the couch and inspected her nail polish as Hannah picked up her catalog and perused a page on daffodil bulbs. Her eyes soon slid back to the window and Naomi's blue and white house as she feverishly speculated about what was going on inside. Naomi had promised to tell her everything Angie said, but Hannah had doubts that Naomi was one hundred percent reliable. What if she left out something that was important?

Unable to stand the suspense, Hannah threw down the catalog and headed for the door.

"Where are you going?" Kiki asked.

"To Naomi's."

Kiki leaped from the couch. "Hannah, you said you were only going to use your eyes and ears, not your feet."

After opening the door, Hannah stopped and faced her sister. "Morgan told me not to ask any more questions. Well, I'm not. I'm only going to listen to answers. There's nothing wrong with that."

"Then if you're going, I'm going, too, just to keep an eye on you."

"No, it's not a good idea."

"Hannah, please. I have a right to help find the killer. Freddie was my boyfriend."

"Kiki, I can't let you. What I'm about to do is ethically questionable."

Kiki moved confidently to the door. "That settles it. When it comes to questionable ethics I've had more experience than you."

Hannah didn't have time to argue since the session would be starting any second. "Just follow me and keep quiet."

With Hannah in the lead, the women walked out the front door, down the walkway, and to the sidewalk, making a left turn toward Naomi's.

Hannah knew exactly which window of Naomi's house belonged to her "spirit room," where she held her channeling sessions. The mild Marin climate allowed the luxury of open windows much of the year, and Hannah had often heard Red Moon's chanting drifting into her backyard while she tended her garden. Today was no exception, and the window was open a good ten inches.

"So what exactly are we doing?" Kiki asked in a chipper tone, her previous misgivings apparently changed to enthusiasm now that she was participating in something ethically questionable. They paused while Hannah inspected the window from about ten yards.

"We're going to eavesdrop."

"Oh, goodie."

"But we have to get close to the window and be perfectly quiet. And you have to take off your shoes."

As Hannah took off her crepe-soled flats, Kiki looked at the ground and scowled. "There's gravel everywhere and I'm wearing my good panty hose."

"What's more important, knowledge or your hosiery?"

Kiki acquiesced and began pulling off her boots, but gravity combined with her plump frame worked against her, and Hannah had to hold her arm so she wouldn't collapse onto the driveway.

"You're going to break your neck with those high heels. Why can't you wear sensible shoes?" Hannah asked, keeping her voice low as her sister struggled to pull off her second boot.

"Because sensible shoes make my ankles look fat. There, they're off." Kiki held up her boots to prove the point.

"Now, do exactly what I do, and above all, be quiet," Hannah told her. Holding her shoes in one hand, Hannah tiptoed down the gravel driveway with Kiki right behind. Kiki stopped twice to say "ouch," but Hannah shushed her so sternly that the third time Kiki bore the pain of the gravel in silence.

A large bush beneath the spirit-room window prevented Hannah from getting directly under it, but even from a few feet away she could hear voices. She knew the actual channeling hadn't yet begun because the rhythm of the conversation sounded too casual, with Naomi speaking in her own voice. There was silence for a few moments, then Hannah saw Naomi's head stick out the window. She was wearing her white Shriner's turban and big hoop earrings.

"Hannah, what the heck are you doing here?"

"I want to listen."

"That wasn't our bargain."

"Well, I'm sorry but I have to stay. What happened to Angie?"

Naomi looked behind her. "Keep your voice down. She's using the phone and she'll be back in a minute."

"How did you know we were here?"

"I'm clairvoyant, remember?" Hannah gave her a dubious look. "Okay, if you must know, it's Kiki's perfume. She's wearing so much Opium they're probably getting a whiff in San Diego. Hannah, I insist you leave. Red Moon won't stay very long with you out here. He doesn't like people hanging around."

"Please let me stay. Remember your tai chi class."

"Hannah, you can be so irritating." Naomi let out a rush of air. "Then be perfectly quiet, and Kiki, stand away from the window. Red Moon's allergic to all scented products. Here she comes."

Naomi disappeared from the window. There were another few seconds of silence followed by Angie asking who Naomi was talking to.

"Oh, I communicate with many spirits, dear. Some can be very aggressive and annoying. Take one more sip of tea and we'll perform the Hopi tea ritual," Naomi said, with an edge to her voice.

Hannah and Kiki exchanged a questioning look since Naomi had never mentioned such a ritual in all the years they had known her. Then tea came flying out the window, missing Hannah but hitting Kiki in the face, quickly followed by another splash.

Kiki's formerly smiling expression collapsed into wrath, and Hannah helped her wipe her face. There were a few minutes of conversation between Naomi and Angie, with their voices too low for Hannah to hear much. "Leaving tomorrow" was one of the few things Hannah could make out, the words coming from Angie.

Unable to distinguish anything else, Hannah moved

closer, stepping into the bush as far she could. There was a long silence, then Naomi began chanting. It was the usual procedure, her voice normal at first, then growing deeper. Hannah felt a tug on her sleeve.

"What are we listening for?" Kiki mouthed, but Hannah pressed a finger to her lips.

It was definitely Red Moon's voice that Hannah now heard drifting from the window. Its deepness made the words easier to hear, yet she still couldn't catch everything. She heard him say something about the moon and about animals that walked at night. Then Angie spoke in a tremulous voice.

"Does Brad love me?"

"Night animals cry together at the moon. There is no love. All is forgotten."

Angie began to sob, and Hannah and Kiki looked at each other wide-eyed. It wasn't hard for Hannah to believe that Angie was in love with Brad. What was difficult to swallow was that Angie thought for a minute that he returned her affections. The man never even looked at her, as far as Hannah had seen. But who knew what had gone on before they arrived in Hill Creek?

Red Moon was still chanting, but his voice was now softened and its pitch rose, which Hannah knew from the séances meant that Naomi had come out of her trance. Naomi's voice lowered once more. The difference between this new voice and Red Moon's was barely discernible. You had to listen intensely to notice the change in resonance, but after years of neighborly chats Hannah knew Naomi's voice well. Now was the time for her to say what Hannah had asked.

Angie was weeping, sucking in air.

"Rows of numbers," Naomi said à la Red Moon. This is it, Hannah thought excitedly, her hands clasped under her chin. She nodded to Kiki. "Numbers stand tall and mighty as ancient trees," Naomi continued.

Hannah frowned. Naomi had taken poetic license with the script. The part about the ancient trees seemed overdoing it, but Hannah supposed it did give the message a Red Moon type of authenticity.

"Numbers frighten. Numbers cause pain."

Angie let out a cry.

"You must tell truth about the numbers."

This was followed by a long silence.

"I . . . I can't," Angie said at last. "Poor Fred." She was crying wholeheartedly now. "I don't want to hear any more. I can't."

There was more silence, punctuated by Angie's sobs. Naomi performed some perfunctory chanting, winding down before resuming apparent consciousness and asking Angie what Red Moon had said.

Hannah stared at the ground, her brain spinning. The reference to the expense spreadsheet had definitely affected Angie. Hannah felt a twinge of guilt over manipulating the girl and causing her such misery, but she reminded herself that Angie could easily be a murderer. Hannah wished Angie had said something more specific, but at least now she felt even more certain that the spreadsheet had some connection to Casey's murder. Hannah badly wanted another look at it.

"Let's go," she whispered. She and Kiki walked as fast as they could with their bare feet crunching against the gravel, Kiki emitting a steady stream of soft "ouches."

"My nylons are in shreds," Kiki said, stopping by Angie's car to pick a rock from between her toes. "What was that stuff Naomi said about numbers? I didn't understand it at all and it really sent Angie into a tizzy."

Stopping at Angie's BMW, Hannah peered into it, her hands cupped against the glass. The red leather backpack sat in the front passenger seat. Pressing her face close to the window, Hannah saw that it was stuffed with a thick paperback book, a hairbrush, and a rolled-up wad of clothing. But in the middle of these odds and ends the file folder containing the spreadsheet peeked out. It sat there looking so innocent, yet it enticed Hannah more than she could bear. If what she had heard during the channeling session was right and Angie really was leaving tomorrow, she was probably taking the file with her. Perhaps she would even destroy its contents. In any event, Hannah would never get to see it.

"The numbers Naomi and Angie were talking about are in that file inside that backpack," she said to her sister. Squinting, Kiki looked into the car.

Hannah considered her options. The proper thing to do was to call Detective Morgan and tell him her suspicions. Of course, if she did, she would have to admit how she had come to those suspicions in the first place. Although Hannah felt her behavior regarding Angie and the channeling session had been perfectly reasonable, it was one of those situations that wouldn't sound so reasonable when described to a third party, especially if that third party was Detective Morgan. And being realistic, what information did she really have to give him? Her ideas about the spreadsheet were mostly a hunch and hardly justified Morgan issuing a search warrant. Even if he got one, Angie could easily destroy the data before he could execute it.

A conclusion is only that place where one chooses to stop thinking, and Hannah put a halt to her cerebral processes right there. The only rational thing to do, she decided, was to obtain more information before worrying poor beleaguered Detective Morgan. She would get a closer look at the spreadsheet and she would do it that day. The only remaining question was how.

"Come on, Kiki," she said, scuttling toward the house.

Kiki hobbled after her. "Can I put on my boots now?"

"No time." Hannah stopped on the porch. "I'm going to follow Angie."

"In the car?"

"No, in a fighter jet. Of course the car. I've got to see that spreadsheet and I'm going to need you with me."

"Now listen here, Hannah," Kiki said, shaking a warning finger from where she stood on the lower porch step. "A little eavesdropping is one thing, but following Angie could get us both in a mess. What if Detective Larry found out? He could say we were obstructing justice."

"Stop being such a crybaby. We're both over sixty years

old and we've spent our whole lives being good girls and doing what we're told. It's high time for a change. We're not frightened mice, are we? Of course not,'' she said, giving the air an emphatic punch. "We're women."

"No, Hannah. It would be deliberately going against what Detective Larry said to us."

"But, you see, we're going to be helping him in the long run. If we get a good look at that file, we'll help him solve the murder, which will boost his career, which will make him happy and help him forget Lauren."

Kiki stood motionless, lips parted as she absorbed this information. "I see," she said slowly. "And I'll be back in time for my date with Bernie?"

"Yes. Now run inside and get my purse and the car keys."

In a twitter of excitement, Kiki went into the house while Hannah lurked on the porch, keeping an eye on Angie's car. If Angie left before Kiki returned, Hannah wanted to know in what direction she drove.

After what seemed forever, Kiki returned carrying a shopping bag.

"What took so long?" Hannah asked.

"I got us a few things."

Hannah was curious about what those things were but didn't ask, because at that moment Angie walked out of Naomi's front door.

"Quick!" Hannah said. "Out the back door to the car!"

They hurried through the living room and kitchen with Sylvia and Teresa close at their heels, the pets excited by seeing the women rushing about. Hannah reached into the cookie jar on her way out and hastily tossed them each a dog biscuit as she and Kiki exited through the back door.

The detached single-car garage stood at the right rear of the house, the Cadillac parked outside it. Angie had just pulled out of Naomi's driveway as Hannah started the engine. Hannah tried to put up the automatic convertible top so they would be less conspicuous, but the mechanism made a grinding noise and the top refused to budge.

"Watch which way she goes," Hannah told Kiki as she backed out the driveway.

"Poop," Kiki said. "I can't see."

In the heat of excitement one of Kiki's false eyelashes had come unglued, hanging over her right eye like a caterpillar crawling for freedom. Hannah snatched it off her sister's eye and stuck it to the dashboard.

"Careful!" Kiki howled. "These things cost me twenty dollars."

Hannah headed out after Angie, who drove the little black convertible far faster than Hannah was accustomed to driving the ponderous Cadillac. At the end of Walnut, Angie turned left and Hannah followed. Attempting to be stealthy, she stayed as far back as possible, but Angie's car darted through the traffic and Hannah struggled to keep up without getting too close.

Bending over, Kiki scrounged through the shopping bag at her feet. "Put this on." She shoved a wide-brimmed peach-colored cloth hat onto Hannah's head.

"I can't see!" Hannah said, pulling it off, but Kiki put it right back on her, placing a pert little straw hat with a polka-dotted band on her own head.

"If we're going to tail Angie, we need to disguise ourselves, don't we?" Kiki said. "This is such fun."

"We're not doing this for fun. We're trying to learn something."

Kiki flapped a hand at her sister. "You're always so serious, always trying to accomplish something or learn something. There's no crime in just enjoying yourself. I'll drive if you want, then you can sit back and relax."

Hannah cast her a sidewise glance. "Someone around here has to be serious, and no thank you, I'd rather drive." Kiki was a notoriously bad driver, moving much too slowly yet still managing to run into things, so that the Cadillac always had a dent in it. As soon as Hannah got one dent fixed, another one turned up.

They followed Angie to Center Avenue, heading toward the main part of town. Angie drove erratically, driving at a speed far above the posted limit and crossing a double yellow line to pass the car in front of her. Luckily a red light stopped her, leaving the Cadillac a safe distance of two cars behind. A group of about twenty young children, all holding hands so they wouldn't stray, marched across the street led by their teachers.

"Hannah! Hannah!"

Turning, Hannah saw Evelyn from the Rose Club waving to her from the street corner.

"She wants to talk to you," Kiki said.

"Ignore her," Hannah replied. "We don't want to draw attention to ourselves."

But Evelyn would not be ignored. She kept waving and gesturing until Hannah decided it would be more discreet to talk to her than have her continue shouting. The light had turned green but a few straggling children were still making their way across the street, so the cars couldn't move. Hannah rolled down her window and Evelyn trotted up.

"Hello, girls. Beautiful day, isn't it?" Evelyn gushed. "Loved your poem in last week's *Sun*, Hannah. One of your best. The part about the gray walls whispering or murmuring or something. So poignant. Adore the hats."

Kiki leaned across the front seat of the car until she was practically in Hannah's lap. "Got them at Macy's White Flower sale. Aren't they cute?"

"For God's sake, sit back," Hannah told her. The children safely across the street, the cars began to move, with Angie's car darting ahead. With a quick good-bye to Evelyn, Hannah drove forward, following the BMW through town, with Kiki waving at everyone she saw.

Irritated, Hannah gripped the steering wheel more tightly. "For your information, Kiki, the objective here is to *not* attract attention to ourselves."

Kiki adjusted her hat in the rearview mirror, turning it toward her so it was unusable for driving. "Oh, take a chill pill. Angie didn't see us. This is such excitement. Lordy, what a week it's been."

They were through town now, and Angie had turned onto a two-lane stretch of road that led to the highway. The

BMW was three cars ahead. Hannah pressed her foot on the accelerator and felt a tingle. Kiki was right. This *was* excitement. Speeding along in hot pursuit of a suspect made her feel twenty years younger.

"How long are we going to follow her?" Kiki asked.

"As long as it takes."

"Just so I get home in time for Bernie. Now tell me again what we're doing?"

"We want to see a spreadsheet that's in a file folder inside her car."

Kiki thought a moment, looking puzzled. "But if she leaves it in her car, she'll probably lock the car. And if she takes it with her, then what? I'm not understanding the plan. What *is* the plan?"

"I don't actually have a plan. We're going to be creative, flexible."

Kiki looked skeptical. Angie turned south on Highway 101, taking the Sausalito exit. They followed her down Bridgeway a couple of miles. A light turned red. Angie rushed through it, leaving Hannah and Kiki behind a more law-abiding driver who had stopped.

"Darn!" Hannah said, hitting the steering wheel with her hand. "We're going to lose her."

"No, she's turning left up there into the boat dock," Kiki said. "Why would she go there?"

"Maybe she's going out for a sail with somebody. Or she could be staying on one of the boats. A lot of them are big enough to live on and people even rent them out. Or she could be seeing a friend."

The light turned green. Hannah drove down the street and parked across from the dock. She could see Angie's car in the parking lot. Angie got out carrying the backpack.

"Out of the car," Hannah told Kiki. "We have to see where she's going."

"Are you sure we should, Hannah?"

"We're not going to see that spreadsheet by sitting here. Besides, you don't have to worry. I have a plan now."

Kiki didn't look reassured but she got out of the car and followed Hannah. They crossed the street, waiting on the sidewalk while Angie walked down the wooden pier between the boats. The Sausalito berths had ten parallel wooden piers that housed a variety of boats, from small sailboats to hundred-foot yachts. Hannah and Kiki stood inside a Plexiglas bus-stop shelter as Angie walked toward the pier farthest to the left.

Angie stopped in front of a twenty-six-foot sailboat, fished through her backpack, and pulled out a set of keys. After tossing the pack onto the rear of the boat, she stepped on board, unlocked the door to the cabin, and disappeared inside.

Kiki and Hannah moved closer, ducking behind a garbage bin. "Only tell me the plan," Kiki said eagerly.

"It's simple. You go up to Angie, tell her you need to speak with her, and get her away from the boat."

Kiki's forehead furrowed. "Under what pretense?"

"Tell her you have something of Casey's you want to return and that you thought she was the right person to give it to. Tell her it's in the car."

"The only thing in the car is my makeup bag, those hats, and some candy wrappers."

"I have a copy of Emily Brontë's poems in the glove compartment that I keep in case of traffic jams. You can tell her that Casey gave it to you the night he died and that you want to return it. Say you're flustered, so flustered that you left the book in the car, and ask her to go to the car with you. While you're there I'll steal the file folder from the boat."

"You call that a plan?" Kiki said, perplexed. "It'll never work. She'll never believe me."

"She will if you sound convincing. Go on," Hannah said.

"I can't, Hannah. You do it and I'll look for the file."

"You don't know what to look for. You have to be the one who distracts her." Hannah gave her sister a nudge, but she remained unmovable. The sisters continued bickering until they saw Angie emerge from the boat carrying a towel, a bundle of clothes, and what looked like a shampoo bottle. Hannah pulled Kiki behind the garbage bin out of view.

"What's she doing now?" Kiki asked.

Hannah peeked around the side of the bin. "She's going to use the showers." She pointed out to Kiki the men and women's showers at the far side of the dock. "This is perfect. I can go on the boat while she's washing up. Do you have your beeper? I need it."

After a few seconds of rummaging, Kiki pulled it from her handbag and gave it to Hannah.

"Here's what I want you to do," Hannah said. "Go to that phone booth down that walkway beyond the showers. When you see Angie come out of the shower, I want you to call your beeper number. When I hear the beep I'll know she's coming and I'll get off the boat."

"I don't like this, Hannah. What if she sees you?"

"She won't. I'll just go the opposite way down the dock and I can hide behind that big cabin cruiser until she's back on the sailboat. Once she's inside, I can get away, but it's critical that you beep me as soon as she comes out of the shower." Hannah peeked at the showers as Angie walked inside. "We have to make our move."

"Hannah, I'm still not sure—"

Before Kiki could protest anymore, Hannah took off, and with a worried sigh, Kiki hurried to the phone booth, casting nervous glances around her. It was only after she had entered the booth and closed the door that she realized she was confused on a critical issue. How long a delay was there between the time she called the beeper number and when it actually beeped? It wasn't something she had ever thought about before. She started to go after Hannah, but Hannah was already halfway down the dock, and she couldn't call out her name. What if Angie heard and came out of the shower? Kiki chewed her thumbnail as she considered the problem. No, it was best to stay put. Hannah probably knew exactly how long it would take for her to receive the beep. Hannah didn't have a beeper, but she was so knowledgeable about everything. Certainly this would turn out all right. But Kiki felt a flutter in her stomach that told her it wouldn't.

THIRTEEN

HANNAH FLEW DOWN THE DOCK to the sailboat, her crepe-soled shoes making a mushy squeak against the wooden planks. She had to hurry. Judging from Angie's appearance, the girl didn't squander a lot of time on personal hygiene and wouldn't stay in the shower long.

Cautiously glancing around her as she racewalked, Hannah saw a couple of people working on their boats, but they were too far away and too absorbed in what they were doing to notice her. Her heart pounded as she gingerly placed one foot on the boat. It shifted precariously in the water and she steadied its side with her hands before climbing aboard. She stepped through the cabin's narrow opening and down three ladder steps.

A damp mustiness filled Hannah's nostrils as she looked about the cabin's interior. It was dark and cramped, strewn with clothes and papers. A tiny stove and sink were situated near the stairs with two narrow bench seats along each side of the cabin and a bed in the back. Angie was definitely staying here, because female lingerie, toiletries, and clothes were tossed everywhere, and her heavy boots lay on the floor.

Hannah moved through the cabin, her hand brushing

against a soft cotton bra lying crumpled on a countertop. Being so close to Angie's intimate belongings made her feel like she had walked in on a secret, as if part of Angie were in these inanimate objects and knew Hannah had trespassed. The cabin's contents revealed a different side of Angie than she showed to the world. A lacy teddy, white and covered with little red hearts, hung on the edge of a small lamp. Copies of *Glamour* and *Self* magazines lay open on the bed, the beautiful smiling models on the pages displaying a very different image than Angie's brusque exterior. The sight of them along with the frilly lingerie saddened Hannah. This was what Angie wanted—to be different from who she was, to be blond, pretty, and laughing. Hannah remembered feeling that way herself many years before. It took a while to accept yourself, she knew from experience.

It was then she felt the first jolt of apprehension, realizing what she was doing. She had entered Angie's living quarters without her knowledge and it was surely criminal, a misdemeanor or worse. And despite Angie's lacy lingerie, she could still be a killer and might be less than understanding if she found someone going through her things. Hannah wondered if the new postmenopause herbs she had been taking had affected her head.

Hannah turned toward the short ladder that led outside, but after putting her foot on the first rung, she stopped. The truth was, she had come too far to turn back. She had already committed a crime, the damage was done, so there was no point in scurrying off without getting some benefit. She would find what she needed, get out of there, and in the future strive to be a more law-abiding person.

Hannah's eyes searched the cabin until she saw the backpack tossed on the bed between two pillows. Grabbing it, she pulled out the file folder.

A quick perusal confirmed that it held the *Pirate John* expense spreadsheet as well as other related documents. The first page showed the general budget, with several expense lines highlighted. The next few pages were budgets broken down by month, but near the back she saw what appeared to be details on the expenses. It listed the names of various firms and the amounts they had been paid, along with the check number and to whom the check had been written. Some were highlighted in yellow with question marks next to them, and next to the question marks notes had been scribbled, some in red ink, some in pencil. A few of the notes were extensive, the jottings running down the margins. Angie must have contacted these people and written comments on the conversations. Hannah noticed that two of the jottings were marked with that day's date.

On this last document she noticed something curious. Several checks hadn't been written to the firms themselves, but to individuals. Hannah had done enough accounting to know that writing checks to individuals in a firm rather than to the firm itself was odd.

Her interest heightened, she thumbed through the other pages. Clipped to the back of the folder was a sheet labeled *Investors*. Scanning it, she saw Roger Burke's name with the incredible amount of fifty thousand dollars next to it. Roger had told her that he had become an investor but claimed to have made the decision the day of the opening-night party. This document bore a date six months earlier, and the paper looked too worn to be only two days old. She stared at the document in bewilderment before remembering that she was in a terrific hurry.

Hannah wanted to take the folder with her so she could study the documents, but she knew Angie would miss it. She pulled a pen from her purse, grabbed a piece of paper off a shelf, and began writing down the names of the high-lighted firms on the expense list, along with the names and phone numbers of the people who had received checks. She had written information on only two companies when a sudden beep startled her so much she dropped her pen.

With a cry of dismay she realized Kiki had beeped her. Angie must have skipped soaping a few body parts, because it seemed like only a couple of minutes had passed since she entered the shower. Frantically Hannah stuffed the folder back into the backpack, tossed it on the bed where she had found it, and scrambled up the ladder and out the cabin door.

She jumped from the boat to the dock and stumbled, her shin hitting the dock's hard edge. As she regained her balance she saw Angie turn the corner, coming her way. Why hadn't Kiki beeped her earlier? Angie was dressed in a dark skirt but diverged from her usual dark clothes with a bright red hip-length sweater. Rubbing her wet hair with a towel, her eyes were directed downward, but she would look up at any minute.

Hannah was trapped. Not knowing what else to do, she ducked and slid onto the boat docked next to Angie's. It was a small motorboat with no cabin, so she had no choice except to crawl under a tarp.

Curling into a fetal position, her shin throbbing, a remorseful Hannah found herself settled between a coil of smelly rope and equally foul T-shirts she felt certain had been used to clean fish. What had started out as an adventure had turned into epic absurdity. Why had she ever started it in the first place? She was, after all, a grown woman, and hiding in the midst of stinking sea gear was no place for a person with her quantity of experience. But hopefully she wouldn't have to stay long. She could hear Angie's footsteps coming closer. As soon as she heard Angie go down the ladder into the cabin, she would make her escape.

Hannah sighed with relief when she heard Angie step onto the next boat and start down the steps, but her relief evaporated when she heard a man call Angie's name.

"Staying on the boat tonight?" he asked. Hannah heard heavy footsteps against the dock as he approached.

"Yeah, I'm sleeping here one more night," Angie told him. "It's more homey than a hotel room. Cheaper, too."

"You got that right," the man said with a laugh. "Jake wanted me to check out the engine. It's been making a noise. I guess I can do it tomorrow."

"You can do it now if you like," Angie said. "I'm off. I won't be back until late."

"Got a hot date?"

"Just some plans."

"Okay then. I want to take my boat out for a while before it gets rough. I'll look at Jake's engine when I get back."

After this exchange, Hannah heard the man open one of the metal lockers that sat on the dock near the boat. At least Angie was leaving soon, she told herself, trying to be optimistic, and the man said he was taking his boat out for a while. As soon as they both left, she would steal away unnoticed.

Within moments Hannah heard Angie tell the man good-bye, followed by the sound of her footsteps down the dock. Now all she had to do was wait for the man to leave as well. She was in the middle of making a solemn promise to herself never to get into such a ridiculous situation again, when, to her dismay, she felt the boat shift. The man stepped onto the very boat where she was hiding.

A dozen awful thoughts ping-ponged through her head. What was the man doing on the boat? Would he find her? What was Kiki doing, observing this fiasco from afar? How on earth would she escape? Could she stand the smell of the T-shirts much longer?

She heard him rummage through his gear. This is ridiculous, she told herself. The only thing to do was to emerge from the tarp and offer some explanation. She could claim she thought she was being followed and was trying to hide, or that she was having an LSD flashback, or that she was in a cult that worshiped tarps and the smell of dead fish. This *was* Northern California after all. The important thing was to regain a few shreds of dignity and she couldn't do that hiding like a scared rabbit.

But just as she was about to expose herself, she froze at a dreaded sound. The man had started the boat's engine. She could feel the boat moving.

Then she heard the sound of Kiki's high-heeled boots clicking down the dock.

"You've got my sister!" Kiki shouted, the staccato of her boots coming rapidly closer. Then Hannah heard a loud "oops" followed by a scream and a splash. Hannah jumped out from under the tarp, yelling Kiki's name. Kiki's head emerged from the water, the man in the boat staring down at her in stupefaction just before Hannah leaped into the bay to save her.

$\mathscr{F}$OURTEEN

γ&

$\mathscr{R}$EGRET WAS A USELESS THING, Hannah had always told herself. If you made a mistake the best thing was to learn what you could from it and move on. But as she sat in her living room next to a warm fire conjuring up images of her sister and her flopping in the bay like two demented flounders, regret loomed large.

Why hadn't she just told Detective Morgan what she suspected about the spreadsheet instead of chasing after it on her own? Hannah sidled closer to the fire's heat to ease the chill still deep in her bones. At least Angie hadn't seen them. The worst part for Hannah was that she hadn't gotten much for all that trouble. Just a couple of names she had jotted down. What good would those do?

The gentleman on the boat took the whole scene gracefully, Hannah had to admit. He let out a yell when Kiki hit the water but it was nothing to match the yelp that blasted from him when he saw Hannah jump out from under the tarp and leap into the bay after her sister.

To his credit, as soon as he regained his senses he pulled both women out of the freezing water and wrapped them in blankets. He even tried to pick sea grunge off Kiki's sweater until Hannah explained with chattering teeth that it was wet rabbit fur and permanently attached. He introduced himself as Bob Bailey, a boat mechanic, and then he drove them home in the Cadillac, accepting Hannah's story about the new family therapy she and Kiki were undergoing. It included an adult version of hide-and-go-seek, Hannah said, which allowed them to explore their abandonment issues. Moved by this, Bob admitted he had a few abandonment issues himself and asked if next time he could play, too. Hannah assured him they would give him a call, then paid for his cab back to Sausalito.

"He was awfully cute," Kiki said, swaddled in a chenille robe, wiggling her toes by the crackling fire. "I got his phone number. Should I ask him out?"

"He's ten years younger than you." Hannah was meeting Hinkley Bowden for drinks in less than an hour, and though she had bathed she still needed to dress and do something with her hair. To be honest, after what happened at the boat she didn't feel like going anymore, but she refused to be a wimp and cancel. She held a piece of paper near the fireplace screen, the one on which she had taken notes on the *Pirate John* expenses. Though a bit blurry from the water, she could still read it.

"It doesn't matter that he's younger," Kiki said. "I'd like to try younger men."

"I guess a younger man would last longer."

"He certainly would," Kiki said with a wink.

"I was talking about the amount of time you get to spend with him. Boyfriends your own age have had a disturbing tendency to die on you."

Kiki looked hurt. "It's hardly my fault poor Freddie was murdered. Before him I only had two boyfriends die, and one was from natural causes."

"My point, exactly. At least Mr. Bailey appears to be in good health and doesn't seem the type to inspire murderous feelings in anyone," Hannah said. "Though I wouldn't have suspected Frederick Casey to inspire them either." Picking up the fire iron, she poked at a log, her mind churning another issue. "Did Roger Burke ever mention anything to you about investing in *Pirate John*?"

"No, why?"

"Just curious." Hannah very much wanted to share with Kiki the fact that Roger had lied about the timing of his investment, but she decided against it since Kiki might fly off the handle and phone him about it.

Crossing her arms, Kiki looked grimly at her sister. "I'd make you tell me exactly what's going on in your head right now, but to be honest I'm sick as spit of this whole mess. That's the coldest water I ever felt in my life, like jumping into a tub of ice cubes. But when I saw that boat take off with you on it, I just went crazy, and I guess my heel caught on something."

"May I repeat for the one thousandth time that you should wear flat sturdy shoes."

"It's not my shoes that are the problem here. We never should have followed Angie in the first place. I don't know what we were thinking. The girl could be a murderer. And I don't want you to meet Hinkley Bowden tonight. He could be a murderer, too, and he could be dangerous."

"I'll be in a public place."

"It doesn't matter. He could slip something in your drink, just like he might have done with my Freddie."

"I'll be careful," Hannah answered. "I'm probably safer than you with Bernie on Viagra." A distasteful image formed in her mind that she quickly squashed.

Kiki chattered about Bernie, with Hannah only half listening. The paper was dry now. Hannah placed it in her lap and studied it. The limited information it contained wasn't enough. She had to have more, if only to justify the dunking in the bay. On an impulse she got up and went to the kitchen.

"Will you get me some tea?" Kiki called out from the living room.

"In a minute."

"What are you doing?"

"I'm not sure," Hannah answered softly. She dialed information in Los Angeles and got the phone number for Creative Filming, the first company name on the paper. The check had been written to a Paul Lancome for $162,000.

Hannah dialed the number and asked the woman who answered for Mr. Lancome. In a few moments a man picked up and issued a gruff hello.

"Mr. Lancome? I, um, work for the *Pirate John* production."

There was a delay in his response. "What do you want?" He didn't sound thrilled.

"I'm calling about the check you received."

This was followed by a good five seconds of dead air. "Listen," he finally said, keeping his voice low. "I'm not doing any more. Who the hell are you, anyway? I've always dealt with Casey. Don't call here. I'm out of this." He hung up.

Hannah placed the phone back on the receiver. The man had sounded angry, even afraid. What had he meant when he said he wasn't "doing any more"? A disturbing yet provocative thought burst into her head. *Pirate John* could have been a front for selling drugs.

All at once Hannah felt new vigor. She knew it was wrong to be excited about such an unpleasant possibility, but at least she had something tangible to pursue. After making tea for Kiki, she dressed, got in the Cadillac, and drove to meet Bowden.

Café Lucca had been in Hill Creek for over twenty years. For a time business had slowed, the old-style Italian restaurant with its dim lighting and red vinyl booths not appealing to the town's increasingly trendy population. But two years earlier it had been remodeled top to bottom, its interior changed to light amber colors, the walls converted to glass and the decor to high-tech Italian. Now it was packed seven nights a week.

Hannah moved through the crowd of patrons swishing down silvery martinis and goblets of golden wine, lucking into a table in the far corner of the bar. Personally she preferred the restaurant when it was dark enough to make you look good on a bad hair day, when half the tables were empty and you could eat in peace and quiet. But Paulo, the owner, was making a bundle and had donated five computers to the middle school the previous year. You couldn't argue with success.

She had just tucked her purse under her chair when she saw Bowden at the captain's stand. Spotting her, he squeezed between the crowded tables. It wasn't until he reached her that she realized she was nervous, feeling a small fluttering in her stomach.

"You look nice," he said as he sat down, giving her a stiff smile. Hannah had worn her favorite calf-length brown skirt and long gold sweater topped with a paisley silk shawl. She knew the gold accented her auburn hair, and suddenly she was embarrassed by it. Was she trying to impress him?

A young good-looking waiter in jeans and a white shirt bearing the name of the restaurant came to the table and Bowden quickly ordered a Scotch, Hannah ordering a soda with lime. "Thanks for meeting me," he said when the waiter left, leaning back in his chair and looking a little more relaxed. Hannah remembered that feeling from her heavy drinking days—that wave of gratitude you felt when you knew your liquor was on its way. They exchanged a few more pleasantries, Bowden asking and answering polite questions with weariness. Even in the enhancing glow of the café's lighting he looked older, his eyes flat. Something in this man had broken in the past twenty-four hours, she thought, and even though she knew he could be a murderer, she still felt sorry for him.

"Why did you want to meet me?" Hannah asked him, her nervousness heightening.

The waiter bringing their drinks delayed his answer. Bowden wrapped his fingers around the glass, then downed half the amber liquid in one gulp. He closed his eyes for a few seconds, and when he opened them again a little of their glow had returned.

"Couldn't we have some small talk first?" he said, the edges of his mouth curling upward. "You know, flirt a little, discuss some poetry. Make a few callous comments about these other, dare I say it, younger patrons?" He filled his cheeks with air, then let it out. "You're not going to let this be fun, are you?"

"You'll have to excuse me. I've had a rough day."

"No problem. You're right. A man has been murdered. We must bow under the weight of its ugliness. But if you don't mind, I'd prefer to do it under the influence."

After gulping the rest of his Scotch, he held up a finger for the waiter, then lowered it with a frown when he saw the waiter's attention consumed by a group of young women at the next table. He tightened a little, returning his attention to her. "Here's why I wanted to meet you. I want to know what your interest is in Fred. Angie's emotional balance has always been shaky, but in certain matters her judgment is unerring. And she thinks you've been nosing around where you shouldn't, and not just for a little gossip to share during bridge."

Hannah took a long gulp of soda. Thank God Angie didn't know where she had nosed around that afternoon.

"I told you before that I feel some responsibility for what happened to Mr. Casey," she said, then reminded him of the letter she had written the man. Bowden gave her a quizzical smile. "I want to help find out who killed him and I intend to keep at it, regardless of who it annoys. So I've answered your question," she told him with a great deal more conviction in her voice than she actually felt, but she knew that Bowden wouldn't give her a shred of information if she wasn't assertive. "Now I need you to answer mine. Why is everyone so edgy about the *Pirate John* accounting?"

Bowden's smile dimmed. "Who is everyone?"

"You and Angie." She let a few seconds pass, then lobbed a missile. "Paul Lancome of Creative Filming."

Bowden's smile now collapsed completely. Suddenly he looked like he had eaten a bad shrimp.

Gaining courage, Hannah pressed on. "I called Mr. Lancome this afternoon. He reacted very oddly when I asked him about the *Pirate John* production."

"How did you get his name?"

"I remembered it from seeing the expense sheets in your hotel room."

"I don't believe you. You only saw that stuff for a few seconds."

"I have a photographic memory," she said, knowing that she couldn't remember a short grocery list. She was now deep in a lie and she didn't like it, but the train had left the station.

Bowden stared longingly into his glass, obviously wishing there were still Scotch in it. "I suppose people will know soon enough anyway, so what the hell." He looked around for the waiter, said a couple of stern "excuse me's," but the waiter was still too interested in the girls to be concerned with Bowden's alcohol requirements. Bowden turned back to Hannah. "Fred was bilking the *Pirate John* investors, the ones who gave him start-up money."

Swallowing, Hannah tried not to look astounded. "How?"

"By claiming false expenses. Big ones."

"I don't understand. I didn't see any checks written to Casey or to cash either."

"You *do* have a photographic memory," Bowden said wryly. "That way would have been too obvious. Instead he would contract with a small firm that was financially and ethically challenged. Take Creative Filming, for example. Lancome and Fred had an arrangement. Lancome would bill the production for, say, a hundred thousand dollars, for bogus consulting on the script, scouting locations, story research, whatever. Just as long as it was a consulting service and not an actual lease or equipment that could be traced. Fred's accountant would pay the bill, thinking it was a legitimate expense. Lancome would keep fifty thousand and give the rest back to Fred in cash. This had been going on for a year. Fred got almost a million dollars and was on his way to getting more."

"And he admitted all this?"

"Not at first. Angie started getting suspicious about two months ago. When Fred told her she wasn't going to be a producer on *Pirate John,* she came crying to me. I've never liked her that much. She's strange, all soft one minute and shrewish the next. But what Fred did really pissed me off, so I told her I'd give her some decent work to do for the movie. No brain surgery but at least some higher-level responsibilities that she could put on her résumé.''

''What work did you give her?''

''A couple of different things, but the main task was to start working on a cost estimate for the special effects. *Pirate John* has a volcano eruption and an explosion. She didn't want Fred to know yet that she was working with me, so she started looking through the expense records to see if he had already done any contracting for the special effects. She found the name of this off-the-wall little company in La Jolla that she had never heard of. She called them and after a couple of questions realized they had gotten paid an exorbitant amount for work that had never been done.''

''Didn't any of the investors ask questions about how the money was being used?''

''No, not at this point. Later on, when a studio picked up the project, there would be financial controls. But Fred had gotten a group of neophytes to put up the seed money. You know, doctors, businessmen who like the idea of investing in a movie.'' Like Roger, Hannah thought. Bowden continued. ''Those types are too dazzled to ask questions and wouldn't know what to ask anyway.''

''But eventually they would want to look at records.''

''If they had brains they would. That's what made it so stupid on Fred's part. There was a good chance that he'd get caught. He had to know that. It just shows how out of control he was.''

''So Angie confronted him with what she'd found out?''

''She asked him about it the week before the film festival, but he blew up, yelled like crazy, and said it wasn't true. Then the next morning he came to her, meek as a lamb, confessed to everything, and said that if she didn't tell anyone he'd pay all the money back.''

Hannah wondered what could have happened overnight

to convince Casey to confess the fraud. "When did you find all this out?"

"The day after he died," he replied, and Hannah wasn't sure she believed him. "Angie was scared that one of the people at the firms he was colluding with might have killed him."

"Have you done much research on what firms were getting payoffs?"

"No. We'll get to that later, I guess."

But Angie had gotten to it already. The notes in the file folder proved she had begun making calls. Was Bowden lying or did he really not know?

A peal of laughter shattered Hannah's stream of thought. The restaurant's crowd grew thicker and noisier and she saw the girls at the next table seized by a giggling fit, induced by the waiter, who was still entertaining them. He was tall, no more than twenty-five, and, Hannah had to admit, very sexy if you happened to like young handsome, broad-shouldered men in tight jeans. Bowden examined him with an unpleasant combination of annoyance and envy, his need for a fresh Scotch intensifying, his fingers nervously stroking the rim of the empty glass.

Watching Bowden, Hannah felt suddenly depressed. She sat back in her chair and considered the fact that no matter what people achieved in life, it never seemed to be enough. Casey wanted more money. Bowden wanted his youth back, and he was never going to get it. He also wanted a Scotch, and it looked like he wasn't going to get that either.

"You look upset," Bowden said. "It wasn't your money."

"It's just hard for me to believe that a man with so much talent—"

He interrupted her with a mirthless laugh. "God, I'm sick of hearing about Fred's damn talent. Okay, talent, yes. I'll give him that. But scruples, morals, ethics, or the barest shred of decency, no. Granted, the man had a marvelous gift for creating a story. For developing characters and dialogue. For placing all of it in the right setting and with the right soundtrack so that you sit in a dark theater and get transported someplace more fucking real than your own life," he said with colossal bitterness. "But he was a human pustule. A selfish, depraved, people-using, teenager-fucking, gin-guzzling pervert. He went through money the way you go through soda water, lady, and he left a trail of emotional carnage that went from New York to L.A. I've had it up to here with people telling me how fucking wonderful he is."

Another titillated squeal came from the next table. Bowden stood up, seized the waiter's shoulder, spun him around, and planted his fist on the young man's jaw. The girls screamed. The waiter fell back onto the table with a clattering of broken glass.

Hannah leaped out of her chair. The waiter, recovering from the blow, was pulling himself up, preparing to slug Bowden. Instinctively Hannah grabbed Bowden's hand and in an instant had dragged him outside.

Bowden seemed dazed, as if the punch surprised him as much as it had the waiter. "This way," she said, pulling him into an alley that ran along the side of the restaurant. They jogged half its length and heard voices far behind them. She pushed him into a doorway, following him into its darkness, both of them panting from the exertion. When she caught her breath she looked at Bowden and saw him smiling.

"Sorry about that. I guess things have been building up," he said, rubbing his hand. "I hope we tipped the guy."

"We didn't even pay the bill. You realize that waiter will probably sue you."

"The jerk deserved it. I'll just get him a bit part in a movie and he'll release me from liability. It's happened before. I didn't even hit him that hard. I'm sixty-three, you know."

"It seems silly to hit a person because he doesn't bring you a drink."

"I didn't hit him because of the drink."

"Then why?"

"I hit him because I want to be him. I want to be young, handsome, and ignorant."

"Is it so bad being who you are?"

"Not right now. Not while I'm with you," he said with a smile.

She smiled back. "You better go home and call your lawyer."

"No," he said. "I want to keep talking to you. You just saved me from having my jaw broken." Punching out a waiter had invigorated him, Hannah decided, for he sounded happier. "I'm yours now. You can barrage me with questions if you want, solve Fred's murder, and ease your conscience. Just stay with me. I haven't felt this good in months. I have to remember to slug people more often."

Hannah laughed out loud. He slipped his fingers around hers and they began walking, their shoes on the pavement echoing against the alley walls.

"Here's my first question," she told him.

"Shoot."

"Was Brad having an affair with Angie?"

Bowden assumed an expression of mock horror. "An affair, of course not. No, he was just banging her when he felt like it and making her run his errands for the privilege. Brad may not have grown up with his father, but he's displaying all the Casey traits."

"Why didn't Brad grow up with him?"

"Fred didn't even admit Brad was his son until five years ago. Fred was never married to Brad's mother. He lived with her a few years in the late sixties, then dumped her when she got pregnant."

"What changed his mind about his child?"

"When Brad's mother died Fred got sentimental. Realized he was getting older, didn't have any kids and all that. He's been good to Brad in the past few years, but too good, if you ask me."

"Why do you say that?"

"Fred managed to be selfish in everything he did. He bent over backward to get Brad a career in film but he did it so he could tell himself what a great guy he was. Which meant he never let Brad stand on his own feet. Fred got the kid every job he's had. As a result Brad's got the self-esteem of a garden slug. His fling with Angie is a manifestation of that.''

''I'd think an actor with a self-esteem problem would go out with gorgeous blondes.''

''Oh, Brad dates his share of bimbo would-be models, but he's always quietly afraid they're just going out with him in hopes of getting connected to his father. Which, of course, they are. So in between those girls he prefers women who remind him of his mother—slightly dowdy, shy little women with no lives of their own that might compete with his. He makes himself believe they truly love him for himself, poor sap. Angie fit the role perfectly.''

Hannah felt an unpleasant twinge. Lauren fit the model as well.

Bowden continued. ''And that woman he lives with. She's got the brains of plankton. They're actually engaged now.''

''He's engaged to a woman?'' Hannah's twinge turned into a sickening wrench.

''I wouldn't call her a woman. I think she's all of nineteen.''

They reached the parking lot and Bowden stopped by a station wagon. He casually leaned against it, unaware of the effect his words had on Hannah. ''Of course, Angie was used to terrible treatment from Fred. He had been sleeping with her, too, until about six months ago.''

''Angie was sleeping with the father *and* the son?'' Hannah asked, shocked.

He looked amused. ''Not in the same bed at the same time,'' he said with a wag of his finger. ''That sort of thing still raises a few eyebrows. No, when Fred got tired of Angie on a physical level, which happened relatively quickly, Brad took her up. She's convenient to have around. Not only does she sleep with you, but she fetches your Chinese takeout, takes the Porsche in for tune-ups, and doesn't complain about fiancées. Unfortunately for Angie she doesn't inspire long-lasting attachments. Brad dropped her about a month ago.''

''She must be angry.''

''In some people getting dumped doesn't inspire anger, only self-loathing. She's still following Brad around like a sick dog. That's why she came to Hill Creek. Fred didn't need or want her here. He refused to pick up her expenses, but she came anyway.''

That explained why she was staying on someone's boat and not in a hotel, Hannah thought. ''She might not have been angry at Brad, but she was sure angry at Fred. It was obvious the night of the party.''

''But that was because he screwed her professionally.''

''Maybe that's why she dug so hard into the *Pirate John* finances. To get revenge against him.''

''At first, probably. But when she told me everything the other night she wanted my promise that I wouldn't tell anyone else. She wanted my help in trying to keep the whole thing covered up.''

''But how would you do that?''

''It would be fairly easy once we got the studio backing to go into production. With an average fifty-million-dollar-movie budget, one million isn't that hard to hide.''

Hannah heard a police siren and saw a flash of red light at the alley's end. ''They're looking for you.''

''Good.'' He put one arm around her and pulled her close to him. ''Let's act like we're eighteen and have sex right here. You know, get really enthusiastic. Think of it,'' he said, his tone dramatic. ''The danger. The thrill. The complete sleaze.''

Laughing, Hannah pulled away. ''I don't think so.''

His smile softened. ''Are you in a relationship?''

She hesitated, thinking it rude to admit she thought he could be a murderer. ''That's one reason, yes.''

''Even better,'' he said, his grin returning. ''You'll be cheating. All the ingredients of great sex.''

''Mr. Bowden,'' she said with feigned seriousness. He reached for her again, but she stepped backward.

He caught her hand. ''Hannah, I'm going to Palm Desert

next week. I want you to come with me. I'm not joking now."

She kept a jovial tone in her voice to counteract his increasingly somber look. "I don't think I believe you."

"Why not?"

"Because I'm sure you can get any number of much younger women who—"

"I don't want those women." He gave her hand a gentle tug, pulling her closer. "I want you. I can talk to you."

"I can't."

"Can't talk?"

"Can't go."

"You have to. My therapist would really think I'd made a breakthrough. Besides, I need you. I just realized it tonight. Younger women make me feel old and burned out. You're my age yet you still have spark in you. I want some spark, too. You can give it to me."

Hannah shook her head.

"Just think about it. Promise me you'll think about it."

"Okay. I'll think about it."

"At least that's something. Now that we've got the romantic scene out of the way I've got to head over to the theater." He checked his watch. "Brad's doing the first part of the lecture, so if I hurry I can make it."

"Go around the back of this building and turn right when you see the wooden bridge. That will take you back to the theater without having to pass the restaurant."

"Thank you. I prefer not to go to jail. I need my comforts. Good-bye, Hannah." He started to walk away, then stopped and turned back. "Oh, yeah, one thing I should tell you. Your letter isn't what brought Fred to Hill Creek. I'm sure it was a great letter, but it wasn't your prose that did the trick."

"Then what did?"

"He knew there were a lot of rich people that live around here. He wanted to get new investors to cover the lost expenses, and if he had gone to his earlier investors or his standard sources in L.A. and New York, they might have gone over the accounting. Instead he decided to charm the

Ralph Lauren shorts off some Marin County movie-producer wannabes. He'd already gotten some money off of one guy around here, so Fred figured there'd be more like him.''

"You mean Roger Burke?"

"Yeah, him. Guys like him don't understand the movie business. In fact—'' Bowden paused to chuckle. ''Burke called Fred a month ago and actually wanted his money back. We got a good belly laugh out of that one. But you see, that's the only reason Fred came. Money. You didn't lure him to his death. Money did.'' He lifted her hand to his lips and kissed it. ''Isn't it always money?'' he said with a wry smile, then walked away.

FIFTEEN

THE BLACK-AND-WHITE POLICE car in front of Café Lucca looked festive, its cherry top blinking happily into the night. As Hannah passed the small crowd on the sidewalk, she heard them talking with amazement about the fistfight. It was a novelty, she supposed. People seldom punched each other in Hill Creek. If angered, they made witty but scathing remarks behind each other's backs, boycotted charity events, or, in rare cases, called their lawyers. But socking someone in a bar. It was so unheard of it was almost chic.

No one noticed Hannah as she glided by the crowd, and she couldn't help chuckling to herself. Only twenty minutes earlier she had escaped with the crime's perpetrator, yet she could slip past all these people, including two policemen, and no one noticed. Being a woman over sixty had advantages, no question about it. You could slip through the world anonymously, watching and listening, flying below all radar.

When she decided she was a safe distance from the restaurant, she slowed her pace and tried to get her thoughts to do likewise, but they didn't cooperate. What Bowden had said about Brad being engaged plagued her. Maybe it wasn't as critical as murder, but it certainly hit closer to home. Lauren would be devastated.

Her conversation with Bowden had eased her mind in at least one way. She wasn't responsible for bringing Casey to Hill Creek. He had come because of his own greed, although it was a disappointment that it hadn't been her artful prose that had persuaded him.

As she walked down the street toward her car, Hannah considered more of the fascinating elements that had been added to the puzzle. Casey had been committing fraud. If any of the *Pirate John* investors had known, it would have given them an excellent motive for murder, which brought up the disturbing idea of Roger's involvement. He had lied to Hannah about the timing of his investment in *Pirate John,* and there was the question of why he had wanted his money back. Perhaps he had known about the fraud. But how?

Hannah approached a corner and, glancing around her, realized with alarm that the street was ominously dark. Hill Creek was normally such a friendly place, but Casey's murder had made it feel threatening, especially on this black street. Pulling her silk shawl more tightly around her and quickening her steps, she made a mental note to suggest more streetlights at the next town-council meeting.

She sensed someone behind her. At first she chided herself for an overactive imagination. She walked farther. Though the steps were faltering, they were definitely behind her. She increased her pace, and the other person's steps quickened to match hers. A hand brushed her arm. She gasped, spun around, ready to use the knee-to-the-groin maneuver she had learned in self-defense class. Luckily for Ed, she recognized him just in time.

Her hand against her chest, Hannah exhaled with relief. "You frightened me," she said with a nervous laugh. "What are you doing out after dark?"

"Walking," he replied.

The idea of him walking around town after dark didn't sit right with her. She looked at him more closely. His face looked troubled. He opened his mouth to say something else, but no words came.

"Ed, is something wrong?"

"The police . . ." He didn't finish the sentence.

"Did the police talk to you again?"

His lips moved but he didn't answer. He simply stared at her as if he would burst with whatever was inside. She studied him, wanting to comprehend, but he was like indecipherable handwriting, with the information in front of you but hidden at the same time.

"What are you trying to tell me, Ed? Do you know something about Casey's murder?"

He grabbed her hand, his skin feeling warm and bone-dry against hers. "It's sad," he told her, then let her hand fall from his. He turned and walked away.

"Ed, wait. Let me drive you home," she called after him. She caught up with him. He kept his eyes downward, his head shaking slightly.

She wanted to talk to him, to find out what was bothering him. But she knew putting pressure on him would only make the situation worse. She would find him tomorrow. She would try again when he was calmer.

"Let me drive you home, okay?"

He nodded. He lived about a mile away in an old two-story house with a Mediterranean façade. The front yard was much larger than Hannah's, made up mostly of weed-infested lawn that his kind neighbors mowed. Every time Hannah saw it she landscaped it in her mind—roses on the south side, hydrangeas by the shady fence, and morning glories climbing up a trellis near the front door.

She pulled the Eldorado to a stop in the driveway, turned off the ignition, and studied Ed's profile. He could easily know something about the murder. He had been sitting near the foyer the night of the party. Maybe he had remembered something he had seen or heard that night and now it worried him, perhaps so much it gave him more trouble than usual in speaking. She found it ironic that she had just been with Hinkley Bowden, a man whose words flowed so easily, and now she was with Ed, a man whose silence communicated volumes.

She helped him out of the car, took his keys, and let him into his house. It was only then the notion entered her head that his current confused state could be illness. To be safe, she decided to stay with him a few minutes to make certain he was okay, so she made the excuse of needing to call her sister.

Using the phone in the living room, she dialed home. The call was just for show since Kiki was out on her hot date with a Viagra-laced Bernie. Hannah checked her watch. It was eight-thirty. Bernie didn't like to stay up late, so about this time they would be finished with dinner and headed for his house. But surprisingly Kiki answered the phone. Not wanting to take the time just then to hear the details, Hannah told Kiki she would be home in a few minutes.

As Hannah hung up she noticed a silver frame containing two photos sitting on a small table near the phone. Picking it up, she saw handwritten music in the right photo frame and in the left saw a photo of Ed's son. From his apparent age, she estimated that it would only have been a few years after the picture was taken that he committed suicide. Her stomach tightened, the thought of Lauren grabbing hold of her. Ed's son would have been only a little younger than Lauren when he died. Hannah remembered him as shy and impressionable, much like Lauren. People like that were so vulnerable, especially in their twenties. A few disappointments, a bad love affair. That sort of thing broke their hearts.

Hannah felt a wave of dull nausea and quickly put down the photo as if touching it too long would cause bad luck. She knew Lauren better than anyone, well enough to know that she was completely infatuated with Brad despite having known him only a couple of days. What would happen when she found out he was not only living with a girl but engaged to her? Other women might get over that sort of disappointment, but not Lauren.

When she was certain Ed was all right, Hannah headed

home. As she pulled into the driveway the friendly visage of her house, its yellow light streaming from the front windows, eased her anxieties. She entered through the back door, walked through the kitchen, throwing her shawl and her purse on the table.

Dressed in her bathrobe, Kiki lay sprawled on the couch reading a paperback novel Wanda had loaned her. The cover showed a huge-breasted, scantily clad woman and a steroid-poisoned, half-nude man locked in a torrid embrace. On the coffee table lay a pile a wadded Moon Pie wrappers and a hand-painted teacup half-full of a clear liquid Hannah guessed was vodka. Apparently the evening with Bernie hadn't been all Kiki had hoped.

"How was your date with Hinkley?" Kiki garbled through a mouthful of chocolate and cookie. Putting down the book, she turned her head to Hannah, her cheeks bulging with the last of her Moon Pie delights.

"It wasn't a date. Still, it was interesting. He punched the waiter, asked me to have sex with him in the parking lot, then invited me to Palm Desert." Hannah plopped into a chair and put her feet on the coffee table.

After swallowing, Kiki frowned. "Why can't you be serious for one minute?"

Hannah smiled inwardly. In spite of all her misgivings, she had found Bowden's advances toward her deliciously wanton. It was ironic that what would be considered sexual harassment to a woman of twenty-five was a compliment to one of sixty.

"I thought you had a date with Bernie," Hannah said.

"I did. After I got so decked out and so excited, he ended up having to go home early because he said his hip was acting up. But to tell you the truth, I think he was lying."

"Why would he do that?"

"I think there's gossip going around just because I've had a few boyfriends die," she said, sitting up. "After Bernie had a couple of gins, he admitted that people around town are calling me the Black Widow."

"That's cruel and stupid."

"I know that's what was wrong with Bernie. He acted

really nervous. I offered to show him my Wonderbra and he practically jumped out the car window. He got so upset he almost ran the Buick into the 7-Eleven.''

Hannah assumed an expression of mock seriousness. ''You should consider the possibility that your bra has some sort of curse attached to it. Or maybe the underwiring is getting negative psychic transmissions.''

''Don't joke, Hannah. This is my life we're talking about.''

''Relax. In a few weeks it will all be forgotten.''

Kiki stood up and ran her hands along her hips, a largely lateral gesture. ''It better be. I'm a woman. I need affection.''

''You really should get a hobby. Needlepoint. Drag racing.''

''Men are my hobby. Besides, it's easy for you to be sarcastic,'' she replied, sniffling and walking across the room. ''Your men are alive and breathing.'' She stopped and faced Hannah, her expression accusatory. ''And you've been having sex. I haven't had sex in three years.''

This last revelation grabbed Hannah's attention. ''But Arnold Lempke's undershorts were in your bedroom only a few months ago.''

''That doesn't mean anything happened, if you get my drift. Hannah, what's wrong with me?''

''Nothing, dear. You've just had a dry spell.''

''The Sahara Desert's had a dry spell.''

The doorbell rang. Grateful for the interruption, Hannah answered it and to her surprise found Detective Morgan.

''Hi,'' he said. Even with handcuffs and a pistol hanging off his belt, he didn't seem very tough. He stood there on the doorstep, a big lump of misery stuffed inside a cop suit, his shoulders slumped and his eyes wearing a sad-dog expression. ''I'd like to talk to you. About Lauren.''

As if she couldn't guess. Opening the door wide, Hannah welcomed him into the land of the lovelorn, his handcuffs rattling as he walked in. Upon seeing a male, even one half her age, Kiki's eyes narrowed lustfully, her mouth widening into a welcoming smile. Hannah could see long-dormant hormones rising to attention in her sister. This combined with that teacup of vodka made Hannah think it wise to take precautions, and she steered Morgan out of her sister's reach.

"You want a cocktail?" Kiki asked.

"Thanks, but I'd better not," he said. "I'm off duty but I'm still in uniform."

"Very prudent," Hannah said. "Please, make yourself at home."

He sat down on the sofa, perching uncomfortably on its edge, and his uneasiness touched Hannah. It occurred to her that although he was blond and baby-faced, he had an appealing masculinity. There was an old-fashioned goodness and dependability about him that was very attractive, if only Lauren would notice it again. Not to mention that Morgan was unattached.

After staring at his hands awhile, he picked up a book of poetry off the coffee table and thumbed through it. The book contained some of Anne Sexton's more suicidal confessional verse. Thinking it wouldn't be good for him in his anguished state, Hannah decided to get a conversation going before he could read any of the poems.

"We're so glad you dropped by," she told him.

"I'm sorry to barge in this way," he said. "I'm embarrassed."

"No need to be," Kiki said, sitting down next to him. She crossed her legs, separating the sides of her robe so that her pink knee peeked through. Hannah cocked an eyebrow. Would Kiki try to seduce her very own niece's boyfriend? It seemed unlikely. On the other hand, he wasn't really Lauren's boyfriend anymore, but he was still thirty years younger than Kiki. Hannah sat down on the sofa, wedging herself between them.

"There's something the matter, Larry. What is it?" Hannah gently asked.

"I just saw Lauren."

Hannah looked hopeful. "You went out with her?"

"No. I just went over to her house. That actor was there." He put an unhappy edge on the word "actor."

Crossing her arms, Hannah settled back into the sofa and eyed Morgan's suffering expression. What an interesting development. He was eaten up with jealousy, that much was plain. Whatever moderately romantic feelings he had previously felt for Lauren, her dating Brad Casey had heated them into agonized yearning. It was a fascinating situation, with so much potential. Hannah's eyes grazed the cover of Kiki's romance novel, still sitting on the coffee table, and for an instant she saw Morgan and Lauren's faces on the lust-inflamed couple.

Kiki reached over and placed her hand on his knee, but Hannah tossed her a chilling look and she removed it as quickly as if she had touched a hot stove.

Morgan raised his eyes to Hannah. "Mrs. Malloy, you and I have always been able to talk, and you know Lauren better than anyone. You fixed us up in the first place."

"I thought the two of you were a perfect match."

"Me, too," Larry said.

A look of wistfulness crossed his face that made Hannah smile. This is a man to lose your virginity to, she thought. A man with quiet strength of character. A man with noble virtue. A man with a uniform and handcuffs.

"That's why I need to know," Morgan said, twisting in his seat, the words causing him pain. "Is Lauren in love with this Brad guy?"

"Probably," Kiki answered. Hannah gave her another scolding look, this one close to nuclear. If Brad was going to dump Lauren, and everything indicated that he was, it was their solemn duty to make sure Morgan would be waiting for her with open arms. Nothing soothed the loss of one man like having another in the wings.

"This is only a brief infatuation for Lauren," Hannah reassured Morgan, "if it's anything at all."

"Oh, right, absolutely," Kiki chimed in, finally catching on.

Hannah gave Morgan's shoulder an encouraging pat. "This infatuation with Brad Casey will be over in a week or so." Mainly because Brad would be out of town by then and back to his nineteen-year-old fiancée.

"Really?" Larry said hopefully, obviously grasping at whatever bones anybody threw him.

Hannah thought it best to end this part of the conversation on that optimistic note. Although under different circumstances she would have gladly discussed his love life for hours, that particular evening she had other issues she needed to explore.

"Yes, I definitely think so. Now, if you don't mind, I'd like to talk about the murder case just a little. I've learned some things, inadvertently, of course, that I think might be useful for you."

He sat up at attention. "I know I should be angry at you, but to tell you the truth, I'd like to hear whatever you have. Things aren't going so well with the investigation and every day that passes just lessens our chances."

"What's the problem?" Hannah asked.

"A lot of things. There were hundreds of people at that party, and we don't know who most of them were. As far as the people we do know about, we've connected some people to the—" He hesitated. "To the substance Casey was killed with, but we still don't have enough to press charges."

He obviously didn't want to give out details, and Hannah didn't want to let on that she already knew about the digoxin. Instead she told him about her meeting with Bowden. It was strictly a social engagement, she assured Morgan, but she told him how in the course of perfectly casual conversation she found out about Casey's embezzling.

"We know about the embezzling and we're checking to see if anyone at the party was an investor," Morgan said. "We already know of one."

"You mean Roger Burke," Hannah said. "Bowden said Roger had asked for his money back and Casey wouldn't give it to him."

Morgan nodded. "Mr. Burke came to the station voluntarily and told us all about it. He said his daughter got into law school and that he needed the money for her tuition. He said the whole thing had been embarrassing and he hadn't wanted anyone on the festival committee to know.''

"But his admitting that surely doesn't take him off the suspect list,'' Hannah said.

"No, he's still a suspect, but we haven't been able to connect him to the stuff that killed Casey.''

"His story about his wanting the money back for his daughter's law school sounds benign,'' Hannah said. "But what if he's lying? What if he knew that Casey was embezzling? If he knew he would have been angry.''

Kiki leaned forward, eager to be included in the conversation. "But how would Roger or any other investor even know that they'd been cheated?''

Morgan considered this question. "I suppose Angie or Bowden could have told Mr. Burke, though I don't know what would be their motivation.''

"No,'' Hannah said. "They were trying to hide the fraud, at least according to Bowden. But I think Angie and Bowden are better suspects than anyone. They both had grudges against Casey.''

"We've interviewed them and they each pointed out what a grudge the other one had against Casey. We questioned Angie again today for a couple of hours. That girl's got a mouth like a sewer. Earlier she said she hadn't refilled Casey's prescription for his heart medication, but we checked pharmacies in Los Angeles. She picked up a fresh bottle for him a few days before they left town.''

"So she had enough pills to kill him?'' Kiki asked.

"More than enough. She says she picked up an order for Casey at the drugstore, some vitamins and blood-pressure medicine, and the pills were included, but she didn't realize it.''

"I suppose that's possible,'' Hannah said thoughtfully. "What about fingerprints on the flask?''

Morgan shook his head. "It was made out of pounded metal wrapped in tooled leather. The edges around the cap were serrated. We couldn't get a usable print.''

"Did you learn anything from Ed Kachowski?'' Hannah asked. "He was sitting near the foyer for quite a while at the party, and he could have seen something.''

''We talked to him but didn't get much. I'm not so sure his mind's right.''

''The stroke slurred his speech,'' Hannah told him. ''But I've known Ed for so long. As far as I can tell, he's perfectly lucid. He just doesn't sound like it sometimes.''

''Hannah's always had a soft spot for Ed,'' Kiki chimed in.

''Ed is friends with a lot of people in town,'' Hannah continued. ''I just spoke to him a while ago and he seems upset, like he may know something he doesn't want to tell.''

Kiki turned up her palms. ''Why wouldn't he tell?''

''I don't know,'' Hannah said. ''Maybe because it would hurt someone. He knew a lot of people at the party.''

''I'll talk to him again,'' Morgan said, then drew a breath. ''What about Brad Casey? Have you dug up any motives for him?''

The edges of Hannah's mouth turned upward. ''I'm not investigating this case, remember?''

''Of course you're not,'' he answered, returning the smile. ''So what have you found out?''

''Brad could have had a grudge against his father. But then, it was his father who kept him afloat in his career.''

''Must be nice to have a powerful daddy,'' Morgan said with tartness. He shook his head and leaned forward, resting his elbows on his knees. ''Bertha Malone is still our best suspect anyway.''

Hannah's face registered concern. ''Why?''

''She sent Casey that threatening note.''

''No!'' both Hannah and Kiki said, the single syllable bursting out of them simultaneously.

''How do you know?'' Kiki asked.

''She admitted to it under questioning. And she does volunteer work at the hospital. She could have accessed medications.'' Morgan stood up. ''Listen, I'd better go.'' He moved toward the door and put his hand on the knob, pausing. ''You really think Lauren's not serious about this Brad guy?''

"I think you still have a fighting chance," Hannah answered with a smile.

"I always suspected Bertha had a violent nature," Kiki said as soon as the door closed behind Morgan. "She's been very belligerent with the Rose Club, the way she insisted that we pull out the Royal Sunsets and put in the Climbing Iceberg. So aggressive."

"Don't be absurd," Hannah said, picking up Kiki's teacup off the coffee table. "She only thought the flower beds at the Rose Club needed a touch of white. There's hardly enough evidence to prove that she's a murderer." But privately she wasn't so sure.

At two in the morning Hannah sat curled on the sofa in the living room, her face washed by the gray glow of the television. She hadn't been able to sleep, so she had fixed hot chocolate, put the *Midnight in Manhattan* tape in the VCR, and turned the volume down low so she wouldn't disturb Kiki.

By her calculation this was the tenth time she had watched the movie. Every time she saw it she found something new to enjoy, some nuance in the script or a look on an actor's face she hadn't noticed before.

She smiled as one of her favorite scenes began, a scene where the hero, drenched with rain and missing a shoe, runs into the diner and sees the love of his life sitting in the corner of a booth with tears running down her cheeks. Hannah always loved the look on his face at that moment. So full of adoration and compassion.

She remembered the terrible things Bowden had said about Casey. It amazed her that the man who conceived of this story, who created these touching characters and wrote the witty dialogue, could be such an abusive person. Was Frederick Casey always an abominable human being or had the years corrupted him? It made her question her own ability to judge people. That was one of the bad things about getting older, she supposed. You became disillusioned as your eyes opened to the world's harsh realities. And there were few things more eye-opening than murder.

$\mathcal{S}$IXTEEN

$\cancel{\approx}$

"$\mathcal{H}$ANNAH, YOUR CHI WAS CHOKED this morning," Naomi said as she poured hot water over a Red Zinger tea bag. Lifting up the steamy mug, she took a sip. Then, apparently moved by a spiritual impulse, her eyes lifted to the ceiling, her head cocking slightly as if to get telepathic communications from the overhead light fixture. "Your life energy, as always, was strong, and yet . . ." She paused, holding up her hand, index finger pressed against thumb. "I felt you were holding back. Now that I think about it, your aura had a strange dark cast around the edges. You're not troubled by something, are you?"

Naomi was still in her floppy white tunic and Hannah in her sweatsuit as the two women stood in Hannah's kitchen. Buttery morning sunlight poured through the window, giving the room a cheerful glow that contrasted starkly with Hannah's bleak mood. Yes, she was troubled, Hannah answered silently. She looked out the window at Lauren and Kiki sitting happily in the garden with their morning coffee.

Naomi shivered, throwing off the bad vibrations. "On the other hand, you probably just weren't focused," she continued. Though Naomi loved to brag publicly about how her body was free of toxins, Hannah noticed her sneak a

spoonful of refined sugar into her tea when she thought
Hannah wasn't looking. "You won't reach divine peace
and wisdom unless you focus." She leaned over the kitchen
counter and inhaled the perfume of the Double Delight
roses arranged in a jam jar. "Look at me. I'm focused and
I'm feeling so centered, so light." With this last statement
she swept an arm upward.

"You won't stay light if you keep putting all that sugar
in your tea," Hannah replied, washing an apple at the sink.

Naomi's beatific smile dimmed to slightly less wattage.
"Was that sugar? I must still be in a bit of a trance, the
class this morning was *sooo* fulfilling." She closed her eyes
and breathed deeply.

Hannah turned off the faucet. "I apologize for not being
a good student. I have things on my mind."

Naomi's eyes opened, the opportunity for a little news
snapping her out of her trance. "I knew it. Things about
the murder?"

Hannah nodded. Detective Morgan's revelation about
Bertha having written the threatening note to Casey had
been a shock. Up until then Hannah believed deep down
that Bertha was innocent. Now she was reevaluating that
position, but she didn't want to tell Naomi what she knew.
It wouldn't be right. Instead she wanted to pick Naomi's
mind about something else.

"Naomi, at the film-festival party, do you remember seeing Ed sitting near the foyer?"

Naomi thought a moment. "Yes. I remember seeing him
there chatting with some people. Why?"

Hannah dried the apple and sliced it into fourths. "I'm
trying to remember how long he was there. I first led him
to that spot right after Casey gave his introductory speech."

Naomi groaned. "Oh, yes, that speech. A little pompous,
I thought."

"More than a little. Remember after the speech when
Casey was in the big leather chair with everyone sitting
around him?"

"And Kiki sitting on top of him?" Naomi said with a

laugh. "And Roger Burke flitting around nervous as a flea."

"He did? Look nervous, I mean."

"You didn't notice?"

Thinking back on it, Hannah had noticed, though at the time she assumed Roger was anxious about the party.

"But what did you want to know about Ed?" Naomi asked.

"I was trying to remember if he sat near the foyer that whole time until we left the party. I think he did."

Hannah offered Naomi a slice of apple. She took it with a shrug. "I wasn't paying much attention to him, to be honest. Why are you so interested?" She held up a finger. "Of course. Ed could have seen who tampered with Casey's flask. But the murderer wouldn't have done anything if Ed was watching."

"But Ed was outside the foyer, not in it. Maybe he didn't actually see the killer put the pills in Casey's flask, but he could have seen him walk into the foyer."

"But the rest rooms were in the foyer. Ed could have seen fifty people walk in there."

"Maybe. But there's a larger set of rest rooms in the back of the building, so the foyer was empty a good deal of the time."

"You're right. I used the rest rooms in the back."

"Someone could have easily slipped Casey's flask out of his jacket on the coat rack and taken it outside or in the rest room to put in the pills."

"Then what could Ed have seen?"

"I don't know yet. Something odd that caught his attention. Something that didn't look right."

Hannah put the cutting board in the sink, dropping the small knife she had been using. It made a cut on the linoleum and she muttered a mild curse.

"Is dwelling on this what's making you so unfocused?" Naomi asked.

"That and other things. I can hardly think straight, I have so much on my mind."

"Like what, dear? You know you can confide in me."

Hannah looked at her friend. She knew that Naomi, despite being so far up the divine-wisdom food chain, adored gossip, and that at this moment she had high hopes of getting some juicy morsel. Hannah hated giving in to such base impulses, but in addition to her cogitation on Casey's murder, she was worried sick about Lauren and needed someone to talk to. It wasn't as if she could discuss matters of *amore* with Kiki. She hadn't even told her about Brad being engaged. What was the use? Kiki thought any love problem could be solved with see-through underwear and massage oil. But Lauren's situation was delicate. Lauren's soul was that of an artist—emotional, gentle, with a heart as fragile as a sparrow's. How could Hannah tell her that Brad Casey was engaged to a teenager and that he had a history of using shy, insecure women just like her?

Hannah placed her hands on Naomi's shoulders and looked her right in the eye. "All right, I want to discuss something with you, but you have to promise to keep it a secret," she said. If Naomi had nodded any more eagerly, her head would have bobbed right off her neck. Hannah went on. "I'm still concerned about Lauren and this Brad character."

Frowning with disappointment, Naomi flapped her hand. "Oh, we've gone over that ground. Lauren's a big girl. Leave her alone."

"I can't," Hannah said, not wanting to tell Naomi all the bad details, since she might let them slip to Wanda. "I want to know how deeply involved she is with him." Hannah looked out the kitchen window to make sure Lauren and Kiki were still outside. "I want to know, and I don't know how else to put this," she whispered. "I want to know if Lauren is still a virgin."

Naomi's mouth formed an excited "Oh."

Hannah continued. "I know that Lauren's virginity isn't any of my business, but based on certain information that I cannot reveal, I feel I need to discourage her relationship with him. But I need to do it gently. I need to know how attached she is to him."

"And whether or not she's slept with him is critical."

"Bingo."

"Why not just ask her?"

"I couldn't. She'd think I was prying."

The two women looked at each other, then out the window, their eyes fixed upon Lauren sitting blithely in a garden chair next to Kiki.

"Perhaps if we go outside and observe her closely," Naomi suggested. "Then we can come back and compare notes."

"What would we look for?"

Naomi considered this. "A glow, I should say. Or perhaps an expression of guilty joy."

Perplexed, Hannah again glanced out the window, trying to imagine what an expression of guilty joy looked like. She knew she had felt guilty joy before, but unfortunately she hadn't been looking in a mirror at the time. "This is the sort of information you get from watching *Oprah*, I suppose, but I've never seen it."

"Well, you know *I* don't watch television."

Hannah gave her a sidewise glance. "That's odd. I could have sworn I heard *The Young and the Restless* coming from your bedroom window the other day."

Naomi looked suddenly pinched. "Just your active imagination, dear. All that poetry swimming through your head. I've just had a marvelous idea. Maybe Red Moon can tell if she's a virgin."

"Don't try to be funny," Hannah said with sarcasm.

"Don't be so cynical. He might get a reading on her chakras that could be helpful."

"And how would Red Moon go about this?"

"If I could get my palms near the back of her head, I think I might get a reading."

"Seems to me it's another body part we're interested in," Hannah said dryly. "And she might object to you waving your hands down there."

"Very amusing. Do you want me to give it a try?"

With reluctance, Hannah agreed. She was ready to try anything in order to avoid a direct confrontation with Lauren on the subject. She and Naomi joined Lauren and Kiki in the backyard by the rose garden. On nice days Hannah and Kiki often had their breakfast there, and that morning Lauren had dropped by unexpectedly. She had been behaving in such an odd manner—cheerful, nervous, and worried all at the same time. She had stumbled on the patio step, gotten her shoe caught in a garden marker, dropped her coffee twice, and now had a glob of honey sitting on the end of her nose. Yet she was blissfully unaware. It was as if she were bewitched, Hannah thought with misery.

After wiping the honey off Lauren's nose, Hannah took a seat and observed her niece. She's definitely in love, she concluded, the idea leaving her with a queasy feeling. But how far had the relationship gone? Upon closer observation it occurred to her that if Lauren had lost her virginity the night before, she wouldn't be nervously dropping things. Having sex would relieve tension, not increase it.

"You're looking at me funny." Lauren eyed her aunt over the top of her coffee mug.

"Don't mind her," Kiki said, heaping jam on a bran muffin. "She's been looking at people funny her whole life. She's always been peculiar. Mother used to say so all the time." She took a bite of muffin, quickly chewed and swallowed. "When Hannah was a little girl she used to wear a ballerina's tutu with cowboy boots and a coonskin hat. Wouldn't take it off even for Sunday school."

During this discussion Naomi slipped behind Lauren's chair and, with her eyes closed, moved her hands, palms downward, in a circular motion over the back of Lauren's head. Since both Lauren and Kiki were facing the same direction, neither of them noticed.

"Never mind, Kiki. You've told the story before," Hannah said, trying to keep her eyes off Naomi.

Lauren smiled. "Only about a hundred times."

There was a brief lull in the conversation. Kiki buried her nose in a new issue of *Cosmopolitan* and Lauren seemed lost in thought while Naomi performed an odd-looking dance behind them that Hannah assumed would bring forth Red Moon. She attempted to communicate to Naomi via eye contact that she should stop the ridiculous dancing, but Naomi was too wrapped up to notice. It was then that Hannah saw a blush creeping up Lauren's face.

"There's something I wanted to mention," Lauren said, her cheeks now bright pink. "Something Brad said yesterday."

"What?" Hannah asked, still trying hard not to look at Naomi, who was now back to palm waving. "He wants me to go to Hawaii with him for a couple of weeks. He says he needs to get away, you know, to help get over his father's death," Lauren said with obvious excitement. "Me in Hawaii with Brad. Wouldn't that be something?"

"When would you go?" Hannah asked.

"In a week. I have some vacation time coming at work."

Naomi's hand movements grew faster and she moved her lips, chanting silently.

Kiki looked up from her *Cosmo,* her face alight. "Are you two getting serious?"

"Well, I don't know about that," Lauren answered shyly. "He's the type of person who doesn't verbalize his feelings." Sensing something behind her, she twisted around and saw Naomi with her eyes closed and her hands raised. "What are you doing?"

"Yoga pose," Naomi told her, doing a quick side bend. "Just stretching, feeling my energy." As soon as Lauren turned back around, Naomi looked at Hannah, shrugged, and mouthed the word "nothing."

Hannah was now gripped by a dismal reality. If Lauren wasn't in love with Brad now, a week in Hawaii would nail her coffin shut. The palm trees, the white beaches, the balmy air, the sound of the surf pounding and pounding against the shore . . .

"Lauren, dear," Hannah said quickly, shoving the image out of her mind. "How come you're not wearing a business suit? Aren't you going in to the office?"

When Kiki heard Hannah's query her eyes widened. A lightbulb had gone off in her head and she suddenly understood what might have happened the night before.

Kiki leaned her chin on her hand, her lips pursed into a smug little smile. "Is something going on? Hmm?"

Lauren shifted uncomfortably in her seat. "No, I'm just taking the day off, that's all. You're always telling me I work too many hours. I thought I'd just take it easy for once. Have my legs waxed."

Upon hearing the last sentence, Hannah, Naomi, and Kiki all stiffened as if nudged simultaneously by the same cattle prod. Lauren might as well have jerked up her sweater and exposed a T-shirt that read GETTING LAID TONIGHT, for they all knew, at least on this occasion, what a leg waxing meant.

Still behind Lauren, Naomi mouthed the words "legs waxed," her eyebrows lifted. Kiki's smile widened while everything in Hannah clenched up. She had to do something. Fate had brought Lauren to her that morning so she could break Brad's spell. But how could she say something to Lauren that would break her heart, especially in front of other people? She would just have to, that's all.

Hannah pulled her chair next to Lauren and settled herself more firmly in it. Kiki saw this and, knowing something was up, scooted her own chair a little closer. Naomi quietly lowered herself onto a nearby garden bench.

Hannah inhaled deeply. Neither Kiki nor Naomi breathed or moved a muscle. Lauren innocently sipped her coffee, oblivious to the high drama around her.

"Lauren, I'm going to tell you something," Hannah began. "Something you're not going to like."

Lauren paused in mid-sip. "What?"

"I've heard some bad things about Brad."

There was a pause. "It's just gossip," Lauren said.

"It's from a reputable source."

Lauren grew rigid. "Then it's someone who's jealous of him. He says a lot of people are jealous of him. He's the best thing that ever happened to me. I won't hear a word against him."

"But, Lauren, what I heard is very serious," Hannah said, losing the little confidence she had.

"Why is this any of your business?" Lauren asked.

"It's not, really." Hannah knew she was on shaky ground, but it was too late for retreat. "But you know how

much I care about you and I don't want to see you hurt."
She changed her mind. She couldn't break the news about
Brad's fiancée in front of Kiki and Naomi. It would be too
cruel. She decided to try a softer approach. "I just don't
think he's the right man for you to . . ." Hannah paused
then started again. "The right man for you to . . ." Another
pause.

"To what?" Lauren asked, her anger rising. The words
stuck in Hannah's throat. Naomi and Kiki edged forward,
eyes like saucers, both of them about to burst with the suspense.

Hannah's expression grew more pained as she put out
one more attempt. "To share that special part of you
that . . ."

"That opens your lotus blossom," Naomi said energet-
ically. Lauren gave her a blank look.

Bouncing in her seat with excitement, Kiki gave it a try.
"And envelops you with an animal fire that makes your
loins . . ." She paused, grappling for the word.

Naomi turned to Kiki. "Tremble with a yearning
that . . ."

"Melts into a rapture . . ." Kiki said with a sweep of her
arm.

Naomi clasped her hands in front of her. "And sweeps
you breathless into a sea of desire that—"

"It's sex! Have you had sex with Brad?" Hannah said
loud enough for the neighbors to enjoy, unable to stand
another second of romance-novel verbiage.

Lauren jumped up from her chair, her face crimson with
embarrassment and fury. "I never should have told you that
I'm a virgin. But I won't be for long. And if I want my
loins to tremble for Brad Casey, that's my business!"

Grabbing her purse, she stomped off as Hannah's heart
sank.

"You can't just blurt out the sex word like that. You scared
her," Kiki said as she and Hannah picked their way through
the dirt piles in front of Bertha's house. "That was the
problem. I was trying to break it to her gently."

Kiki was still upset about the way Lauren had stormed out of their house an hour earlier, but not as upset as Hannah. It was all Hannah could do to keep from crying.

"I just thought it was best to say it directly," she said.

"And she got mad and left directly."

Hannah still hadn't told Kiki about Brad's fiancée and certainly wouldn't until she had told Lauren first. "It's hard to know the right thing to do. She's so young."

Kiki let out a "hmmph." "She's no spring chicken. She's got to be the only twenty-eight-year-old virgin in California. Another couple of years and they may start putting little plastic figures of her on dashboards. If you want my opinion she should do the wild thing with the first construction worker who whistles at her. Lord knows I would, if one would whistle at me."

"If you could find one that old, he wouldn't have the strength to pucker up much less do anything else," Hannah replied with irritation. Kiki gave her a frigid look as they reached Bertha's door. "I'm sorry, Kiki. I shouldn't have said that. It's just that I'm so upset about Lauren."

"Then you should be at home calling her and apologizing."

"I tried to call her three times. She wasn't there."

"And I still don't understand what we're doing here at Bertha's. Why are we paying a social call on a murderer?"

"Keep your voice down. We don't know she's a murderer."

"She sent that threatening note to Freddie, didn't she? What other proof do you need?"

"The police haven't arrested her, have they? There could be a reasonable explanation."

"There is. She sent it to him to warn him not to make any more movies. He wasn't going to do what she wanted, so she killed him, simple as that. You were always the smart one, yet sometimes the easiest concepts fly right past you."

"I'm familiar with the concept of innocent until proven guilty, and that note proves nothing." Hannah stabbed the doorbell with her finger.

Rolling her eyes, Kiki scowled. "She's probably going to murder us both, cut us up into little pieces, and use us for fertilizer."

"I will not dignify that with a response." Hannah rang the doorbell again, but there was no answer. She heard sounds from the back of the house. "She's probably in the garden. Let's go."

With Kiki muttering protests, they started along the walkway that led to the backyard. Upon reaching the gate, they stopped and listened. Hannah heard the sound of metal hitting dirt.

"She's shoveling," she said, then called Bertha's name. The sound stopped.

"Who is it?" Bertha called out, her voice booming.

Hannah identified herself. After what seemed a long time Bertha came to the fence dressed in her gardening clothes and wearing leather workman's gloves. Even covered with dirt, her despondency showed through.

"I don't want any company."

"We need to talk," Hannah told her.

She shook her head. "Sorry, but I'm busy moving my rosa cressida. I found another pottery shard and I need to dig right where it's planted. Can't talk." With that, Bertha stomped away.

"Moving her rosa cressida? How strange. It's climbing up her fence and hardly in the way of her digging," Hannah said to Kiki.

"Forget her rosa cressida. She can move her biggus butt-sida out of our lives forever. That's the rudest woman I've ever met, and after all you've done to help her. Let's go," Kiki demanded.

Standing on her tiptoes, Hannah reached over the top of the gate and unlatched it.

Kiki's face scrunched. "What are you doing?"

"I came here to talk to Bertha and I'm talking to Bertha. I'm in no mood for stubbornness." Hannah marched into Bertha's backyard.

"Well, isn't that the spinach calling corn a vegetable, or whatever that silly saying is. You're the queen of stubborn.

You're the most stubborn woman on the planet," Kiki called after her, then followed.

Hannah was shocked by what she saw. The whole yard was an excavation site, so much worse than the day before, with Bertha's camellias, lavender, and roses dug up and tossed in a heap.

Bertha was in the corner shoveling like a madwoman, her rosa cressida lying in a sad green heap on the ground. Hannah winced at the sight of the poor rosebush with its roots exposed.

Bertha glowered at her visitors. "What are you doing back here?"

Hannah walked right up to her, getting as close as she could without burying her feet in dirt. "Bertha, you should have told me you wrote that threatening letter to Casey."

Bertha plunged her shovel into the ground. "You're invading my privacy. Why should I tell you anything?"

"I don't understand your attitude," Hannah said, affronted. "You're the one who asked me to help you."

"No need to help me. I'm as good as tried and convicted." Bertha repeatedly stabbed at the dirt with the shovel as if to beat it into submission.

Seeing Bertha's pain, Hannah softened. "Writing a letter doesn't prove you're anything except a little foolish. Let's talk about it. I want to help you if you'll let me."

That was when the dam burst. Bertha's entire body began to tremble, which considering her size was like an earthquake. Tears, large enough to match the rest of her, flowed down her dirt-streaked cheeks. She threw down her shovel and covered her face with her hands. "This is all such a nightmare. I would never kill anyone."

Hannah placed a hand on her shoulder. "We'll sort this out."

"I only wrote that stupid letter to scare him a little," Bertha said between sobs. "I didn't mean anything terrible. Now the police think I killed that wretched man. But I have to defend women as a sex, don't I?"

"I don't need any defending. I can defend myself just fine," Kiki snapped.

"Ignore her, Bertha. Why don't you sit down and try to calm yourself? Would you like me to make some tea?" Hannah asked.

Bertha shook her head. "Let me make it. I'll feel better if I'm doing something. I have to keep busy. That's why I'm digging everything up."

She clomped across the yard and into her house. Hannah turned to Kiki. "You were rude."

"Well, she's never been nice to either of us. She's only being friendly now because she's in trouble. And just because she says she didn't kill my sweet Freddie doesn't mean she didn't."

Hannah shook her head. "I simply don't think she's a murderer." Just then she noticed the poor forgotten rosebush. "I have to get that rose back into the ground. She can't possibly mean to destroy it. She always loved it."

"Now you're doing her yard work for her," Kiki said, throwing up her hands. "Such a Good Samaritan. She's probably in there right now getting her scissors so she can plunge them into our hearts."

Ignoring the remark, Hannah rolled up her sleeves and grabbed the shovel, her eyes falling upon a fresh mound of earth on the south side of the yard. "I'll put it over there. Kiki, go get the hose so we can give it water."

"Kiki, go get the hose," she mimicked. "Go get this. Do this. Let's be gardeners for the murderer. Let's wax her floor and rinse out her underwear."

Hannah pushed the shovel into the ground, lifted out one clump of dirt, then dug some more.

"I can't find the hose," Kiki called out.

"It's got to be there somewhere."

"Well, you look for it, then." Kiki walked over to Hannah just as she finished shoveling.

Leaning over, Hannah took hold of the rosebush and placed it in the hole.

"It doesn't fit," Kiki told her.

"I can see that. The hole's too shallow." After removing the bush, Hannah picked up the shovel and put it into the earth once more.

It was when she pulled out the shovel's blade that the hand popped out of the ground.

Both women screamed and jumped backward. Beneath streaks of dirt, the hand was grayish white, its fingers curled into a claw. Dirt fell from it and it seemed alive, the bent fingers angry, grabbing upward for vengeance. Hannah then noticed its smallness. For one horrible second she thought she saw it quiver.

"What's going on?" Bertha shouted, lumbering into the garden carrying two mugs, but when she saw the hand she dropped them both. "My God. What is it? What's it doing in my yard?"

"Murderer!" Kiki wailed. "Murdering people and burying them in your backyard!"

"It's not true! Hannah, tell her."

Recovered from the first shock, Hannah grabbed at the dirt, digging it away from the body's head and neck. Within seconds she saw a face. In revulsion, she averted her eyes.

"Who is it?" Kiki asked, crying. Hannah could feel her and Bertha close behind.

"It's Angie. Frederick Casey's assistant," Hannah said slowly.

The top of Angie's head was covered with a sticky black substance Hannah recognized as blood, the same stuff that was mixed with the dirt around her. Angie had to have been buried while the blood was still fresh.

Kiki raised her eyes to Bertha. "Just because that girl embarrassed you at the theater, you killed her?" she wailed through tears. "That so excessive."

Bertha let out a howl. "I didn't kill anyone!"

The shouting between the women continued, but Hannah no longer heard them. She thought only of Angie. The girl had been restless and angry, someone who had yet to find her way in life. Then to die like this. Hannah wasn't especially religious, but she found herself murmuring "God rest her soul."

It was then that she noticed a sprig of foliage tangled in Angie's hair. Hannah touched it with one finger. It was dark green and frond-shaped, its delicate leaves crushed from the dirt. It occurred to her that someone had placed it in Angie's hair, a last adornment for a funeral, but a closer inspection proved it hadn't been placed there lovingly. It was twisted in the dark strands. Angie probably fell into a bush after whoever it was bashed in her head. Hannah turned and looked at Bertha.

Seeing the expression on Hannah's face, Bertha's mouth opened in horror. "You can't possibly think I know how she got there?"

"Call the police," was all Hannah replied.

$\mathcal{S}$EVENTEEN

$\mathcal{F}$OR WEEKS WALNUT AVENUE RESIDENTS had jested behind Bertha Malone's back about the scant possibility of her yard being an archaeological treasure trove. As they carried out their recycles or spread organic fertilizer on their lawns, they quipped to each other with knowing smiles that nothing interesting would ever be dug up in Bertha's garden. In this they were proven wrong, for right after the police arrived that morning the news hit the neighbors that a fresh corpse had been found in the very hole where Bertha claimed she would find Indian artifacts. But Bertha had the last laugh, for she had been right about one thing. Her yard was indeed a burial ground.

Neighbors gathered on the sidewalks, coffee mugs in hand, temporarily abandoning their TV talk shows, meditation sessions, and home offices to watch the drama unfold. Speculation flew concerning the corpse's identity and how it had ended up in her yard. All anybody could find out for the moment was that the unlucky victim was associated with the film festival. The neighbors shook their heads and called it a tragedy, secretly hoping the corpse would turn out to be somebody interesting. That would have a certain panache, while finding just any old corpse smacked of social decay, not to mention it being a slap in the face to the Neighborhood Watch program.

The Hill Creek police had arrived within moments of Kiki's call and an hour later Bertha's yard was a frenzy of activity, its perimeter cordoned off with yellow crime-scene tape. The police were as astounded as anyone that another murder had occurred in normally peaceful Hill Creek, and they had called the county sheriff's department for assistance.

Feeling drained and frightened, Hannah and Kiki held on to each other, standing by themselves in the narrow alley that wrapped around the side of Bertha's house where they had been instructed to wait. Hannah had already told her story to Detective Morgan twice, with Kiki adding embellishments that Hannah had to constantly correct. Hannah gave him the name of the man who had fished them out of the water at the dock, thinking that perhaps he had seen Angie with someone back at the boat later in the evening. She also told Morgan that she and Kiki followed Angie to the dock, but left out the part about sneaking onto her boat.

"Angie had financial records for Casey's movie production," she said to Morgan. He scribbled everything down in a small notebook, perspiration beading on his forehead. "You should take a look at them. I think they're connected to what happened to her."

He shook his head. "You never should have followed her, Mrs. Malloy. You're putting me in an awkward situation. I can't protect you from the chief, you know."

"I'm not asking you to. Just find out who killed this girl."

He walked away, leaving Hannah alone to console a weeping Kiki. Hannah had not shed a tear, even though she felt the shock of Angie's death more deeply than her sister. Her reaction to a crisis was to try her best to do something about it rather than stand around despairing. And right now all she could think about was who would have wanted Angie dead.

Hannah peered around the corner of the house, her attention focused on the three officers and the medical examiner huddled around Angie's body, which still remained partially buried. The medical examiner pointed to the bloody gash at the top of Angie's skull.

"This is so horrible. Two film-festival guests murdered in one week," Kiki said. Hannah turned to her sister and saw tears streaming down her cheeks, her smudged mascara forming black rings underneath her eyes. "It's going to be hell getting a guest of honor next year."

"That's an absurd thing to think about right now. A young woman has lost her life."

"But don't you see, Hannah? That's just it. The film festival is cursed."

Hannah didn't believe in curses, but the thought was disquieting nevertheless. She watched as an officer used a trowel to remove the rest of the dirt from Angie's body.

The scene at the Hill Creek Theater flashed through Hannah's mind. Angie shouting at Bertha in the lobby with Bertha standing in front of half the town looking embarrassed and angry. Angry enough to kill, some people might say.

Bertha came out her back door escorted by one of the officers. Hearing the screen door slam, both Hannah and Kiki stepped forward to get a better look. When Kiki saw Bertha, she pointed a condemning finger, like in a scene out of a witch trial.

"Murderer!" Kiki shouted, still crying.

"Kiki, please!" Hannah said, horrified by her sister's outburst and not wanting to make things any worse for Bertha. But it was too late.

"It's not true!" Bertha said, both her voice and her body shaking. She aimed the words at the police, then looked at Hannah. Hannah felt almost as sorry for Bertha as she did for Angie, but not quite. "I haven't killed anybody."

Gaining confidence, Kiki pivoted her finger to Angie's corpse. "What's that in your garden, then? Mulch?"

With this last insult Bertha's fear turned to outrage. She lunged for Kiki, her hands reaching out in a way that implied a strong desire to perpetrate strangulation. It was an unfortunate gesture, for it didn't substantiate her claims of innocence. Bertha looked definitely homicidal.

Screaming, Kiki jumped behind Hannah, so that Hannah saw with consternation that Bertha now headed straight for her. The policeman next to Bertha threw his arms around her waist, but she outweighed him by fifty pounds. To Hannah's relief, although the officer failed to stop Bertha, he at least slowed her down, since she couldn't move very fast dragging an adult male behind her. Detective Morgan leaped in to assist, and he and his fellow officer together wrestled her to the ground.

"You see, she's violent!" Kiki shouted. "You saw her. She tried to kill me."

While Hannah shushed her sister, Bertha broke out into a maniacal fit. With Detective Morgan and the other officer holding on to her arms, she kicked her feet at the air like a bull that had been lassoed, crying and shouting at Kiki.

Hannah took a firm hold of Kiki's arm. "Look what you've done! You just made everything worse." Apparently the police felt the same way, because a policeman hauled Kiki into the house.

With Kiki out of sight, Bertha stopped kicking, her anger reduced to sobs, and Morgan let go of her arm, leaving her to the other officers.

Hannah walked up to him. "Detective Morgan, could I speak to you?"

He turned. "What is it?" He sounded cranky, but Hannah knew that brawling with Bertha would unnerve the best of men. "I'd like to take a look at that bit of leaf in Angie's hair. It might be significant."

He gave her a look of vague puzzlement, then told her to wait. He walked over to the officers still collecting evidence and returned with the sprig, now encased in plastic. "You can't touch it."

"No need to." As she took the plastic bag from him, it shook in her hand.

"Are you okay, Mrs. Malloy?" He placed his hand gently on her wrist in a kind yet unpolicemanlike gesture.

"Yes, I'm fine. Just a little shaken up." Hannah examined the bag's contents carefully, taking note of the coarse frond that had just begun wilting. "This is woodwardia."

"What's that?" he asked.

"A giant chain fern. It's native to this area."

"I don't have time for a botany lesson."

"What I'm telling you is that it's not growing in this yard."

Morgan glanced around the remains of Bertha's garden. "There's not much of anything growing in this yard. The plant could have been here before and there could still be leaves on the ground."

Hannah shook her head. "No, Bertha's never had this plant and she never would. This grows in a woodland setting in deep shade under trees. Bertha's yard faces south and gets all-day sun. So you see, this plant couldn't have been here. It's healthy. Look at the deep green. It was planted where it thrived."

Morgan's eyes moved from the frond to Hannah. "So you think the woman was killed elsewhere?"

"I don't see any other explanation. Everybody in town knew that Bertha had dug big holes in her yard hoping to find artifacts. It's the town joke. Someone could have killed Angie then brought her here. Everyone knows Bertha's under suspicion for Casey's murder. And her yard backs up to the park. If the killer brought the body in that way, no one would have seen him."

"But Bertha could have killed Angie, then brought her back here herself."

"Kill someone then haul the body all the way here, to bury it in her own yard? That would be a stupid risk."

"It would be a risk for anyone."

"A risk worth taking if it would focus attention on Bertha."

Out of the corner of her eye she saw Bertha looking at her and realized she overheard the conversation. With one swift jerk of her arm, Bertha broke free from the policeman, ran to Hannah, and threw her arms around her.

"Thank you, Hannah! I knew you'd help me."

"Bertha, please, I can't breathe," Hannah said, her voice muffled by Bertha's powerful embrace. Over Bertha's

shoulder Hannah saw Kiki watching with alarm from the
kitchen window. Apparently misinterpreting Bertha's display of gratitude for something more lethal, Kiki ran out
the back door waving a wire whisk as if it were a saber.

"Unhand her!" Kiki yelled.

"Kiki, no!" Hannah shouted. But Kiki still barreled
across the lawn, wire whisk held high. The police moved
to stop her from whipping Bertha into meringue, but Hannah knew it wasn't necessary, since with Kiki's high heels
she was incapable of running more than a few yards without falling. True to form, her heel caught on a lump of
loose sod, sending her sprawling onto the dirt.

It took a good ten minutes to get Kiki upright and
calmed, but once she realized she was being attended to by
a good-looking policeman, she quieted easily. When Hannah was sure that her sister was okay, she found Morgan
and tapped him on the shoulder.

"We didn't get to finish our conversation. I think I may
know where Angie was murdered," she told him. "The
only place around here I've ever seen that fern growing is
off the deck at the old winery."

Roger Burke's front door opened, revealing a woman about
thirty wearing stained sweatpants and a T-shirt. Hannah assumed she was Miranda, the housecleaner he always spoke
about during the casual chatter that went on before committee meetings. Miranda had a master's degree in sociol-
ogy but for some reason preferred cleaning houses to
working in her field. Roger thought it very chic to have a
maid with such an excellent education. But that was Roger,
always concerned with appearances.

"Hi," Miranda said flatly, wiping her hands on a dish
towel. She wore the wooden expression people reserved for
door-to-door salesmen. When Hannah told Miranda she
was a festival-committee member, she relaxed. "Roger's
on the back deck."

Following Miranda through Roger's living room, Hannah focused on stopping the trembling in her hands. She
had left Bertha's house only a half hour before, dropping

Kiki off at Wanda's so Wanda could look after her. Hannah
needed some looking after herself but didn't have the time.

Finding Angie's body had done something to her. Before
that morning she had been looking for a murderer because
she felt morally obligated, because she wanted to help right
a wrong. But seeing Angie with her head bashed in and her
body buried like a discarded pet had wrenched her soul.
She wanted this person punished. Her hands wouldn't stop
shaking or her heart thumping, but she had steeled herself
and drove the Eldorado to Roger's house. She knew that if
Morgan found out what she was doing he would be furious
and that his chief could probably throw her in jail if he felt
like it, but she didn't care.

Hannah saw Roger through the picture window, looking
silly in a long blue cotton kimono. She could hear him
warbling in falsetto a tune Hannah recognized from *Madame Butterfly*. Bending over, a golf club in his hands, he
positioned his bare feet shoulder width apart, wiggling his
hips comically as he settled into his stance. When she
walked outside she saw that the deck's railing was on a
hinge, making an elongated gate that had been pushed aside
so he could practice golf shots unimpeded. She wondered
how he kept from knocking out his neighbors' windows.

An assortment of bird feeders hung on a tall Japanese
oak next to the deck, with at least twenty birds taking advantage of them. When Roger's club hit the ball they twittered nervously but apparently were used to the noise.

"Oh, Hannah, what a lovely surprise!" he said, though
his tone didn't reflect the welcome. He punctuated the
greeting by whacking the ball with his club. As he swung,
Hannah noticed his strong hands, strong enough to hit
someone hard over the head if he had a weapon and the
inclination. Despite the forcefulness of his swing, the ball
flew only about twenty feet, dropping onto the brush below.
This confused Hannah until she saw a small bucket filled
with the balls and realized they were plastic practice balls.
"Would you like a cinnamon bun? They're right out of the
oven."

She noticed the plate of pastry on a small table. Normally

they would have been tempting, but at that moment the sight of them made her want to puke.

"So what do I owe the pleasure this morning? Do you play golf?" He hit another ball, shooting it straight off the deck with a high arc.

"No, I don't."

"You should. Fabulous game. Very Zen. Lord knows I need it now with everything that's been going on."

He didn't look upset, she thought as he picked up another plastic ball and placed it near his feet in front of him.

"Have the police been giving you a difficult time?" Hannah asked.

"About what?" He swung back his club and Hannah jumped back to be well out of the way. Then he struck the ball, it cutting to the right. He muttered a soft curse.

"About your investment in Casey's movie."

"Why would they care about that?" he asked, busily setting up another ball.

"Because you told lies about it."

Roger again swung his club, the ball glancing off the tip and shooting wildly left, ricocheting against one of the bird feeders and sending the birds shrieking. He spun around and glared at her. "Look what you made me do. I smacked the little birdies. What did you mean? I haven't told any lies."

"You told me you invested the money the day of the opening-night party. I know it happened months before that."

"Ridiculous."

"Roger, I saw some of the financials on the project. Your name was down as an investor, and the dates proved you invested the money long before the festival. Why didn't you tell the truth?"

Angrily he picked another ball out of the bucket, swung the club, and whacked at it, missing the ball completely. He groaned, bracing the small of his back with his hand, and turned to her with an aggravated sigh.

"Honestly, Hannah, you're a pain in the tush sometimes. If you must know, I told you that little fib because that investment was an embarrassment and a mistake and I just wanted to forget the whole thing. I never would have mentioned it to anyone, but I was afraid Casey would blab about it at the party.''

"But if you were embarrassed by the investment, why did you invite him to be the festival guest of honor?''

"First of all, it wasn't the investment that was embarrassing. It's the way he treated me afterward. And I didn't invite him to the festival. You did. When you brought his name up at the meeting, I didn't want to tell the committee members about my connection to him. So at the next meeting I just said I called Casey and that he had refused. But you couldn't leave well enough alone. You wrote your little letter. Well, that really put me in a fix.''

"Why did you want your investment back?''

He went rigid. "I told all this to the police and they didn't think it important at all.''

"So there's no reason you shouldn't tell me.''

"If you must know, my daughter got into law school and I don't want her to take out so many loans that she'll have to pay back later. I just wanted my money back from *Pirate John* to give to her. But Casey acted like I'd asked for his underwear. I threatened to sue him, but he just laughed at me. The horrible man ridiculed me, making the rudest comment about the silk bow tie I was wearing, and I had just bought it.'' He started to set up another ball, but Hannah grasped the shaft of his club. Roger looked at her with high irritation.

"How did you get involved in *Pirate John* in the first place? How did you know Casey?''

"In my position with the festival committee I meet people, I make connections. I even get invited to film openings and parties occasionally, and I always try to go.'' He smiled with pride. "I mentioned to someone at a party in L.A. that I was interested in making an investment in a film project. It was just cocktail talk, but this man took my name down. A few days later I had Frederick Casey himself on the phone. I was wowed, I admit. It didn't occur to me until later how manipulative the man was. He charmed the money out of me. Later I felt very used.''

"Were you angry?"

"Oh, yes—" he started, then cut off the sentence. "Just because I was angry doesn't mean I wanted him dead. He's still a genius. And I think it's very impolite for you to even ask these questions.'' He turned away, picking a ball from the bucket and slapping it against the deck.

"The time for politeness is over, Roger. Frederick Casey's assistant was found murdered.''

Bending over his club, Roger froze. He straightened and turned slowly to her. "No. I don't believe it. That strange girl? Found when?"

"I shouldn't say anything else.''

"How do you even know about it?"

"I just heard.'' She purposely didn't tell him about finding Angie at Bertha's. He was an excellent suspect for Angie's murder as well as Casey's and she didn't want to let any facts slip that he could use to his advantage later.

Putting down his club, he sat wearily on a bench. Hannah sat across from him in a wooden deck chair. His arms resting on his knees, he stared downward. "Poor girl. Why would someone do it?''

"Maybe in retaliation because they thought she had killed Casey,'' Hannah told him. "Where were you last night, Roger?"

"It's none of you business. How dare you insinuate what you're insinuating. Why would I kill her?"

"It's possible that Casey's murderer killed her because she could identify him.''

"Him or her, Hannah. Him or *her*. I didn't kill anybody and I resent your nosing around and saying slanderous things. To be honest I haven't liked you being on the festival committee, you're so pushy and always think your opinions are better than everyone else's. You'd better be careful.''

"Or what?'' she asked, standing.

Roger stood up and grabbed his golf club. Hannah flinched, but he headed for the ball that he had set up a few minutes before. With no fanfare he hit it hard, the ball shooting straight off the deck, going much farther than the ones before it.

He turned to her. "There's a murderer running around town. There's always the chance you might get a little more information than you bargained for."

EIGHTEEN

*N*O HILL CREEK GARDEN EVER blossomed more abundantly than Lady Nails bloomed with speculation after the arrest of Bertha Malone. Still kicking her feet and shouting her innocence with the fervor of her antiwar protest days, Bertha was carted off by Hill Creek's finest around lunchtime, and by mid-afternoon every woman in her circle of friends and enemies suddenly found herself in desperate need of a manicure or pedicure.

Ellie had never enjoyed such brisk business and even called Shiloh to come in to work, though it was the girl's day off. The women flocked in, not caring how long they had to wait, packed side by side in the wicker chairs like chickens in a coop. In fact, waiting was preferred, for it gave them more time to explore the fascinating minutiae of Bertha's descent into crazed carnage.

Ellie put an empty mayonnaise jar with a label taped to it reading *Bertha Malone Defense Fund* by the cash register. It already contained twenty-eight dollars and some odd cents, twenty of it donated by Hannah. Yet the wave of public opinion at Lady Nails had turned against poor Bertha.

As it turned out, Bertha's closest friends had suspected

for years that she nursed homicidal tendencies, and each one tossed her own ingredient into this bubbling stew of conjecture. Ellie had noted criminal leanings in the aggressive way Bertha chewed her nails. Wanda had observed it in the way Bertha manhandled fruit at the grocery, cruelly squeezing the oranges until the poor things were bruised. Louise, a neighbor, had seen murderous inclinations in Bertha's cramming her trash into the bin, then crawling on top and stomping madly on the rubbish until the lid would close.

But when it came to "Bertha Babble," Kiki reigned supreme, for she had seen up close and personal the horrific results of the woman's murderous rage. Naturally Kiki played this to the hilt, retelling for everyone the story of how she personally discovered Angie's body. Maximizing poetic license, she amplified it with each recital, until the last time she told it, it wasn't just a hand that came out of the earth but Angie's whole torso, the corpse popping out of the ground like a jack-in-the-box.

Perusing a magazine in a wicker chair by the window, Hannah listened to all this with increasing consternation. It wasn't Kiki's embellishments that annoyed her. Those were to be expected. What irked her was the fact that Bertha hadn't been behind bars more than a few hours before her supposed friends had as good as convicted her. Friends were supposed to rally to each other's aid, not condemn them. And if everyone had known all along that Bertha was a homicidal maniac, why had they been friends with her at all since the woman obviously couldn't be trusted with salad tongs?

Hannah squeezed her eyes shut and tried to remember all the words to "Blue Suede Shoes" in a futile attempt to block out Wanda's gossiping ad nauseam about Bertha leaving rat poison for a gopher. Bertha had done no such thing. She had trapped the animal and released it down the street. Hannah knew it for a fact because the gopher had later destroyed her agapanthus.

Of course, the circumstantial evidence did cause one to strain in order to believe in Bertha's innocence. Ellie's cousin's best friend Misty had recently gotten a job as a part-time dispatcher at the police station, and Ellie had phoned her right after Wanda broke the news about the arrest. A promise to Misty of free manicures for a month had secured most of the late-breaking information, and none of it looked good for Bertha.

The police went to the winery immediately after Morgan's conversation with Hannah and they found strands of Angie's hair in the woodwardia ferns off the deck, confirming Hannah's suspicion that Angie had been killed there. Unfortunately this fact hurt Bertha rather than helped her. While the police were bagging the hair, the caretaker told them he had seen a dark blue Chevy Suburban climbing the steep driveway the previous night when he left for home. This happened sometime before the murder took place, and Bertha drove a dark blue Suburban. But the bleaker things looked for Bertha the more Hannah found herself wanting to help her.

"We shouldn't convict Bertha on circumstantial evidence," Hannah announced loudly to the Lady Nails patrons just as Wanda started giving new details on the gopher story. The chatter quieted as all heads turned toward her.

"Don't be silly," Kiki said. She was sitting at a manicure table where Shiloh was putting little gold stars on her freshly lacquered nails. Kiki had just had a manicure a few days before, so the stars were the only excuse she could think of for coming to the salon. "We found Angie's body in Bertha's backyard."

Sitting in the elevated pedicure chair, Wanda cast her eyes upon the other women with the air of a queen peering down from her throne. "May I remind you that Bertha's car was seen at the winery."

"But there's an explanation for that," Hannah said. "Bertha was probably going to pick up the wine she loaned the film festival for the opening-night party. You know, the bottles everyone brought for the wine racks to make them look realistic. She could have left before Angie and her murderer arrived."

Wanda narrowed her eyes. "I suppose that could be the

case, but that excuse is awfully convenient."

"That doesn't mean it isn't true," Hannah told her. "Besides, Bertha never would have buried anyone in her yard when she was expecting someone from Berkeley to drop in and dig around the yard for artifacts."

"Hannah, Berkeley called Bertha a week ago," Wanda said with real concern. "They told her that her so-called ancient pottery shard came from Pier One Imports. She made me promise not to tell, but under the circumstances I feel it's my duty to let you know."

Shiloh lifted her gaze from Kiki's hands. "So Bertha kept digging even though she knew there wasn't an Indian burial ground there?"

"She said she was going to keep at it because she truly believed she was going to find something. At the time I just thought she kept it up because she was embarrassed," Wanda said. "She'd made such a big deal out of that shard, broadcasting it to everyone in town. I assumed she was going to dig a few more holes, then stop and hope people would forget." She paused, leaning forward in her chair. "Of course, the holes turned out to be very useful, if you know what I mean."

"Of course!" Kiki said excitedly, waving her hand.

"Don't wreck your stars," Shiloh warned her.

"Oh, right," Kiki said, putting her hands back on the manicure table. "Bertha probably planned Casey's murder for weeks and used the whole pottery-shard thing so she could dig his grave."

"Don't be absurd," Hannah said. "Why would Bertha be digging a grave for Casey if she poisoned him at the film-festival party? There's no connection."

"So she dug the grave for Angie," Kiki replied.

Hannah shook her head. "She started digging holes in her yard before she even met Angie."

Ellie looked up from Wanda's toes, which she was painting a vivid red, making Wanda's feet look like she had just tiptoed through bull's blood. "Remember that spat Bertha and Angie had in the theater? Bertha turned the color of a tomato she was so mad. Everybody knew about it."

Tossing her magazine on the chair beside her, Hannah
stood up. "That's just it. Lots of people knew lots of things.
They knew that Bertha was a suspect in Frederick Casey's
murder."

Kiki got a faraway lovelorn look on her face and let out
a loud melodramatic sigh, which she did anytime Casey
was mentioned. Everybody rolled their eyes.

"Everyone knew that Bertha and Angie had that scene
at the theater," Hannah went on, jabbing the air with her
finger for emphasis. "Things are so public in this town.
Whoever killed Angie knew that Bertha was perfect to
frame. Bertha even provided a good place to bury the body.
Not only did she have the holes in her yard, but her property backs up to the park. Someone could have easily put
the body in her yard at night without being seen."

Finished with the polish, Ellie blew on Wanda's toes.
"But how did the murderer know where Bertha lived?"

"If Hannah is right, though I doubt she is," Wanda said,
"Angie's murderer would have to be someone who knew
Bertha."

Hannah walked to the window and gazed out at the
street. "And whoever killed Casey had to be at the film-
festival party."

Ellie gave Wanda's toes one last blow then looked at
Hannah. "So the same person killed both of them?"

"I think so," Wanda said, sliding to the edge of her
chair. "But that's another thing that's damning for Bertha.
She had angry scenes with both victims and the evidence
points to her. Ellie, I smudged my little toe."

Ellie frowned. "If you wouldn't move around so much
it wouldn't happen."

"If you'd use that quick-dry polish like I asked you,"
Wanda said.

"You hated the colors," Ellie replied testily.

"Ladies," Hannah said, interrupting. "We're all upset
about what's happened to Bertha, but we should be trying
to clear her name. There are other people who could have
wanted both Casey and Angie dead." She had more to say
but she stopped there. All the distressing talk about Bertha

had pushed Roger Burke to the back of her mind, but now he returned, kimono-clad, to the forefront. What if Roger found out from Angie that Casey was cheating the *Pirate John* investors? Fifty thousand dollars was a lot of money to lose, and on top of that, Casey had ridiculed him. Roger could have killed Casey, then murdered Angie to cover it up. But if he did kill Casey, how did he get the heart pills?

"Hannah, pay attention," Wanda commanded. "We're making progress here. Ellie's theory is that Angie's murderer met her at the winery because he or she wanted a private place to talk. The winery's deserted when it's not rented for a party."

Her hands raised to keep her stars from smudging, Kiki got up from her chair and walked over to her sister. "So do you think whoever murdered Angie asked her to the winery specifically to kill her?"

Hannah glanced down while she ruminated on the idea. "I think the murder was an impulse. A carefully planned murder would have taken place somewhere much more remote. No, I think Ellie's right. Angie and the killer probably met there just to talk. The killer got angry and in a rage bashed in Angie's skull with a rock or something." All the women scrunched up their faces. "Sorry for being graphic. Maybe the killer was startled by Bertha driving up and then got the idea to frame her. See? It's simple."

"It sounds simple when you explain it like that," Wanda said. "But that doesn't mean that's the way it happened. I'm sorry to say it because Bertha's my friend, but she still looks guilty to me."

"You act like you want her to be the killer," Shiloh said.

"It's the last thing I want, but facts are facts. The evidence certainly points to her. If Bertha is a murderer she must pay the price. Not to mention the fact that she committed the murders in such a disgusting way. Poisoning a man so he ends up dead in my guest room."

"The rudeness," Hannah muttered as she again looked out the window.

"But I'm going to make a major contribution to her defense fund," Wanda added. "I think claiming insanity is the only way to go. She eats all that junk food. It could have affected her mind.''

"Hannah, why do you keep looking out that window?'' Ellie said. "If you're bored you can read a magazine.''

Hannah smiled. "Sorry, but I don't like the brain candy you keep here. They're years out of date, anyway. Throw them out and I'll bring you a stack of this year's gardening magazines.''

Kiki twittered. "Hannah thinks everyone's fascinated by gardening.''

"They should be,'' Hannah replied, then turned again to the window, her brow furrowed. "Has anyone seen Ed today? I'm looking for him.''

Wanda shook her head. "Why?''

"I need to talk to him.'' Hannah had gone by his house right after she dropped off Kiki for her manicure, but he hadn't been at home. Waiting for Kiki at Lady Nails was a good excuse to keep an eye on the street in hopes of catching him.

Kiki still needed a coat of clear sealer, so Hannah had another ten minutes to wait. She sat down and was considering going to the Book Stop for a quick coffee when out the window she saw Naomi rushing down the sidewalk, her canvas shopping bag hanging off her arm, celery sticking out the top. Naomi opened the door to Lady Nails, the Buddhist prayer chimes announcing her arrival.

"Hello, Ellie. Hello, everyone,'' she said, out of breath. "Ellie, I was wondering if you could give me a manicure.''

Ellie tilted her head, trying to look surprised when she knew exactly why Naomi was there. "But you always do your nails yourself.''

"Yes, well, I'd like something more reflective of my inner self, and it requires a professional. I was wondering if you could paint each nail with a swirl of two shades of polish. You know, a ying-yang effect.''

"I think I can work you in,'' Ellie told her.

Naomi dropped into a chair next to Hannah. "So, is there any news? I just heard about Bertha's arrest at the grocery,'' she said, her voice low and conspiratorial.

Hannah filled her in on the facts she knew as well as the current speculations.

"It's all such a worry and so terrible for Hill Creek," Naomi said, settling back in her chair. She picked up one of the most worn *People* magazines from the stack on the floor. It had a photo of a smiling Mel Gibson on the cover. "I'm thinking of doing a death cleansing in the plaza. I could cleanse the whole town of negative spirits."

"I don't think the town council has death cleansing in the budget," Hannah said with a smile.

"Oh, it would be pro bono, naturally," Naomi said very seriously. "After all, it's my civic duty." She began idly flipping through the pages of the magazine. Hannah had opened her mouth to ask a question about Angie when Naomi said, "Oh my."

"What is it?" Hannah asked.

"Right here," she said, tapping the page with her finger. "It's a photo of Frederick Casey. How prophetic."

She handed the magazine to Hannah. The photo was in the section on celebrity parties, and Casey had attended a benefit for a charity. The camera caught him smiling, drink in hand, wearing his usual buckskin jacket. So very much alive, Hannah thought, and now so awfully dead. There were several other people in the photo with him, but only he was named. Two other people in the photo, one in particular, looked familiar to her, but she couldn't place them, so she assumed they were television actors.

"It's so terrible for Lauren and Brad," Kiki said loud enough for everyone to hear. "Here they are starting off a new romance, and to have all this tragedy." She sighed. "I wonder if Lauren's picture will be in the newspapers or magazines. They have a date tonight, you know. It could be a big night." She gave Hannah a wink. Hannah cringed.

"If Lauren and Brad get serious, I guess they'll move to La Jolla," Ellie said.

Hannah looked at her. "Why La Jolla?"

"Brad Casey has a house there. It was his mother's house. I read about it somewhere."

The idea of Lauren moving anywhere distressed Hannah

and she turned again to the window. The street was bustling with shoppers—people walking their dogs or sitting on the benches outside the Book Stop having coffee. She had visited La Jolla once, and it was a lovely town right on the ocean and not that far from Los Angeles. She hadn't thought about La Jolla in years, yet for some reason it sounded very familiar, like someone had mentioned it the day before.

Out the window Hannah saw a young man throw a Frisbee that accidentally hit the hood of a new Porsche waiting at a stop sign. The driver shouted. The young man shouted back.

Hannah's hand involuntarily raised itself to her mouth. She suddenly knew why La Jolla was so familiar.

NINETEEN

AFTER DROPPING OFF AT HOME a freshly manicured and gossip-gorged Kiki, Hannah returned to town and searched for Ed at the Book Stop, the Urban Farmer Nursery, and the grocery. No one had seen him. Increasingly concerned, she decided to try his house.

As she walked up the curved brick walkway she considered all the reasons she shouldn't be so worried about his absence from town. Maybe he was visiting a relative. Maybe he had a cold and was staying at home. She mounted the steps and knocked on the door. He didn't answer.

She stood there, her hand pressed against the porch railing's peeling paint, racking her brain to figure out where he could be. Ed knew something about Casey's murder. She felt more certain of it with each passing hour, which was why she had such an ominous feeling. Angie had known something and she had ended up as fertilizer in Bertha's garden. Ed could be in danger as well.

Although every bone in her body resisted, she had to admit that it was possible that Bertha was the murderer. Everyone else could be right and she could be wrong. Of course, if Bertha was the killer, then at least Ed was safe as long as she was in jail. Unless Bertha had gotten to him before her arrest. Propelled by this horrible possibility, she flew down the walkway and got in her car.

Fifteen minutes later she was at the police station parked on a plastic chair, waiting for Detective Morgan, inhaling the aroma of the potpourri on the information counter. She knew they had just changed it because the lobby now smelled like peach and the day before it had definitely smelled like apple. But the fragrant atmosphere didn't calm her mood. Too antsy to sit, she walked around the room, glanced at the whale pictures, tried sitting again, then settled for some pacing.

Morgan walked briskly into the lobby. "How can I help you, Mrs. Malloy? We have to make it quick. I'm really busy right now."

"I know, and I wouldn't have bothered you, but it's very important. I'm worried about Ed Kachowski."

Morgan's face registered concern. "What about him?"

"He's usually around town during the day, but today nobody's seen him."

"Maybe he's at home."

"I tried him there. When was the last time you saw him?"

"First thing this morning, around eight. After what you told me last night I went over to his house and questioned him again. He didn't tell me anything new." He studied her. "Why are you so worried?"

"Because he never misses a day in town."

"Listen, try not to fret over it. He was safe and sound this morning." His thumbs hooked in his belt loops, Morgan looked at the floor a moment, then back at her. "I tell you what. I'll drop by his house on my way to the sheriff's office. It'll only be a couple of hours from now. How's that? If he's not there I'll have someone check around."

Hannah relaxed a little. "Thank you. Call me, will you? Leave a message if I'm not home."

"Where are you off to?" Morgan asked with a trace of suspicion.

She took a breath. "To run an errand." It was an errand

of a sort, but it would be best if Morgan didn't know about it.

The small cocktail lounge at the Marin Inn smelled of damp bar rags mingled with the stale odor of cigarettes from when they still let people smoke in California. Hannah stood near the entrance and allowed her eyes to adjust to the darkness. Bowden was the only customer sitting at the bar. He was perched on a bar stool hunched over his Scotch, staring into the amber liquid as if the ice cubes were talking.

Steeling herself, Hannah approached him. "Thanks for meeting me."

His eyes darted to her then back to his drink. "You're the one who found Angie."

"Yes. I feel terrible about her."

"Yeah, well, nice little burg you have here. Love the welcoming committee," he said, his tone harsh behind its slur. Hannah wondered how many drinks he'd had. "I'd like to get out of here before I end up dead like my friends, but the police want to question me again tomorrow. My attorney's flying up from L.A." His eyes moved to her again, this time staying. "That Malone woman's still in jail, right? She's not out on bail or anything?" Hannah nodded and he visibly relaxed. "Why did she kill Angie? The kid was harmless."

He sniffed, his eyes starting to fill, and Hannah didn't know if it was the liquor or genuine grief.

"I'm not convinced that Bertha Malone killed Angie," she told him.

"The cops charged her with it."

"They could be wrong."

He lifted his shoulders. "You got a point there. The police questioned me this afternoon like they think I might have friggin' killed somebody. But I didn't. Why would I?"

Hannah pulled out a stool and sat down next to him, laying her purse on the bar. "They might think you killed Fred so you would have *Pirate John* all to yourself."

"That would be stupid. I needed Fred." The words came out harshly. He paused. "And he needed me," he added, this time softer. "He realized it, too. Took him long enough."

To Hannah his words sounded genuine. She supposed you could murder someone then miss him afterward.

He sniffled again. "We worked together when neither of us had shit. We shared a dump apartment, shared liquor, shared women. We did some great work." He lifted his glass to his lips, his eyes closed like he was saying a prayer, then tossed the last swallow down his throat. "I need to get out of here, get away from all this crap. Are you coming to Palm Desert with me?"

"I'm sorry, I can't."

"It's not because you think I'm a killer, is it? I mean, if you thought that, you wouldn't be here talking to me."

"I'm here because I want information from you."

"That's what you always want." Her hand rested on the bar and he ran his finger across it. "Why don't you want me, Hannah?"

She could think of several reasons. Number one was the fact that he could be a murderer. Number two was that he was very likely an alcoholic. Those were bad enough. But the third reason, one she only realized fully at that moment, was that she didn't want to tell him about her mastectomy. She had been able to share it with John Perez and he had understood. John's wife had died from cancer. But there was something about Bowden that made her think he couldn't handle it. From their conversations she knew he had this image of her as being completely strong and wise, someone who could help mend his broken soul. He would be frightened by the reality of her scarred chest and its tattooed garden. He would be disappointed by the knowledge that she was broken, too, no matter how well she disguised it.

"I'm sorry. I can't."

He looked at her a moment, shrugged, then said, "You want a drink?"

He got over rejection pretty quickly, she thought. She

would have liked it better if it had taken a few minutes.

"No, I don't drink anymore."

"You miss it?"

"Every day."

One side of his mouth turned upward. "When you used to booze, did you ever get as drunk as I am right now?"

"Yes, but I was more ladylike about it. I did it in my living room."

"Very classy. Me, I drink anywhere. Booze was one of the things Fred and I had in common. We used to like it to excess."

"You still do. You have a drinking problem. I know the signs."

"No, I don't. Honest," he said, feigning innocence. "It's just this situation the past few days. It would drive anyone to drink." Bowden raised his glass. "I'm just sentimental. It's for old times' sake that I've been drunk since Fred died." He frowned when he remembered that there was no liquid left in the glass.

"Hinkley, I came here to ask you about La Jolla."

He blinked, taken aback by the change in subject. "Nice town but too many hardbodies. We'll like Palm Desert better, trust me. We'll be two of the youngest people there."

"That's where some of the consultants lived, the ones that got the payoffs from *Pirate John*."

"Maybe. So?"

"La Jolla is where Brad lives."

He touched one finger to her chin. "No, babe, Brad lives in L.A."

"He grew up in La Jolla. He still has a house there. He must have friends and connections who would help him with the fraud."

"Maybe Fred had connections there as well," Bowden said but without enthusiasm.

The bartender, a man in his seventies with a long gray ponytail, asked Hannah what she wanted. She asked for a plain soda with lime. Bowden wanted another Scotch.

"I think Brad was the one embezzling from *Pirate*

John,'' Hannah whispered so the bartender wouldn't hear. "Not Fred."

"Why would you think that?"

"The La Jolla connection, for one reason. But I know that Angie was doing research on which firms got the pay-offs. She made at least some of the calls to these companies after Fred's death. Why would she do that if she were so certain he was the one responsible for the fraud? If the man was dead, why not just drop it?"

"How do you know she researched it?"

"I've seen the accounting documents, all her notes, everything."

"Angie had all that stuff," he said grimly. "How did you see it? And don't give me some crap about your photographic memory."

"I sneaked onto the boat where she was staying. You can turn me in to the police if you like," she said, hoping he wouldn't take her up on the offer. "What's important is that she had written things down. There were notes from conversations, dates, amounts."

"Maybe she was trying to get the money back."

"If anyone was going to get the money back, it would have been you, and you'd use a lawyer, not an underling like Angie." Hannah hesitated, another idea entering her head. "Unless—" She stopped talking when the bartender approached. He pushed their drinks in front of them, then left.

"Unless what?" Bowden asked.

"Unless you and Angie were trying to get more money laundered through these people. Angie could have been calling for that."

"No," he said with new potency. "That's not it. And please don't say anything like that to the cops. I've got enough troubles."

"Then talk to me."

He picked up a cocktail napkin, crushing it in his hand. "Listen, what you said earlier was right. Angie thought Brad was doing the fraud and that Fred was covering for him. That's what we were talking about in my hotel room when you came by. She said she was going to look into it and find out the truth. I said leave it alone. Fred was dead, so what did it matter? Stirring things up would only cause trouble for the movie project. I told her that if she'd drop the whole thing, I'd make her an associate producer on the film.''

''She didn't take your advice?''

''Not even close. After all the shit Fred gave her she wanted to protect his memory. I couldn't believe it. She said she didn't want him taking the blame for something he didn't do, even after he was dead. Especially after he was dead, is what she told me.''

''She could have also wanted revenge against Brad for dumping her.''

Wiping a tear with the back of his hand, Bowden softly chuckled. ''Probably. But you know what's funny? I think she really admired Fred. In her own way, she was as tough and self-serving as he was. She was going to be a producer and nothing was going to stop her. If she had to grovel, fine. If she had to get treated like dirt, no problem. Then in the end she was willing to give up her one real shot because she didn't want to think badly of him.''

''And she felt sure she'd found the truth about the fraud?''

He nodded. ''She called me yesterday and told me that she knew for sure, that some guy confirmed it over the phone. Brad was embezzling from *Pirate John*, not Fred. And Fred Casey, the biggest asshole walking the earth, was willing to take the blame for it to protect his son. I guess he felt he owed him. Fred and Angie both ended up noble creatures and they both ended up dead. I think I'll stay a son of a bitch. You live longer.''

Hannah felt something very much like dread in the pit of her stomach. ''When Angie called last night, did she say she was going to confront Brad with what she knew?''

''No. She didn't say she was meeting anybody.'' He leaned closer to her and whispered. ''Listen, I know what you're thinking, but Brad couldn't have done it. He had dinner with some local girl,'' he said, with Hannah tensing, knowing that the local girl was Lauren. "Then he was with me. The cops grilled both of us today about where we were, but we told them. We were preparing for tomorrow night's lecture."

"What time did you finish?"

"I don't know. Really late. Way past midnight, maybe later. Trust me. Brad didn't kill anybody. It had to be that woman who kept yelling at everybody or that chubby film-festival guy."

"You mean Roger Burke?"

"Yeah, the one that looks like the Pillsbury Doughboy. According to Angie, that guy was so mad about his money he could have killed somebody, given half a chance."

"How did Angie know he was mad?"

"He took her aside at the party and tried to wheedle information out of her about getting his money back. She had just had that ugly scene with Fred on the patio and she was still pretty pissed, so she told the guy he'd never see his money again and for him to take a hike."

"Did you tell the police all this?"

"Sure. I'm certain Angie told them, too. Trust me. Brad may be an embezzler but he's no killer."

Hannah believed him, but it didn't lessen the sick feeling inside her. "Where's Brad right now?"

"I don't know. Probably out spending what he believes will be his inheritance. He'll be so disappointed when he realizes Casey didn't have a nickel."

Hannah picked up her purse. "I have to go."

Bowden grabbed her wrist. "Don't. Stay and talk to me."

"Can't. I have business."

"What business?"

His fingers hurt. She wrenched her arm away from him. "Brad's a crook, and I've got to protect my niece from him."

TWENTY

ARMS CROSSED AND MOUTHS SET tight, Hannah and Kiki sat in the Eldorado in front of Lauren's house, the convertible top up and the windows rolled down, allowing in the evening chill. The sweet smell of the eucalyptus trees tantalized Hannah's sensitive nose but she felt too gloomy to enjoy it.

They had looked for Lauren everywhere, including every restaurant and coffee bar. Then they called Lauren's friends but no one knew where she was. Was there a problem? her friends asked. Yes, there was a problem, Hannah thought but didn't say. How big a problem she wasn't certain.

"This is hopeless," Kiki said, her knees bent, feet pushed against the dashboard. "I don't know why you asked me to come along with you in the first place."

"I thought you might be able to help."

"Help with what? So what if Lauren has sex with Brad? And we don't know for sure he's done anything terrible."

"I told you. He's engaged to a nineteen-year-old girl."

"You don't know for sure."

"Hinkley Bowden told me so. He also said that Brad committed fraud."

Kiki waved her hand dismissively. "That's just hear-say."

"And there's still a possibility he could be a killer."

"Pooh. That good-looking boy wouldn't hurt a fly. Bertha killed Angie and Fred. You just don't want to admit that you could be wrong."

"I have no problem admitting that I'm wrong," Hannah said, feeling cranky. "It's just that I rarely am."

"Oh la-di-dah. You were wrong about that pottery shard. You said Bertha wouldn't have buried Angie in her yard because archologists were going to dig it up."

"Archaeologists."

"Whatever. You were wrong about it. Bertha already knew her yard didn't have old Indian pottery in it. You were wrong, wrong, wrong. But you can't ever accept the fact that you're not totally right and not totally in charge. You meddle in everybody's life, especially Lauren's. If you knew Brad was engaged, why didn't you tell her?"

"I tried but she got so upset, and now she won't return my calls."

"Well, you only have yourself to blame. You're always tossing out advice on what work she should do, what she should wear, who she should date, and now who she should sleep with!"

Hannah leaned her forehead against the steering wheel, wondering if her sister was right. Had she been meddling too much in Lauren's life? She soon felt a sisterly pat on her shoulder.

"Honey, I'm sorry. I didn't mean to hurt your feelings," Kiki said. "But let little Lauren have a night of unbridled lust. She's probably at his hotel room right now doing the wild thing, and no matter how much it irks you, there's nothing you can do about it. Truth is, it's just none of your beeswax."

Suddenly Hannah straightened and started the ignition.

"What are you doing?" Kiki asked.

"Making it my beeswax. I'm sorry, but I just have to butt into Lauren's life one more time, then I'll stop, I promise. I can't let her lose her virginity to Brad Casey. She'll regret it the rest of her life.''

"What does it matter who you lose your virginity to, just as long as you're lucky enough to lose it? You and I don't sit around thinking about who we scrambled the sheets with when we were in our twenties.''

"But Lauren's not like us, thank God. We're going to the Marin Inn. If what you say is right, then that's where they are.''

"Oh, God, Hannah, you're so difficult. He's not even staying at the Marin Inn anymore. They couldn't be there,'' Kiki blurted, then pressed her hand against her mouth.

Hannah gave her a hard look. "What do you mean? Where are they?''

"I can't tell you. Not that Lauren told me not to tell, but I know I shouldn't.''

"Where is Brad staying? I want to know now,'' Hannah said, using the gruff tone that usually worked with her sister.

Kiki sucked in some air and held it. "Oh, poop,'' she said, letting it out. "You'll get it out of me anyway. He moved to the Wyndam after Freddie died. He told Lauren it was more private.''

Also more luxurious, Hannah thought, remembering what Bowden said about Brad thinking he had an inheritance coming. "Did she say what room he was in?''

"No. Why would she tell me that?''

"Then we'll phone his room.''

"Get your brain on straight. If he and Lauren are doing what I think they're doing, they're not going to answer the phone.''

"Then we've got to find out what room they're in and go get her.''

"Please, Hannah, let's go home. I'll let you watch the Discovery Channel all night.'' But dangling that prize had no effect. Hannah turned off the ignition and jerked out the keys. "Now what?'' Kiki asked.

"I'm going inside Lauren's house. She might have Brad's room number written down somewhere.''

"Lauren gave you her house key in case of an emergency. This is not an emergency."

But by this time Hannah was outside the car and walking up the sidewalk.

"I'm not coming with you. You're as good as breaking and entering. I won't be a part of it. You're on your own, missy!" Kiki shouted out the car window. But by the time Hannah opened Lauren's front door, she heard the sound of Kiki's shoes clicking up the sidewalk.

Upon entering Lauren's living room, Hannah gave her usual small gasp. The room looked as it always did, as if a tornado had swept through, leaving clothes, pillows, newspapers, and every other object randomly scattered. It was a sight Hannah never got used to.

"Now, where would she have written down his room number?" Hannah muttered.

"She wouldn't write it down. She'd keep it in her head. She's good with numbers," Kiki said, following Hannah into the kitchen.

"She's terrible with numbers." Hannah checked under an open bag of potato chips near the phone.

"She's an accountant!"

"But only a mediocre one, thank God. Lauren should be a famous chef. She's a creative spirit, a free-form thinker, as the state of this room proves."

It was in Lauren's bedroom where Hannah found it. On Lauren's nightstand next to a novel titled *Dangerous Desire* was a used envelope with *Wyndam Hotel* followed by a phone number and the digits "608" written on it. Drawn over the rest of the envelope were little hearts as well as the name *Lauren Casey* scribbled again and again in different-sized letters. She wanted to see what her name as Brad's wife would look like, Hannah realized, and it made her heart ache.

Hannah shoved the envelope in her purse. "Got it. Let's go."

"Go and do what?" Kiki said.

"Get Lauren out of there."

"If you think Brad's a criminal, then why not call the police?"

"Because the Hill Creek police wouldn't have jurisdiction over the kind of fraud he's committed. Besides, I'm not concerned about the fraud. That's someone else's business. I just don't want Lauren involved with a two-timing swindler."

"If you're going to get that picky over men, she'll never lose her virginity at all. Most men are two-timing swindlers. At least the really cute ones."

Hannah drove slowly, carefully navigating the Eldorado up the hairpin curves that led to the Wyndam Hotel. Nestled in the posh hills of Sausalito, the hotel, which had been a spa in the 1920s, sat back among the trees, with golden lights washing its ornate facade. It looked like a magical palace.

"We're not dressed well enough to go in here," Kiki said after they had parked and were approaching the door.

"We look fine."

"But I have a mustard stain on my blouse and you're wearing those horrible old loafers."

"Just walk in with an air of confidence and no one will notice."

Kiki stopped and concentrated a moment. Then, lifting her chin and holding her hands away from her sides, she put a touch more wiggle in her walk as she and Hannah entered the hotel's front door.

The lobby was large and elegant, with a marble floor, potted palms, and walls of gleaming wood. Kiki followed Hannah as she whisked past the front desk and to the elevator.

Barry Manilow crooned through the elevator speakers as Kiki glared at her sister. "I still don't like this," she said as the elevator doors parted on the sixth floor. "It's an invasion of privacy."

"Wait in the car if you like," Hannah told her, knowing that her sister, despite her protests, wouldn't miss this adventure for the world.

They stopped in front of room 608. Now feeling pangs of trepidation, Hannah paused, eyeing the door while Kiki eyed her.

"Lauren's going to be spitting mad, Hannah. I wouldn't knock if I were you. I sure wouldn't."

Having received the final impetus she needed, Hannah rapped firmly on the door.

"Shit's gonna fly," Kiki said with a moan. "And I'm going to catch it the same as you, even though I'm one hundred percent innocent. But is Lauren going to see it that way?"

When no one came to the door, Kiki sighed with relief and tugged on Hannah's arm. "God has saved us. Let's go have some tea somewhere. My nerves are shot."

Hannah didn't budge, for at that moment she saw a young hotel maintenance man in blue work pants and a blue shirt carrying a tool chest. He stopped at the end of the hall, pulled a paper out of his pocket, and studied it.

Hannah hastily conceived a plan. She began knocking lightly on the door.

"Brad, dear, it's Aunt Hannah. Are you there? I've lost my key."

"What kind of nut are you?" Kiki whispered. "You're not his aunt and he's not in there anyway."

Ignoring her, Hannah continued knocking and calling for Brad, her voice becoming more pleading. Out of the corner of her eye she saw the maintenance man watching her.

"Could you help me?" she asked in her best helpless woman-of-a-certain-age voice. "I'm staying here with my nephew and I've lost my key."

The young man approached her. "Sorry. I'm not allowed. You'll have to go to the front desk and ask them."

"See, Auntie Hannah?" Kiki said, her voice loaded with sarcasm. "He can't do it. We'll just have to go to the front desk." She pulled on her sister's arm.

Hannah pressed her hand to her chest and did her best to emit a believable wheeze. "I just don't know if there's time." She softened her knees, slumping downward. Looking panicked, the maintenance man grabbed her.

"Are you sick?" he asked.

"I just need my inhaler. It's in my bag." Hannah pointed a trembling finger toward the door. Kiki's eyes narrowed and her mouth opened. The young man looked worried.

"Asthma?" he asked. Hannah nodded and watched his forehead scrunch. Within a few seconds he pulled a card key from his pocket, slipped it in the door, and it clicked open. "I'll just let the front desk know I let you in. They'll send a new key up."

Kiki grimaced.

"Thank you," Hannah said with a small choke.

"You're sure you're okay?" he asked, slipping his hand under her elbow. "I could have the front desk call a doctor."

"Oh, I think she's going to be just fine and dandy," Kiki replied, irritated.

He walked down the hallway and Hannah hurried into the room, with Kiki right behind. Brad's room was neat, the bed still made, which Hannah considered an excellent sign. The sound of rock music came from the next room.

"Nice room," Hannah said, "but you'd think a nice hotel like this would have thicker walls."

"Forget that. What the hell are we doing here?" Kiki demanded. "He and Lauren are someplace else."

"I want to look around."

"For what?"

"Papers. Notes. Phone numbers. Anything we could use to link him to the fraud and convince Lauren to stay away from him."

"I thought you said you didn't care about the fraud."

"I'm not interested in talking to the police about it, but I'd like to prove to Lauren what kind of man he is." She began quietly opening drawers and looking through the contents.

"But, Hannah, that maintenance man said he was going to tell the front desk he let us in. They'll know we don't belong here."

"Then we better hurry."

Kiki released a series of fretful whimpers as Hannah continued searching the room. Brad's expensive clothing lay neatly folded in the drawers. She searched them all but she couldn't find anything interesting.

"As long as we're doing this, look and see what kind of undies Brad wears," Kiki said, standing close to the door. "Is he tightie-whities or boxers?"

"I already checked," Hannah said, going through some magazines on a table. "He wears little dark things that look like a Speedo swimsuit."

"Let's take a pair," Kiki said.

"What for?"

"In case he ever gets famous," Kiki said. "Then we can show them to everyone. They might even be worth some money."

"You're a sick woman, Kiki Goldstein," Hannah told her as she checked the drawers in the nightstands on either side of the bed. It seemed odd to Hannah that he didn't have a notebook or a Day-Timer in the room. She opened the door to the closet and began going through the pockets of his clothes.

Kiki remained by the door, keeping it open a crack so she could tell when someone was coming. "Has it occurred to you, Hannah, that all your information about this supposed fraud has come from Hinkley Bowden? I mean, he accused Freddie of being a crook, then he accused Brad of being a crook. Maybe *he's* the crook and you're not seeing it because you think he's cute."

Hannah stopped looking through the clothes and turned to her sister, stunned at the simple truth of her statement. Why couldn't it have been Bowden who had stolen the money from *Pirate John*? Which meant he had an excellent motive for killing both Casey and Angie since they both knew about the fraud. But instead he accused everyone else of the fraud and the murders.

"I'm such a fool," Hannah said slowly.

"You are?" Kiki replied, sounding surprised.

"I did think of Bowden as a suspect for Casey's murder, but I've been blind to the possibility of anything else.

You're right. I've accepted too much of what he's told me. Thank you for opening my eyes.''

"My pleasure. Can we go now?''

It was then Hannah noticed the small ficus tree in the corner with its branches droopy, a handful of leaves scattered on the carpet. "Overwatered,'' she said out loud.

"What?'' Kiki said.

"That ficus is waterlogged. You'd think a hotel would take better care of its plants.'' Unable to abandon any plant in need of help, Hannah went to it, reached into the decorative basket, and stuck her finger in the space between the plant's pot and the dish in which it sat. "Full of water. Its poor roots are rotting.'' She grabbed the plant by the base of its narrow trunk and lifted it upward. "Kiki, get over here and lift out the dish, then pour the water in the bathroom sink. I'll send a note to the hotel management tomorrow and let them know what terrible condition this plant is in.''

"Have you lost your mind? They're going to send the police up here any minute to arrest us and you're worried about that plant.''

"They'll send up a manager, not the police, and I can deal with him.''

"This is just like that time you got me to smoke that cigarette in the girls' rest room.''

"That was in the seventh grade. Now hurry up and help me.''

Kiki scooted across the room. Hannah grabbed the ficus by the rim of its pot and lifted it.

Kiki wrinkled her nose. "The water's all icky brown.''

"Just empty it.''

"Wait a minute,'' she said, looking at the base of the plant. "There's something stuck here.'' Kiki reached down and pulled out a Ziploc plastic bag covered with brown slime. Hannah put the plant down, forgetting about its being waterlogged. She immediately thought the bag held drugs, but when Kiki opened it, she pulled out a folded paper.

Hannah took it from her, recognizing it immediately. A chill climbed up her spine. It was the page from the expense summary, the one she had had seen on the boat. She recognized the names, the handwritten notes jotted on the side. But there was an addition to the page that hadn't been there the day before. The right edge of the paper was streaked with blood.

$\mathscr{T}$WENTY-ONE

$\mathscr{A}$T THE SIGHT OF THE blood-splattered paper inside the plastic bag, Kiki dropped onto the bed, her hands pressed against her face. "Hannie, what is it?"

Hannah held the bag with two fingers, the way she would have held a dead rat by its tail. "The expense information from Angie's backpack." For a moment she stared fearfully at the bag as if it contained pure evil. "Kiki, when you saw Angie leaving the boat last night, did she have her leather backpack with her?"

Kiki's expression became puzzled. "I'm not sure. I was so worried about you sailing off in that boat, I wasn't noticing much."

Hannah sat down beside her sister. "Think, Kiki. It's critical."

Squeezing her eyes shut, Kiki concentrated. "Okay, I'm visualizing. Let's see, Angie was wearing the long red sweater, probably to hide her hips, and she had on those awful heavy boots." Her eyes opened. "Yes, I remember. She threw the backpack over her shoulder like it was a purse, except it was a lot bigger than a purse. What does it mean?"

Hannah rose. The hotel room, despite its size and elegance, now felt claustrophobic. "It means we've got to get this evidence to Detective Morgan."

"Oh, no. I think we should leave it here. You're not supposed to disturb evidence."

"But we can't leave it. Brad could skip town with it or destroy it. No, it's better to just call the police from here and wait until they arrive."

"And then how do we explain how we found it?"

"I'm afraid we're going to have trouble with that anyway."

"No, Hannah," Kiki said, jumping up from the bed. "Let's get out of here. We can call the police from the lobby. Go ahead and take the bag with you, but please, let's go. I didn't like being here in the first place, but now it's downright creepy. I mean, how on earth did Brad get that thing?"

Hannah looked at her sister, stupefied. "Kiki, don't you get it? That paper belonged to Angie. Now it turns up in Brad's possession with blood on it." Kiki wore a glazed look, indicating that the message wasn't sinking in. It sometimes amazed Hannah how her sister's synaptic connections could fire off at the speed of smell. "He's a murderer," she said, emphasizing the last word. "And our Lauren's with him."

Kiki let out a shriek as the reality of the situation seeped into her cranium. The music in the next room quickly lowered. Hannah shushed Kiki, then the women headed for the door, Hannah taking the plastic bag with her. Suddenly Hannah inhaled sharply, freezing in place.

The unexpected stop caused Kiki to bump into her. "What are you waiting for?" she said, giving Hannah a push. "We've got to hustle. We've got to find our Lauren."

"But I just heard her voice," Hannah said slowly.

Kiki gave her another shove. "Listen, honey, this is no time to turn psychic. You can have a long talk with Red Moon later."

"No, I mean I heard it next door. Lauren is in there," Hannah said, nodding toward the next room. "This is a suite. I should have realized it before. Lauren's in there with Brad.''

In the next second Hannah bolted toward the door that separated the two rooms, moving too quickly to hear Kiki's protests. All in one movement she twisted the doorknob and threw her body against the door, bursting into the adjacent room with the ferocity of cops on a drug raid. She stood there, physically stunned, and for a moment her eyes, ears and brain didn't connect. Split seconds later, as the fog in her head lifted, she saw a dazed Lauren sitting on the couch with her blouse off. Brad let out a grunt of astonishment as he hastily pulled on his pants.

''Aunt Hannah!'' Lauren cried out. ''What—''

''Lauren, you have to get out of here,'' Hannah said, the words coming out between gasps for air. ''Get your clothes on.''

''Please, Lauren,'' Kiki said, poking her head into the room. ''Do what Hannah says.''

''Kiki, go call the police!'' Hannah told her.

''The police?'' Lauren whimpered. ''I just want to have sex. It's not a crime!''

For an instant everyone was frozen in place, each person totally bewildered, uncertain of his or her next move. But the desperate reality soon crystallized for at least two people in the room. Brad's gaze moved downward to the plastic bag and bloodied paper still in Hannah's hand.

His eyes moved back to Hannah's, and she knew what a mistake she had made. She should have called the police before rushing into the room, but her only thought had been of Lauren, of getting her away from a murderer. It was too late to correct the error and too late to run.

With one hand Brad pulled Kiki fully into the room and kicked the door shut behind her.

Still on the couch, Lauren watched this with dazed confusion. ''What's happening?''

''Shut up,'' he barked at her.

''What?'' Lauren said, her tone hurt, her face crumpling.

Hannah and Kiki stood motionless by a chair while Brad paced jerkily about the room, his eyes frantic. He had to know that his options were seriously limited, Hannah thought. He halted in front of her. "Give me that bag."

Her eyes filling with tears, Lauren stood up. "I want to know what's going on here," she said. Brad shoved her back on to the couch.

"Don't you touch her," Hannah shouted, moving to her niece, but he stepped between them. He glowered at Hannah with such hate that she froze, afraid he would hit her. Lauren curled into the corner of the couch.

Slowly Hannah raised the plastic bag and handed it over. He shoved it in his pocket.

"I'll tell you what's going on here," Hannah said, directing the words at Lauren but keeping her eyes on Brad. "He killed Angie. The paper I just found in the next room was in her backpack hours before she died. That's surely her blood on it. He killed that poor girl and buried her in Bertha's garden."

"I didn't kill her," he spat. "I told the police. I was with Lauren, then I was with Hinkley until early morning."

Hannah shook her head. "Bowden's been sotted for days. My bet is that he doesn't know if you were there or not."

"Then why would he tell the police I was with him?"

"Maybe he didn't want to admit that he's a drunk. Maybe he thinks you're innocent and wants to protect you. I don't really know."

He stepped closer to her, his hands curling into fists. "That's right. You don't know shit."

"I know you killed that girl and buried her in Bertha's yard."

"But, Hannah," Kiki said, peeking out from behind her sister. "How would he have known where Bertha lived?"

Hannah gently nudged Kiki back toward the door, trying to keep her as far from Brad as possible. "Lauren told him. She did it innocently. She just told him a story about our crazy neighbor Bertha who was digging up her yard looking for artifacts."

Lauren covered her mouth with her hands, looking at her now former boyfriend with repulsion. She grabbed her blouse off the floor and pulled it on, hastily buttoning it. Being half-clothed in front of your boyfriend was one thing, but to be so in front of a killer was apparently in bad taste.

"The maintenance man called the front desk just a few seconds ago," Kiki said to Brad, her voice cracking. "Someone will be up here any minute."

Hannah closed her eyes and mouthed a silent no. She had hoped to calm Brad, to reason with him. Kiki's statement only panicked him more.

He grabbed his leather jacket off the back of a chair, reached into the pocket, and pulled out something dark and oblong. Hannah heard a click. She saw the gleaming blade pop out and her skin prickled with fear. Grabbing Lauren by the hair, he jerked her toward him, and she yelped with pain. Kiki yelled out, "Lauren, baby!" He pulled Lauren in front of him and pushed the knife against her throat. "We're getting out of here. You both do exactly what I tell you or I'll cut her."

His voice was commanding, his eyes bright with rage, yet every part of him quivered, betraying his fear. He's a child, Hannah thought. He was just as afraid as they were, and this made him even more dangerous. Cornered, he would act desperately and irrationally. It was those qualities that had left Angie dead.

"I don't think you meant to kill Angie," Hannah said to him, struggling to keep her voice low and soothing when what she wanted to do was shriek her head off. "When she confronted you so suddenly you couldn't help but be angry. I'm sure you didn't plan to kill her. It just happened."

"Oh, yeah, of course," Kiki squeaked. "You could plead temporary insanity or something. They'd probably just put you in one of those, you know, country-club prisons. I had a friend whose cousin went to one and he met up with a very high-class circle of people."

"I'm not going into any prison," Brad spat, beads of sweat forming around his lips. Dragging Lauren with him, he moved to the door, opened it a crack to see if anyone was in the hall, then motioned Hannah and Kiki out. "The stairs," was all he said.

"Look what you've done," Kiki whispered tearfully to her sister as they moved into the hall. Hannah saw a door to the right of them that had STAIRS written across it. "I told you we shouldn't come up here, but would you listen?" She sniffed back a sob. "Lauren would have had a little fun wham-bam-thank-you-ma'am, and that would have been the end of it. But could you accept it? There's a lesson to be learned here."

"Yes. Don't go out with men in the movie business," Hannah whispered back. "If you and Lauren hadn't gotten your heads turned by a little Hollywood glitz."

"Like you weren't having hot flashes over Hinkley?"

"Shut up," Brad said, a few steps behind. "Get in the door."

Hannah's heart pounded. Kiki had been right about one thing. It was her fault they were in this current situation.

She and Kiki moved into the stairwell, stopping on the landing. Brad followed, still holding on to Lauren, his knife at her throat. Lauren, her face white, slumped beneath his grip.

"What do you think you're going to accomplish?" Hannah asked, trying to keep her voice steady.

He pushed the knife a little closer to Lauren's flesh. "I'm getting the hell out of here."

"Then go, but leave us," Kiki said. "We won't tell anyone anything."

The ridiculousness of her statement just angered him more. Hannah didn't think he realized it, but his knife had pressed deeper into Lauren's skin, a tiny rivulet of blood trickling down her skin. "Just get down the stairs, you stupid bitch."

Kiki scowled. "Do what he says," Hannah told her, nudging her down the steps. She followed Kiki, hearing Brad's footsteps close behind. Even though she couldn't see him, his desperation was palpable. She could smell his perspiration, hear his breathing becoming heavier. She thought if she listened closely enough, she would hear his heart pounding in his chest. But his fear was no stronger than her own. She knew she had to do something and it had to be fast, but she didn't know what. She couldn't risk yelling for help. Lauren's throat could be cut within seconds. The only thing she had in her purse even close to a weapon was the metal nail file she kept in the outside pocket.

Hannah tried to take a deep yoga breath, but anxiety kept the air stuck in her throat. Think of your strengths and use them, she told herself. Brad was panicked, out of control. She could be calm if she tried hard enough. She was intelligent and had seen a quantity of life. He was young, inexperienced, and, from observation, no rocket scientist.

Just then something clicked in her mind. Why not? It had worked with the maintenance man. If she feigned illness she didn't think for a minute that Brad would rush to help her, but it might at least cause confusion so she could use her nail file on him.

She wrapped her hand around the file, cried out, then faked a stumble. But as she went down her foot slipped and she stumbled for real. She fell hard against the concrete step, pain shooting through her knee. Kiki, now several steps below her, shouted her name.

She felt Lauren and Brad falling into her. Hannah grabbed the railing, the nail file slipping from her fingers. Brad's hand, the knife in it, shot toward the railing to steady himself, Lauren's legs now tangled in his. He cursed as he stepped down to get a secure footing, but his foot, between two steps, hovered in the air right in front of Hannah's face.

Hannah grabbed his shoelace in her right hand and with all her strength jerked hard on Brad's foot. Years of gardening had made her strong and he lurched forward. Both he and Lauren fell into her, the three of them tumbling down the stairs, a confusion of arms and legs. Hannah heard the knife skipping down the stairs.

A small landing stopped their fall. It hadn't been that far a tumble, only about five steps, but they ended in a pile on the concrete floor. The impact left Hannah disoriented. Brad was on top of her, scrambling up. She saw Kiki standing on the step above them.

"The knife!" Hannah yelled to her, raising herself on

her elbows. Lauren sat up, her back to the corner. On his hands and knees, Brad searched wildly for his knife.

Hannah spotted it first. It lay on the floor half-hidden beneath the stair riser only inches from Brad's foot. She lunged for it. As her fingers pressed against the handle Brad slammed his foot down on her hand. Hannah groaned with pain.

Lauren shoved her foot into his groin. He howled, doubling over. Hannah grabbed the knife. Kiki took off her high heel and hit Brad over the head with it, sending the spike heel onto his skull and neck. Lying curled on his side, he moved his hands to his head to protect himself from the blows. Then with a grunt he raised himself up, knocked Kiki away, and staggered down the next flight of stairs, gathering speed with each step until he disappeared from view.

"He's getting away!" Lauren said, crying.

"Let him go. They'll find him," Hannah said. The sound of his footsteps echoed inside the stairwell. Then there was the sound of a heavy door opening and slamming shut. The women were silent. Lauren, sobbing, threw herself into Hannah's arms.

Kiki sat down next to them and stroked Lauren's hair. "He was a crummy actor anyway. I never liked him," she said soothingly.

It was Hannah who called the police. She hadn't specifically asked for Detective Morgan but wasn't surprised when he got out of the squad car. A small crowd of onlookers gathered near the corner.

"Lauren, dear," Hannah said, moving in front of her niece to shield her from view. "Rebutton your blouse."

Lauren's eyes moved downward. In her haste to dress she had misbuttoned her blouse, a situation she quickly remedied.

Hannah told the story to Detective Morgan in as much detail as she could manage. The only item she left out was the state of Lauren's clothing when she and Kiki burst in upon them. Somehow it didn't seem crucial to the case.

TWENTY-TWO

FIVE SETS OF ARMS SWEPT through the Saturday-morning air, greeting the Universal Spirit with variating levels of spiritual harmony and grace.

To start making good on her promise to Naomi, Hannah had talked Ellie and Wanda into taking Naomi's tai chi class, and now they, along with Kiki and herself, stood in Naomi's front yard slowly waving their arms while Naomi shouted about oneness and the flow of life-force energies. Hannah's own energy would have flowed a little freer if Naomi hadn't been shouting her instructions so loudly, but she knew that Naomi, thrilled to have finally expanded her class, wanted all the neighbors to know of her success.

Unfortunately the class had not been conducted in total spiritual harmony. The women had tried their best to focus on their chi, but the chilliness of the damp grass on their bare feet made it difficult, and the desire to regurgitate the news of the past twenty-four hours made it impossible. In fact, in their current state of agitation, even remaining completely upright was hopeless, and they kept bumping hips, hands, and feet.

Much of this discord was because Wanda and Kiki had resumed with new vigor their competition for the job as

Roger Burke's assistant, a few barbs having already been exchanged. Twice Kiki had "accidentally" knocked down Wanda, the last time into a distressingly fresh lump of doo left by the Epsteins' Labrador. This incident Kiki sorely regretted, for it left a small yet aromatic streak across the rear of Wanda's Donna Karan sweatpants. Luckily Wanda had yet to notice, and everyone pretended it wasn't there, fearful of the volcanic eruption it could cause. To prevent further mishap Naomi suggested that each woman place one hand on the shoulder of the woman next to her. The procedure kept them relatively upright but also made them look like a chorus line of over-the-hill, New Age Rockettes.

"Does anyone know what Brad Casey did when they picked him up?" Kiki asked, grunting as she raised her left foot, following Naomi's lead. Naomi called this posture "Flamingo Flies Then Lands So Happy." It was by far the most difficult she had concocted, requiring the women not only to stand on one foot but to raise their arms especially high. "Did he struggle?" Kiki continued. "Of course he was probably weak after the beating I gave him. I used my highest heels."

Her arm lifted, Wanda improvised on the posture by pointing her finger, resembling John Travolta in *Saturday Night Fever*. "He was at the Mexican border when they caught up with him. Supposedly he confessed to killing Angie right away, blabbering on like a baby about how he hadn't meant to do it, how they had an argument, and how sorry he was," Wanda said. Her ex-husband-number-three, the entertainment lawyer, knew Brad's current attorney and had offered to provide Wanda whatever gossip he reasonably could in exchange for the Andy Warhol lithographs she had won years before in the divorce settlement.

Naomi, looking at the sky with an expression of supreme oneness with a nameless, genderless deity, cleared her throat. "Ladies, we must focus. We must not chitchat." She brought her left foot slowly down, then lifted her right, the tiny bells on her toes jingling cheerfully. After a moment her beatific expression turned perplexed, her supreme serenity compromised by her even more supreme curiosity.

"I still don't understand why he wanted that paper so much he killed Angie for it."

"He didn't kill her for the paper," Hannah said, struggling to stay balanced. She longed for the days when you could just do some jumping jacks and not worry about your psyche. "Brad killed her because he was afraid she would tell everyone that he'd been defrauding the *Pirate John* investors."

"But I thought Angie was in love with Brad," Wanda asked. "Ouch. Kiki, you stepped on my foot again."

Kiki said a quick and suspiciously pleasant "sorry," not wanting Wanda to twist her head around for a sharp retort and get a whiff of her own backside.

Hannah continued. "But he had dumped her. She must have met him at the old winery to tell him she knew what he had done. She took the paper along as proof."

"A scorned woman wants revenge," Wanda said.

"Or maybe," Kiki added, "she thought she could use it as blackmail to get him back."

"Possibly," Hannah said. "Anyway, I think after Brad killed her he took the paper because it was a direct connection to him. But then he realized that the notes were useful. They told him which companies Angie had talked to."

"Why was that important?" Ellie asked.

"So he'd know where to cover his tracks," Hannah replied. "Wanda, do you know if he confessed to his father's murder as well?"

"Don't know," Wanda said, giving the air a puzzled sniff. "We'll never know the truth now. Brad's lawyers have taken over and he's not talking. The important thing is that Bertha's out of jail. I, for one, always knew she was innocent."

"Well, so did I," Kiki said. Hannah's eyes rolled upward as her sister went on. "She's in the clear for Angie's murder, but I guess there could still be some suspicion hanging over her for killing my Freddie if Brad hasn't confessed to it."

"Your Freddie," Wanda mimicked, followed by a dismissing "pffft" sound. "They never had any real evidence against her on that. Everyone knows Brad committed both murders."

Naomi now had both feet on the ground, leading the women into an uncomfortable squat.

"It's hard for me to believe that the same person committed both," Hannah said, wincing when she heard her knee crack. "The first killing was done in such a passive way, putting pills in Casey's flask. But Angie's death was so violent."

"Both were opportunistic," Wanda said. She was having difficulties with squatting, and Hannah knew it had to irk her after all those tantric sex classes she and Walter had taken where supposedly they contorted themselves into pretzels. Wanda tried gently bouncing herself down. "Brad Casey is nothing if not an opportunist. All he cared about was money and ambition. He committed fraud for the money. He killed his father so he could produce *Pirate John* on his own and get all the glory."

"I don't find it plausible that he would kill his father," Hannah said. "Brad was too dependent on him for his career."

"Seems to me he just got tired of living in his father's shadow. Some people just snap," Ellie said. "They roll along for years all nice and normal and one day they go nuts. I've seen it in the manicure business." She was supposed to be facing north like Naomi, but she turned to Hannah, who was behind her. "How's Lauren doing?"

"Still upset," Hannah answered. "But she'll get through this."

"Poor girl. There's been a lot of fallout from this situation," Wanda said, now fully squatting. "Poor Bertha's still nerve-racked. She's spent the last two days shoveling dirt in those holes. She says she's going to cement over the whole yard and turn it into a shuffleboard court."

"And then there's Ed," Ellie chimed in. "Louise at the gas station told me that he had a heart attack last night. She saw the ambulance pick him up at the grocery."

"What?" Straightening, Hannah dropped her arms to her side. "How is he? Will he be all right?"

"I'm so sorry, Hannah," Ellie said. "You didn't know?"

"There was a message on my machine from Detective Morgan, saying that he'd found Ed and that he was okay. But it was from yesterday afternoon."

"Well, I guess he was okay then. All I know is that he's in the hospital."

Kiki shook her head sadly. "Poor man. Always shuffling down the sidewalk, so pathetic. He looked like a big old bird, that beak nose of his and his bug eyes."

Naomi looked at Hannah with vexation. "Hannah, your flamingo has flopped," she said. "The arms must be lifted high, high toward the sun."

But Hannah stood rooted to the ground, her gaze off somewhere in the distance. "You'll have to excuse me," she replied distractedly. "Ed being in the hospital. I didn't know. I have to visit him."

"But we're right in the middle—" Naomi said, but it was useless. Hannah took off toward her house with a rapid stride.

"She forms attachments to the oddest people," she heard Wanda say behind her. If she hadn't been in such a hurry she would have chastised Wanda for such a remark. Ed wasn't odd. He was the victim of a stroke. The same thing could very well happen to Wanda herself one day, or to any of them. But Wanda was the sort of person who had lived such a protected life, her idea of a tragedy was if the caterer canceled.

Not bothering to change her clothes, Hannah grabbed her purse and keys from the kitchen and got in the Eldorado. As she backed out the driveway she saw Naomi and the rest of them still in the yard. They were all standing now except for Wanda, whose knees appeared permanently bent. "Flamingo Flies Then Lands So Happy" had become "Crab Squats, Gets Stuck So Sadly." Naomi and Kiki had taken hold of her arms and were trying to lift her out of it.

Hannah drove down Walnut, taking a right at the intersection and heading for the freeway. Thinking of Ed sent a distressing wind through her mind. It was more than his illness. It was what might have caused it. If he had some knowledge about Casey's murder that he hadn't shared, the stress of keeping it bottled up could have precipitated a heart attack.

Fifteen minutes later she pulled into the Marin Hospital parking lot. She knew the hospital well. The Breast Cancer Counseling Center was in the east wing and Hannah had been going there for over eight years, first as a client then as a counseling volunteer. She walked quickly through the parking lot and into the lobby, recognizing Barbara, the volunteer at the information desk.

Ed's room number didn't show up on the computer, so Barbara called, learned that he had been moved out of intensive care only minutes before, and directed Hannah to the third floor. When Hannah exited the elevator she steeled herself as the aroma of disinfectant filled her nostrils. Her mastectomy years earlier had been a terrifying experience. The hospital wasn't to blame. Her medical care had been excellent, the doctors and nurses well trained and caring. But regardless, the emotional pain of the surgery had stayed with her. Every time she came to the hospital to visit a breast-cancer patient, the sights, sounds, and smells of the hospital ward brought all her memories back.

As always, she reminded herself of her purpose, pushed the negative thoughts out of her mind, and marched to the nurses' station. The nurse on duty, a stick-thin woman with heavy glasses, was busily scribbling something on a chart.

"Excuse me, where could I find Ed Kachowski? He's a patient."

The nurse finished writing before she looked up. "No visitors right now. You'll have to come back this afternoon."

"Couldn't I see him just for a moment?" Hannah pleaded, but the nurse responded with a firm no. She returned her attention to the papers on the desk, silently dismissing Hannah, but when she looked up again Hannah was still there. The nurse's face softened.

"I can't let you into Mr. Kachowski's room, but his brother is over there talking to the doctor." The nurse nodded toward two men down the hall. "Maybe he can tell you something."

Thanking her, Hannah took a closer look at Ed's brother and was amazed she hadn't noticed him immediately. He looked so much like Ed, with the same nose and eyes. As soon as he finished his conversation with the doctor, Hannah walked up to him and introduced herself.

"My name's Ron. Nice to meet you," he said. He was pleasant enough but he seemed a bit disoriented, which Hannah understood. Ron was taller and thinner than his brother, with a soft-spoken politeness that made Hannah think he lived somewhere other than the Bay Area.

"How's Ed doing?" she asked.

"Not good." Ron took off his glasses and with two fingers rubbed the bridge of his nose. "He had a heart attack seven years ago and he wasn't laid up nearly this bad."

"Does the doctor think he'll be all right?"

He shook his head. "He doesn't know. Listen, I've got to phone my wife," he said, putting his glasses back on. "I flew out here last night and I haven't had the chance to call. She'll be worried."

He made a move to leave, but Hannah touched his arm. "One more thing, please. Do you know if there was anything that caused Ed's heart attack? Some kind of stress?"

"Ed can't hardly talk, so I can't ask him. The doctor said he got a few words from him and it turns out Ed hadn't been taking his heart pills lately."

The information jolted Hannah. "Do you know what kind of pills he was taking?"

"The doctor told me, but I forget."

"Does digoxin sound familiar?"

"Yeah, that sounds right. The doc said not taking them could have messed him up. I've really got to go now. Nice meeting you."

Hannah watched Ron walk away and she cogitated on why Ed would have stopped taking his medication, an ugly answer taking shape in her mind. Because someone had stolen the pills. That could have been what Ed was so upset about. But why wouldn't he tell the police?

"Can I help you with something?"

Hannah looked up and saw the nurse, still behind the desk, looking at her. "Oh, no, I'm fine," she said, even though she wasn't. The nurse gave her a concerned look, picked up a clipboard, and walked off, disappearing around a corner.

Taking advantage of the nurse's absence, Hannah headed down the hallway in the opposite direction, reading the small name labels posted at the right of the doors until she found *Kachowski*. She stepped into the doorway. A curtain was drawn halfway around the bed, so only Ed's head and shoulders were visible. The sight of the tubes snaking from his nose wrenched her.

He could have carried his pills in his coat pocket, Hannah thought as she watched him lying there, looking shrunken and helpless. It made sense. When she had pills that had to be taken throughout the day, she always carried them with her, so if she forgot to take one she could do it as soon as she remembered. If Ed did the same thing, then someone could have stolen the pills from him at the party. If so, he didn't tell anyone, but why? Apparently he wanted it to be a secret so badly that he didn't even have his prescription refilled right away, probably because he thought the pharmacist would alert the police.

Hannah wanted so much to talk to him. Ed coughed, shifting under the covers. She couldn't understand how anyone knew he even had the pills. She had never known. But someone at the party could have seen him take one. That person could have asked him what kind of medication he was on. It's common knowledge that digitalis is lethal. But why didn't he tell the police? There was only one reason she could think of. Because telling would have implicated a friend in Casey's murder. The dilemma must have weighed on him, the burden increasing every day until his heart rebelled under the pressure.

He was deep asleep now and she knew it wouldn't be

good to disturb him, especially for the conversation she needed to have. She turned and left.

The sun beat against the concrete entry to the hospital, the cleansing heat welcomed her as she stepped outside. For a long time she sat in the Eldorado, hands on the steering wheel, staring straight ahead, her head flooded with questions.

She had always wanted to be smarter, but never more than at that moment. And another idea nagged at her. There was something familiar about Ed's brother, more than just the sibling resemblance. She felt she had seen him before. And strangely, after giving it more thought, she decided it wasn't the similarity to Ed's face that made her think she had seen him. It was the fact that he looked different. He was younger than Ed, his face smoother and longer, his features more refined.

A gnawing in her stomach reminded her that she hadn't eaten. There was some poached salmon salad in the refrigerator that would be a minimum of trouble if she got to it before Kiki did, so she started the car and headed home, her mind still fixed on Ed.

Stopped at a red light a few blocks from home, she heard the tap of a horn next to her and saw Roger Burke. Sitting in his white sporty convertible, dressed in a bright red golf shirt, he looked like a cherry atop a scoop of vanilla ice cream. He smiled and waved, apparently no longer annoyed with her. She smiled and waved back, hoping he wouldn't want to talk. No such luck. He leaned over the passenger seat to get within chatting distance.

"Have you heard? I filled the assistantship post. Happened this morning," he said brightly.

This got Hannah's attention, since the information directly affected the quality of life in her own household. "Who's the lucky winner?"

"Shiloh. You know, from One Hand Clapping. She spoke to me about it last week and sent me a résumé. Charming girl. Seems so efficient."

Shiloh getting the coveted film-festival job? That news was almost as surprising as Roger's description of her as efficient. Hannah wondered how such a change in the winds had come about. Shiloh, hearing Wanda and Kiki vying for the position, must have sneaked in and stolen the job out from under them. Served Kiki and Wanda right, the way they had squabbled. But why had Roger chosen her? Hannah checked his hands resting on the steering wheel to see if they were freshly manicured. They were, naturally, but free manicures couldn't have been the lure. There was no point beating around the bush. Hannah just flat out asked him.

"Well," he began, looking sheepish. The light turned green but there were no cars behind so they stayed put. "The truth is both Wanda and Kiki, well, I don't mean to be offensive. They're lovely women, of course, but they tend to prattle on about nonsense. But Shiloh . . ."

Hannah waited eagerly for the rest of the sentence. When it came to talking nonsense Shiloh could keep up with anyone.

"To be honest, Shiloh reminds me so much of my daughter when she was that age," he finally spit out. "They have the same eyes and mouth, even the same little cute smile. And with my daughter living on the East Coast . . . well, I know it's an emotional decision but the job requires no skills and it's only a couple of hours a week." He hesitated. "Hannah, do you think you could help me with the politics? Wanda and Kiki are going to be a touch miffed."

"When Iraq invaded, the Kuwaitis were a touch miffed," Hannah said. "This will be worse."

"Please, Hannah. You're so diplomatic with these things."

She should have known he wanted something from her. "I'll do what I can."

A driver pulled behind them and, anxious to use the road for actual travel, honked, so Roger and Hannah took off. As she drove she rehearsed how she would break the news to Kiki. "She reminds him of his child," she would say. "That sort of thing tugs at a person's heartstrings. Makes them behave irrationally." She would remind Kiki how Frederick Casey had admitted to a crime he didn't commit in order to spare his son. Certainly Kiki could understand Roger wanting to give the assistant job to a girl who reminded him of his daughter.

Hannah made a left turn on to Walnut Avenue, drove a block, then slammed on her brakes. "My God," she said out loud. She quickly pulled into a driveway, backed out with a screech of tires, and headed toward Lady Nails. Ellie didn't open until one on Saturdays, but Shiloh might be there.

She parked in a no-parking zone in front of the shop and jumped out of the car. The sign on the door read CLOSED, but she saw a light in the back room, so she banged on the door. Looking surprised but curious, Shiloh emerged from the back wearing her usual ankle-length dress and clogs.

She opened the door about six inches. "We don't open for another half hour, Hannah, and we're pretty booked today."

"I don't need a manicure. I just want to look at your magazines," Hannah said. Shiloh's lips parted, her expression puzzled. "I can't explain right now. Could I look at them? It's urgent."

It was ten A.M. on a Saturday, but Hannah didn't think it being a weekend morning accounted fully for the look of complete noncomprehension on Shiloh's face. Hannah wondered if Roger had seen this expression on her.

"They're gone. After what you said the other day about them being brain candy, Ellie threw them out."

Hannah's heart took a nosedive. The magazine she wanted was an old one, and she felt sure the library wouldn't keep old issues of *People*. They might have a copy on film, but the photographs on those were always so blurry. She needed the real thing. She was about to thank Shiloh and leave, when the girl's face lit up.

"They're probably still, like, you know, in the Dumpster. They don't pick up until late this morning."

Hannah perked up. "Where is it?"

"In the alley." Shiloh opened the door wider. "I'll show you."

Excitedly, Hannah followed her through the shop and out

the back door. As soon as they reached the alley she saw the Dumpster, a big green metal bin overflowing with stinking garbage. Hannah's enthusiasm dampened.

"Pretty disgusting, huh?" Shiloh said. "We share it with that Chinese takeout place." That explained the aroma of rotting egg rolls. "And there's a dead mouse in there. I threw it in yesterday."

Every pore in Hannah's body yearned to make a hasty exit, but she forced herself to stay. She took a deep breath, but immediately regretted it. The odor was awful.

"Could I borrow some rubber gloves?" she asked.

Shiloh brought the gloves, and once Hannah had them on she dragged a wooden crate up to the Dumpster, stepped on it, and began sorting through the rubbish. Shiloh watched while Hannah worked, never offering to help. Hannah couldn't blame her. There were old yogurt cartons, banana peels, the dead mouse, a pile of slimy noodles, and various things repulsive beyond identification. Just as she was making a mental note to pour Clorox over her arms when she got home, she let out a yelp of delight. The *People* magazines were lying beneath some decaying bok choy, covered with sauce. Digging through them, she found the one she was looking for, the years-old, tattered issue with Mel Gibson on the cover. Magazine in hand, Hannah stepped down off the crate.

"You really like Mel Gibson, huh?" Shiloh asked.

"Crazy about him," Hannah said. "Thanks for your help." She returned the gloves to Shiloh then hurried down the alley. As soon as she was around the corner she stopped and thumbed through the magazine. At first she couldn't find what she was looking for. Again she flipped through the pages. When she finally found it she stared at the page for a long time. Just imagine, she thought. The answer had been in *People* magazine all along.

TWENTY-THREE

THE ROOM'S DIM LIGHT MUTED everything inside it, softening all edges. The chair, the bouquet of flowers on the chest, the chrome rails of the hospital bed, and even Ed himself—they all seemed in the process of disappearing, dreamy images caught in the final seconds before melting away.

As she stood in the doorway Hannah's eyes fixed on Ed. He lay perfectly still, arms at his sides, a pink blanket pulled up to his chest. Near him sat a low white machine with a dozen gauges. It was a machine-mother, an umbilical cord in the form of a long plastic tube connected to Ed's arm, its soft hum gently reminding him to live.

His eyes were open and directed at the ceiling. His faded hospital gown fell from one shoulder, revealing childishly pale skin.

She stepped into the room. Sensing her presence, he turned his head toward her. He lifted his hand.

She sat in a chair next to the bed and clasped his hand. His fingers squeezed hers with surprising strength. He opened his mouth, struggling to speak, but only gasps came out.

"It's okay," Hannah whispered. "I know what you've

been wanting to tell me. That day at the Book Stop when I told you about Casey's murder. I think you tried to tell me then. You said that he'd died too young. I thought you meant Casey.'' She reached into her handbag and pulled out the page she had torn from the magazine. It was the photograph of Casey from the charity event, him smiling at the camera looking half-drunk and arrogant. But it was the nameless person standing behind him and to the left that drew Ed's eyes. Slowly Ed reached out and with one finger touched that person's face.

''He looks like you,'' Hannah said. ''He's your son, isn't he? And he worked for Frederick Casey. When I was at your house I saw the framed piece of music. He must have wanted to compose for the movies.''

Ed began to cry quietly, and the sight of it broke Hannah's heart.

''I killed him,'' he said, the words faint. He pulled Hannah closer. She felt his body stiffening. ''He killed my boy.''

''I know you must have blamed Casey for what happened to your son, for the drugs and the alcohol. For the disappointments.''

Ed gave a shuddering sigh and then relaxed, his body sinking back into the white sheets. They sat quietly for a while, with Ed weeping and Hannah holding on to his hand. She wanted to cry, too, but didn't let herself.

''I'll tell the police that you couldn't have planned it,'' she said to him, her voice soft and soothing, her hand stroking his hair. ''You didn't even know about the film-festival party until I told you about it that day. You couldn't have known that Casey was the film-festival guest of honor.''

It must have been a shock for Ed to see the man he felt was responsible for his son's death, Hannah knew. Ed's decision to put his own medication in Casey's flask had been a disastrous impulse, for he had killed not only Casey. By using his heart medication to end Casey's life, he couldn't use it to maintain his own. If Ed had gone to the pharmacist and asked for more digoxin, it might have alerted the police. So he went without. He committed a murder, then levied the death sentence on himself.

Hannah grabbed a clean tissue from a box on the small dresser and wiped the tears from Ed's face, struggling not to cry herself. "I have to tell Detective Morgan the truth. We can't let anyone else take the blame."

Ed nodded. There was a knock at the door. Hannah twisted around and saw Ron. She turned back to Ed. "I better go now. I miss you, Ed. I miss seeing you downtown."

Bending over, she kissed him lightly on the forehead and left.

TWENTY-FOUR

❧

ONLY A FEW MINUTES BEFORE, the hero's girlfriend had unceremoniously dumped him. Brokenhearted, he now jogged through Central Park, the autumn leaves swirling across the narrow, winding trail. He wore a dark suit covered by a trench coat, the back of the coat flapping behind him as he ran faster, his shoes beating a desperate rhythm against the pavement. Finally, breathless, he stopped, collapsing onto a wooden bench, looking so lost and miserable.

Hannah watched the last scene of *Midnight in Manhattan* alone in her living room, with Kiki long off to bed. Curled up on the couch in her robe, she smiled and popped another jelly bean into her mouth. No matter how down she had ever been, seeing this movie had always lifted her spirits. She needed it now, with Ed's funeral that morning still weighing on her.

She knew the film so well that she played the scenes in her head, knowing precisely what the characters would do moments before they did them. After the events of the preceding week, she would never again see the movie in quite the same way. But she was gratified that in the end Frederick Casey turned out to not be the complete ogre everyone thought he was. He had love in his heart. It was this love that took the blame for a fraud he didn't commit in order to save his son. It was this love that had created Hannah's favorite movie.

A schnauzer trotted up and sniffed the leg of the hero. The hero picked up a stick, threw it, and the dog chased after it, barking joyfully. The hero smiled. He rose from the bench and meandered down the path, hands in pockets, whistling, right before the words THE END flashed across the screen.

Hannah always imagined she knew what the hero was thinking at that moment. He was thinking that despite the loss and disappointment that inevitably comes with being human, you sometimes stumble across nuggets of such joy if you'll only look around yourself and be open to them. And it's knowing that a nugget could be just around the corner that makes it so remarkably wonderful to be alive.

"Okay, explain to me again. Why the heck are we sitting in Bertha's bushes with twigs up our butts?" Kiki whispered with irritation, her request punctuated with two quick spits and the ejection of an oleander petal. While she, Hannah, and Lauren hid behind Bertha's oleander hedge, Bertha clomped with her usual intensity around her yard, wearing her rubber boots and Winnie-the-Pooh hat. With military fervor Bertha adjusted her spray nozzle to a stronger stream and blasted the aphids off the new Crimson Glory rosebush she had planted in the spot where Angie's body had been found.

"I told you. There's something I want to do," Hannah said, her voice lowered. "And I can't do it until Bertha leaves. But it won't be long now. See the big mug on the step? When she drinks coffee she goes to the bathroom every fifteen minutes."

"Ouch. Aunt Kiki, you're stepping on my foot," Lauren whispered.

"Oops, sorry. There's not enough room here for three people," Kiki whispered back. Still in a squatting position, Hannah sidled to the left to make more room. When Lauren dropped by for breakfast an hour earlier, Hannah invited her along on this current escapade, hoping it would lift her from her lovesick torpor over Detective Morgan.

Not that Hannah blamed Lauren. That awful night at the Wyndam Hotel, Morgan had been every inch the romantic hero, chivalrous yet professional as he wrapped a blanket around Lauren's shoulders and, his jaw set and his expression determined, took notes on a small steno pad. But several days had passed and he hadn't called. Lauren now realized what a mistake she had made. She had cast away a diamond for a piece of glittering cheap glass, and she feared that her brief ill-fated fling with Brad Casey, a man now referred to by Kiki as "that piece of pond scum," had forever torpedoed her chances with Morgan. This possibility Lauren deeply regretted, for when she saw Morgan that night, so strong and serious, his baby face bathed in the flattering red glow of the police-car light, Lauren suddenly realized what a hunk he was. And as he dashed off to track down Brad Casey and make the world a safer place for children and small animals, Hannah distinctly heard Lauren mutter, "Gawd, he's so cute."

How did Hannah know all this? Although Lauren didn't talk about it, Hannah saw the truth in her forlorn eyes. Kiki thought she was grieving over Brad, but Hannah knew the truth and had it confirmed the night before when she stopped by Lauren's house and found her in her bathrobe watching *Cops* and weeping. Now Hannah schemed of ways to get Lauren and Morgan back together.

An apparent sudden itch caused Bertha to twist around and inspect her posterior, and in the process pointed the spray at the oleanders. The water hit Kiki in the face and Hannah clamped her hand over Kiki's mouth to muffle the resulting yelp.

"Grannie sucking eggs," Kiki whispered through gritted teeth after Hannah released her. "I'm soaked and my knees are starting to hurt." She shifted her weight backward, paused, and then emitted a low whine. "I just squished a snail."

Hannah shrugged. "As a gardener, I have to consider a dead snail a good snail."

"But I've got snail guts all over my knee."

"You're the one who begged to come with me."

"You said it was going to be fun."

"I'm having a good time," Lauren said in a brave attempt at cheerfulness.

"See?" Hannah told Kiki. "When it's over we'll be so proud of ourselves. Bertha's going to be so happy."

"She should already be tickled pink," Kiki said grumpily. "We've all been killing her with kindness trying to make up for thinking she was a murderer. Wanda gave her that lunch party. Ellie's giving her free manicures for a month and I bought her that red Wonderbra. What else could she need?"

"Something more unique," Hannah replied.

"Unique?" Kiki said with amazement. "Why, I had Bertha's initials monogrammed on the left cup."

"Aunt Hannah, tell us what you're going to do," Lauren said.

Hannah gave her a sly smile. "You'll see in a minute."

"That's so typical of you lately," Kiki said. "You've been running around doing all these nice things for people. You told Wanda about that poodle at the SPCA that looks so much like Bon Bon. I know she loves the dog, but why did you do it? You never did anything nice for Wanda before."

"I guess everything that happened with the film festival taught me some things."

"Like what?"

"About the power of love."

Kiki grinned. "You're just thinking about love because John Perez is coming home tomorrow."

Hannah smiled back. "I meant the kind of love in families. Between fathers and sons, for example. Between aunts and nieces." She gave Kiki a playful nudge. "Between sisters."

"And that's connected to your finding Wanda a new dog?" Lauren asked.

"I thought Wanda was so silly for having Bon Bon stuffed and then I realized she loved that dog like it was a child.'' Hannah pushed back the bush and peered through the leaves. ''Good, Bertha's gone inside.'' She reached in her pocket and pulled out an arrowhead.

''What's that for?'' Kiki asked.

''Follow me.''

Kiki and Lauren crawled behind Hannah as they pushed their way through the oleander. Near the west end of the garden sat a Madame Alfred Carrière rose fresh from the nursery and still in its black plastic bucket. Hannah had given it to Bertha the day before, suggesting that she plant it in a particular spot where it would get the best morning sun. The plant currently sat next to its new home, waiting to be planted.

Quickly Hannah pulled a small spade out of her handbag and dug up some earth where she knew the rose would go, and placed the arrowhead about three inches down, recovering it with dirt.

''I've had that arrowhead since I was ten,'' she said.

''Is it real?'' Lauren asked.

''Oh, yes. It came from around here.''

Kiki punched her fists into her hips. ''Bertha's just going to find that thing, get all excited, and dig up her yard again.''

''Maybe, but it doesn't matter,'' Hannah replied. ''Wanda told everyone in town that the pottery shard came from Pier One, and Bertha was so humiliated. Now she'll be able to show people this arrowhead and save some face.''

Hannah, Kiki, and Lauren tiptoed back into the bushes. It took about five minutes for Bertha to return and begin digging the hole for the new rose. After overturning several shovelfuls of earth, she froze, knelt down, and sifted the dirt through her fingers. Picking up the arrowhead, she inspected it a moment, at first not appearing to believe what she held in her hands. Then suddenly, her face beaming and her arms outstretched, she leaped into the air, letting out a loud and joyful whoop that all Walnut Avenue could hear.